DAKOTA LUCK

BOOK SIX OF THE TOUCH SERIES

STONI ALEXANDER

SILVERSTONE PUBLISHING

This book is a work of fiction. All names, characters, locations, brands, media and incidents are either products of the author's imagination, or have been used fictitiously. Any resemblance to actual persons living or dead, locales, or events is entirely coincidental. The author acknowledges the trademarked status and trademark owners of various products referenced in this work of fiction, which have been used without permission. The publication/use of these trademarks is not authorized, associated with, or sponsored by the trademark owners.

Copyright © 2020 by Stoni Alexander LLC

Developmental Edits by Johnny at Better Together
Copy Edits by Nicole at Proof Before You Publish
Cover Photo by Tijana Vukovic
Cover Model Dusan Susnjar
Cover Design by Johnny & Stoni Alexander

All rights reserved.

In accordance with the U.S. Copyright Act of 1976, the scanning, uploading, and electronic sharing of any part of this book without the permission of the publisher is unlawful piracy and theft of the author's intellectual property. Without limiting the rights under copyright reserved above, no part of this publication may be reproduced, stored in or reproduced into a retrieval system, or transmitted, in any form, or by any means (electronic, mechanical, photocopying, recording or otherwise) without the prior written permission of the above copyright owner of this book.

Published in the U.S. by SilverStone Publishing, 2020
ISBN 978-1-946534-14-9 (Print Paperback)
ISBN 978-1-946534-15-6 (Kindle eBook)

To my parents

Mom
You are missed every single day.
Your beautiful smile and loving nature surround me...always.

Dr. J.D.
A brilliant physicist I called Dad.
Klaatu barada nikto.

ABOUT DAKOTA LUCK

He's as dangerous as he is irresistible...

I'm angry...angry in my bones.

Fury fuels me to find the monster who took my wife. To exact vengeance for her death. He'll look forward to meeting the devil when I'm done with him.

My salvation? My precious child. She's my entire universe. There's nothing I wouldn't do to keep her safe.

Nothing.

I'm living two completely different lives. When the sun goes down, this real estate mogul and doting daddy becomes a dangerous, ruthless, and lethal vigilante. Every kill leaves another blemish on my tarnished, tortured soul.

But I don't give a damn.

I'm broken...until *she* storms into my wicked world. She's bold, brilliant, and so damn beautiful. I'm drawn to her in ways I can't explain and can't control. She's what I crave, what I need... what my daughter needs. Then, I learn the shocking truth about her.

She's been sent on a mission to destroy me.

And only she has the power to save me.

1

DAKOTA'S SLEEPY LITTLE PRINCESS

"But wait, Daddy." Samantha Luck twisted around and stared at him, her bright eyes brimming with excitement.

"What, punkin?"

"This princess is different."

Dakota Luck smiled at her. "It would appear that way, Sammy Lynn. Should we see what she does next?"

"Okay." His daughter snuggled back into his lap. He loved the way she trusted him without question. And his heart melted at how her tiny hand clutched his as he gripped the picture book resting on his thigh.

Dakota continued reading about the defiant princess who refused to take orders from anyone, not even her dad, the King. A woman so strong-willed, she carved out her own damn path. He liked this badass princess.

Forcing himself to focus on the story, he continued reading until his precious bundle had fallen asleep—a small lump, out cold in his lap. He set the book on the side table next to the custom rocker he had purchased when Beth had been pregnant. The cushions hugged his large frame, his broad shoulders forced into that too-tight space. He was twice as big as she had been. Though he had contemplated replacing the rocker with something larger, Dakota thrived on being uncomfortable. Hunting down the motherfucker who took his wife gave him purpose. That, and the precious angel asleep in his arms.

With tender care, he laid his child onto her toddler bed. Her eyes fluttered open. "I'm not sleepy."

Every night, she fought hard to stay awake. *I don't like to sleep, either, sweet baby.*

He squeezed into the opening between the wooden slats of her small bed and gently moved the hair from her face. "I'm going out, but the sitter is here."

"Where's Mrs. Morris?"

"She's on vacation, visiting her son." He leaned down and kissed her forehead.

"Uh-huh." Sammy's eyes closed. "I remember."

"Tomorrow is Saturday, so you don't have to get up early for daycare," he whispered.

Her brow furrowed, but she didn't open her eyes. "I'm a big girl," she murmured. "I go to *school*."

"Right, school." He tucked the sheet around her neck. "How 'bout pancakes for breakfast? You can add the blueberries."

"I love can-cakes," she said before slipping her thumb inside her mouth.

"And I love you."

Her eyes flew open and she flung her small arms around his neck and gave him a tight squeeze before settling back down.

A damn lump formed in his throat every time she did that. Ever since turning four, she'd blossomed into a little girl. His waddling, pudgy toddler had vanished. The only remaining trace was the baby blanket she dragged around the house, the worn cloth fraying at the edges.

Dakota pushed off the bed and stared down at his child. He would kill for her. No way in hell would he let her down, like he had her mother. If it took him the rest of his undeserving life, he'd avenge his late wife. For no other reason than to quiet the raging demons in his head that plagued him every moment of every good-for-nothing day.

He left the lamp on. Somehow that oversized princess nightlight helped stave off her nightmares. After closing the door, he squinted in the harsh hallway light. He needed to get a dimmer switch. Or lower the bulb wattage. Hell, he needed to do a lot of things around the house. Right now, there was only one thing on his mind. *It's time to focus.*

He trotted downstairs. Marcus Freethy stood by the pillars in his two-story foyer. Built like a brick building, Marcus took shit from no one, and that's exactly how Dakota liked it.

"Is the sitter here?" Dakota asked.

"Living room."

In addition to owning and managing a private security company, Marcus was Dakota's part-time bodyguard. Marcus only smiled when he wanted the asshole standing in front of him to see his gold front tooth. He had a shaved head and large diamond studs in his ears. And Marcus would catch a bullet with his teeth if he had to.

"Who's watching the house tonight?" Dakota asked.

"Craig will run surveillance out front. Hillendale in the back."

Dakota could never understand why Marcus called Craig by his first name and John by his last. But he never questioned Marcus about irrelevant bullshit because Marcus had his back. And Sammy's back. Hell, probably even Mrs. Morris's back.

As Dakota walked into the front room, he spied the sitter hunched over a textbook on the sofa. When she saw him, she sat tall and arched her back. Her shoulders glided back and she gave him a sultry smile.

"Hello, Mr. Luck."

"How's the semester treating you?"

"Good. I'm going the pre-med route."

She slid the book off her lap, revealing a very short skirt. His cock twitched. She was a sweet piece of twenty-something ass.

"I've been practicing my blow jobs." She stood and her protruding nipples pressed against the too-tight sweatshirt.

He stepped close enough to her to smell her just-washed hair. "Practicing that swirl on those lucky frat boys?"

A pinkish hue covered her cheeks. He loved making women blush. Drove him fucking wild. She tilted her face toward his and nodded.

It would be easy to kiss her, then unzip and let her demonstrate her newfound talent, but he had a job to do that had nothing to do with getting blown by the sitter.

He grabbed her ponytail and yanked it back. "Take good care of my angel." He released his hold and a moan slipped from her lips. "If she wakes, stay with her until she falls back to sleep."

She cleared her throat. "Of course."

"You can fall asleep on the sofa or in the guest room."

She batted her lashes at him. "Your bed?"

He'd never take a woman into his bed. The one he'd once shared with his wife, the mother of his child. The woman who'd paid the ultimate price because he couldn't keep her safe. He clenched his fist, wanting to punch it straight through a fucking wall.

"Sofa or guest room." He walked into the foyer and waited for her to catch up. "I'll be home before dawn. Bolt the door behind me and open it for no one. Understood?" He hitched his brow as he waited for her response.

"Right. Of course not."

Marcus opened the front door and Dakota grabbed the backpack by the door before stepping onto the porch. A glance to the left. Another to his right. The suburban Northern Virginia neighborhood was peaceful. Though night had fallen, four boys played glow-in-the-dark Frisbee two houses down. He recognized their voices. Middle schoolers. *That's a fucked-up time.*

He inhaled the night air, savoring the crispness that smacked his lungs. Early April meant they could enjoy another month, maybe two, before the suffocating humidity hit the DC region. As soon as she snapped the bolt, he set off toward the black SUV parked in the driveway.

"How old is that girl?" Marcus asked.

"Old enough to swallow," Dakota replied, and slipped inside the waiting vehicle.

2

MISS RHODE ISLAND

Dakota opened a document on his laptop as Marcus drove into the parking lot. The long line of young men and women, dressed in their sexiest duds, stood outside the unmarked three-story brick building in Arlington. Some glanced around, eager to make eye contact, but most were too engrossed in their phones.

"Technology is the bane of man's existence," said Rhys, staring out the tinted window. "Those kids don't know how to talk to each other."

Dakota glanced up from the back seat. "Technology is the reason we have six kills."

Rhys ran his hand through his hair. "And I'm so ready for lucky number seven."

"This dossier is extensive. Are you confident he's our man?" Dakota asked as he scanned the page.

"One hundred percent," Rhys replied. "But he's altered his looks since his last arrest, so I accessed the FBI database for confirmation."

"But he's not *the one*?" Dakota asked.

"Unknown at this time. Maybe he'll tell you."

His guts burned with frustration. *If it takes me the rest of my sorry-ass life, I will find Beth's killer.*

Marcus drove around to the back of the building, turned off the headlights, and pulled up to the unmarked fire door. Normally bathed in darkness, a glaring light bulb illuminated the area.

What the hell?

A phone buzzed and all three reached inside their sport coat breast pockets.

Rhys answered. "Go." He listened, then hung up. "We've got company."

The door burst open and a woman stepped outside. Dakota's brain screeched to a halt. She was fucking loaded for bear with a handgun in her grip and a wild glint in her eyes.

Using her ass as a doorstop, she stood in the doorframe's shadow, her short, dark hair framing her sharply-angled face. From what he could tell, she was all woman and rocking hot. Dark tank top that stretched against her full breasts. Tight, black shorts hugged her hips and showed off her toned legs. If he could glimpse her ass, he'd be golden.

Marcus rolled down his window. "Good evening, ma'am."

"Use the *front* door like everyone else," she bit out.

"Tell her I'm getting out," Dakota said.

"Ma'am, Mr. Luck is exiting the vehicle."

Dakota stepped out and she cocked her weapon. Her feistiness hit him like a tsunami. Nice and slowly, he extended his hand.

"Dakota Luck. I'm an L3 Dungeon member and a friend of Stryker's. We play poker in the Travesty Room and I've got a key to unlock this door."

Dakota needed to emotionally disarm her. Since the gun was pointed at his scrotum, he'd tread lightly. No smile, few words, no sweet-talking or checking her out. She wasn't a pushover and she wasn't a player.

His goal? Get his guys inside that building. Loitering outside was like chum to a shark. She lowered her arm and his balls dropped back into place. He had to admire a woman packing heat.

With her eyes locked on his, she stepped forward and the door slammed shut.

Rule number one. Never cut off your escape route.

She shook his hand. Two firm pumps that sent a shock wave up his arm and down to his twitching dick.

"Where's Mavis?" he asked, hitching a brow.

When she moved into the light, he got a better look at her. Fucking gorgeous. Untamed, gray eyes that bore into his soul. His hollow, empty soul.

"Sabbatical."

This hardcore gatekeeper had a sense of humor, but he kept his face expressionless, on purpose.

The left side of her mouth lifted. Was she mocking him or smiling?

She eyed the vehicle. "Tell your boys to step out. No weapons or I'll blow off your teeny tiny boy-balls."

That smart mouth around his cock would feel so fucking good. "Slowly," he said to Marcus while keeping his gaze trained on her.

The guys emerged like synchronized swimmers. She gave each a once-over, then flipped her poignant stare back to Dakota.

"I'll take them upstairs, then you and I will discuss your bullshit membership."

She turned to unlock and open the heavy, metal door.

Rule number two. Never turn your back on your enemy.

Instinctively, he wanted to disarm her, put her in a choke hold and restrain her, but she wasn't the enemy. Only one damn hot roadblock.

He glanced back at his team. Marcus was stone faced with a clenched jaw. Rhys looked amused. That man was rarely fazed.

Again, she held open the door with her ass. It took a megaton of restraint not to glance at the curve of her backside.

With a toss of her head, she motioned for the men to step inside. Each offered a polite acknowledgement as they passed, but she said nothing. Dakota gripped the steel door above her head. "Go ahead."

Pausing, she eyed him from head to foot while swirling sparks ignited the air between them. Her wild eyes seared him with a welcomed ferocity.

Who is this woman?

His peripheral vision afforded him a shadowed image of her body. Like a moment ago, the large swell of her breasts protruded from her black tank top, but he wasn't stupid enough to look. Sounded like he was two minutes from getting an earful. In exchange, he'd take an eyeful.

Until tonight, they'd entered and exited the club via the back stairs without incident. The fewer eyes watching their comings and goings, the better.

With the men in tow, she climbed the stairs two at a time, unlocked the third-floor fire door, and marched through it.

The Dungeon was located in an unmarked building outside DC. Though the structure appeared unremarkable on the outside, anyone interested in kink knew this was *the* place to play.

Two years ago, the club had changed owners. That's when Dakota and his team had claimed a room on the third floor in a dark alcove next to the back stairs. The sign on the doorframe said *Travesty*. Seemed fitting, so they left it.

Though the Travesty Room was stocked with playing cards and poker chips, Dakota and his team never played. The soundproof, surveillance-free room provided a secure location for their clandestine meetings.

But Mavis, the club's former General Manager, had never used the Dungeon's surveillance system. Based on the actions of this *new* employee, she was all about controlling mayhem and enforcing rules.

Once, Dakota had been an excellent rule follower himself. But he had buried that man three-and-a-half years ago. Now, he lived by his own set of rules.

The pistol-wielding vixen tried the door handle. Locked. She flipped Dakota a saucy look, then used her master key. With a sweep of her hand, she gestured for the men to enter. Once inside, she followed.

Quincy looked up from his computer and blinked. "You pussies needed a private escort?"

"Unfortunately," Rhys replied.

The scuffed walls were bare, the lighting dim. The dingy room wasn't inviting, which was how Dakota liked it. Six mismatched chairs surrounded the table with its neatly stacked poker chips.

Dakota hoped the master key didn't work on the unmarked door on the *other* side of the room. But he'd never call her attention to that. With any luck, she hadn't noticed it.

A server entered, balancing a tray of glasses on his palm. "Here you go, my darlings!" After distributing the drinks, he shut the door behind him.

"Okay, cowboy, ready to chat?" The woman eyed Dakota with a hard stare.

"Back in fifteen," Dakota said as he lifted an ice-cold glass of water from the table.

She raised her brow. "You'll be back when I say so."

Eyeing the guys, Dakota tapped his watch. "Fifteen." He opened the door and waited for her to walk through it. *Damn, she smells good.* Before closing the door, he stuck his head inside. "She could have installed a security cam in here. Sweep the room."

As he followed her down the red-lit hallway, he eyed her perfectly rounded ass. His breathing shifted. My God, she was hot. Shoving down a smile, he pushed on.

In flip-flops she was, maybe, five eight. This smile he couldn't hide. Every woman he screwed wore five-inch fuck-me stilettos. Was this a sign she was all business and not to be fucked...or fucked with?

Her shoes, her garb, and her tight ass were irrelevant. Women were distractions—beautiful ones—but distractions, nonetheless. A way to spend a few hours and try to forget. Then, he'd be on the warpath again, hunting for Beth's elusive killer.

But this one was more than a pretty face and a sexy body. Her defiant energy turned him on in ways he couldn't explain. This woman's aloofness sparked something. Could be as simple as not getting his way or her waving a gun at his junk. Whatever, it would be over in less than fifteen minutes, and he'd get on with his evening.

Their next hit.

This one, a serial killer who'd gotten away with murder one too many times. Tonight, the son of a bitch would breathe his very last breath. Dakota would make sure of that.

She pulled a keychain from her pocket and unlocked her office door. He hadn't been inside Mavis's office in a few months, but the over-crowded, cluttered space had been gutted and sanitized. It no longer stank of the cigarettes Mavis chain-smoked, despite club rules. The stacks of old magazines and faded newspapers had been cleared. Gone was the putrid yellow sofa with so many cigarette burns he couldn't believe the joint hadn't gone up in flames.

The clunky metal desk once covered in debris, and the rickety, unstable chair he was convinced would crack under Mavis's weight, had been replaced with a sleek glass desk and a mesh chair. The sticky slate flooring had been cleaned and polished, removing the layer of god-knows-what that crunched beneath his feet.

The office had *uptight* written all over it in invisible ink.

Flanking the desk and positioned like interrogation lights stood two steel floor lamps with octopus arms sticking out in haphazard directions.

A fresh coat of paint covered the once peeling walls. Was that taupe? No, more like a muted gray. *That's upbeat.*

With a titty jiggle that lit his insides on fire, she sauntered over to the credenza that was once piled high with Mavis's crap and tapped a keyboard. The six monitors mounted on the back wall went dark...the ones that displayed live surveillance video from inside and outside the club. He suppressed the urge to roll his eyes and groan. *Whatever happened to a little damn privacy?*

She sat behind the desk and, suddenly, this hard-assed woman looked uncomfortable, like the slick digs didn't jibe. Would Mavis's mess have been more to her liking? With her jaw set in a hard line, she looked like she was about to hold court.

Cementing his gaze on hers, he sipped the ice-cold sparkling water, then sat on the sofa arm. Instant mistake. The thin, metal sunk into his ass crack like quicksand, so he moved to the ultra-modern chair across from her desk. This one felt like a slab of cement. *My poor ass.*

But it afforded him the perfect view. Maybe a glass desk was the way to go. He had an unobstructed view of everything from her toned thighs down to her shiny black toenail polish. In the five seconds he stole to check her out, he gained a whole new appreciation for ultra-modern furniture. He fucking loved it.

With less than ten minutes to get his ass back to that room, he pinned her with an ardent stare. "You got a name?"

Her gaze floated across his face, lingered on his chest and torso, then meandered back to his eyes. "Providence."

This time, he couldn't hide his smile. "Like, Rhode Island?"

"Providence means divine guidance and care." She leaned back and crossed her arms. Besides hoisting her phenomenal breasts onto a makeshift platter, her body language screamed closed-off. He'd have her spread eagle and loving every submissive minute before he was done with her.

"You've got a lot of nerve trashing my name when you're named after a state."

He couldn't miss the gleam in her eyes. She liked messing with him.

"Touché." He steeled his spine. *Enough small talk.* "What's the problem?"

She leaned forward and dammit if he didn't look at her cleavage. Fuck his dick. He couldn't control himself. And it was worth the eye scolding he was getting.

"Besides having a key to the building, that I'm going to confiscate, you and your idiot friends owe this club a cool million. You want to explain yourself, Mr. Luck?"

"I'd be happy to." He took a mouthful of water and swallowed it down. "When the club traded hands and the current owner bought it, I negotiated a deal that provided me and *my idiot friends* with lifetime L3 memberships at no cost."

She pushed out of her chair and sashayed around the desk, sandwiching herself between it and him. Holding out her hand, she said, "May I?" Before he could figure out what she wanted, she took the drink and tossed back a mouthful. And then she placed the glass against her chest. His gaze hung hungrily where that lowball rested. She was doing an incredible job of teasing him. And he was loving every damn minute of her mind fuck.

When she removed it, beads of condensation rolled between her breasts and vanished where he wanted to place his dick.

He started to harden and he crossed his legs to hide his burgeoning bulge.

She'd eaten up seven minutes and all he'd gotten out of their conversation was a fantasy to jerk off to. This Providence chick was starting to get on his nerves.

"I don't care about your negotiations," she said. "As the new GM, I'm all about the bottom line. You and your poker pals are *not* getting a free pass." She shrugged. "If you don't like my rules, take your games and your kink elsewhere."

Her office door flew open. With lightning speed, Dakota grabbed the Glock strapped to his ankle and stood, taking aim at the intruder.

"You fucking shoot me and I'll be so damn pissed," Stryker said.

On an exhale, Dakota returned the weapon to its holster. "You're an asshole, you know that?"

Stryker Truman laughed. "Yeah, man, *that* I know. And you're fucking crazy to pull a gun on me at my own club." His dark brown hair touched his shoulders. Ten days ago, Stryker was clean-shaven. Tonight, he had a scruffy beard. The men stood almost eye-to-eye.

"You look good, bro," Dakota said. "If you're trying to look like Sasquatch, mission accomplished."

Chuckling, Stryker slapped Dakota on the back before kissing Providence's forehead. The fire in her eyes and the hardness around her mouth vanished. Her smile, though brief, halted Dakota's breath. She had the ability to stop a locomotive with that smile. This hard-ass gatekeeper was fucking beautiful.

"You've been giving my boys a hard time?" Stryker asked.

Ah, hell, he's replaced Mavis with his girl. A sexy-as-hell woman he'd been keeping under tight wraps. As Dakota flushed every late-night fantasy down the commode, his twitching dick stood down. He'd never screw another man's woman, especially not a member of his crew.

Providence handed Dakota his drink. "Stryker," she began, but her gaze stayed pinned on Dakota, "I've been doing clean-up this week. Your friends are cutting some serious corners by skipping the membership fees." She grabbed her beat-up handbag from the credenza behind the desk and popped two squares of gum into her mouth.

"When did you become a gum chewer?" Stryker asked.

"When I quit smoking."

After pushing out of the chair, Dakota checked his watch. Four minutes to spare. And he was confident his guys had placed wages on whether he'd get there in time. "I've gotta bolt. Can you handle this and join us?"

Stryker nodded, then turned back to Providence. "The men in Travesty get a pass. No questions asked."

"Thanks, man." Dakota turned back at the door. "Miss Rhode Island, it's been a pleasure."

She flipped him off and folded her arms.

Dammit, she needs to stop doing that.

"You might get to play for free, but I'm keeping an eye on you," she said.

I like the sound of that. "Yes, ma'am."

"Providence, this is the man who saved my life," Stryker said.

"You would have done the same for me," Dakota replied, but couldn't take his eyes off Providence. Why did his best friend's girl have to be so freakin' hot?

He'd never sleep with her. His loyalty toward these men went blood deep. And Stryker was one crazy motherfucker. He'd kill Dakota in a heartbeat.

The new gatekeeper was off limits. *Stay the hell away from her.*

Suddenly, Miss Rhode Island had become absolutely irresistible.

3

THE KILL

With fourteen seconds left, Dakota high-tailed it to the Travesty room. All four men were staring at their watches. He chuffed out a laugh. "Well?"

"Two seconds left." Marcus collected the pile of money in the middle of the poker table. "I had faith you'd make it back in time."

"You suck," Quincy grumbled.

"Is the room still secure?" Dakota asked as he joined them at the table.

Rhys glanced up from his laptop. "Yes."

"Prep us," Dakota said to Quincy.

By day, Quincy ran a DC firm that helped underprivileged youth get accepted to college. When he joined Dakota on a hit, he scouted locations, and met their targets, when feasible. "Last week, I took a meeting with Ralph Meyers—AKA Mr. Ralphy—in the back room of a strip club in Baltimore," Quincy said. "I offered him ten grand to complete a hit. Five tonight, and another five after. I instructed him to come alone. He won't."

"Why not?" Dakota asked.

"His two bodyguards flanked him during the meeting and followed him out after."

"Run down tonight's time frame," Dakota said.

"We arrive in by midnight," Quincy continued. "Fifteen to get inside the warehouse and into position. Meyers is expected before one."

Dakota glanced at his watch. "Where's the hit?"

"An abandoned warehouse, southeast side of Baltimore," Quincy said. "I instructed him to enter through the back of the building. Rhys will run down Meyers's priors."

Dakota shifted his attention to Rhys. He looked every bit a Marine as the day Dakota met him, but his military career ended when half his unit got killed in Afghanistan. He got out with full honors and a heavy heart.

"Ralph Meyers has been on the FBI's Most Wanted List for two decades." Rhys turned the laptop around and showed the guys the mug shots of Meyers. "His killing sprees hug the East Coast, primarily along the shoreline. Law enforcement believes he's behind forty-two abductions, but there could be dozens more. Not one body has ever been found intact. He's spending his weeks in Baltimore and his weekends at Ocean City. Most likely prepping for another abduction. Over the years, he's been arrested twice. The first time he was released. The second time he escaped before his trial started."

A chill careened through Dakota. Had this monster abducted Beth? "We're going to put a permanent stop to Ralph Meyers's horrific beach plans." Dakota raked a hand through his unkempt hair. "Run down his SWOT."

Rhys guzzled his water. "*Strength.* Ability to use a knife. He can dismember his victim in minutes. *Weakness.* Greed. *Opportunity.* He's not killing for sport anymore. He's branched out for-hire. *Threat.* The usual. Crazy. Dangerous. Armed. At least two guards."

"The warehouse doesn't have electricity," Rhys added. "So, you'll need a headlamp. Do you have Beth's picture?"

Dakota nodded.

Their plan was simple. Dakota was hiring this serial killer to murder his already deceased wife. He would show Meyers the picture of Beth. If he recognized her as one of his victims, Dakota would finally have his answer. If he didn't, he would continue searching for her abductor. Either way, this was the end for Ralph Meyers.

"If everything goes according to plan, we'll be back here by two thirty." Quincy pulled off his Howard University college ring and set it on the table. "What's the trigger sentence?"

"'That's exactly what I needed to hear,'" Dakota replied.

"On hearing that, Stryker and I will eliminate the bodyguards," Rhys said.

For the next eleven minutes, the men reviewed every conceivable scenario. Under no condition would they leave one of their own behind. Not on Dakota's watch.

After knocking twice before stepping into the room, Stryker said, "Time to go." He locked the door, strode across the room, and unlocked the door on the far wall.

"Providence has activated the surveillance system," Dakota said. "She saw us arrive tonight and was there to...*greet* us."

Stryker chuckled. "She doesn't like members using the back door."

"And?" Dakota asked.

"I took down that security cam," Stryker replied. "Problem solved."

"No pushback from the new sheriff?" Dakota asked.

"Hell, yeah, but I'm the boss."

Relieved, Dakota stood and eyed each of the men. "If you aren't up for this or can't move forward, now's the time to back out."

He was met with silence. They all knew they were walking into a dangerous situation, but that had never stopped them before. And it wouldn't stop them now.

After several more seconds, he dropped his phone and wallet on the table. "Good luck."

"Don't you mean *Dakota* Luck?" Rhys slapped Dakota on the back, then tossed his phone and wallet on the table.

With the exception of Marcus, who kept his driver's license and cell phone, the men carried no identifiers. After dropping their wallets, phones and jewelry on the table, they entered the back room and opened their lockers. Like before, Stryker locked the door from the inside. Everyone, except Dakota, dressed in full tactical gear, down to their combat boots. Since Dakota was primary, his only defense against a spray of gunfire was the Kevlar vest he wore like a second skin beneath his shirt.

After checking their weapons, they collected their NODs— night observation devices. Dakota shouldered the backpack, opened the door, and they filed down the metal fire escape.

In silence, they rode north.

While Dakota could have phoned in an anonymous tip to the FBI hotline and let the feds capture Meyers, he and his team would ensure this long-time serial killer did not get off on a technicality...again. After two decades of being an abductor, sexual predator, and serial killer, Ralph Meyers's luck was about to run out, Dakota Luck style.

An hour later, as the twinkling high-rises of Charm City sprouted into view, Dakota, Stryker, Quincy and Rhys strapped on their NODs. They slid on their skintight leather gloves as Marcus drove into the rundown neighborhood. Dakota listened for uneven breathing and watched for fidgeting. These were solid, honorable men who'd joined him of their own volition. Nevertheless, he needed to confirm they were up to the task.

"It's go-time. Everyone in?"

"Absolutely," Quincy replied.

"Affirmative," Rhys echoed.

"No reservations," Stryker said.

"Hell, yeah." Marcus street parked two blocks from the abandoned building. In an eerie silence, the four men got out.

Eleven thirty-three.

Marcus stayed behind. If all hell broke loose, he was tasked with getting them—or their bullet-laden bodies—the hell out.

Under cover of a new moon, Dakota switched on his goggles and adjusted the headband. Then, he shouldered the backpack and tossed Marcus a nod before closing the door of the black SUV, one of several Dakota kept at his black site.

The foursome jogged toward the building, Stryker and Quincy at the head followed by Rhys and Dakota. Dakota's heart rate increased, but with the amount of adrenaline pumping through him, he expected it. The beats would slow once they settled into position.

Two dealers lingered on the street corner at the end of the quiet block. When they saw what looked like a SWAT team barreling toward them, they fled.

As planned, Stryker and Rhys headed toward the back of the building while Dakota and Quincy entered through the front. Several rats scurried across the cavernous space. Before venturing down a dark hallway to the back offices, Dakota stopped and listened.

Upon hearing nothing, Dakota signaled that he was heading in while Quincy acted as lookout.

Dakota ensured each office was clear before wedging open the door leading out back. He entered the office across the hall and dragged a metal table and two chairs into the center of the room. He removed the NOD and replaced it with a headlamp from his backpack. Then, he sat, pulled off his leather gloves, and dropped them on his thigh.

And there, he waited, his steady inhale and slow exhale his only companion.

"Dakota," said Marcus through the comm device.

"I'm here."

"We've got a police cruiser rolling by the building."

"Probably making the rounds."

"He turned the corner."

"I've got eyes on it," Quincy said. "The car stopped out front."

"Let us know if they get out," Dakota said.

Four minutes later, a vehicle pulled up out back. The engine cut off. A door opened, then a second and a third.

"Quincy," Dakota murmured. "Where are the police?"

"Still out front," Quincy replied.

Fuck. Meyers had arrived with his bodyguards.

"Hello?" called a man.

"In here," Dakota replied.

Meyers's bodyguard entered.

"Who the hell are you?" Dakota asked.

"Mr. Ralphy's assistant. Here to check the place out."

Dakota spit out a grunt. "I hired Meyers to murder my wife. Why the hell would I tell anyone?"

"Relax," said the bodyguard. "Mr. Meyers is outside."

"Police drove away," Quincy said into the comm.

"Good," Stryker replied from the rear of the building. "Here comes Meyers."

"I'm here," said a gruff voice. Ralph Meyers stepped into the room and Dakota's blood ran cold. Staring into the eyes of a cold-blooded serial killer filled him with hate.

"I'll be outside, Mr. Meyers." The guard left the room.

"Let's do business." Dakota adjusted the headlamp toward the ceiling. "Sit."

Meyers folded into the second chair. "I got word you need my help."

Dakota slid the photo across the rusty, metal table. "This is my wife." If Meyers recognized Beth as one of his victims, Dakota and his team would move fast.

"Pretty lady. Why off her?"

"You recognize her?"

"Nope. Should I?"

"This job needs to happen in the next two days. She's going on a business trip, only she's not. She's meeting up with her pig boyfriend."

"You got the money?"

"I need assurance her body won't be found."

"Do you know who I am?" Meyers asked.

"I only know you can help me."

"I've been around, kid."

"I'm not going to prison because some guy tells me he's been around," Dakota bit out. "I need proof you're going to take care of this with no loose ends."

"Karen Barberry, Missy Lynn James, Mary Watson, Becky Martin, Flo Patricks. You want more names?"

"I have no fuckin' idea what that means. Is that code?"

"Those girls will never be found because they were cut to pieces. But not before I had my fun with them. And there were dozens more just like them. At some point, I lost count, but I'd say sixty-two or sixty-three. Is that sufficient?"

Jesus.

"Now, where's my payment?" Meyers bit out.

Dakota shone his headlamp into the backpack. "Five now. Another five after."

Meyers pulled out a banded wad of cash and smelled it. "Mother of God, this gives me a rush."

"I'll need confirmation she's dead."

"Does she wear a wedding ring?"

"She has one, but I have no idea if she wears it when she's whoring around." Dakota needed to wrap this up. Beneath the table, he slid on the leather gloves. "What do you normally do?"

"I keep everything from photos to jewelry. I can take a picture of her severed head if you want absolute confirmation."

Oh, my God.

"So, you'll kill her?" Dakota confirmed.

"Jesus H. Christ, yes, I'll kill her and anyone else you want me to." Meyers leaned forward. "Taking your wife's last breath is what I live for."

"That's exactly what I needed to hear." The trigger sentence Dakota had been waiting to utter.

Stryker and Rhys pumped each bodyguard with five bullets made quiet by silencers. Still, the popping sound shattered the otherwise quiet night. One body, then the second, collapsed on the ground.

"What the――" Meyers blurted.

As Dakota pushed out of the chair, he wrapped his gloved hand around Meyers's neck, yanked him out of the chair, and shoved him against the wall. "Do you like killing innocents?" he growled.

"What the fuck," Meyers gasped. "Who the hell are you?"

"Do you feel powerful, godlike even, when you watch the light fade from their terrified, innocent eyes?"

"I…" Meyers squeezed out.

"I might go to hell for this, but I own what I'm about to do. Someone has got to fucking stop you."

In one quick, skilled move, Dakota spun him around, put him in a choke hold, and snapped his neck. Meyers dropped to the floor. Stryker entered and shot Meyers in the forehead and the chest. Dakota shoved the photo of Beth into his pocket. Then, he and Stryker pulled out microfiber cloths and, with efficient precision, wiped down the rusted, metal furniture while Meyers bled out.

Careful not to step in the expanding pool of blood, Dakota threw the headlamp into the bag before turning back to Meyers. Seeing his lifeless body brought Dakota no joy.

He and Stryker exited through the nearby fire door. After Dakota shut it, he, Stryker, and Rhys jogged to the front of the building, picked up Quincy, and continued on to the waiting vehicle.

A block away, Marcus flashed the headlights, once.

Safe to approach and enter.

"I'm making the call." Dakota pulled the burner from his backpack and dialed.

"Good evening, FBI tip line," said the operator. "With whom am I speaking?"

"Karen Barberry, Missy Lynn James, Mary Watson, Becky Martin, Flo Patricks." Dakota spoke in a raspy growl.

"Sir, what can I help you with?"

"These victims were innocent, young women killed by Ralph Meyers, AKA, Mr. Ralphy. His killing spree spans decades and he admitted to murdering over sixty women. I'm calling to report he's dead. His body can be found in the abandoned warehouse on Fleeger Street, in southeast Balmer."

He said "Balmer" as a native Baltimorean would.

"Sir, we follow-up on every credible lead. How do you know his body is there?"

Dakota disconnected.

Because I fucking put him there.

Rage billowed up and he ripped the flip phone in two. With each death, the blood on his hands grew. Sammy had already lost one parent. If Dakota got killed or ended up in prison, she'd lose him, too.

As soon as the men piled into the vehicle, Marcus pulled onto the quiet street. After a few blocks, he stopped at the curb. Dakota pulled the ski mask out of his backpack and covered his face, then got out. He tossed the broken burner into the dumpster. Once back in the SUV, Marcus took off.

Dakota waited until they were on I-95, heading back to Virginia, before he broke the silence. "Injuries?"

"None," Rhys replied.

"I'm good," Stryker said.

"Ditto," Quincy added.

And just like that, it was done. A serial killer exterminated, like a damn cockroach. But not the one who'd taken his Beth. While

Dakota should have felt like the scales of evil had shifted, he didn't. Pride did not fill his heart, for he knew the devil himself was grinning in anticipation of his arrival. Just because Dakota justified what he and his team did, didn't make it right. And it certainly didn't mean God justified it, either.

But Ralph Meyers would kill no more and that was Dakota's sole goal.

No one spoke as they drove back. After Marcus parked at the back entrance to The Dungeon, the team trudged up the fire escape to the third floor. Though the men never spoke about their feelings, Dakota wondered if their hearts were as heavy as his.

He never took the killing of another lightly. And he'd never intended to take the law into his own hands. But when his wife went missing, and he'd gone off the rails, someone close to him had offered him a lifeline. By searching for his wife's killer, he'd become one himself.

Stryker unlocked the door. They retreated into the Travesty equipment room and removed their gear.

Dakota turned to his vigilante brothers. "Excellent work, tonight. Live with the demons or make peace with your actions. I'm here if you want to talk."

"Want me to stick around?" Marcus asked.

"Take my SUV," Dakota replied. "I'll get it from you tomorrow."

"I can drop you at home, Marcus," Quincy said.

After Marcus handed the keys to Dakota, he and Quincy took off, followed by Rhys.

Dakota eyed Stryker. "You doin' okay?"

"Who the hell knows, anymore," Stryker replied.

Dakota wanted to gather intel about Providence. Instead, he'd ask about the previous GM. "What happened to Mavis? Did you let her go?"

Stryker slipped his wallet and phone into his pocket. "She's recovering from surgery."

"Is she okay?"

"She'll be back in a coupla weeks. And no doubt giving me a shit-ton of grief about remodeling her office."

What's Providence's story? No way in hell was he going there. "Headed downstairs for a drink?"

Stryker pulled on his black, devil mask. "I'm using the dungeon tonight." With his hand on the knob, he turned. "You okay?"

"I'm never gonna find Beth's killer," Dakota bit out.

"Probably not, but I've got your back, no matter what kinda crazy shit you pull." Stryker shut the door, leaving Dakota alone with his thoughts.

Which was never a good thing.

His late wife popped into his head. They'd found out they were having a baby and, as tears streamed down Beth's cheeks, she stared at the pregnancy test.

"I don't know how this happened," she said.

Laughing, Dakota pulled her into his arms. "Our children are going to be very lucky to have you as their mom."

Through misty eyes, she stared up at him. "Children?"

He nodded. "Lots of stinky ones who will all adore you."

Blinking away the bittersweet memory, he checked his phone. The sitter had sent a photo two hours ago. The pic was of Sammy, cuddling with her blanket on the family room sofa. "Woke for water," she had texted. "Couldn't sleep. Reading princess story."

He replied, "Thanks for the update. Is she ok?"

No dots appeared. He locked the Travesty Room door before heading down the hall toward the stairs.

As he strode past the GM's office, the door opened and Providence stepped into the hallway. "Hey, cowboy, how'd your poker game turn out?"

Damn if her beauty didn't send his heart pounding. He hadn't reacted like this to a woman in a long time. He tossed her a nod. "Sheriff."

Her smile sent a jolt of energy through him. *Wow, she's gorgeous.* "Heading to the dungeon?"

Confusion flashed in those intense gray eyes of hers. "Making the rounds."

No woman kept Stryker waiting. But, clearly, this one did.

"I'll walk with you to the second floor," he said. "I'm headed there for a drink."

"Last call was at two."

Ah, Christ, here we go. Mavis instructed the staff to serve him at all hours. Dammit, the new gatekeeper was pissing him off again. Yanking open the fire door, he waited while she sauntered past. Her feminine, flowery scent grabbed his attention. She smelled so damn good. Good enough to eat.

Club members rarely used the back stairs and he found himself alone with her. The door slammed shut and he hung back so he could admire her hourglass figure, the curve of her ass and the sway of her hips as she made her way down. God, he loved women, and this one had hijacked his complete attention.

After placing her hand on the second-floor door handle, she turned back and pinned him with another fiery gaze. "But you look like the kinda man who takes what he wants without permission or apology."

A ravenous need overcame him and he grabbed her hands and lifted her arms over her head. Pinning her body against the cold, metal door, he kissed her, *hard.*

She groaned into his mouth and stroked his tongue with wild abandon. He ground against her, the desire building to a maddening frenzy.

And then his brain kicked in and he broke away. Panting, he stepped back. Her straining nipples stretched against the thin layer of fabric.

Fuck me.

He'd done the unthinkable. He'd kissed Stryker's girl.

She sucked in a harsh breath while her laser-focused gaze

never left his. Dragging her fingers through her short hair made his balls ache. "Mavis let the bartenders serve past two," she said as if that scorching kiss hadn't just happened. "I hate to be a ballbuster, but I'm following strict orders. The bars on all three levels are closed."

Her voice didn't quiver. She didn't bat her thick black lashes and her cheeks didn't flush with color. But her pupils were fully dilated and it wasn't from the dimly lit stairwell. She wanted him to believe that kiss hadn't affected her, but her body was screaming for more. And he wanted to accommodate her in every possible way.

All he could think to say was, "When did Stryker become a rule follower?"

He hated when useless shit came flying out of his mouth. He'd kissed Stryker's girl. He'd have to tell him. And then block Stryker's right hook. No, Stryker would clock him with a left sucker punch because he wouldn't expect that. Whatever Stryker gave him, he'd take, like a man.

She shrugged. "He's always been that way. I've got to head downstairs and clear out the young, wild things. See ya."

She didn't wait for an answer. She didn't glance over her shoulder at him, either. She just left him standing alone in the stairwell with a raging hard-on and an aching, suffocating need to kiss her again.

His vibrating phone shifted his attention and he read the incoming text from the sitter. "Sammy woke again. Didn't feel well. Temp 99.2."

"Be there shortly," he texted back. As he strode down the steps and out into the night, his desire for a whiskey and a fuck were replaced with an urgent need to care for his child.

4

THE PRODIGAL SON

Providence Reynolds eased onto the cold, park bench, coffee cup in hand. At ten minutes past seven, she had the area to herself, so she reread the text from her boss.

"Langers Park, Arlington, Sat, 7AM."

While it was unusual that Lou would request an off-site meeting so early into the investigation, she didn't question it. She was a damn good team player, but this assignment had her pissed off. Babysitting a playboy real estate broker was total BS.

She didn't care that his piercing blue eyes had stripped her bare and locked in on her with an intensity that made her crazy with lust. It didn't matter that men sporting some facial scruff drove her wild, and that Dakota Luck wore his to perfection. And so what if she could have stared at him and his rock-hard body for days?

She had a job to do, so she'd ignore her raging hormones, act like the pro she was, and get it done. Period.

Maybe Luck is the perfect assignment for me.

She'd just come off an intense, twenty-one-month gig where she'd worked all the angles, made dangerous connections, and even went so far as to step inside the bizarre world of a cult in order to find several missing persons. Because of her efforts, their bodies had been found, and the son-of-a-bitch cult leader had been arrested.

Then, she'd gotten "selected" by management to work this case. "What a crock," she grumbled before downing a mouthful of joe.

The crisp, morning air should have invigorated her, but she couldn't shake the sleep from her eyes. The four hours in bed had been spent tossing and turning, her mind consumed by her newest target.

Dakota Luck.

That man took up way too much head space. Rather than push out the thoughts, she let them rattle around until they seeped into her soul. She was good at her job because she became one with her target, and she was prepared to do it again.

That was always how she worked a case, and this one was no different. Except for the fact that she'd kissed him. But that hot-as-hell smooch was nothing when compared to all the other things she *wanted* to do. The moment he stepped out of that vehicle, her brain had shorted. Dakota Luck was gorgeous, loaded with testosterone, and a total alpha.

But she'd fallen for all that macho shit once before, only to be gutted when the relationship ended. She promised herself 'never again' and she had meant it.

She had been working her newest gig for a whopping week and all she'd been able to confirm were two things. Dakota Luck was a cocky bastard and a damn good kisser.

As far as her *actual* assignment, she had gleaned nothing. While she hated taking the nightclub's GM spot under false pretenses, she needed to get close to Dakota, and The Dungeon provided her the perfect opportunity, no questions asked.

A car door closed, plucking her from her thoughts. A middle-aged woman opened the back door and a mutt hopped out. *No fucking way. What's she doing here?*

Special Agent in Charge Patricia Stearns managed the *entire* DC office of the FBI. Had word gotten back to the SAC that Providence was not okay with this assignment?

After leashing the pooch, Patricia and her pet walked into the park, and over to the bench. "Can I join you?"

"Sure."

As the woman eased down, the dog approached, tail wagging, and Providence stroked its soft fur.

"Did Lou call in sick so he could sneak off to the links?" Providence asked.

Patricia chuckled. "I wanted to speak with you myself."

Maybe there was more to the wealthy playboy than Providence had thought.

"How'd your first week go?" Patricia asked.

"Aside from the fact that I know absolutely nothing about managing a kink club, I'd say I did one helluva job."

"I knew you'd be the perfect person for the case," she said with an approving smile.

Providence returned her attention to a large oak tree a hundred feet away. Rather than dance around the subject, she said, "You asked for me because I've got a connection with the club owner."

"True, but you're smart, level-headed, and a skilled agent."

That politically correct answer made Providence chuckle. The two women grew quiet and Providence sipped her black coffee, appreciating the robust blend that nipped at her tongue.

"I'm sorry I wasn't able to speak with you before today," Patricia said.

"No worries. I just met Luck last night."

"What have you learned?"

"They don't use the surveillance system and the exterior cam at the rear entrance was taken down."

"Hmm, that's noteworthy. What else?"

"In general, people like their kink," Providence continued. "They hang from ropes. And they enjoy getting spanked. Pain, the great stimulant."

Patricia chuckled.

"Members wear masks to hide their identities and call themselves Ecstasy and Midnight so no one knows who the hell they really are."

"I need to get out more."

"I'd be happy to offer you a complimentary pass, but an annual membership starts at five grand."

"Ouch. I'm a government employee on a government salary with two kids to put through college, so I'll pass on the kink. Plus, I like to keep the fun at home with my hus—"

"Okay, so thanks for that." After shooting Patricia a brief smile, she said, "Regarding Luck, I haven't learned a thing. His file was redacted. What's ALPHA?"

"I don't know. There's nothing anywhere about an organization with that name and I've asked around. No one knows."

"How can I build a profile if there's no information on him?"

"The old-fashioned way. Keep your eyes and ears on him."

I can think of a few other body parts I'd like to press against his. She tried shaking that thought. And failed.

"Lou didn't have much to tell me about this gig," Providence said. "What's Luck suspected of?"

A car pulled into the lot and Patricia glanced over her shoulder. "Killing men on The Most Wanted List who have eluded us for years."

"Hmm, a vigilante."

Patricia rose and paused while a pair of joggers ran past. "Several months ago, an anonymous caller using a burner led Philadelphia police to the body of Kevin Ericson. He'd been on

The List for over a decade for the abduction and deaths of thirty coeds. He was arrested for the murder of three, but there were mistakes made with the evidence and he got released. When his body was found, he had a broken neck, a gunshot wound to the head and another to the chest. Same M.O. for a handful of murders over the past few years."

"I see," Providence said.

"We've never gotten a break, until a couple of months ago," Patricia continued. "Another murder, same M.O. This criminal had been on The List for a string of violent crimes against homosexuals in southern Virginia. A DNA match linked him to several of his victims. While in custody, he escaped. An informant at the crime scene caught a partial license plate. That was linked to Luck and about three hundred other people, but a majority of those have been ruled out."

"Have you had eyes on him before me?"

"An undercover agent out of the Virginia FBI office is a licensed real estate agent. A perfect cover, if you ask me." Patricia paused to pat her pup. "Anyway, she got a job working at one of Luck's real estate offices in Virginia. Her husband works for the State Department. He recently got transferred, so she put in for a relo."

"What did she find?"

"Not a damn thing. In her report, she stated he was the most ethical broker she'd ever worked for. Since he spends a fair amount of time at The Dungeon, I need someone who can get close to him."

Providence wanted to ask her exactly how close she wanted her to get, but decided against that. Instead, she said, "I'm using my real name. I've never done that before and I feel vulnerable."

"Your legend as a marketing consultant with time on her hands works for this case."

"I've gotta be honest. I'm not happy with this assignment."

"Your last gig was intense and everyone—even you—needs a breather between jobs. It's easy, it's local, and this beats a desk job. That would drive you crazy."

"True." Providence downed more coffee. Though she'd voiced her concern, she was stuck working this one.

Patricia opened her handbag and offered Providence a name tag. "Speaking of sticking close to Luck, he's got some upscale real estate event. And you'll be attending."

She glanced at the name on the tag. Elaine Jones, Larke Realty. "What's my story?"

"You're an agent with Larke Realty. Stagehand set up a realtor profile for you on their website that expires in twenty-four hours. I heard you're great with accents. Can you pull off a Boston one?"

"I've got one that'll pass," Providence said.

"Good. You just moved to the area from Boston."

"He already met me...as me."

"The event has a masquerade theme, so you can use one of those sexy club masks. It's at the National Harbor from seven to ten. There will be a few hundred realtors, plus their guests, so it'll be easy to blend in."

"When?"

"Tonight."

"I'm going to have to beg out of working at the club."

"Migraines always worked for me."

"You were undercover?"

"I was once young, like you."

"Not sure thirty-three counts as young."

"It is when you're fifty-four."

A car pulled in and two children and a man exited the vehicle. The little girls' laughter snagged Providence's attention and her heart clenched. The kids bolted past, big smiles filling their small faces. "Slow down, you two," the man called after them.

Time for Providence to move on. She tossed Patricia a nod. "I'll be in touch."

"Good luck."

Providence returned to her car and locked the name tag in her glove box. As she drove out of the park, she wondered how she was going to beg out of work while she sleuthed around at the realtor event.

Though she was ready to go home and crash, she'd been invited to her parents' house for breakfast. Her mom had mentioned she was excited for Providence and her sister to see "the big surprise".

As she jumped on the beltway, her phone rang. Providence glanced at the nav screen before hitting the speaker button. "Hey. Need a ride?"

"How'd you know?" asked her sister, Megan.

"I'm a genius."

Megan laughed. "Where are you?"

"On the way. Be there in twenty."

"Thanks." The line went dead.

Megan Sharpe was younger by eighteen months. She was a structural engineer, a whiz with numbers, and a volunteer puppy raiser for a national organization that trained guide dogs for the blind.

As Providence drove toward her sister's, her thoughts drifted back to Dakota. A cold-blooded killer? That seemed extreme, but not inconceivable. In her line of work, anything was possible. And Patricia Stearns had a rock-solid reputation. She wouldn't have asked for undercover if she didn't need eyes on her suspect.

She pulled into her sister's driveway and hopped out. As she made her way up the walkway, the front door opened and Megan exited the house, her four-legged companion by her side. Beacon was wearing his guide dog vest.

"Where's Leigh?" Providence asked.

"She had to work today," Megan replied. "The pharmacy was short-staffed, so she went in."

After situating the dog in the back seat, Megan jumped in as Providence got behind the wheel.

"So, what do you think the surprise is?" Providence asked.

"I assumed it was a puppy, so I asked, since I bring Beacon wherever I go."

"And?" Providence headed out of the neighborhood.

"No animals, but that's all Mom would say. Did you ask?"

"No," Providence replied. "I'm guessing they might be putting the house on the market and downsizing."

"There's no way that house is anywhere near ready for showing," Megan said. "The garage is stuffed with everything Dad won't get rid of. If I ever owned a home with a garage, I would park my car in it."

As Providence pulled onto the entrance ramp for the Dulles Toll Road, Megan asked, "How did this job with Stryker come about?"

"Marketing consultants aren't in great demand these days. But Stryker needed a GM to fill in while his stepped away for a few weeks."

"That's cool. How do you like managing a night club?"

"Ask me again in a week. I'm still trying to figure out the damn software and don't get me started on which kind of bondage rope is best."

Megan slid a smirk in her direction. "I can kinda see you working there and kinda not. Do you like it?"

"Sure." Providence needed to redirect the conversation. "How's Beacon's training going?"

"He's doing great. He learned how to open and close the refrigerator door by using a rope. Hey, maybe I should check out the rope you order for the club." As Megan chatted about Beacon's latest accomplishments, Providence relaxed.

She hated having to change the subject, hated living a lie. Anxiety tinged her vague conversations about work simply because she couldn't share her real career with anyone, not even with the ones she loved the most.

When Providence parked in front of her parents' brick-front home in Reston, the two-car garage door was open, revealing boxes, old bikes, and miscellaneous junk piled so high both women stood there gawking at the mess.

"I'd lose my mind," Megan said before pulling a small plastic doggie bag from her pocket. "I'll be right in. I'm taking Beacon for a quick walk."

Providence headed up the path, rapped on the front door, and stepped into the foyer. "Hello!"

Her dad hurried out of the kitchen and toward her. "Hello, dear." He kissed her cheek. "Where's Megan?"

Gordon Sharpe was grinning like he'd won the damn lottery. "Okay, Dad, you're dying to tell me. What's the big surprise? You bought a new sailboat, didn't you?"

Her dad shook his head. "Megan texted that you were picking her up."

"She took Beacon for a walk."

Gordon put his arm around her and escorted her into the kitchen. Her mom sat at the table, sipping what looked like a mimosa. Neither parent drank much, and never in the morning. Heather Sharpe rose, but grabbed the table and slammed her eyes shut.

Her dad was by her side in a flash, helping steady his wife. "Easy does it, honey."

When Providence hugged her, she couldn't help but notice her mom was shaking. "What's going on?"

Her mom inhaled and squared her shoulders. "I got up too fast and was a little light-headed, that's all. It's nothing."

Providence shifted her attention to her dad. His brows were knitted together, his concern apparent.

The front door opened and shut. "Sit, Beacon. Good boy." The three of them grew silent while Megan spoke with the dog. A few seconds later, her sister and the pup entered the room. "Why do you guys look like you've seen the dead? Mom, you're so pale. Oh, God, is someone sick?"

"Mom got up too quickly," Providence said. "She was light-headed." Providence studied her mom. "Are you okay?"

Heather Sharpe, a vibrant, healthy sixty-five-year-old, was a psychologist who specialized in helping her patients overcome sexual challenges. "Yes, yes. All good. Are you two ready for the big reveal?"

"The suspense is killing me," Megan said before filling a bowl with water and setting it on the floor in the corner. "Beacon, water."

A man walked into the room, an explosive smile brightening his face. Providence stared at him for a few seconds, then blurted, "Oh, my God."

"No way," Megan whispered.

"Surprise!" Randy exclaimed. "The prodigal son has returned!"

"Wow," Providence said as he threw his arms around her and offered her a warm embrace. While Randy hugged Megan, Providence slid her gaze to her mom and dad. "You guys must be thrilled."

"We are," her mom said with a delighted smile.

Over a decade had passed without so much as a phone call from her half-brother. At forty-one, a smattering of grays blended with Randy Maddox's short, dark hair. Creases etched his forehead and crow's feet accented his eyes, but he appeared as fit as he'd always been.

Randy stepped between his mom and stepdad, placed his arms around their shoulders and grinned at his sisters. "These two have been incredible. Before we catch up, I have a surprise of my own."

A cute blonde with a sweet smile took a few tentative steps into the kitchen and gave a little wave. "Hi."

"Providence, Megan, meet my wife, Lizzie Maddox."

Though reeling from the surprise, Providence smiled. "Welcome to the family."

"It's great to meet you both," Lizzie said.

"I'm Megan and this is Beacon."

"How 'bout I make you guys mimosas?" Randy asked his sisters.

"Sounds good to me!" Megan said.

Providence shook her head. "It's too early for me to hit the sauce."

Randy got busy making more drinks while Megan chatted with Lizzie. As Providence's mom headed for the fridge, she swayed ever-so-slightly. Providence took her by the elbow and ushered her to the counter. "Why don't I get out the eggs?"

"Lizzie and I made two quiches yesterday," her mom replied. "And Lizzie made a hash brown casserole."

While the family got caught up, Providence helped her mom heat up the food. Normally whizzing around the kitchen, her mom seemed unsure on her feet.

"Mom, another cocktail?" Randy asked from across the room.

"How many mimosas have you had?" Providence asked her mom.

"I'm still nursing my first one."

"Ah, Mom, have another," Randy chided. "It's a celebration."

"I'm good, Randy."

Her dad brought in extra chairs and everyone sat around the kitchen table. Once the food had been served, Randy raised his glass. "Here's to Mom and Gordon. Thanks for showing me tough love when I needed it and welcoming me back when I—*when Lizzie and I*—needed a place to crash."

They're living here?

After everyone toasted, Megan asked, "What brings you back to town, Randy?"

"I just got my real estate license. I've already got a couple of clients looking to buy in the area." He puffed up his chest. "Might be close to listing a home, too."

"Which company do you work for?" Megan asked. "The big one in the area is Goode-Luck, but their realtors are seasoned."

Oh, crap. I hope he's not going tonight.

"I'm with Larke Realty," Randy replied.

Years earlier, Randy had flunked out of college freshman year and returned home, unsure of what to do with his life. Providence, eight years younger, had been in elementary school. Her brother was there day in and day out, a total lump on the couch playing video games. Then, Randy had become consumed with get-rich-quick schemes and borrowed money from her parents to kick off a computer-based business that went nowhere. Six months after that, their mom gave him an ultimatum. Pay rent or join the military. After a heated argument that went on for days, Randy joined the Marines. For eleven years, he stayed in touch, but sometime around his thirtieth birthday, he ghosted on them altogether.

"How long were you in the Marines?" Providence asked.

"I retired after twenty years."

"Lizzie, what do you do?" Megan asked.

"I'm an educator. I love teaching the little ones, so I got a job at a preschool."

"What have you been up to, Providence?" Randy asked.

I'm an undercover FBI agent with the Violent Crimes Division. "I'm a marketing consultant."

The doorbell rang and Randy pushed out of his chair. "That's the guy to check out the lawn mower. Gordon, you wanna join me?"

"You've got this," his stepdad replied. "Take your pretty wife. She can help with negotiations."

Lizzie set her plate on the counter. "Heather, I'll be right back to clean up."

And with that, they headed toward the front door. Once

Randy closed the door behind him, Providence leaned back. "If you had given us a hundred guesses, I would never have picked this one."

"Ditto," Megan said. "When did they come back?"

"About a week and a half ago." Providence's mom pushed out of the chair, but gripped the table.

Again, her dad was by her side, offering an assist. "Heather, I think you should see the doctor."

"I'm fine, honey, really." Providence's mom ambled over to the sink, moving slower than usual. "It's probably just the excitement of having the kids home."

Providence and Megan exchanged glances. "Why are you selling your mower, Dad?" Providence asked.

"It's the old one I don't use. Randy offered to clean out the garage. He's already hauled a trunkful to the dump and is selling a bunch of things."

Her mom stopped loading the dishwasher. "I cannot wait to have my garage back," she said with a smile.

A few moments later, Randy and Lizzie returned, and Randy plunked down the cash. "Lizzie wouldn't budge from your asking price."

"A deal is a deal," Gordon said, pushing the cash toward Randy. "You sell it, you keep the cash. You have no idea how happy you're making your mom. I would say I'm going to clean out the garage—"

Providence's mom barked out a laugh. "You don't have to tell me that anymore, dear."

Megan pinched her nostrils shut. "Ew, I smell cigarettes. You still a smoker, Randy?"

"Hell, no." Randy sat back down. "I quit years ago. The dude who bought the mower was smoking and it stunk like hell."

"Randy is one of those annoying reformed smokers," Lizzie added. "Even vaping makes him sick to his stomach."

"A couple will be here soon to buy the kayak," Randy said, after checking his phone. "And I'm going to sell that, too." He grinned. "I'm a born salesman, what can I say?"

The go-getter sitting across the table was a completely different person from the lazy, angry, young man Providence had known all those years ago. Had her mom not shown him tough love, what would have become of her brother? As she marveled at the changes in him, she couldn't help but wonder what kind of life he'd had that had brought him right back to the beginning.

5

GOODE-LUCK

Dakota stashed the thermometer in the kitchen cabinet before returning to the family room. Sammy's fever had vanished. Even so, he'd opted to skip her Saturday morning karate class.

"How do you feel, punkin?"

"Good." Sammy was too busy building LEGO Duplo to pay him any attention.

He sat on the floor beside her. "What are you building?"

"A house for my Barbies."

"Need some help?"

As Sammy told him what to do, he smiled. She had a clear image of how she wanted her house to look. She told him how high she wanted it and which colors he should use. He did as she instructed, father and daughter working silently side by side. When finished, Sammy collected her dolls and got busy playing, while he stepped into the kitchen to check in with his guys. He worried about them, especially after the intensity of a kill. Saving Stryker for last, he dialed.

"Hey." Stryker sounded groggy.

"Doing okay?"

"I'm still here on planet earth. Aliens haven't abducted me and I'm breathing. You?"

He wanted to ask about Providence, but they rarely discussed women. "Good. I'm good."

"Why don't I believe you?"

Sammy started crying and Dakota leaned around the corner. "Hold on," he said to Stryker. "What's going on in there?"

"My house fell apart." More crying.

"I have a LEGO disaster. Later."

Kneeling beside his child, he eyed the remains of her structure. "Sammy." He waited while she continued crying. "Samantha Lynn." She threw a piece of LEGO across the room.

As much as he wanted to laugh at her temper tantrum, he did not. "Okay, so when you're ready to fix your house, let me know and I'll do what I can to offer you some structural engineering ideas." He'd thrown in some big words, knowing that would snag her curiosity and disrupt her tantrum.

"I don't know what that is," Sammy replied, still indignant. "What's ructure neering?"

As he explained the importance of a strong foundation, the frustration in her eyes faded away. He showed her the difference between a tower and a solid structure. Once she got the hang of it, she started to rebuild. He wished life's traumas were as easy to fix.

"Samantha," he said with an authoritative tone, "you threw a piece of LEGO across the room. We don't throw our toys."

Big blue eyes stared up at him. "Can you get it for me, please?"

While he was a total sucker for his four-year-old, he wasn't budging. "I wasn't the one who threw it across the room. Please pick it up and don't throw your LEGO again."

The Samantha Lynn stare down began. "I'll get it later."

"No. Now."

Silence. He was not budging on this one. He would win this one if he had to wait there all morning. After a moment, she walked over to the leather chair in the corner, picked up the block, and returned to her building.

One lesson down, a million more to go. "Thank you," he said. "Do you need my help?"

"Uh-uh."

"I'm going to make us breakfast. You want to add the blueberries to our pancakes?"

With her attention glued on her rebuild, she shook her head.

Fifteen minutes later, he spooned out scrambled eggs, then cut up her pancake. He poured a small amount of syrup into a plastic bowl as she climbed onto her booster seat.

His cell phone rang with a call from his real estate partner, Juanita Goode. "Hey, Juanita. What's going on?"

"Daddy, I'm thirsty," Sammy said. He poured milk into her sippy cup and handed it to her. "Thank you," she said. He winked at her, then ran his hand down the back of her hair.

"My Larke cohost has the flu and can't attend," Juanita began. "There's no way I can do it solo. Any ideas?"

"No worries. I've got your back and can fill in."

"Thank you. By the way, I spoke with Matt and asked him to swing by the office at two."

Dakota sighed. He hated having to let an agent go, but he had no choice. "I'll see you then," he said and hung up.

After sliding the rest of the eggs onto his plate, along with a stack of blueberry pancakes, he smiled at his daughter as he sat beside her. "You were hungry."

"Uh-huh."

They ate in silence. When they'd finished, he said, "I have a surprise for you."

Her face lit up.

"You've been invited to a sleepover at Uncle Lalla and Aunt Evangeline's."

She clapped her small hands together and squealed. "Hurray!" And then, she started to climb down. "Can we go now?"

"Let's stop at the playground first. They're expecting you a little later."

Because his brother and sister-in-law had no children, Dakota filled a duffle with some of her dolls and toys, then packed her overnight bag.

As they were leaving, he grabbed a sippy cup from the cupboard. Feeling like he was forgetting something, he glanced around the kitchen. "Sammy, Daddy's forgetting something."

She shrugged. "I can't know."

He loaded the truck, buckled her into her car seat, started the vehicle, and backed out.

"Where's Blankie?" she asked.

He hit the brakes and turned to look at her. "We forgot your snuggle blanket." After pulling back into the garage, he cut the engine, closed the garage door, took his keys, and unloaded her. Together, they hurried back inside for the blanket, which he found under her bed. *I'm beat and the day hasn't even started.*

It was a brief ride to the playground. As Sammy ran to the slide, he spotted several parents he knew from the neighborhood.

"Hey, Dakota," said one of them. "How ya doing?"

"Good to see you." He watched Sammy slip down the slide and run over to the jungle gym.

"Aren't you a realtor?" the dad asked.

"I'm a broker with a real estate company."

The neighbor knitted his brows together. "I didn't know there was a difference."

"Are you guys moving?" Dakota asked, his eyes trained on Sammy.

"I want to, but the wife likes it here." The neighbor droned on and on about the pros and cons of moving. Like Dakota had never heard them before…ever…from anyone.

In reality, Dakota had been a licensed realtor for twenty years and had heard *everything*. When the guy finally stopped talking, Dakota handed him a card.

"Call my office if you decide to sell. Ask for my business partner, Juanita Goode. Her name is on the card. She can pair you with a realtor from our team."

"I was hoping *you* could list our house."

"I have over two hundred realtors who work for me," Dakota explained. "I run the company and they work with our clients."

"Thanks." The neighbor shoved the card into his stuffed wallet. Dakota threw him a smile and walked toward the jungle gym. Never one to refuse business, he could spot a prospective client from someone who would drag his feet for a year before deciding not to move after all.

Sammy ran over to him, breathing hard. "Can Noah come over for a playdate?"

Dakota glanced up to see a little boy talking to his mom. She shot him a friendly wave and the two headed in their direction. He'd seen the mom walking her dog, most times her son in tow. She was cute, but Dakota wasn't looking to start anything, especially in the neighborhood.

"Looks like our kids are having fun together," she said.

"Daddy, can Noah come over?"

"Not today, but maybe another day. Why don't you guys go play before we have to head out?"

"Let's play on the slide," Noah blurted and ran off.

"I'm one of those hovering dads." Dakota started walking back toward the slide and the neighbor fell in line beside him.

She was friendly and personable, chatting about the April temps. He glanced over, but kept his attention on his child. He was the first to admit he was overprotective, but he didn't give a fuck what others thought of him.

"Maybe we could take a break from our kids and have dinner together sometime." He glanced over. Her cheeks flushed a little. "I'm divorced. I've seen you here with your daughter, but I've never seen her mom. Are you divorced, too?"

"I'm a widower."

"Oh, I'm sorry. I had no idea."

"It's okay."

"No!" Sammy yelled before shoving Noah back. "Daddy!" She raced over. "Noah spit at me."

Noah hurried over. "She cut in line."

"Noah, we do not spit," said the boy's mom. "What do you say to Sammy?"

"She cut in front of me. She's a stupid butthead."

Staying quiet, Dakota glanced at Sammy, waiting to see how she handled things.

"I'm sorry I cut in front of you," Sammy said, "but I don't want to be your friend if you spit. Spitting is bad."

"Nice job using your words, Samantha." Dakota held out his hand and she slid her small one inside his.

He waited for Noah to say something, but the boy stared at the ground. His mother looked meekly at Sammy. "Noah's sorry, Sammy." Then, she smiled up at Dakota. "If you give me your number, I can shoot you a text."

"We've got to get going," Dakota said. "Good talking with you." As he and Sammy headed back toward the car, he said, "You handled that very well, Samantha. Do we need to head home and clean you up?"

"He wasn't a good spitter, so it never got on me."

Dakota laughed. "Good to know. How do you know Noah?"

"He goes to my school."

"Does he spit there?"

"Sometimes, but he's never spit for me before."

Rather than correct her grammar, he just smiled. After strapping her into her car seat, they took off for DC By the time they arrived at his brother's, Sammy was out cold. But the second he cut the engine, she blurted, "Yay! Uncle Lalla's."

Dakota's sister-in-law, Evangeline Develin, swung open the door. "There's my sweet girl." She lifted Sammy into her arms and hugged her. "Uncle Lalla and I have been so excited to see you."

"We are going to have sooooo much fun," Sammy declared. Dakota's twin walked into the room and Sammy held out her arms. "Uncle Lalla!"

Evangeline handed her over and Sammy wrapped her arms around Sin and hugged him.

While Sinclair Develin was known around the region as The Fixer, he was simply Uncle Lalla to his niece. Dakota breathed easier knowing Sammy was with family. He would be able to attend his event without worrying about her.

"Aunt E-Leen, will you play with me?"

"Of course. Maybe Daddy can stay for a little while and see the present Uncle Lalla and I bought you."

Sammy's eyes grew large. "A present?"

"Before presents," Sin said, "we have to go over the safety rules."

"Uh-huh."

"No touching or playing in the waterfall."

"I remember."

"Good job," Sin said. "If the doorbell rings—"

"Stranger danger," Sammy said proudly. "Never open the door without the peeping first."

"Peep hole," Dakota said.

"Okay, you ready to unwrap your present?" Sin carried her into the living room and her eyes grew wide.

"That's soooo big."

He set her down and she ran to the middle of the floor where a large, wrapped gift waited.

The youngster beamed. "Can I open it now?"

"Go for it," Sin said.

Sammy unwrapped the present and squealed. "A dollhouse with furniture!"

"That present stays here," Sin explained. "Every time you come over, you can play with it."

The child got busy examining everything and Evangeline offered Dakota a drink.

"Coffee, leaded."

"Honey?" she asked her husband.

"I'm good, babe."

Evangeline left the room and the brothers relaxed on the sofa.

"I saw the news report about Ralph Meyers," Sin said.

Dakota nodded.

"How are you doing?"

"I don't know."

"What does that mean?"

"I feel like I'm treading water and the sharks are circling my feet."

Evangeline handed Dakota a mug before sitting on the floor beside her niece. "I have a night light for later," she explained to Sammy. "That way, we can light up the house and keep on playing."

Sammy smiled. "That's good." She got up and headed out of the room.

"Where are you going?" Sin asked.

"To get my dollies."

Evangeline pushed off the floor. "Wait for me."

When his daughter was out of earshot, he said, "I'm chasing a damn ghost. Every elimination is a blemish on my soul. No matter what I do, it doesn't bring justice for Beth. And nothing can bring her back."

"You can't change the past," Sin said. "You have a great daughter and a thriving business. You don't have to do the other."

"I can't sleep knowing there are predators out there preying on the innocent." Dakota sipped the coffee.

"That won't ever change," Sin said. "You know that. Find yourself a woman and have a meaningful relationship."

"Did that. It didn't end well."

The girls returned, each holding a doll. "Tell us about your event tonight," Evangeline said.

"Every year, we hold an awards banquet with our biggest rival. For one night, we're one big real estate family. This year, it's at National Harbor."

"Nice," Evangeline said. "Are you staying there?"

"No. I'm swinging by The Dungeon on my way home."

"Come by tomorrow for brunch, unless something comes up and you need more time. Either way, we're happy to keep Sammy all day tomorrow." Evangeline smiled at her niece. "We've got some other surprises planned."

Sammy popped up on her knees. "More surprises?"

"Samantha, it sounds like you're going to have a great time." Dakota finished his coffee, then pushed off the sofa. "She had a slight fever last night, but she's been fine all morning. I packed a liquid fever reducer if you need it."

"We've got this," Evangeline said. "Just enjoy your evening."

"Thanks for taking care of her." He hugged them both before lifting his child into his arms. "I love you, honey. Have fun and be a good listener, okay?"

"Okay. I love you, Daddy."

He left, feeling somewhat free and kinda like he was leaving the best part of himself behind. Being a parent was a blessing. Being a single parent was a full-time job.

After returning home, he packed his tux and took off for the office. Slogging through Saturday traffic, he thought of Providence, the feisty club manager.

If there was anything that turned him on, it was a confident woman. Her rockin' hot body and those swaying hips had snagged his attention, and her extreme beauty had held it. But it was her pissed-off, take-no-prisoners attitude that had spiked his curiosity and kept her in his thoughts. He had to see her again. Had to find out what the new sheriff did besides bust his balls.

But not before he talked to Stryker.

As he pulled into the parking lot of his flagship office in Tysons, he forced the stunning brunette from his thoughts. Time to let one of his employees go. Gritting his teeth, he walked inside the high-rise that bore his name. The elevator split open on the top floor, and he stepped into the highly competitive and fast-paced world of real estate.

Goode-Luck was the largest residential real estate company in the Washington region. With twelve offices in Virginia, DC, and Maryland, he employed over two hundred seasoned agents. As a licensed broker, and the company's CEO, he managed a ten-person executive team, along with branch directors at each location.

After greeting his receptionist, he headed past the rows of cubicles on his way to his partner's office. The floor was abuzz with activity, realtors eager to close their active listings while always on the lookout for new ones. At Goode-Luck, dozens of homes were bought and sold on a monthly basis.

He'd first met Juanita Goode when he'd moved to the area after college and started working at a real estate company in Fairfax. She had over twenty years of experience and a stellar track record. They'd struck up a friendship, then decided to join forces and operate as a team. That move proved quite lucrative. At the urging of Juanita's husband, she and Dakota ventured out on their own. One office grew to multiple locations and, thirteen years later, they were the most successful real estate company in the region.

Dakota stopped in Juanita's doorway, and she glanced up from her computer. "You ready?"

She collected her laptop and rounded her desk. "I couldn't sleep last night. My stomach is in knots."

Dakota offered an encouraging smile. "We've let agents go over the years."

"But never for cause," Juanita murmured.

DAKOTA LUCK

Together, they headed toward the smaller of two conference rooms.

"He'll move on," Dakota said as they entered the conference room, "and learn his lesson."

As he gestured for her to take the chair at the head of the table, she chuffed out a laugh. "You sit there. I'm much more comfortable being your wingman for this one."

As Juanita sat, Matt Hastings strolled in.

At six-four, Dakota towered over most. In this case, Matt was several inches shorter, but all muscle. The twenty-something hotshot never hesitated to boast about his sales, but he had the numbers to back them up.

Unfortunately, greed had provoked Matt to engage in unethical business practices. Time to put the brakes on him.

"Hey, guys." Matt shook Dakota's hand, then sat across from Juanita. "I'm guessing you're about to tell me I won Realtor of the Year, but I should act surprised at the banquet." He waggled his eyebrows. "I'm right, aren't I?"

Dakota eased into the plush chair at the head of the table. "You had a strong year, Matt."

Matt smiled. "What can I say? I'm good at what I do."

Opening her laptop, Juanita spun the device toward Matt. "It's been brought to our attention that you've been taking kickbacks from a mortgage broker."

"*What!?* That's insane." Matt's cheeks reddened while he squinted to read an email. "Oh, c'mon. That's so not true."

"Matt, what you did is a violation of RESPA rules," Dakota said. "You've exposed the company and yourself to lawsuits."

"Aw, c'mon. Everybody does it. It's no biggie."

Dakota steeled his spine. "No, everyone does *not* do it and our company ethics policy makes this clear. You've left us no choice but to let you go."

Matt jumped up. "Screw you, man!"

Juanita and Dakota exchanged glances. "Sit down, Matt." Juanita kept her voice low.

"You can go to hell. You both sit in your offices counting your goddamn money that *we* bust our asses to make, and *you* have the nerve to accuse *me* of doing something unethical. You're the ones stealing from us. That's way worse."

As Matt continued ranting, several realtors stopped to watch through the wall of glass lining the conference room. The last thing they needed was an audience.

Dakota rose. "I need your keycard."

Matt tossed it on the conference table.

"Clear out your desk," Dakota said.

"You do it," Matt said. "I'm outa here. I can do way better than this shithole." Matt pointed his finger at Dakota. "You're going to regret firing me."

"Stop taking kickbacks," Juanita warned.

"Assholes," Matt muttered as he left the room.

Dakota followed him out, ensuring he left the building, then returned to the conference room. "You okay?"

"I'm fine." She pulled her laptop over. "I'll draft a letter to send to the affected clients, indicating that we'll be conducting an investigation and providing appropriate consideration to anyone who might have been impacted by Matt's actions."

"He got greedy."

"And he was making good money without the kickbacks." Juanita shook her head. "Moving on, let's discuss tonight's agenda."

Dakota sat back down. One of the reasons he appreciated Juanita so much was because she handled things and kept going. No dwelling, no discussion. She was a damn good business partner. The best, as far as he was concerned.

"Matt was slated to win Realtor of the Year," Juanita continued. "I'll check the stats and we'll award the person who came in second."

"Thanks for doing that," Dakota said. "I'm going to make an announcement to the realtors who are here. Can you send out a company-wide email?"

"Of course. Thanks for co-hosting with me tonight."

"It'll be fun."

That made her laugh. "Standing in front of hundreds of people is *not* my idea of fun."

After their meeting ended, Dakota walked into the bullpen. He stood there a moment while agents finished their conversations and phone calls. Once all eyes were on him, he said, "Matt Hastings no longer works for Goode-Luck."

"We heard him," said the office director.

"What happened?" asked a realtor.

"Juanita is sending out a company-wide email." Dakota painted on a smile. "So, who's excited about tonight?"

A chorus of affirmatives filled the air, and, just like that, he redirected them away from the brouhaha of Matt Hastings. After a few moments of chatting with employees about their listings, he left. Instead of heading to the hotel, he made a quick stop for a mask.

At four thirty, The Dungeon was closed, so he used his key to enter through the front door. As he rounded the corner, a hit of adrenaline fueled him forward.

Providence was sitting at the bar while Stryker stood behind it. And he'd said something to make her laugh. When she turned in Dakota's direction, her expression of joy and amusement stirred an emotion that had died inside him a long time ago.

"Hey!" Stryker called. "What are you doing here? I thought you had your awards banquet tonight."

Dakota tossed Stryker a nod before turning his full attention back to Providence. The closer he got, the harder his heart pounded. No one had ever been able to jump-start his heart like this. Not until now.

"I need a mask," Dakota replied. "Got one I can borrow?"

"Take one from my store. Don't you have one of your own?"

He still couldn't drag his gaze from Providence. Her tight jeans clung to her thighs and she'd rolled up her shirt sleeves. His conclusion? No matter what she wore, she was a total knock out. He slid his gaze from one to the other. *Those two are too damn relaxed around each other.* "Hello, Miss Rhode Island. What's the latest?"

"I'm already wreaking havoc on Stryker." She pushed off the barstool and the front of her white shirt opened, revealing a bright pink tank top. *Jesus, she's hot.*

"Quitting already?" he asked.

Her husky chuckle landed in his groin. She took a few steps in his direction. "I have a commitment tonight, so I'm abandoning him until later."

"And she hasn't even worked here a damn week." Stryker laughed. "Go on. Enjoy your evening. I'll catch up with you later."

"Thanks for being flexible." Her steel gray eyes found Dakota's. "An awards banquet? Sounds swell."

Her sarcasm wasn't lost on him and both men chuffed out a laugh.

With her sultry gaze cemented on his, she strolled right up to him. And with a smarmy expression and a glint in her eyes, she said, "I hope you win."

My God, she loves busting my chops.

6

THE REAL ESTATE SHINDIG

Providence strolled into the Gaylord Resort and Convention Center at National Harbor and followed the signs for the Cherry Blossom ballroom. The nearby atrium was packed with masked realtors, dressed in gowns and tuxes, clustered in pairs and groups chatting away. The majority were waiting in a long registration line, something Providence could skip thanks to her SAC, Patricia Stearns.

First stop, a restroom. After finding one at the end of a quiet hallway, she ducked inside. She ran her fingers through the dark brown wig and adjusted her purple mask. Providence tended to have a light hand when it came to applying makeup, but tonight, she'd concealed herself in dark eye makeup and bright red lips. Normally, she liked to show a little skin, but when she was playing the part of someone else, she needed to blend in. The less skin showing, the less to remember. Tonight's number was a simple, black evening gown. The only identification she carried dangled from a lanyard around her neck.

I'm Elaine Jones with Larke Realty.

When finished, she headed toward the ballroom, keeping an eye out for her target and for her brother. With dozens of masked attendees crowding the area, she doubted she'd run into Randy. If she did, her disguise would conceal her identity.

She didn't stop at any of the nearby bars, nor did she stop at the vendor booths lining the hallway between the atrium and the ballroom. As she meandered around the mingling attendees, her only goal was finding Dakota.

Almost as soon as she entered the ballroom, she spotted him. He towered over the podium, looking so damn hot in his black tuxedo, his face framed in a simple, black mask, his dark hair a tousled, sexy mess. The woman standing beside him, wearing a deep red gown and matching mask, was his business partner, Juanita Goode.

Providence had read every article she could find about the self-made multimillionaire. At thirty-five, Dakota Luck was the youngest broker to win the Billionaires Club award for selling over a billion dollars in residential real estate in a single year. From his middle-class upbringing, to the decision to get his real estate license during college, he was living proof that hard work could pay off…big time.

But Providence didn't care about his millions and she wasn't there to mix-n-mingle. She was there to track his every move and assess how he handled himself in various situations. She was there to gather evidence as to whether he was or wasn't a cold-blooded killer who took the law into his own hands.

Never mind those bright blue eyes or his unruly head of hair. His hard-muscled physique was irrelevant and she'd barely noticed that killer smile.

Barely.

She stood in the back of the ballroom, eyeing the large, round tables, searching for an empty seat. Purple and dark pink spotlights bathed the room in a relaxed, upscale glow. Tall floral centerpieces brightened the reserved tables while modest bouquets adorned all the other ones.

"Hi, there, do you want to join us?" A masked man nearby

gestured to an empty chair at his ten-person table.

Providence walked over. "Sure, thanks."

"I'm Matt Hastings, soon to be with Larke Realty." He glanced at her name tag. "Hey, you're with Larke, too."

"I'm Elaine Jones," Providence said, trying not to push her faux Boston accent. "Which office do you work out of?"

"I worked for Goode-Luck up until five hours ago," Matt said. "But I quit."

"Why'd you do that?"

Raising his shot glass in a mock toast, Matt tossed back the booze. "The broker there is one messed-up dude. He and his partner are difficult as hell to work for."

This oughta be interesting. "I'm new in town. Who are you talking about?"

"Dakota Luck and Juanita Goode. But I made one phone call —*one damn call*—and I'm gonna have a new job by the end of the night." He drained the alcohol from his glass. "I can't pass up free liquor. Want something?"

"I'm good, thanks."

"Can I get your drink tickets? You got two when you checked in."

Since Providence wasn't officially registered, she said, "I already gave mine away."

"Damn," Matt said before lumbering away.

Providence returned her attention to Dakota, still standing at the podium. Now he and Juanita were speaking with a man. Dakota's sexy-as-hell smile sent a burst of heat traveling through her.

That man is some looker.

When the conversation ended, Dakota headed toward the back of the room, pausing to speak with several guests. She kept her gaze trained on her target, but when he got closer, she broke contact to avoid catching his eye.

The woman seated beside her called out, "Hey, Dakota."

Oh, no. Providence turned away.

"Good to see you, Mia," Dakota said. "How's Larke treating you?"

"I've been nominated for Realtor of the Year, so I'm doing okay."

"Congratulations. I hope you win."

"I'd love to chat with you about joining Goode-Luck."

"I'll let Juanita know to expect your call."

"Oh. I was hoping *we* could meet." Providence couldn't miss the disappointment in her voice.

"Juanita does all the prelim screening."

Matt returned to the table and set down two shot glasses, plus an unopened beer bottle tucked under his arm. *He's a class act.*

"Hello, Matt," Dakota said.

Providence loved the deep timbre of Dakota's voice, but this time, a sharp edge caught her attention.

"You didn't think I'd show, did you?" Matt asked. "I've got a meeting with the CEO of Larke and I'm gonna have a job—a *better* job—by the end of the night, no thanks to you." He tossed back a shot.

Like a cat stalking its prey, Providence slowly pivoted toward them.

Dakota leaned down. "You should be thanking me you've still got a career in real estate. Don't push your luck with me, Hastings."

"Fuck you, Luck," Matt growled.

"Dakota, can I buy you a drink later?" Mia asked.

"Unfortunately, I can't stay." Dakota slid his gaze from Mia to Providence and a zing shot through her. He extended his hand to her. "Dakota Luck with Goode-Luck."

As Providence rose, she slipped her hand into his. His shake was firm, his skin warm. "Elaine Jones with Larke." Strangely, she did not want to let go.

His piercing blue eyes drilled into her. "Have we met?"

She released his hold. "I just moved here from Boston." Being that he went to college there, she hoped he didn't call her out on her accent. It was good, but it wasn't authentic.

"One of my favorite cities. Enjoy your evening." Dakota peered into her eyes for another second before moving on.

As she slid her gaze to Matt, she inhaled a calming breath. In a room of five hundred masked attendees, she'd come face-to-face with her target. *He might have made me.*

The woman beside Providence held out her hand. "Look, I'm shaking." Providence eyed her trembling hand. "He's the reason I became a realtor."

"Seriously?" Providence asked.

"Oh, puhleeese." Matt guzzled half the beer down. "He's a total douche."

"He's so beautiful, it hurts to look at him."

Providence barked out a laugh. "Isn't that a bit over the top?"

"No, that man is absolutely gorgeous. And smart. And successful. And filthy rich. He's the perfect storm that I could get swept away in."

Both Providence and Matt laughed.

And he could also be a murderer.

The woman extended her hand. "I'm Mia Jefferson with Larke in College Park."

Providence shook her hand. "Elaine Jones. Good to meet you." Since she was there to learn as much about Dakota as possible, she addressed Matt. "So, what's your beef with Luck?"

"Can you keep a secret?" Matt asked, before tossing back the second shot.

"That's what I do for a living," Providence replied.

Both Matt and Mia cracked up.

"Good one," Matt said. "Can I use that with my clients?"

"Go for it." Providence needed to know what happened before the event started and Matt got too shit-faced to utter a string of coherent words.

"You wanna sit?" Matt gestured toward the chairs. After they did, he continued. "I won tonight's Realtor of the Year award, but they fired me instead."

"How'd you manage that?" Providence asked.

A crooked smile lifted Matt's lips. "In a word...kickbacks. It's the secret to my success."

Mia shook her head. "Not cool."

"Everybody does it," Matt insisted.

"No, they don't." Mia's frustration wasn't lost on Providence.

Dakota entered the ballroom and made his way to the front of the room. He couldn't move five feet before someone stopped him to say hello. The man was striking from any angle and Providence found herself craning her neck to stay connected to him. As she glanced around, she wasn't the only one tracking him. His energy rolled off him like turbulent waves crashing against the rocky shoreline.

Once at the podium, he turned on the mic. His relaxed smile sent another blast of heat through her.

"Wow." Mia leaned toward Providence. "Is it me or is that man absolutely beautiful?"

Beautiful. So beautiful. "He's handsome."

Mia's mouth dropped. "I would give my right arm to work at Goode-Luck."

Providence chuckled. "Again, that's a little over-the-top for me. I'll admit he's a head turner, but, he could also be a first-class jerk or super-high maintenance."

"He and his partner have the best reputation in the business. He's won more real estate awards and accolades than most of us in this room combined. He might be high maintenance, but I'd be happy to be the one maintaining him."

"I was married to high maintenance and I can speak from experience," Providence said. "No one is worth the aggravation that comes with a pretty face and a boatload of heartache."

"You're pretty cool, Elaine." Mia tossed her long cornrows off her shoulder. "You must make one kick-ass realtor."

That made Providence smile. "I do okay."

"Good evening and welcome to the Larke, Goode-Luck annual awards banquet. I'm Dakota Luck." With his signature, sexy-as-hell smile, he paused while attendees hollered and applauded.

As he laid out the evening's agenda—from dinner to awards—Providence studied him. Was it possible he was leading a double life? Realtor by day, vigilante at night? She'd met cold-blooded killers who had families, full-time jobs, and appeared to be model citizens. Could Dakota be one of them?

During the meal, Matt talked as much as he drank. By the time the awards ceremony began, Matt's mask was on the floor, his eyes were glazed over, and he was hitting on Mia, big time.

Dakota announced the categories and nominees, and Juanita announced the winners. One by one, people made their way to the front of the room to receive their awards and offer their thanks.

"Our final award is for the coveted Realtor of the Year," Dakota said into the mic. He read the list of nominees and stepped away from the mic so Juanita could announce the winner.

After a pregnant pause, Juanita said, "This year's winner is Larke Realty's Mia Jefferson."

"Congratulations," Providence said as Mia—looking somewhat stunned—headed toward the front of the ballroom.

"That's my damn award," Matt blurted. "I sold more houses than she did." He pushed out of the chair and half-walked, half-staggered toward the front of the room.

Oh, boy. This won't be pretty.

Mia accepted the award from Juanita, but instead of shaking Dakota's hand, she hugged him. Providence smiled. Mia hadn't won by being passive or subtle. Providence admired a woman who went after what she wanted.

Matt stumbled onto the stage, grabbed the mic, and stood swaying in front of the podium. "Helloooooo, people. I'm Matt

Hastings with Goode-Luck. Well, I was, but I got fired." He glared at Dakota and Juanita.

The room grew pin-drop silent. Dozens of guests lifted their phones to record whatever crap was about to fly out of Matt's mouth next.

"I would stop now." Juanita gestured for him to step away from the podium.

"I got accused of taking kickbacks." Matt leaned against the podium to keep from swaying. "Hey, guys, newsflash. Everybody takes kickbacks from someone. That's the biz, baby."

"Dude," someone shouted. "Sit down."

"All you fuckers out there are doing the same damn thing," Matt blasted into the mic.

"I'm not," a realtor called out.

"You're drunk," an attendee yelled. "I'd shut up if I were you."

Dakota moved beside Matt, his hands clenched into tight fists. "That's enough, Matt. You need to—"

Matt swung and hit Dakota in the chin. Moving with lightning speed, Dakota grabbed his arm, spun him around, and put him in a choke hold. "Take it down a few," Dakota rasped in Matt's ear, the mic catching his words.

"Fuck you, Dakota. I don't work for you anymore, and I sure as hell don't take orders from you."

The second Dakota released him, Matt took another swing.

This time, Dakota blocked him. "Calm the hell down." The anger in his voice was palpable.

"Got it," Matt said, raising his arms in surrender. He started to amble away, then turned and charged Dakota, head down like a bull.

Matt rammed into him, but Dakota body-slammed him onto the floor. Several in the audience screamed, while a collective gasp filled the room. Then, silence.

More silence.

Two men from Dakota's dinner table rushed onto the stage.

"Let's go, Matt," said one of them as they pulled him to his feet.

"You're gonna regret that," Matt slurred out. "I'm gonna press charges for assault."

Dakota glared at him before addressing the men. "Get him the hell out of here, but don't put him behind the wheel."

Both men escorted Matt toward the back of the room. As he passed Providence, his face was flaming red and he was muttering obscenities.

Dakota spoke quietly with Juanita before moving back to the podium. His jaw was set in a hard line and he stared out at the group for several seconds. "That was one helluva finale, don't you think?"

"We love you, Dakota," one woman shouted.

"Right back atcha," he said and flashed that killer smile. "On behalf of the managing partners of Larke and Goode-Luck, thank you for your efforts throughout the year. We might be rival companies, but we're all—well, most of us—are trying to do right by our clients. A home should be filled with love, starting with the process of finding the right one. Make it your mission to do that for all your clients and you'll win every single time."

The room erupted in applause. "This concludes our awards ceremony," Dakota said once everyone settled down. "If you aren't staying at the hotel, take a taxi if you've had too much to drink."

After flipping off the mic, Dakota hung at the podium with Juanita while people started moving through the ballroom. Providence positioned herself in the hallway waiting for him to exit, but the area soon grew crowded. Some stayed and mingled, while others made their way over to the atrium and sidled up to the bar.

She eavesdropped on a group of realtors cluttered together nearby.

"That drunken outburst was a career-killer for Matt," one said. "Do you think he was taking kickbacks?"

"I can't imagine Juanita or Dakota would fire him for no

reason," said another.

"I'm keeping my head down and doing my job," said a third.

Twenty long minutes later, Dakota emerged, surrounded by a dozen people, mostly women. He was smiling, but he didn't appear to be talking to any of them. He stood in the hallway while agent after agent came over to speak with him.

Keeping a low profile, Providence edged in his direction, but she couldn't get close enough to hear him over the cacophony of voices surrounding her. Rather than head into the atrium, Dakota walked down the hallway. Though several stopped him, he kept the chatting to a minimum.

Providence followed. He stopped in front of an elevator in the lobby and pressed the "up" button. After standing there for several seconds, he strode toward the stairway, opened the door, and ducked inside.

Where's he going?

She waited another fifteen minutes for him to reappear. When he didn't, she returned to the atrium, now packed with attendees. Matt was leaning with his back against the bar while a small crowd of realtors hovered close. They might have been impressed with Matt's antics, but she wasn't.

Since her reason to stay had disappeared in a stairwell, she headed toward her car, parked in the nearby garage. After stopping at home to change, she drove to the club. On the way, she replayed the evening.

Providence had gotten a glimpse into Dakota's world and had witnessed his charm firsthand. He kept the awards ceremony moving along, had what appeared to be great camaraderie with his business partner, and handled the debacle at the end without getting sucked into Matt's drunken drama.

She'd also seen him put Matt in a choke hold in a split-second. *That's how you break someone's neck.*

The evening's events had given her more insight into her target than she would ever have expected.

7

OVERTAKEN BY RAPTURE

With energy to burn, Dakota took the stairs to his hotel suite while anger bit at his heels. He entered his room, stripped off his mask, and changed out of his tux and into black pants and a black shirt. While he should have stayed and mingled, Matt's drunken antics had monopolized every damn conversation.

Dakota had better things to do than spend his evening discussing a piss-ant lying, cheating realtor who should get booted out of the industry. Rather than get caught up in the drama, he needed to leave before he put Matt in his place with a few choice words and a black eye.

He left his room and took the stairs to the lobby, then strode into the parking garage. As he approached his truck, his brain stuttered to a stop. "No fucking way."

The word ALPHA had been spray painted in red across the side of his vehicle. Feeling like eyes were on him, he peered into the parked cars, but saw no one. Had the word ASSHOLE been plastered on his truck, he would have assumed Matt guilty of that.

But ALPHA? He hadn't been with the top-secret organization in three years, not officially, anyway. And the *only* person he'd confided in had been his brother, Sin. He'd have to get his truck repainted. *Fucking pain in my ass.*

As he drove to The Dungeon, he replayed the evening. As far as he was concerned, Matt's childish behavior would be forgotten by tomorrow. For the rest of the evening, he would chill with a strong drink and an enthusiastic play partner. Reality could wait a few damn hours.

He parked around back and tied on the black mask. Rather than wait in the long line, he used his key and entered through the back door. He'd hoped the new fire-breathing sheriff would be waiting to give him a ration of shit. But he stood there alone. So, he headed upstairs to L2.

The Dungeon's layout was simple.

Level One—L1—members were hard-core partiers. Mostly, young professionals who worked hard and played harder. Five thousand a year bought a basic membership. They'd meet up on the first floor, but hookup elsewhere. As an L3 member, Dakota never hung out on the first floor.

Level Two membership provided three strip bars of varying heat levels on the second floor. A dozen private rooms were available for lap dances on L2. The wealthy threw down twenty-five grand—year in and year out—in exchange for a VIP membership.

Level Three was designed for those with eclectic tastes. An L3 member annually shelled out seventy-five big ones. Seven private, third-floor suites, nicknamed after the seven deadly sins, came stocked with the finest liquor, the silkiest sheets, the plushest towels. These rooms afforded a variety of toys for the serious-minded. Consenting adults could play in luxury, knowing their fetishes and sexual desires were safely guarded and protected from the real world.

But the basement, known as the dungeon, was how the club got its name. And only two people had access to that sacred space. The owner and Dakota. Since Dakota had forked out the money to buy the building and turn it into a hotbed for debauchery and sin, he was entitled to the key to hell. But he'd never gone downstairs to check it out. Medieval-like torture before, during, or after sex wasn't his thing.

Most wore masks on L1, but everyone wore masks on L2 and L3. As mainstream as tattoos, they heightened sex appeal, created mystery and, in some cases, were a necessity. The club catered to high-profile members. Not all members were single and none wanted to end up on the front page of *The Washington Post* or trending on social media.

Dakota entered L2. The alluring music, paired with the sea of masked members, washed away his frustration. Here, his goals were straightforward. Enjoy a strong drink and a willing kink partner. The bar was packed, so he found an empty booth. After the server took his order, he watched a stripper make love to the shiny silver pole.

Hoping to spot Providence making the rounds, he glanced around. He shouldn't be thinking about Stryker's woman, but he was. Her fiery energy, paired with those sexy eyes, were a dangerously delicious combination.

Dakota needed to know her story, so he sent Stryker a text. "I'm on L2. Join me for a drink."

Dots appeared, then Stryker's reply. "Later. Talking to my GM."

Of course, he's with Providence. I'd be with her, too, if she weren't his.

After slipping his phone into his pocket, Dakota adjusted his mask. He hated wearing the damn thing, but when he played, he used it. In reality, it did little to conceal his identity, but it created a necessary shield between himself and his partner. Masked sex kept things anonymous. No need for small talk. Just two consenting adults enjoying some hedonistic fun.

Like his club name—Maximus—it was one more layer devised to keep everyone at a comfortable distance.

In twenty minutes, he would head upstairs to the Lust Room

to exorcise his inner demons with a woman named Rapture. He met her a couple of months back, but she hadn't pinged him for a connection until this week. She was into two of his favorite fetishes—sensation play and role playing—and he was looking forward to seeing where those sexy distractions would take them.

The server set down his Macallan and left. The whiskey went down easy as the topless performer left the stage, only to be replaced by another.

"Hey, Maximus, want some company?"

Three masked women were hovering like drones. One of them slid into the booth across from him. "I'm pretty sure this is you." She showed him her phone. The entire fiasco with Matt was playing out on social media. *Fuck. Fuck me.*

"That was hot, what you did to that creep," she said. "He should never have hit you."

"So, you're a real estate broker," said the second one. "I've got my license and I would *love* to work *under* you."

"I don't care who you are or what you do for a living," said the third woman. "I just wanna get wild. Come play with us."

Before he could refuse them, the two squished into the booth beside their friend. Then, they started jostling for more room. Elbows butting against elbows. One of them yelped.

The server returned. While the women agonized over what drinks to order, Dakota jumped on his phone in search of the video. *Hell, no. It's everywhere.*

Putting Matt in that choke hold was the last thing the public should see. Dakota had unleashed the monster that lived inside him, the one that sucked the life out of him day by day.

But, what was the big deal? That could have been a simple self-defense move. Matt had just charged to the front of the room, behaved like a drunken fool, then clocked him in the chin. Granted, it was a sloppy punch, but still.

Dakota watched the video again. *Damn, I am fast.*

"Your online profile says you're into sensation play," said one of the girls. "Me, too."

"I like calling my partner Daddy," said another. "That really gets me off." She batted her eyelashes. "Will you be my daddy, Maximus?"

"Can you handle all three of us?" asked the third.

"I'm sure he can. You know, you are the most beautiful man I have ever seen. It's sick how handsome you are."

"I'm soooooo horny, big Daddy. Please say yes."

Dakota's phone buzzed with an incoming club message from Rapture. "I'm not into talking and I'm up for sensation play."

"Works for me," he replied.

After downing the whiskey, Dakota caught the attention of the server. As she hurried over, he pushed out of the booth and handed her two Ben Franklins. "This covers the drinks. Keep the change."

She thanked him and left.

"Wait, you're leaving us?" asked one of the women.

"What about role playing?" asked another.

"Sorry, ladies, my evening is booked." With a wink, Dakota headed toward the stairs.

He stood outside the Lust Room while the scanner captured a shot of his retina. The light flashed green and Dakota entered the darkened room.

A table lamp with a red bulb illuminated the corner of the room where Rapture sat, naked, in a stately armchair. Accessorized in fantastic fuck-me pumps and an ornate full-face gold mask, she made his aching dick throb. Her long hair was pulled into a ponytail.

Her crossed legs hid her pussy, but her arms lay on the armrests, revealing her voluptuous feminine form. *Nice tits.* She looked relaxed, composed, and so damn fuckable.

"Hello, Rapture."

"Maximus." Her voice, muffled behind the mask, had a sexy southern lilt to it.

He stood there admiring her for several more seconds. Then, with a cat-like grace, she pushed out of the chair and sashayed in his direction. With each step, his cock firmed. When she stopped, inches away, he wanted to rip off his clothes and dive into her. But there was something sexy about being that close and not stroking her silky skin that caused his breathing to hitch. Not only could he feel her electricity, he believed he could see it burning from her eyes, framed behind the mask.

She placed her hands on his chest, as if marking her prey, and raked her fingernails down the material. Then, one at a time, she flicked open the buttons of his shirt and his cuffs before dragging it over his shoulders and tossing it on the floor. She sucked down a steadying breath as she unhooked his belt and dropped his pants. Since he hadn't bothered with underwear, his hard-on was front and center.

With her gaze fixed on his, she collected his cock and balls in her hands and massaged. The anger and frustration rolled off him and he moaned through the pleasure.

Normally in complete control, he liked how Rapture didn't wait for him to set the tone. She knew what she wanted and she took it. She doled out a few more glorious strokes before she slowly circled him, as a hungry mountain lion would its prey. While standing behind him, she trailed her hands down his back and ass while her soft moan filled the silence.

Because he was known as a Dom, the women he played with tended to be submissives. But Rapture had usurped his power and her sensual touch sent waves of energy surging through him.

Facing him, she stroked his shoulders and arms. He closed his eyes and listened to her steady breathing. When she placed his hands on her breasts, energy surged through him, and he opened his eyes to admire her.

Behind his mask, he groaned while cupping and squeezing her

beautiful, full tits. His thumbs brushed her nipples and they responded by pebbling and firming. Another groan shot out of him as she sucked in one harsh breath after another.

Then, she stepped away and placed her hands on her hips. With her head cocked in a playful manner, she waited.

Time to take control. Something he relished doing.

"What's your poison, Rapture?"

She pointed to him and he smiled.

"Since you've chosen to be silent, nod or shake your head so I know what you like and what you don't."

She nodded.

"I received a text that you want sensation play. Is that correct?"

Again, she nodded.

"What about edging? Do you want me to bring you to the edge and make you wait to come?"

She didn't move. He waited, giving her time to decide. After a few seconds, she shook her head.

"Penetration?" he asked.

She retrieved a condom from the display box on the night table. He pulled one from the pocket of his pants. "I bring my own."

After nodding, she returned the one in her hand to the box.

Pausing, he let his gaze roam over her body. He didn't remember Rapture being so damn hot, but he'd only met her once. His cock grew firmer still. He couldn't wait to sink inside her hot, wet pussy. But, first things first. He needed to take care of his partner.

Ready to play, he pulled a leather flogger, a crop, and anal beads from the assortment of toys hanging on the wall. Turning back to her, he lifted each of the items, one at a time. She liked the first two, but not the beads. "Ice?"

She nodded.

"Warmed wax?"

She shook her head, before pointing to the Tantra chair in the corner. Each of the seven Deadly Sin rooms housed one of the curvy, ergonomic chairs. Covered in a soft, dark leather, it had a sloped back and a small hump at the foot. Since he was all about hard fucking against flat surfaces, he'd never bothered to use one.

As she made her way over, he admired her heart-shaped ass. *Fuck, she's phenomenal.* "You are so fucking sexy. I can't wait to make you come again and again."

Behind the mask, she moaned, the sultry sound landing in his cock. Straddling the chair, she eased down. When she arched back against the curvy backside, her voluptuous tits stole his full attention. He needed to suck them. Now.

Joining her on the chair for two, he sunk down in the center facing her so his straining cock was poised to go inside her. But rather than enter her, he ran the flogger across her chest and over her breasts. Her eyes fluttered closed and she sucked in a jagged breath.

Again and again, he teased her. He dragged the toy over her abs and down to her snatch, then trailed the strands of soft leather over her hairless pussy. Her throaty moan made his cock bob. She lifted her head and pointed to the crop in his other hand.

"Pain?"

She nodded.

"Light, medium, or intense?"

She held up two fingers.

He smacked her thigh with the implement and she groaned. "Turn over and I'll smack your beautiful ass."

When she offered her ass, he wanted to plunge inside her hot pussy until she screamed with ecstasy. Instead, he smacked her flesh with the crop. Once, twice, three times. Each time, he increased the intensity. Her moans turned raspy and he reached beneath her and cupped her breast, stroking her plump nipple between his fingers.

Then, *whap, whap, whap!* Each time he smacked her ass, she

arched in response. When finished, he held his hand over her heated skin.

"Are you okay?"

"Yes," she whispered.

"Again?"

"Yes."

After another round of crop spanking, he soothed her skin with his hand. When ready, she turned back over. Though he wouldn't ask, he wanted her to remove her mask. He hated that he couldn't see her face, couldn't feel her hot breath on his face.

"Fuck me." Her harsh command snapped him from his thoughts.

She lay against the slope, forcing her back to arch. Her large, erect nipples protruded into the air and he took one into his mouth.

Her deep groan had him sucking harder while adrenaline coursed through him. He fondled one tit while biting and licking the other.

"Finger me," she groaned out.

He slid two fingers inside her dripping wet heat and groaned through the pleasure. She pushed into him as he thrust again and again.

And then he did something he'd never done with a play partner. He withdrew his fingers and waited until she lifted her head from the chair. With her fiery gaze on his, he slid his wet fingers into his mouth.

Her body trembled against his and she dropped her head onto the chair and opened her legs wider.

And then, he tunneled inside her heat, groaning from the euphoria spiraling through him. And he pounded into her again and again, the pleasure taking him hard and fast.

"From behind," she whispered through jagged breaths.

He withdrew and she turned over. He slid back inside her and resumed his thrusting. The intensity of the sex had him hurtling toward an orgasm, but he wanted her to climax first.

"Come for me, Rapture," he said between clenched teeth, trying to hold himself back.

"Fuck me harder."

Her insistent words triggered his release. Wave after wave of ecstasy freed him from his demons. For those precious seconds, the nirvana helped him forget about the hell he'd created. Everything fell away, leaving only the purest of pleasure.

When it was over, he withdrew and relaxed against the chair. Turning around, she faced him. As she got her breathing under control, they stared into each other's eyes for several long and intoxicating seconds. Instead of floating back to earth, he grew riled from the intensity of their connection. He wanted her again, and his desire to make her come had him pressing his thumb to her clit.

She shook her head, so he removed his hand. He was confused. All the other play partners who allowed penetration wanted to climax.

"Remove your mask and tell me what you need," he said.

In silence, she pushed off the chair. Then, she collected his clothing.

What the hell? "Whoa. We aren't finished."

"Yes, we are."

"Let me take care of you."

Again, she refused him.

"After care?"

She didn't want that, either.

"Can I buy you a drink?"

She'd sent him flying high, only to reject him again.

All she offered was her hand.

Pushing off the chair, he placed his large hand over her delicate one. Energy traversed his arm, heating him from the inside. After escorting him to the bathroom, she laid his clothes on the vanity, turned on the shower, and walked out.

After thirty minutes of screwing, she'd bolted. What he thought would be the start of their evening, had been the end. Surprised by her abrupt exit, he had an unexpected urge to chase after her.

Had he done something wrong? Not done something to her liking? He always took care of his play partners, and his failure to do so left him frustrated. After removing his mask and the condom, he stepped into the shower.

Of two things he was certain. He wanted more of this mysterious, sensual partner. And the woman he'd just hooked up with had *not* been Rapture.

8

THE RULE BREAKER

Rule number one. Don't fuck the clientele, especially not the one you're targeting.

A sly smile tugged on Providence's mouth. From time to time, she had been known to bend the rules, maybe even break a few. But this? This was over-the-top insane. She had crossed a line.

After pulling on her clothes, she bolted from Lust. Once safely behind the locked door of her office, she removed her mask and wig, then sucked down a lungful of air.

Still trembling from their steamy romp, she gave herself a few moments to relive their connection. Dakota Luck was one hot handful she could easily get lost in.

She couldn't blame him for not bringing her to orgasm. That was all on her. But he *was* guilty of being so damn irresistible. It was bad enough that Providence had gotten the nightclub gig under false pretenses, but to have screwed her target?

In all the years she'd been working undercover, she had never had sex on the job, with anyone. Ever.

While she didn't want to wash away his delicious scent, her skin glistened with perspiration. She flipped on the shower in her private bathroom, stripped naked, and stepped into the stall. As the hot water pounded her, she deliberated on which of her latest sins was worse.

Having sex with her target or tampering with the club's accounts.

Her interest in Dakota had morphed from curiosity to full-blown desire, so, with a quick stroke of her mouse, she'd canceled his hookup with Rapture, blocked the notification from pinging his account, then replaced it with a different connection.

Her.

The second he had stepped out of the SUV, everything in her world had shifted. Stryker had talked about him for so many years, he seemed more god than man.

Sure, he was gorgeous, but she needed more than a pretty face and big muscles to hold her attention. She needed a man with conviction. She needed a man with purpose that went beyond his dick or his wallet. And since that man didn't exist, she'd settle for thirty minutes of carnal bliss. Thirty damn minutes. Had that been so wrong?

As Providence rinsed off, she thought about Dakota's achingly beautiful blue eyes. They reminded her of an abyss that she'd be willing to fall head first into, if she were the kinda woman who was in love with love. But she was a hard-core realist, and that connection was nothing more than a fuck. A damn good one, but a fuck, nevertheless.

The more she thought about their hookup, the more aroused she became. More than anything, she wanted to have *unmasked* sex with him. And kiss him for days.

Shut that shit down. Not gonna happen.

In a huff, she turned off the water, dried off, and dressed in jeans and a black halter shirt. After toweling her wet hair, she returned to her office to shut down. It was time to clear out the members and close up for the night.

Knock, knock, knock.

She shoved the mask and wig into a drawer before opening

her office door. Her heart skipped a beat, then took off in a frenzy.

Dakota filled her doorway. His dark, damp hair was a tousled mess, but it was his just-got-fucked smile that made her cheeks flush with heat. *I put that smile there.* While Providence was rarely happy, she got a rise out of knowing she'd done that...to him.

"I didn't think you'd be here," he said.

She hadn't expected to see him, either. "So, were you planning on slipping a note under my door?" Men baffled her. This one, in particular.

"Can I come in? I need to talk with you in private."

Ah, shit, shit, shit. He knew it wasn't Rapture. "Sure." She swung open the door and he stood close enough to see his whiskered cheeks, the ones he'd scraped over her breasts minutes ago.

He smelled of soap...and sex. Her insides tightened. She wanted to drag her fingers down his rock-hard pecs and continue where they had left off.

Stop it.

Squaring her shoulders, she gestured toward the guest chair. Once he walked in, she closed the door. Being alone with Dakota only turned up the heat. While she could have sat beside him in the second guest chair, putting distance between them was smarter. So, she sat behind her desk and stared into his glowing eyes. *Jesus, this one brings the heat all the mother-lovin' time.*

"Alright, cowboy, I don't know about you, but my bed is calling my name."

He dropped his mask on the guest chair next to him. "*My* bed is calling your name, too."

Her chest warmed. "While that *line* might sound original to you, I'm confident some man, somewhere, has uttered those inane words before."

"You like to bust my balls, don't you?"

She bit back the smile. *If only you knew.* "All right, Dakota, what can I help you with?"

"I know you're new here, but I'm hoping, *together*, we can figure this out."

She raised her eyebrows.

"I had a connection tonight in the Lust Room with someone new."

"Was there something wrong in the suite?"

"No, it was fine. The reason—" He stopped mid-sentence and stared at her damp hair. "You showered?"

I need a cigarette. She crossed her legs beneath her glass table and his gaze tracked her movement. "Stay on point, Dakota."

He stared into her eyes. "Seriously, you showered."

"You are a keenly observant man."

His attention stayed glued to hers while the right side of his mouth lifted ever so slightly. Was he mocking her?

"Good grief," she said, feeling like she was under a damn microscope. "I really don't see how my hygiene habits are relevant to this conversation, so I'm giving you one more chance to tell me why you're here or this scintillating conversation is o-v-e-r."

Leaning back, he crossed his legs. "The woman I hooked up with tonight was supposed to be Rapture. There was a computer mix-up and I ended up with someone else."

Intensity rolled off him like morning fog billowing over the San Francisco Bay. She held his searing gaze for an extra beat. "On behalf of The Dungeon, my apologies. I'm still finding my way around the system, but I'll make sure it doesn't happen again."

"Here's the kicker. I *want* it to happen again. Help me find that woman, Providence."

Well, damn. He wants an encore.

"I'm available tonight," Dakota said. "All night long."

Providence hitched a brow. "The club closes in thirty."

"I've got a key and I'll lock up when we're finished." He flashed a smile. "Help a guy out."

"You sound desperate."

"Determined. *Damn* determined." Dakota collected his mask and stood while her eyes trailed up and down his body. This woman definitely wasn't shy about checking him out. If she continued with her eye fuck, she'd be getting more than an eyeful in return. Her heated stare was driving him crazy.

"I'll see what I can do."

"My club name is Maximus. I'll be waiting on L2." He walked to the door and turned back. "Find her for me." He tied on his mask and left, closing the door behind him.

As he trotted down the stairs, Stryker texted him back. "Ready for that drink now. I'm in a booth, L2."

Dakota needed answers. Could Providence and Rapture be the same person? A few months back, he'd spoken with Rapture, but he couldn't remember much about her. She had long hair, but he thought she was a redhead. He didn't remember her having a southern accent. And why would Providence shower at the club right before closing?

Once on the second floor, he pushed through the crowd in search of Stryker, spotting him in the corner booth. He slid in across from his friend. "What's the word?"

"I saw the damn video. It's all over the Internet." Stryker tossed back his drink. "Dude didn't have much of a right hook, but that choke hold you put him in caught my eye."

"Sin will divert everyone's attention with a juicy DC scandal."

"You're the scandal. You look like you know what you're doing, bro."

"That's because I do."

Stryker laughed. "You're a stupid, fucking idiot."

"Fuck you," Dakota said, and both men laughed.

After the server took their drink order, Dakota texted Sin. "I've got a video that's trending. Can you bury it for me?" He sent it, but no dots appeared.

"I never like when any of us gets tagged on social media," Stryker said.

"I'm not worried. The Matt debacle will be dead by this time tomorrow. I need to know... are you and the new GM close?"

Stryker shrugged. "I guess. She's cool. Very chill, you know?"

"How long have you known her?"

"Forever."

"Things serious?"

Silence.

"Say, what?"

"Are you and Providence serious?"

"As in, *together*?"

"Yeah, she's your woman, right?"

Stryker threw back his head and laughed. "Hell, no. She's my cousin."

Dakota couldn't contain his smile. "No, shit."

"You've got a thing for her, don't you?"

"I'm crazy attracted to her. Is she seeing anyone?"

Up went Stryker's eyebrows. "Wow, you do have a thing for her. She's been solo for a while."

"What's her story?"

"She's a marketing consultant, but things have been slow, so she asked if I could bring her onboard. Perfect timing with Mavis out for a few."

The waiter returned with their drinks.

Stryker tapped Dakota's glass. "Here's to..." He paused. "Jesus, my mind blanked. I'm running on empty."

Dakota shook his head. "Story of your life. Here's to your cousin, Miss Rhode Island."

"You asking her out?"

"You know my life is complicated. Plus, I've got Sammy. She's so young. I'd hate for her to get attached, especially if things didn't work out. It's just easier to chill here."

The two men sat in a comfortable silence sipping their drinks. When Stryker finished his, he pushed out of the booth. "Stay out of trouble."

Dakota tossed his friend a nod. "Not possible."

As Stryker walked away, Dakota's phone buzzed with a message from club management. "It's Providence. You connected with Venus."

"Thanks for helping me out," he replied.

Dakota checked Venus's club profile. Though there was no photo, she, too, was into sensory play and role play. Venus identified as a "she" and was into men, but her decision to do anything sexual—kissing, oral, and penetration—was made on a case-by-case basis.

Tonight, she'll be doing all three.

If the mystery woman *was* Providence, he'd play along. But if Venus was a different clubber, he could beg out if he didn't want to play. Communication and consent were key, and a member could change his or her mind at any point during a connection.

He reserved the Greed Room, pinged Venus for a connection, and added a personal note. "Venus, meet me in the lounge on L2. Wear a mask that doesn't cover your mouth. Your profile says kissing is optional. Let's make it mandatory." He sent the message and finished his drink.

A moment later, his phone binged. Venus had accepted his connection and replied to his private message. "I'm into fantasy sex. Let's role play it's your b'day and I'm going to make all your wishes come true. See you in 10. It's your Lucky night. I'm in the mood for kissing a sexy stranger."

His breath hitched. *She knows it's me.*

In all the years he'd played at The Dungeon, no woman had ever suggested fantasy sex. His pulse kicked up speed. He couldn't wait to see who showed up.

A few moments later, she slinked into view. As she made her way over to the table, adrenaline surged through him. She'd changed into a black, leather corset and ass-hugging leather shorty shorts.

Holy fuck. She looks phenomenal. My God, she's gorgeous.

The long dark wig and simple, black mask couldn't conceal the truth. Her piercing gray eyes and pouty lips made it evident. His mystery woman *was* Providence and he was flat-out thrilled to see her. Pushing out of the booth, he greeted her with a peck on her cheek. "Hello, Venus."

She placed her hands on his shoulders, leaned up, and whispered, "Happy birthday, Maximus." Her mouth grazed against his ear and a thrill surged through him.

"You look incredible," he murmured.

Her brief smile halted his breath. "You, too." She'd resurrected the subtle southern accent, but it was the fire in her eyes that claimed his undivided attention.

"Please," he said as he gestured to the booth.

She slid in. Rather than sitting across from her, he sat beside her.

As he reveled in her beauty and sex appeal, a calmness came over him. Time stood still. The trending video didn't matter. The pounding beat of the music became background noise and the mingling bodies searching for a connection faded away. All that mattered was this woman. This stunning, headstrong woman. She lit a fire inside him that burned like the scorching sun.

The server set down two sparkling waters and left.

Providence lifted the glass and sipped. "I ordered these because I want you sober."

Her sultry smile sent him soaring to the damn moon. "I've got to touch you, but I need your permission."

"You have it. If I don't like something, I'll stop you."

Laying his hand over her thigh, he murmured, "Let's choose a safe word."

She leaned close and whispered, "I don't want to play things safe. I don't want a word and I don't want rules. This is like free falling without a parachute. Just for tonight."

"Jesus." He kissed her.

The air turned turbulent and chaotic. He couldn't resist the pull and he kissed her again. Their lips met in a tender embrace, but the desire ripping through him was anything but tender. His muscles tightened and he grew hard in his pants.

"I want to do every filthy thing to you," she murmured. "I want this to be a birthday you'll never forget." Her voice had dropped and her gaze darkened.

"My imagination has gone off the rails, Venus."

As she repositioned so she could peer into his eyes, she shuddered in a breath. "Tell me your fantasies."

His gaze dropped to her mouth while he caressed her silky thigh. Up and down, back and forth. *You, Providence. You are my fantasy.*

Instead, he said, "Rough fucking on hard surfaces. I want to restrain you."

She nodded.

"I want to kiss you for hours and fuck you with my mouth," he continued. "I want to make you writhe with pleasure until you have nothing left to give me."

Her whisper-soft moan landed in his groin.

"Your fantasy will begin with a massage," she said. After a few more sips, she set the glass on the table, then pinned him with a heated gaze. "Time to play, birthday boy."

I could go all night with her.

He pulled a bill from his wallet. "No, it's taken care of," she said, and caressed his back. The currents of electricity running through him could light up the whole damn city. He was that charged.

With his hand firmly cemented on her sweet, round ass, they squeezed their way around members, heading toward the elevators. His thoughts were laser focused on everything Providence. The way she glided across the floor, the confident way she carried herself. He inhaled her flowery scent, slipped his hand around her waist, and pulled her close.

Bypassing the bank of elevators, she continued toward the stairs. The retina scanner mounted on the wall turned green and she pushed open the door.

Though some members used the stairs, most used the elevator. *You're giving yourself away, Providence.*

She climbed two steps, stopped and pivoted to face him. Now eye to eye, she kissed him, her throaty groan turning him harder still. She plunged her tongue into his mouth, stroking his with wild abandon. His body thrummed with an urgent, unrelenting desire. The need to bury himself inside her made him growl. But when she gripped his shoulders and pulled him flush against her, he wrapped his arms around her and he kissed her like she was his. Like she was his beckoning oasis in the middle of the sun-scorched desert.

On a moan, he opened his eyes to find her staring at him. Determined to get a hold on his raging hormones, he slowed them down. He was a grown man, for fuck's sake. Not a pubescent teenager.

Dakota was out of his mind for her. From the searing look in her eyes, to the intensity of her kiss, he had to have her. All of her, all night long.

He glanced at her chest, admiring the small heart tattoo above her left breast. "Nice tat."

A flicker of sadness flashed in her eyes before she continued climbing the stairs. But he hung back to admire her perfect ass, the sexy sway of her hips, and those toned calves made longer by her stilettos. She was mouth-watering hot.

They walked in silence toward the Greed Room, but his throbbing cock could not be ignored. He couldn't wait to play with this goddess. This dirty, fantasy-filling woman who turned up the heat simply because she existed.

The retina scan approved his entrance and he opened the door. Rather than gesturing for her to enter, he snaked his arm around her waist, pulled her close and kissed her. "You are so fucking hot."

A sly smile graced her face, the subtle upturn of her lips made his heart pound harder. She walked into the room and he followed, shutting the door behind him. Alone with Providence for hours and hours. That, alone, was a dream fantasy come true.

This suite included a sheet-covered mattress, a night table filled with condoms, an array of sex toys hanging on the wall, and a Tantra chair in the corner. The red lamp cast the room in a devilish glow.

After removing his shoes and socks, he tossed his condoms on the bed, and he waited. One button at a time, she unfastened his shirt. He studied her face like an artist revels in his muse. She was breathtaking. With his shirt gone, she pressed her mouth to his chest and kissed his heated skin.

He took a deep, relaxing breath. "Mmm, you feel good."

She scraped her fingernails down his back while pressing her mouth over his nipple. Gentle sucking concluded with a nip.

"I love how you're taking control," he murmured.

After giving his other nipple equal time, she bit that one harder and he flinched. "Pain?" she whispered.

Dakota was so used to doling that out, that he paused before uttering, "I want whatever you give me."

She removed his black pants and tossed those, along with the shirt, onto the chair. Then, she retrieved a blindfold from a hook on the wall. "To enhance the experience."

He removed his mask and she slipped the room darkener over his eyes. Then, she led him to the mattress and had him lie on his stomach. After retrieving what he assumed was a bottle of lotion, she straddled him and began rubbing his shoulders. He sighed as the stress began to melt away.

"I like your tat," she murmured, running her fingers over his ink. "It looks familiar."

"It's based on the Vitruvian Man."

"Right... by da Vinci." She continued massaging his tight muscles. "He believes everything is connected to everything else. It's sexy."

"So are you."

Her touch was both firm and soft. At one point, she dipped down and dropped a series of tender kisses down his spine. "I love your touch," he murmured.

After she massaged his back and thighs, she told him to turn over. Now, lying on his back, she continued caressing him. Up and down, back and forth, the tension melted away. With his sight impaired, he focused on her touch. Her fingers worked his muscles with an intense precision. Her breathing was slow and steady, except when she leaned down and kissed him.

When her lips touched his, her breath hitched. And then, she slipped her tongue inside his mouth and stroked his gently. The build was luxurious. He had no recollection of ever being this spoiled by a woman, and never at the club.

One of the things he appreciated about her was her beautiful aroma. At first, she smelled like the club soap, but the more he relaxed, the more her baseline scent became apparent. It reminded him of a garden of spring flowers.

When she finished, she removed his blindfold and stared down at him. She was straddling him on all fours and it took all his strength not to flip her over and drive himself inside her. Her beautiful, relaxed smile made his heart pound.

She tucked a pillow beneath his head. "I want to give you a happy ending. Can I blow you?"

"Fuck, yeah. Jesus, I am so damn lucky. Take off your mask so I can see your beautiful face."

"No," she whispered before silencing him with another searing kiss. Then, she kissed his chest and his abs before coming to rest between his legs, his shaft throbbing with anticipation.

"Watch me take your cock into my mouth and suck you hard."

He blew out a breath as she cradled his balls and massaged gently. When she ran her tongue over his head, then slipped his cock inside her mouth, he released a long, deep growl.

"Oh, fuck," he rasped.

As she rolled her tongue over the head and down the shaft, he rested his arm behind his head and watched. Each time, she took in more and more of him until she was deep throating him again and again.

Pleasure bowed to pure euphoria. His breathing became jagged, his cock turned rock hard in her mouth. The faster she sucked, the higher he flew. Her throaty moaning drove him wild with need. She was unleashing herself on him, stroking him with one hand while pulling him into her until his cock touched the back of her throat. His moans turned to groans; her moans turned to mewls. She had him flying toward a release.

"Pull off if you don't want to—"

And that's when she took him in as far as she could and he exploded in her mouth, the orgasm sending wave after wave of ecstasy pounding through him. And somehow, he'd forced himself to keep his eyes open, so he could watch her taking him.

At that moment, she owned him. To do with as she pleased, for as long as she wanted. Slowly, she lifted off him and vanished into the bathroom while he lay there drifting amongst the stars.

When she slinked back into the room, she turned up the music and started moving to the beat. Inch by inch, she unzipped the corset, revealing her exquisite breasts. His cock hardened as her lids grew heavy. Not wanting to miss a second of her strip show, he leaned up on his elbows to watch.

The corset fell away and she danced her way over to the bed.

As he admired her large breasts and erect nipples, he said, "Venus, you have the body of a goddess."

Then, she turned around and bent over to pick up the corset, giving him a perfect view of her sexy ass. "You are gorgeous from every damn angle."

With her back to him, she shimmied out of her hot shorty-shorts, then rose and faced him. Shaved pussies always did it for him and he groaned out his approval. He dragged his gaze up and down her body while his cock shot to attention.

But watching wasn't enough. He went to her, captured her masked face in his hands, and kissed her.

Their throaty moans filled his ears while she wrapped her arms around him and pressed her breasts against his chest. He caressed her back and her ass, appreciating her soft skin and figure eight curves.

And then, his controlling nature kicked in and he lifted her into his arms and deposited her on the bed. "I need to be inside you," he rasped out. "Now."

"Tie me up and fuck me, hard."

Dakota used the Velcro wrist and ankle straps to secure her to the bed. Then, he rolled on a condom.

"I want to bury myself so deep inside you, you surrender to me, again and again."

Though she was secured to the bed, spread eagle before him, he paused to admire her. "You are so damn beautiful."

She had given him the ultimate compliment by submitting to him, by trusting him enough to let him tie her up.

"You are so fuckable and completely irresistible."

"Fuck me," she commanded. "Fuck me good." He plunged inside her and she cried out while he groaned through the pleasure. "Mmm, yes. I need this so badly." Her voice was gritty and dripping with lust.

His thrusts were deep and fast. The need to bury himself turned him into an animal. Her raspy moans and dirty talk had him barreling toward another orgasm. Through the onslaught of pleasure, they stared into each other's eyes.

He didn't want this to be over. Not yet. So, he slowed down, and then he stopped moving altogether.

Planking over her, he leaned down and kissed her. One soft kiss that turned into several. Her quiet coos matched the gentleness in her eyes. This should be just another wild hookup at the club, but it wasn't.

She slipped her tongue inside his mouth. And the build began again. Their kisses grew ardent while her body undulated beneath his.

Their tongues lashed, the intensity of her kiss stealing his breath. He began moving inside her again while she bit and nipped at his tongue, his lips. She was out of control, arching up and forcing him to sink in deeper.

"You feel amazing," she said between gasps. "Suck my tits."

Repositioning, he kissed her breast, then moved to her nipple and sucked. Hard sucking, then he bit her tender flesh. She yelped and said between gritted teeth, "Untie me. I need to fuck you."

He withdrew, did as she asked, and she pushed him onto his back, mounted him, and repositioned him at her opening. With her wild, fiery eyes locked on his, she sunk down until he was buried deep inside her.

She raised her arms and began gliding on him. Faster and faster, while the pleasure stole his mind. "I want you to come first," he said while breathing hard. "Say my name when you come."

"Dakota," she hissed, and his mind shorted. She'd done what no other play partner had dared. She'd dared to call him by his real name. "Come inside me."

She laid over him and he grabbed her hips, driving himself inside her again and again until he groaned out his release. Fireworks of ecstasy rained down on him.

She kissed him with a brutal wildness, until she slowed down, ending with several soft pecks. This woman wasn't just fucking his body, she was fucking with his mind, too.

And he hated giving anyone that kind of power.

Instead of pulling off, she lay there and he wrapped his arms around her while they both got control of their breathing. He didn't like that she hadn't come, but now wasn't the time to bring that up.

He stayed silent for a few moments knowing that if he spoke, she would probably leave him. And no way in hell was he ready to let her go. When she lifted her face, calmness had replaced the intensity that had radiated from her eyes.

As he predicted, she pushed off him and sat on the edge of the bed. "I hope I was able to fulfill your birthday fantasies."

He stroked her arm and she went rigid. Clearly, she was not into after care. "I'm not ready to say goodbye," he said.

"Can you come again? Is there something else I can do to fulfill your fantasy?"

For Christ's sake, she's still role playing.

He liked *her* voice without the accent and he wanted that wig gone, too. "Venus." He sat beside her. "Do you have orgasms?"

"No."

He ran a soft hand over her breast and teased her nipple with his thumb and the tip of his finger. "I want you to feel good."

"I do feel good. That was amazing." She scooped up her clothing, then shot him a rueful smile. His chest tightened. "I've gotta head out."

He did *not* want to lose her. Not again.

"Do. Not. Leave."

The intensity in his voice stopped her. "Providence."

Oh, God, no. She stilled.

"*Providence.*"

Turning, she faced him.

As he made his way to her, her heart pounded hard and fast, while her body yearned for him, one more time. He started to untie her mask, but she pulled his hands away. She wasn't ready to drop the facade.

"No running away, this time," he said, before kissing the top of her head. "Let's get dressed and go down to the bar so I'm not tempted to climb all over you again."

A few beats passed while she weighed her options. A drink and a conversation...or...going home to the silence and the memories. A familiar sadness swept through her.

"Please," he murmured.

The pull to be near him was undeniable and all-encompassing.

Then, he kissed her. "One drink, Miss Rhode Island." His charm, along with that tempting smile, was the tipping point.

I don't want to leave him. "All right."

After she removed her mask, he kissed her again. One long, searing kiss that made her insides quiver and her arms tighten around him.

"Much, much better." His smile touched his eyes. "Time to lose the wig."

Frozen in place, she studied him. Were those the eyes of a killer? She couldn't read him. She did not know.

After tugging it off, she ran her fingers through her hair. With her disguise gone, she stood there completely naked and feeling totally vulnerable.

"So beautiful," he murmured as he captured her face in his hands, dipped down again, and dropped another panty-melting kiss on her lips.

She gripped his massive shoulders, clinging to something that wasn't even real. The smell of sex hung in the air and her back tingled where he caressed her skin. The truth? She didn't want their evening to end.

But Providence was a die-hard realist. This was her target and she was supposed to be profiling him, *not* screwing his brains out.

He collected his clothing and extended his hand. "I don't want you ducking into the other bathroom. You're a flight risk."

She chuffed out a laugh as they entered the bathroom. This should have been the awkward, post-hookup moment, but she felt at ease with him. Too comfortable, really. She pulled on her shorts and zipped up her corset.

He dressed, then kissed her bare shoulder. "You look amazing in that corset and those shorty shorts are blowing my mind."

"I dressed for you." *Stop blabbing. Get it together.*

His smile sent ripples of excitement skittering through her.

"I'm very attracted to you, beyond the sex," he said. "I wanted you to know the truth."

He wouldn't be smiling if he knew the truth about me.

They exited the suite and she paused at the retina scanner outside the door. Once the light turned green, she tapped the keypad, indicating that the room needed to be sanitized. Together, they walked toward the stairs.

"Where are we headed?" she asked.

"The main lounge on L2."

Dakota stood behind the bar while she got comfortable on a stool. Now, she could breathe something besides his intoxicating scent.

He glanced at the wall clock. "What should we drink at four fifteen in the morning? Too early for a mimosa or bloody Mary? What about a screwdriver? I could put on a pot of coffee. What can I get you?"

More of you.

Her head was still buzzing from the sex. Despite her inability to climax, she'd loved every minute of him. She loved losing herself in his strong embrace...and she loved forgetting, even if just for a couple of hours. Pangs of guilt and sadness washed over her.

He knitted his brow. "What's wrong?"

Either she was terrible at hiding her feelings or he was excellent at reading people. "Nothing. I'm fine."

"I ask you a simple beverage question and you look like someone died."

Her heart dipped. *Oh, God.* Clearly, she sucked at hiding her feelings. She needed to keep a clear head, so she opted for coffee.

As Dakota brewed a pot, she studied him. His private brand of confidence teetered on cocky, but there was a determination in his eyes and an intention in everything he did. Whether he was standing at a podium, or putting Matt in a choke hold, or role playing at the club, he was in complete control. Power and charisma clung like the throng of women who tailed him around The Dungeon. But it was the constant stream of frustration surging off him that intrigued her the most. What dark secrets did Dakota carry around that weighed him down?

What did he do besides run his real estate company and enjoy the late-night company of a masked woman? Only one way to find out. Rather than answer *his* questions, she'd do the asking.

Once the coffee had finished brewing, he poured two cups, slid the container of sugar packets toward her and opened the fridge beneath the bar. "Cream?"

"Almond milk."

He set the container on the bar and pulled out a small pitcher.

"Carton's fine." He slid it over and their fingers brushed as she took it from him. Streams of electricity charged through her. Their gazes held across the bar for an extra beat. Had he felt that, too?

After pouring the remaining brew into a carafe, he sat beside her on the barstool. He was so close and so damn kissable. But she had this perfect opportunity to learn more about him, so she steeled her spine and forged forward.

"What do you do besides hang out here?" she began.

"I run a real estate company."

She sipped the hot drink, savoring the hearty flavor. "That must keep you busy."

A shadow fell over his eyes. "My managing partner runs the day-to-day operations."

"Does that mean you've got a lot of time on your hands?"

As he paused to drink, she wondered if he was composing a canned response. "I've got a few other businesses that eat into my week. There are six of us—close friends from college—and we own several businesses together."

While she had zero expectations he would confide his darkest secrets, she was hoping he'd tell her something about himself that she hadn't already gleaned off the Internet. "What do you do for fun? Got any hobbies?"

She was drowning in a sea of inane questions and vague answers.

"I work, a lot. I play here." He ran his hand down her arm. "I'm much more interested in you. Why didn't you want me to know it was you?"

And just like that, he'd taken the offense. Rather than push back, she opted for the chill approach. Like him, she'd answer his questions, but disclose nothing.

"Stryker said no fraternizing with the clientele." He hadn't actually said that, but it was kinda assumed.

He chuffed out a laugh. "Stryker did not use the word *fraternizing*."

"Well, I'm here to do a job, not screw the members." That part was true.

"You won't hear any complaints from me." He held her gaze while he ran the backs of his fingers down her arm, warming her skin from his touch. How could such a simple act elicit such a strong reaction?

"You are so beautiful," he murmured. "Too beautiful, really."

Her heart skipped a beat, but she couldn't get snared in his web. "I'm not even sure how to respond to that."

"Kiss me."

She'd had her fun. Time to put some distance between them. As she leaned against the back of the stool, she crossed her legs. "That's not a good idea."

"No, it's not. It's a great idea." He leaned close and adrenaline streaked through her. "You are too damn sexy. I can't resist you and I sure as hell can't get enough of you."

A low, guttural moan rumbled out of him while she fought the urge to kiss him. He placed a claiming hand on her thigh and a frisson ripped through her. The tug was too strong to resist, and she pressed her lips to his.

An explosion of passion thundered through her and she released a long, ardent moan. Pushing off the stool, she wedged herself between his thighs, folded her arms around him, and kissed him hard.

Their tongues crashed into each other as the air around them crackled with desire. She released another long moan as he fondled her ass and groaned through the embrace.

Before she could process what he was doing, he'd lifted her into the air and pushed off the stool. She wrapped her legs around him and held on tight.

The kiss intensified, the moans grew grittier, and she started grinding on him. Suddenly, he broke away. While he kept his breathing under control, she couldn't miss the feral look in his eyes.

In one swift move, she unzipped her corset and the leather fell away. As he eyed her breasts, she arched back. He pulled a taut nipple into his mouth and sucked. Together, they moaned through the glorious pleasure.

His sucking grew more intense. With a wild gleam in his eyes, he said, "I have to have you. Take off your shorts and bend over that table." He set her down.

Eager to feel his hard shaft inside her, she peeled off her shorts, gripped a table, and sucked down a jagged breath. Seconds later, his pants were gone and the condom covered his cock. When he grabbed her hips and drove himself inside her, the euphoria made her lightheaded.

Again and again, he tunneled inside her. "Christ, I can't get enough of you." Dakota's deep voice ripped through her and she groaned out her approval.

She didn't deserve so much pleasure, but she succumbed to the nonstop ecstasy. "I love how deep inside me you are."

He reached around and fondled her breasts. The onslaught of his intense thrusting had her flying high.

"Oh, God, you feel phenomenal," she groaned out. "Spank me. I don't deserve to feel this good."

He smacked her ass and she cried out. Pain grounded her. After Dakota groaned through his orgasm, he murmured her name like she was his, like this was the start of something…not the end.

And suddenly, their impersonal fuck had become very, very personal.

9

THE BODY

Dakota couldn't keep his hands off her. Providence was intense, aloof, and all-consuming. Instead of putting on the brakes, he'd gunned the gas and accelerated into recklessness.

He strummed her back, her shoulders. And damn him, but he could not stop kissing her.

Despite his sex high, he couldn't shake the sense of loss. Providence wouldn't let him pleasure her—or even try—and she flat-out rejected his offer to give her a massage. When she slipped into her leather outfit and told him she was showering *alone* in her office, their wild ride came to an abrupt end.

It was just before six in the morning.

"How 'bout I wash your back?" he asked.

"I'm good. You headed out?" she asked.

Up go her walls again.

He pulled on his pants and slipped into his wrinkled shirt. "I'm going down to L1 to make us breakfast."

She didn't even try to hide her surprise. "Don't you have somewhere you need to be?"

He stepped close and breathed her in before running the back of his index finger down her soft cheek. "Yes. Here. With you." He stroked her bare shoulders, unable to stop touching her. She was like a seductive sorceress and he'd fallen under her powerful spell.

She stepped away, severing their heated connection. "I'll be back in a few." She took off toward the stairwell. A few easy strides and he fell in line beside her. "Making sure I don't take off?"

"I couldn't stop you if you were."

He opened the door to the stairs and she thanked him as she walked past. But before the door closed, she was on him. The kiss was raw, intense, and over too fast.

After sucking down a breath, she said, "What is it about you and this stairwell?" Without waiting for a response, she headed up the stairs.

In search of food, Dakota entered the spacious kitchen on L1. The club didn't serve breakfast, so he settled on burgers and fries.

While cooking, he couldn't stop thinking about her. Her feistiness and her aloofness intrigued him. He wanted to get to know her outside the club.

Ten minutes later, he plated the burgers on buns and pulled the fries from the hot oil. Providence entered the kitchen and their eyes met across the room. Beautiful didn't do her justice. He loved how she wore her short hair in wavy layers that drew attention to her eyes. Most women wore their hair long and he appreciated that she had her own sense of style. She'd dressed in the skin-tight jeans and the black halter shirt from earlier that evening.

As she made her way toward him, he took all of her in. She was a breathtaking woman.

"Smells great." She eyed the food. "You must have read my mind. I'm dying for a burger."

They brought their food into the main room and sat beside each other at a horseshoe-shaped booth.

"This is good," she said after a few minutes. "Thanks for making us some grub."

"Next time, we're going out for a real breakfast."

"No, Dakota. No next time."

"Why the hell not?"

"Not a good idea, plus, I'm not..." She broke eye contact. "I don't date."

"It's a meal and a conversation."

She said nothing more, so he let it go. Time to get to know the alluring Miss Rhode Island. Though Stryker had already told him, he asked, "How'd you come to work at The Dungeon?"

"I'm a marketing consultant and things have slowed down. Stryker said he could use a little help while his GM recovered from surgery."

He'd been watching her because she was so damn pretty, but his gut told him she wasn't telling him everything. *What's she hiding?*

The more she wouldn't reveal, the more he wanted to learn about her. "What do you do when you're not here?" He bit into the burger.

BAM! BAM! BAM!

"What the hell?" Dakota exclaimed.

They hurried to the front door and were greeted by two police officers. The female was on the phone. "Someone's here," she said and hung up.

"Good morning, officers," Dakota said. "What's going on?"

"Can we come in?" asked the male officer.

Dakota threw open the door and stepped aside so they could enter.

"I'm Officer Cardin. This is my partner, Officer Braden. Are you Dakota Luck?"

"You got him."

"Ma'am, what's your name?"

"Providence Reynolds."

"We've got a few questions about your employee, Matt Hastings," said Cardin.

"Former employee. I had to let him go." Dakota slid his gaze from one to the other. "Is this about the video?"

"No, it's not," said Cardin.

"He assaulted me, but I'm not pressing charges," Dakota said. "He was drunk."

"His body was pulled from the Potomac this morning," said Officer Braden.

Fuck, no. "Oh, Jesus. What happened? Drunk driving accident?"

"He was bound with rope and tied to a mooring outside the Sequoia restaurant in Georgetown."

Dakota's stomach dropped.

Officer Braden looked around. "Isn't this a kink club?"

Dakota slid his gaze to Providence. The color had drained from her cheeks. Because of that damn video, Dakota was a person of interest.

If the police started investigating him, no telling what they'd find. He wasn't just exposing his secret, he was putting his vigilante team at risk. Not to mention the hit Goode-Luck could take.

But Dakota had not offed Matt, so he'd answer their questions, then send them on their way so they could chase down the real killer. "We were having something to eat. How 'bout some coffee?"

As the officers sat at a table, Providence retreated behind the bar. She returned with four mugs and a small pitcher of cream. To his relief, the color had returned to her face. She offered the police a pleasant smile as she eased down beside Dakota.

"We saw the video," said Braden. "What happened?"

When Dakota finished recounting the events, Cardin asked if he and Mr. Hastings had a history of altercations.

"No," Dakota replied.

"Where did you go following your banquet?" asked the officer.

"I came here."

"What time did you go home?"

"I didn't. I've been here all night."

The officers exchanged glances. "Were you alone?"

Fuck, fuck, fuck me. He glanced at Providence. He did not want to involve her, but he wasn't gonna lie. A lie could backfire.

"I've been here with Dakota," Providence said, steeling her spine.

"Are you a member?"

"I'm the general manager."

"What time did the club close?" asked the officer.

"Two," Providence replied. "The owner, Stryker Truman, closed up. I was in a meeting with Mr. Luck."

Again, the officers exchanged looks. He should have been worried, but he wasn't. He had an airtight alibi.

"How did you know where to find me?" Dakota asked.

"Your brother, Sinclair Develin," replied Braden.

Reacting on impulse, Dakota patted his pants pocket, but his phone wasn't there. He must have left it upstairs in Greed.

"So, ma'am," Cardin said to Providence, "you've been here with Mr. Luck since the club closed?"

"Earlier, actually," Providence replied. "I talked with him around midnight."

Braden eyed Dakota. "Where did you go after your event, where Mr. Hastings assaulted you?"

"I already told you. I came here."

"So, you're telling us you've been here since midnight."

Dakota nodded. "That's what I'm saying. No matter how many times you ask me that, my answer won't change."

"And how long did you spend with Ms. Reynolds?"

"I was with her the entire time, save for about thirty or forty minutes when I was on the second floor having a drink."

"Is there video surveillance that shows you here?"

"Yes," Providence replied. "I deactivated the internal cameras just before the club closed. But the external ones in the front of the building have been on all night."

"Is there a rear entrance?" asked the officer.

She nodded.

"Surveillance there, too?"

"No," Providence replied.

Dakota glanced at her. Having no camera out back just bit him in the ass.

"We'd like a copy of the surveillance video." Cardin rose, pulled out two business cards and offered one to each of them.

Braden also handed out her cards. "We'll be in touch. Thanks for the coffee."

Dakota walked them out, locking the door behind them. He found Providence had moved to a booth. She was staring at him, but looking right through him. He sat beside her. "I'm sorry you've been dragged into this."

"It's not your fault. You didn't do anything wrong."

"I've been through an interrogation before and I've been a primary suspect. They're going for the low-hanging fruit. You know, the obvious choice. If you haven't seen the trending video of what happened at the event last night, you might want to check it out now."

To his surprise, she didn't go for her phone. She had this far-away look in her eyes, like she was buried in thought. "I'm sorry, what did you say about being a primary suspect?"

"Nothing. Don't worry about it." He pushed out of the booth. "I've got to find my phone and make some calls. We need to lawyer up."

Muscles running the length of Providence's back were as tight as piano wire. She'd never been on the receiving end of an interrogation and, while the officers were relaxed and friendly, she wasn't fooled by their delivery. She, too, had played the role of a laid-back law enforcement agent.

Providence needed to speak with her SAC. Patricia Stearns would want answers. No matter how she might try to spin their all-nighter, there was no hiding what she'd done. For starters, she would be removed from the case. Her job was to get close to him, but she'd taken that to the extreme. And now, she was his alibi, unless the medical examiner determined the time of death was before midnight.

Her inability to control her damn libido might very well have cost her her job. Nausea clouded her thoughts. She wanted to throw up.

When Dakota returned, he was talking on his cell phone. "No, I didn't kill Hastings...of course I'm telling you the damn truth. I need to know if your dad will talk to me." Dakota leaned against the bar.

Providence eyed the sexy beast and tried to make sense of him. Was he a vigilante? Had he murdered Hastings? All she knew about him was that he was charming with the ladies, good in the sack, and made a decent burger. She shook her head in disgust. Sleeping with him was a bonehead move—one that could end her career. "Don't embarrass the Bureau" was the unwritten rule agents lived by. *I am so screwed.*

"I'll be by later this morning," Dakota said. "Thanks for your help, bro." He hung up.

Providence needed to get the hell outa there, clear her head, and figure out a plan. She slid out of the booth and started clearing the table.

Within seconds, he was by her side, his hand on her arm. "Leave that." Concern was streaming from his eyes. "Sit down."

Rather than sit, she crossed her arms. He turned a chair around, straddled it and eased down. "I'm sorry you're getting dragged into my mess. My brother, Sinclair Develin, is going to call his dad, Warren Hott. He's a retired chief prosecutor for DC who runs his own legal practice. I'm hoping he'll represent us."

Providence had heard of Develin. He was known as The Fixer and he helped his clients get out of scandals. But she knew Warren Hott personally. Before Providence went undercover with the FBI, she was a special agent who had testified against the criminals she'd arrested. And since Warren had been a chief prosecutor in the nation's capital, their paths had crossed more than once.

"I'm not following the family connection, though at this point, I'm not sure any of that matters." She couldn't hide the frustration in her voice.

"Sin and I were put up for adoption," Dakota said. "Sold, actually. We were adopted by different families, so we've got different last names."

Providence had read a three-part article about them in *Washingtonian* magazine.

"Warren Hott adopted Sin when he was in middle school, but Sin kept his first adoptive dad's last name."

Providence's head was spinning from the police visit, so she didn't question Dakota about his family tree.

"My brother is checking with Warren about representing us. I'll keep you posted." Dakota picked up his phone. "What's your number?"

She rattled it off and he sent her a text. "If the police contact you, don't talk to them until we've spoken with Warren. I'll be in touch once I know something."

To her surprise, he placed both hands on her shoulders and stared into her eyes. "I had a great time with you."

The anxiety gripping her back relaxed a little. The effect this man had on her defied logic. "Sure, the sex was fun, but a man is dead and you're a POI. That's not good."

Surprise flashed in his eyes. "POI? You're throwing around law enforcement lingo like a pro."

Oh, God. She forced out a laugh. "Busted. Must've picked that up from watching all those crime shows."

He dropped a soft kiss on her forehead, then peered into her eyes. "I didn't murder Matt Hastings."

"I'll talk to you later," she mumbled, then she hurried upstairs to her office. She slung her bag over her shoulder, exited down the back stairs and out the back door. The brisk morning air chilled her warm cheeks as she hurried to her car.

Of one thing she was confident...her secret job was going to stay that way for only so long. And when the truth came out, she would become Dakota's number-one enemy.

As soon as Providence walked into her Arlington condo, she called Warren Hott's law office. The outgoing message provided his cell phone in the event of an emergency. She didn't want to disturb him on a Sunday morning, but she needed to speak to him before Dakota did.

"Hello?" She recognized Warren's pleasant voice.

"Warren, it's Providence Reynolds. Some years ago, we worked together on a few cases."

"Of course, I remember you. How've you been?"

She started pacing in her living room. "I need to talk with you about something confidential. Do you have a minute?"

"Sure."

Providence's heart was pounding too damn fast. "I'm involved in something that's...You're going to be getting a call from..."

"Slow down. If I can help you, I will. Why don't you start at the beginning?"

She stopped pacing and stared out the picture window in her living room. "I'm still with the FBI, but I've gone undercover."

"That's wonderful. Congratulations."

"As part of my assignment, I've been managing a members-only nightclub in Arlington. Last night, a man named Matt Hastings was murdered in DC, and Dakota Luck is a POI. Your son, Sinclair, is going to ask you to speak with him."

"For representation?" Warren asked.

"Yes."

"That's easy enough."

"Since I can corroborate that Dakota was at the club last night, he's going to ask you to talk to me. Please don't let on that you know me or that we've worked together."

"Providence, you've put both of us in a tight spot."

"I can't have my cover blown."

"Sinclair is calling me. No worries, Providence. I won't say anything."

"Thank you." She hung up.

She hated that the lies were piling up. She wanted to tell Dakota the truth, but she would never betray the Bureau or blow her cover. She'd already risked too much by telling Warren.

While Providence should have felt relieved that her secret was safe, she knew the truth would come out. It always did.

10

BLACKMAILING DAKOTA

Dakota could not stop smiling. Sammy had been talking nonstop about her fun sleepover for a full ten minutes. She was cuddled on Evangeline's lap, her blankie draped over her.

Listening to his daughter was the best medicine for his troubled soul.

"Daddy, we watched the movie *Cars*! It was soooo good. I'm going to be a race car driver when I'm growed."

"And here I thought you were going to run a real estate company worth millions."

Sin and Evangeline laughed.

"A race car driver sounds great, honey. I missed you, punkin."

She scrambled off Evangeline's lap and hugged him. This energetic bundle of love kept him moving forward day after day.

"Come see my dollhouse." Sammy bolted over to the three-story structure, dropped to her knees, and got busy arranging furniture.

Dakota sat beside her while she explained every detail of the house. "That's where the mommy and daddy sleep."

Dakota's chest grew tight. While he was doing his best as a single dad, his daughter wanted a mom so badly. "This is a beautiful house, Samantha Lynn. What did you say to Uncle Lalla and Aunt Evangeline?"

"I told them thank you and added 'very much'. And I hugged them."

"Good job." He gave her a high five.

"She might crash this afternoon," Sin said. "We were up late." His phone rang. "It's my dad."

Evangeline sat beside Sammy. "Let's play with your dollhouse before you guys take off."

Dakota loved how trusting Sammy was with those she loved. He wanted to tell her about the dangers lurking in the world, but he would never destroy her childhood with the ugly truth.

Dakota pushed off the floor. "Sammy, I'll be right back."

As he and Sin entered the kitchen, Sin answered. "Hey, Dad. You're on speaker and Dakota is with me."

"What's going on?" Warren asked.

After Dakota filled him in, Warren said, "Let me see what I can find out."

"Can you represent me?" Dakota asked.

"Absolutely," Warren replied.

"There's one more thing. My alibi, a woman named Providence Reynolds, needs representation, too."

"Got it. I'll be in touch." Warren hung up.

"This isn't good," Sin said. "I'll do what I can to keep the media off your back."

"Thank you, bro. The police came after me hard when Beth went missing. I was innocent then, and I'm innocent now."

"Unfortunately, that video of you with Hastings shows what you're capable of." Sin headed back toward the family room and Dakota fell in line beside him. "This'll get worse before it gets better."

Frustration curled Dakota's hands into fists. He hated that his brother was right.

Sunday night, Providence texted Patricia Stearns and requested an in-person meeting at FBI headquarters. Not one to level-jump, Providence reached out directly to the woman who had asked her to track Dakota.

Patricia sent her a meeting notice for seven forty-five Monday morning.

Most of the night, Providence tossed and turned. At two in the morning, her phone buzzed with a text from Dakota. And her annoying little heart skipped a beat. She wasn't helping herself by reacting to him this way.

Stop. He's my target, not my lover.

"Warren Hott is checking with police," Dakota texted. "I haven't stopped thinking about you."

Providence stared at the text. Her fingers twitched to text him back, but every text was fodder for the police. For all she knew, someone was sitting outside her condo waiting to track her every move.

But the need to reply wouldn't go away, so, thirty minutes later, she responded. "Thanks for letting me know." She wanted to tell him she hadn't stopped thinking about him, but decided to withhold that information. They'd had one wild night and one wild night only. The end.

She stared out her bedroom window at the twinkling city across the river, the same river where Matt Hastings had ended up dead.

But sleep would not come. At four fifteen, she texted Dakota. "I haven't stopped thinking about you, too."

Damn that man.

Monday morning, Providence stepped off the elevator and headed toward the Violent Crimes Division at FBI headquarters in DC. As she made her way toward Patricia's office, her mouth went bone dry. Despite her churning gut, she was going to play this cool.

Providence was about to knock on Patricia's open office door, when she glanced up. "Come on in and shut the door."

As Providence eased down in the guest chair, Patricia said, "Dakota Luck is front page news."

"That's why I'm here."

"You want to fill me in."

"I went to the realtor banquet and witnessed Mr. Hastings assault Mr. Luck. I spotted Mr. Hastings at the bar after the event, but lost Mr. Luck, so I returned to the club. He caught up with me around midnight regarding a club matter."

"Do you suspect he killed Hastings?"

"No."

"Why are you here, then?" Patricia sipped her coffee.

Providence's stomach roiled. "I was with Mr. Luck from midnight until almost eight in the morning."

Patricia raised her eyebrows. "So, you're his alibi?"

Providence nodded. "I am."

"If you were doing something *other* than the obvious, I would have a stronger argument for keeping you assigned to his case." She adjusted her glasses. "And you did this, *why?*"

"I was hoping to earn his trust so he would confide in me." While her words were filled with conviction, she doubted Patricia would believe her. She didn't believe herself.

"While it's impossible to know if an agent has ever used sex as a tool, I didn't expect this from you." Patricia paused for several seconds. "So, it's unlikely he killed Mr. Hastings."

"Correct."

"Unless you're his alibi *and* his accomplice."

That was insulting. "I made an error in judgment, but I did *not* commit a crime."

"Thank you for telling me directly. Until I can determine next steps, you need to stand down on this case. I'll be in touch."

"Thank you for your time, Patricia."

And just like that, Providence had single-handedly thrown her world into turmoil and derailed her career.

And her career was all she had.

Dakota sipped his coffee while Sammy finished her breakfast.

The door to the basement of the Luck home opened. "Guess who's back?"

Sammy's face lit up. "It's Mrs. Morris!"

Miranda Morris scurried into the kitchen and hugged Sammy. "There's my sweet angel."

When Dakota became a single parent, he hired Miranda Morris to be Sammy's nanny. Sammy had been six months old and Dakota needed full-time help. Miranda had been contemplating early retirement from her career as an elementary school teacher, so when Dakota offered her a six-figure salary to care for his daughter, Miranda accepted. He turned his basement into her private residence and put a lock on the door so Sammy couldn't meander down there at all hours.

Sammy attended daycare twice a week, giving Mrs. Morris an opportunity to grocery shop without his chatterbox daughter, take classes, and see her friends.

Over the past three and a half years, Miranda had become a member of Dakota's family. She was smart and kind, but most importantly, she adored Sammy. He would be lost without her.

"How was your weekend, Miranda?" Dakota asked.

"Wonderful." She poured herself coffee. "I loved seeing my son and his fiancée. I went with them to pick out their wedding cake. It was fun, but there was too much sitting and eating." She shot Sammy a smile. "And not enough action."

"Are you going to your tie cheese class today?" Sammy asked her.

"Tai chi. And, yes, I am, right after I take you to school." She opened the refrigerator and checked the pantry. "And the grocery store, too."

"Dakota, what's your schedule today?" Miranda asked.

"A quick errand, then I'm headed to the office." He wasn't about to tell her that the name of a top-secret government organization had been painted on his truck.

"I'm done." Sammy climbed off her booster.

"Go brush your teeth," Dakota said.

Dakota watched his daughter walk up the stairs before he turned his attention back to Miranda.

"Have you seen the news or been on social media?"

"No. I got back late last night."

After Dakota brought her up to speed on Matt Hastings's death, Miranda said, "That's a lot to digest. How are you holding up?"

"The police have to start somewhere and I'm the logical choice."

"Sammy might hear about this at daycare today. Should I keep her home?"

"I don't want her life to change because mine has. Let's send her today and see what happens. I can't imagine the other kids' parents know who I am."

Miranda chuckled. "Everyone knows who you are. You're a local celeb from the days when you and Juanita did those TV commercials. I'll be even more vigilant to keep Sammy safe."

"I know you will."

When Sammy returned, Dakota kissed the top of her head. "Have a fun day at school, Sammy Lynn."

Dakota took off before they saw the graffiti on his truck. On the way to the auto body shop, he made a call.

"I turn on the news this morning and see a story about a dead body in the Potomac," Luther barked, "and your name is mentioned because of some video that's been trending since

Saturday. It's too early in the day for a damn headache, Dakota. You want to tell me what the hell is going on?"

"We need to talk, in person. Meet me at Precision Auto Body."

"I'm on my way to the Pentagon."

"Trust me, this can't wait."

"Ah, hell. Give me the address."

Dakota finished the drive in silence, unable to shake the anger that had burrowed into him like a tick.

His relationship with Luther Warschak spanned decades. In addition to being Dakota's late dad's best friend, Luther was Dakota's godfather. Luther and his wife rarely missed Dakota's high school football games. They'd been there for his graduations from high school and from Harvard. Luther had been there when Dakota buried his beloved dad, when Sammy was born, and six months later, when Beth went missing.

Their relationship had changed when Luther shared his greatest secret. Luther Warschak ran ALPHA, a top-secret government organization that had been formed decades earlier to hunt down the country's most violent criminals and eliminate them...for good. When Luther needed Dakota's help, Dakota stepped up and offered an assist to the man who had supported him his entire life.

As Dakota parked at the auto body shop, his phone rang with a call from Marcus. "Hey, Marcus."

"I saw the video. How are we handling your security going forward?"

"Business as usual."

"Not loving that idea. What about your six?"

"Marcus, I've got this."

"You want me to put a detail on Sammy and Miranda?"

Silence.

"Dakota?"

"Sammy is at daycare on Mondays and Thursdays. Assign someone on Tuesdays, Wednesdays, and Fridays. I'll tell Miranda."

"Got it. If you need anything else, let me know."

"Hey, Marcus. Thanks."

"You betcha." Marcus hung up.

Luther pulled into the lot, made his way over to Dakota's truck, and stopped short. Always dressed in tailored suits, he kept his Afro cropped and his face clean shaven. As Luther eyed the graffiti, Dakota exited his truck.

"Dammit. This isn't good," Luther said before glancing around. "I don't like you hanging outside like this."

"I've got my vest on and I'm carrying. Whoever did this isn't going to take me out in broad daylight. This is a psychological move designed to scare me. I'm not scared."

"I'll be waiting in my vehicle. Do you have a rental car lined up?"

"It's being dropped at my office."

"I'll drive you there. We can talk on the way." And with that, Luther retreated inside his vehicle. He did not mess around when it came to his safety. He had a beloved wife of forty years, three grown children, and seven grandbabies that were his pride and joy.

Dakota told the shop manager he'd pay double if he could bump his truck to the top of the list.

"Sure," said the guy, "but it won't be ready for a coupla days. We gotta let the paint dry for twenty-four."

"Text me when it's ready." Dakota left and jumped into Luther's car.

As Luther slogged through morning traffic, he asked, "When did the graffiti happen?"

"Saturday night during the realtor event. When I came out, it was there. I didn't see anyone."

"You aren't with ALPHA anymore, but the person who did this thinks you are."

"Or they just want to out the organization."

Luther stopped at a light and glanced at Dakota. "This is definitely an attention-grabber. But why now?"

"That's the question I've been asking myself."

"Did you kill Matt Hastings?"

"Of course not. I take all my termination orders from you."

"Where were you after the event?"

"At the club."

"Until when?"

"Until the police banged on the door the next morning."

"*What*? Don't you sleep?"

"No comment."

"Well, she must be something special to hold your attention for that long."

Dakota chuckled.

"Who is she?"

"I don't want to drag her into this."

"Too late. Who is she?"

"Stryker's cousin, Providence Reynolds. She's the club's temporary GM."

"What do you know about her?"

"She's damn hot."

"Something *relevant*, Dakota."

He stared out the passenger window. "She's a marketing consultant who took the gig to help her cousin."

"I'd like to get the focus of the investigation off you, but that might be tough. I'll make some calls. Cameras in the club?"

"Yeah, but not on the back door."

"So you could have left."

"But I didn't."

"Can your brother get the press to back off?"

"Sin's working his magic. So far, no one has called me or shown up outside my house."

"The spray paint is bad enough." Luther parked at the curb in front of Goode-Luck. "But this young man's death was a targeted

DAKOTA LUCK

hit. Someone saw that video and decided to take advantage of the situation."

"I hate that you're right." He got out. "Thanks for the ride."

"Keep a low profile."

After Luther pulled away, Dakota scanned the parking lot. He didn't know who or what he was looking for. "Pain in my fucking ass," he grumbled as he walked inside.

The second he entered the reception area of his company, the swarm of realtors gathered around the front desk stopped talking. All eyes on Dakota.

"Good morning."

Some replied, most just continued to stare. His attorney, Warren Hott, hadn't called him back yet, so he wasn't going to say anything. Rather than get into it, he strode to his office and called Warren. After a brief conversation, Warren advised him to address his employees with a simple statement.

He opened his email, typed a draft, and read it to Warren.

"I, along with all of you, am shocked and saddened to learn of the unexpected passing of our colleague, Matthew Hastings. During the year that Matt worked here, he was a valued employee of the Goode-Luck family. Because of the ongoing investigation, I am not at liberty to discuss the situation. Rest assured, I am complying with law enforcement to ensure the person responsible for Matt's death is caught, arrested, and brought to justice."

"That's good," Warren said, and Dakota sent the email.

"Can you and Ms. Reynolds meet me tonight at eight?" Warren asked.

"I'll check with Providence. Your office?"

"No, the club. I'll need you to walk me though your evening."

That oughta be interesting.

"Do you need the address?" Dakota asked.

"Sinclair gave it to me. See you tonight." Warren hung up.

Knock-knock-knock.

"Come in," Dakota said.

Juanita stepped in, shut the door behind her, and eased into the chair across from his desk. Normally polished and composed, she looked like she hadn't slept all night. "How are you holding up?"

"I'm fine."

She hitched a brow. "Seriously? Your picture is all over the news."

"Unfortunately."

"You have my full support," she continued. "I'm very sad about what happened to Matt, but I am confident you didn't kill him. Having said that, I'm concerned about the negative publicity, not to mention how this is affecting the team."

Dakota didn't like what he was hearing, but he wouldn't fight her on this. She was protecting their business. "I'll work from home."

"I'm sorry." Juanita rose. "But you know it's for the best."

On his way out, he grabbed the stack of mail on the corner of his assistant's desk, took the rental car keys and left.

The house was empty, but rather than work in the kitchen, he made his way to his first-floor office. Before going through his mail, he called Providence.

"Hello, Dakota." He loved hearing her say his name. "What's the word?"

"My lawyer, Warren Hott, will represent both of us."

"Okay."

"Why don't you sound relieved?" he asked.

Silence.

"It's been a long morning, that's all," she replied, her voice tight.

"You wanna talk about it?"

"No. Thanks for letting me know about Warren."

"He asked for a meeting at the club tonight."

"Why there?"

"He wants us to walk him through our evening."

"Oh, God," she bit out. "Never did I imagine something so private would become this public."

"Would you change it if you could?"

Silence.

"Neither would I," Dakota said. "See you at eight."

Curious about the woman he couldn't stop thinking about, Dakota Googled her. She was a marketing consultant with a polished website and a string of testimonials by happy clients. Besides the website, there was nothing online about Providence. Like him, she had no social media accounts.

Next, Dakota checked email. Juanita let him know that a handful of realtors were leaving. "The nervous ones are jumping ship," she wrote. "They'll regret it."

Like Juanita, he didn't appreciate their lack of allegiance, but he couldn't control their decisions. Dwelling on it was a waste of his time and energy, so he moved on.

He extracted the stack of mail from his bag, tossing aside the junk. One envelope caught his eye. His name and company address had been typed, but in large, block letters, someone had written "Private" across the bottom. Inside was a letter and two photos. The first photo was of his spray-painted truck, and the second, of his crew on a mission. There were four men in formation, dressed in tactical gear, their faces concealed by night goggles.

"No fucking way," he murmured.

The letter had been created from clipped letters and words from magazines, and glued to a piece of white construction paper.

NOW THAT I HAVE YOUR ATTENTION

If you want your ALPHA secret to stay that way, wire transfer $15 million to offshore account 1-87623-487721 Bank of the Princes. You have until midnight Thursday.

He slammed his fist on the desk. "Fuck." *This cannot be happening, again.* He held the note under his desk lamp in search of fingerprints, but saw none. To his naked eye, the letter appeared clean.

When Beth had gone missing, her abductors had extorted money from him, but they hadn't returned his wife. That was a dark time in his life and he hated thinking about it.

Pushing out of his chair, he pressed the hidden button on the underside of a shelf on his built-in bookcase. The shelf slid open, revealing a safe. He keyed in the code, stored his Glock, and removed his ALPHA laptop.

After logging in, he began reviewing some of the cases he'd worked. As an operative, he'd helped capture dozens of criminals. Had one of them decided to exact their revenge?

The security alarm chimed. "Dakota?" Miranda called.

"Office."

She appeared in his doorway. "There's a strange car in the driveway. Yours?"

"It's a rental. My truck is in the shop."

"Got it." She left.

He went back to reviewing past cases long forgotten. The minutes turned into hours. By the end of the workday, he hadn't isolated a single suspect.

The security system chimed. Seconds later, Sammy appeared in his doorway. "Daddy!" She rushed in and he lifted her onto his lap.

"How was school?"

"Good." She grew quiet as she stared at his computer screen. "What's an Alp-ha?"

He closed the laptop. "Just boring work stuff."

"I saw the word, 'kill'."

He moved that computer out of the way, then slid his real estate one over. The plus side of having a full-time nanny was that his daughter was learning to read. Albeit basic words, but she'd seen plenty in those few seconds.

"I liked your question about alpha," he said. "What do you do when you don't know what a word means?"

"I ask you."

He laughed. "What else could you do?"

"Ask Mrs. Morris."

He opened the laptop and clicked over to the dictionary. "We can use the dictionary, Samantha. Why don't you type in the word?" With his help, she did, and together they read the definition.

"Alpha. The 'ph' together makes an 'f' sound."

Big blue eyes met his. "That's funny."

After reading the definitions to her, he changed the subject. "Tell me about school."

"I have a new teacher. Miss Liz."

"Awesome. What's she like?"

"Sooooo nice. She told me that she knew my mommy had died and she wanted to be my special friend."

What the hell?

Sammy scooted off him. "Mrs. Morris is making me a snack plate." Together, they walked into the kitchen to find Miranda slicing an apple. While Sammy ate, he asked Miranda if she had ever told anyone at the school that Sammy's mom had died.

"Absolutely not," Miranda replied. "I've never said more than a few words to the staff."

When Dakota had enrolled Sammy, he'd mentioned Beth's death to the staff director, but he didn't think she had added that to Sammy's file. Dakota was aware that he was on edge, but he needed to touch base with the childcare center.

"Miranda, I've got a meeting tonight at eight."

"Thanks for letting me know," Miranda said before turning her attention to Sammy. "Sammy and I are going to make a lasagna for dinner."

"I want to play with my dolls," Sammy said.

"You can do that while the lasagna bakes in the oven," said Miranda. "I sure could use your help counting out the layers."

She was so good with Sammy.

"Okay," Sammy replied.

"Good girl, Sammy," Dakota said. On the way back to his office, he called the daycare center and asked for the director.

"Hello, Mr. Luck," said the director.

He shut his office door. "Sammy mentioned she has a new teacher."

"Yes, Miss Liz. She's great with the kids."

"Miss Liz told Sammy that she knew her mom had died. Is that information in the file?"

There was a brief silence. "It is, but I find it hard to believe that the teacher would mention something that sensitive to a student on her first day. Is it possible Sammy told Miss Liz about her mom? She has mentioned it to me. Maybe she said something to her new teacher."

"It's possible."

"I'm sorry for any distress it caused you or Sammy."

With nothing left to discuss, Dakota ended the call and made a mental note to meet Miss Liz. He didn't like that she wanted to be Sammy's special friend or that she'd crossed a line on day one.

With a splitting headache, he flipped open his ALPHA laptop and continued searching for an invisible enemy hell-bent on wrecking his life.

11

PUTTING PROVIDENCE FIRST

Providence cut the engine in The Dungeon parking lot. Still angry with herself for getting sidelined, she forced down the emotion as she unlocked the door to the club. Despite her frustration, she needed to stay in control. Behaving badly could arouse suspicion with Dakota.

Once inside, she turned off the alarm and flipped on the lights.

As she got busy brewing a pot of coffee, the front door opened. A man dressed in leather strolled in.

"Hey, where is everyone?" he asked.

"The club is closed on Mondays," she replied.

"Damn. Just my luck." Rather than leave, he stalked toward her. "Can I get a beer?"

The hair on the back of her neck prickled. "No. Come back tomorrow."

"C'mon," he said, getting comfortable on a stool. "Damn, girl, you're hot. And I mean, like, sizzling-inferno hot. You've got some wild-lookin' eyes." His gaze dropped to her chest. "And that ain't all."

She leaned forward. "You want to know a little secret?"

"Hell, yeah, and can I get that beer?"

"I've had a bad day. And I'm pretty fired up."

"Mmm, pent-up anger. I know just how to help."

The guy started to walk behind the bar. Her every muscle tensed, like a cat about to pounce on its prey. *Don't fuck with me, asshole.*

When he grabbed her arm, she kneed him in the groin.

"*AHHHH!*" He doubled over.

She grabbed the back of his shirt and dragged him toward the exit. He swung and his fist made partial contact with her cheek. Then, he took her to the floor. She screamed as the front door flew open.

"Jesus, what the—" Dakota yanked the guy off her and delivered a punishing right hook to his face. The second the guy dropped, Dakota pulled him up, shoved him against the wall, and wrapped his hand around the guy's throat. "I'm gonna fucking kill you," he growled.

"She told me she wanted to fuck," the dude choked out, his nose bleeding.

Dakota tightened his grip and the guy's eyes widened.

With her heart racing and adrenaline pounding through her, Providence whipped her handgun from the waist of her pants and pointed it at the guy. "Go to hell, you lying scumbag."

"You two are crazy," said the guy. "I'm at a kink club, lookin' for a beer and a good time. You don't need to go ape shit, ya know."

She eyed the asshole for an extra beat. "When a rapist gets in my space, I go ape shit."

"Whoa, whoa, bitch. Don't even go there."

When Dakota released him, the guy started coughing, then bent over with his hands on his knees.

"Tell me your name." Dakota's voice was filled with controlled rage. His stance screamed fight, his glare was razor sharp, and his hands were curled into tight fists.

The second the guy uttered his name, Dakota jumped on his

phone. "I killed your membership. When a woman says no, you back the hell off. Understood?"

"Fuck you."

Dakota stepped forward and the guy flinched.

"Get out. *Now!*" Providence barked.

The man took off and the door slammed shut behind him.

Providence shoved her weapon into the back of her waistband. "Asshole."

"Are you okay?" Dakota asked.

"Yeah. Thanks for pulling him off me."

"What happened?"

"I didn't lock the front door." She felt her throbbing cheek. "Scumbag didn't understand the word 'no'."

"That son of a bitch hit you."

"I got a sloppy right hook."

Dakota stepped so close his minty breath warmed her face. He regarded her cheek, then clasped her hand. "Let's put ice on that."

She could have pulled her hand away, but she didn't. His soothing touch helped slow her thundering heart. He went behind the bar and scooped ice cubes into a plastic bag. Rather than hand it to her from across the bar, he sat beside her, then offered her the bag.

"Thank you." She pressed it to her cheek and winced.

Dakota stared into her eyes. "You look beautiful. I missed you today."

His romantic words melted away the fear and anger. But the passion in his eyes would soon be replaced with contempt. Once he learned the truth, he would hate her.

But when he leaned over and kissed her, the only thing she cared about was that moment. Her soft moan filled the silence. Throughout the day, she had thought about him. And while she was pissed she'd been sidelined, she didn't regret what they had done. The more she stared into his eyes, the more she wanted to do it all over again.

He kissed her again, this time letting his lips linger on hers. She closed her eyes and kissed him back.

"Such a badass," he murmured. "Such a sexy, self-sufficient badass."

She stilled while the air grew chaotic around them. "That is the best compliment I have ever received."

The front door opened and banged shut. Providence nudged him away and pushed off the stool as Warren Hott entered the club. "Hello, hello," he called.

Dakota shot Providence an easy smile before he walked toward Warren. The two men shook hands and Dakota introduced Providence.

"Hello, Ms. Reynolds." Warren was playing this like a pro. "I'm Warren Hott."

"Please, call me Providence."

He glanced at her cheek. "What happened?"

"A guy came in here and we got into it," Providence replied.

Warren's eyebrows jutted up. "Are you okay?"

"I'm fine. Royally pissed, but fine."

"Did you call the police?"

"No. They've already been here once to speak with us." She pressed the bag of ice to her cheek. "Nothing a shot of whiskey won't cure." Her cheek throbbed, but the pain would fade away soon enough. Physical pain was nothing when compared with the emotional turmoil she carried with her day in and day out. "Who wants a cuppa joe and who's joining me in a shot of whiskey?"

"Coffee would be great," Warren said.

"Whiskey," Dakota replied.

With mug in hand, Warren made himself comfortable in a nearby booth and opened the case of his tablet. Dakota gestured for Providence to slide in, and he sat beside her. She loved being inches away from him, but she needed to maintain a respectable distance, so she scooted to the corner.

And damn, if he didn't reposition, so his thigh pressed against hers. Energy skittered up her leg. The man brought the heat and she would be more than happy to play in his fire.

No, no playing with fire.

"I've got a source at the police station," Warren said before logging in on his tablet. "She told me that Matt was bound with some type of black rope. They're analyzing it to determine the source. Also, the detective assigned to the case is combing through surveillance video from the convention center the night of the banquet to see who he might have come in contact with."

Oh, God, no. "The club uses black hemp rope," Providence said.

"Hmm, good to know," Warren said. "Dakota, tell me as much as you can about what happened."

As Dakota recounted the events, Providence wanted to add that she'd sat with Matt and heard his rants firsthand. But now wasn't the time to come clean, so she stayed silent. Her guts churned from the guilt.

Warren stopped typing. "And when you got here, what happened?"

"I spent time with a member in a private room, then I had a drink with the club owner, Stryker Truman," Dakota said.

"The security cameras were on," Providence added. "I can forward you a copy of the public areas, but there's no surveillance in the private suites."

Warren nodded. "And then what happened?"

"I spent more personal time with the woman from earlier," Dakota explained.

"I'll need to speak with her so she can corroborate your story."

Here we go.

"It was me," Providence said. "The first time, we were together for about forty minutes. I left the suite sometime around twelve thirty."

Warren slid his gaze from one to the other. "Okay, and then what?"

"I waited in the second-floor lounge for her," Dakota

continued. "Thirty minutes before the club closed, we returned to a private suite."

"How long were you two together?"

"All night," he replied.

"I'm sorry if this is uncomfortable for you, but I have to ask. What did you do?"

"I gave him a massage," Providence said, "then, we had sex. We were in the room for—" she glanced at Dakota and he returned her gaze—"three, maybe four hours. I lost track of time." Though her voice was steady, her heart was pounding out of her chest and her fingers trembled as she clutched the glass. Providence didn't discuss sex with her own mom, and she was a trained sex therapist. But, she had little choice, so she tossed back another mouthful and let the sharp bite burn a bitter trail to her roiling stomach.

"Understood," Warren replied.

She appreciated his professionalism. He didn't smirk, he didn't make an inappropriate comment. He handled these facts like any other, despite their sensitive nature.

"Where were you when the police arrived?" Warren asked.

"Down here, having breakfast." Dakota sipped the Macallan.

"Talk to me about the surveillance system."

"Before the club closed, I turned off the internal cameras, but not the exterior," Providence said.

"Great." Warren resumed his note taking. "So, there's evidence you didn't leave the building."

"Not exactly," Providence said as she and Dakota exchanged glances again. "There's no camera over the back door."

"That's not going to help us at all." As Warren discussed the case from a legal standpoint, Dakota dropped his hand below the table and placed it on her thigh. The heat from his hand seeped through her pants, and she wanted to thread her fingers through his and hold on tight. But she didn't.

Everything private was being made public in a stark, factual way. The sensuality, the intimacy, and the privacy had been stripped away leaving the raw, naked facts.

"All right." Warren closed the tablet case. "Why don't we take a brief tour?"

They escorted Warren upstairs to the Lust Room and the Greed Room, then to Providence's office, and finally to the back stairs that led out of the building. The tour finished at the front door.

"I'll be in touch," Warren said. "If the police swing by to question you again, don't answer their questions and contact me right away."

"Thanks for your help," Providence replied.

"I'll walk you out," Dakota said, before eyeing Providence. "Back in two. Lock the door. I have a key."

After Dakota and Warren left, she locked the front door. Her chest was so damn tight from anxiety and she massaged her muscles as she returned to the bar. There, she poured herself another finger of Macallan and took a swig.

A moment later, Dakota returned. Like every other time, the intensity in his eyes sent a jolt of energy through her. *Damn him. Damn this man.*

He slid onto the stool beside her. "Must've been one helluva day to be drinking alone."

She raised her glass and downed the alcohol. "You have no idea."

"Tell me about it."

Her heart fell. She couldn't. He would never speak to her again, and with good reason. She wanted to live the lie just a little longer.

Dakota placed his hand on her shoulder. "I'm sorry you've been dragged into this."

Their eyes met, he leaned forward to kiss her, but he didn't. The air turned electric and her pulse picked up speed. He was waiting for her to kiss him. As she stared into his eyes, she knew what she was going to do. She was going to kiss him.

They crashed into each other, the explosive kiss filled with so much passion. It was as if they'd been waiting all day for this moment. This wild, sensual moment that seemed so right.

She pushed off the stool and wedged between his thighs. She wrapped her arms around his neck and he snaked his around her waist. Hard-stroked kisses and kneading fingers made her panties damp and her nipples hard.

Then, he stopped. Breathing hard, he said, "I don't want to hurt you."

"What?" she gasped.

"Your cheek."

She smiled. "I can't feel my face right now."

With a smile that made her heart soar, he pressed his mouth to hers and kissed her with so much tenderness, she wanted to cling to him like a lifeboat in a raging sea and, never, ever let him go.

"You're wound tight," he said. "Time for me to massage you."

"Uh. No."

"Yes. But no sex."

"Well, that sucks."

His deep chuckle rumbled through her. When he pushed off the stool and held out his hand, she glanced at his long fingers. Those strong, sexy hands would be all over her. A thrill ran through her.

It was like she was fighting the undertow of the ocean, but she could never win, not against something that powerful, that all-encompassing. She was about to drown in him and she couldn't stop it from happening.

I have to do this.

She took a step toward him, then another. He clasped her hand and she appreciated the gentle way he stroked her skin. Back and forth. Up and down.

In a silence filled with unspoken expectations, they made their way to the stairwell. As soon as the door slammed shut behind them, he pinned her against the wall and kissed her like he was going to strip her bare and fuck her to the moon.

Everything about him screamed power and control, which made her feel safe. His breathing was calm, but the intensity in his eyes was not. Her own breath was coming in short bursts, her body thrumming with a desire so strong, she was dizzy with lust. He'd pinned her arms over her head and was teasing one nipple, constrained behind her bra, while he was grinding into her as if they were two horny teenagers making out beneath the stadium bleachers.

And, oh, my God, did she want to let go, to free herself from the prison she'd placed herself in. But she didn't deserve to be that happy. So, she slowed the kiss down, but Dakota wouldn't let it end. Rather than breaking away, he dropped gentle pecks on her lips. Then, her cheeks and finally, he kissed each wrist and the palms of her hands.

Her knees grew weak.

When he finally pulled away, they climbed the stairs in silence and entered a room on L3. "Take off your clothing." This wasn't a request, it was a demand. Her insides pulsed, her body ached for his.

But she took her time stripping out of her shirt and pants, never taking her eyes off him. When she stood naked before him, he led her to the Tantra chair.

She sat facing him. "Please, fuck me," she begged.

Dakota needed her more than he would admit. But he wasn't going to screw her. Tonight, he was going to help her. Given what she'd been through on his account, he was determined to do something just for her. With the exception of Sammy, he put no one before himself and his own needs. That was about to change.

Ignoring his raging hard-on, he collected the bottle of lavender scented oil, and returned to admire her. She'd leaned against the sloping back and closed her eyes, her chest rising and falling with each breath. Though he could stare at her for hours, he murmured, "Providence."

Her eyes fluttered open and she eyed the bottle in his hand.

"Turn around and lean against the cushion."

The lines between her brows deepened. "So, you're really not going to have sex with me?"

"No, I'm not. I'm going to massage that tension out of your shoulders."

With a playful smile, she arched up. His attention shifted. "As beautiful and tempting as your breasts are, I am *not* going to fuck you. Now, turn around."

Her saucy glare made him smile. She turned, draped her arms over the top of the chair, and grew still. And he dropped into the tight space between her glorious backside and the curve of the chair. He pressed his mouth to her skin and kissed her. Getting lost in her would be much too easy.

But he had a job to do, so he drizzled oil into his palm and started massaging her upper back.

She exhaled a sigh. "Oh, my God, you have got the best hands."

"Let me get you something so you don't stick to the leather." He pulled off a pillowcase and she lifted her face so he could slide it under her. "Better?"

"Mm-hmm."

Save for an occasional sigh, she stayed silent as he glided over her tense muscles, pausing to work on a knot before moving on. He took his time massaging her neck and shoulders, then her back, dropping a kiss or two as he moved down her body.

"I want to rub your legs." He pushed off the chair and an extremely relaxed Providence lifted her face.

He guided her to the bed and she lay face down. He worked her glutes, appreciating her toned bottom before moving on to rub her muscular thighs. As he doted on her, he realized that he hadn't appreciated a woman in a non-sexual way in a long time.

From out of nowhere, the blackmail threat crashed into his thoughts and hung over him like an angry storm cloud. Ignoring the outside world, he stayed focused on the sublime creature before him. Tomorrow would come soon enough.

"Can you roll over?"

"Mmm, you feel amazing," she murmured as she turned.

He continued massaging her upper chest, her arms, legs and feet. And he finished with a tender kiss. "Feel better?"

The serenity radiating from her eyes calmed him. The tension she carried in her shoulders was gone, as was the worry knot between her brows. Her smile was lazy and carefree and his hardened, vengeful heart softened...ever so slightly.

Time had taken on a different meaning, or maybe he had slowed himself down enough to enjoy *her*.

After pushing up on her elbows, she said, "You've worked a miracle on me and I am indebted to you. My offer is still on the table." She spread her legs a little and he glanced at her enticing pussy.

"I'd love to, but I won't. This was my apology for dragging you into this mess."

A shadow fell over her eyes. "You don't owe me a thing. You didn't murder anyone." Then, she broke eye contact. "What I mean is...you didn't murder Matt Hastings, and I will do everything I can to help you."

She started to get up, so he brought her her clothes. After dressing, she stood close, peered up at him, and ran her soft fingers over his beard. "Thank you for going out of your way to do something special for me."

In silence, they left the club. They'd parked beside each other and she glanced at his rental car.

"I pictured you in something—I don't know—bigger."

"My truck is in the shop."

Her smile charged through him like a bolt of lightning. "You, in a truck, makes more sense. Thanks for tonight."

He waited until she pulled out before he left. As he drove through the quiet streets, he wondered if she would think about him. He was convinced he couldn't *stop* thinking about her, even if he had wanted to.

THE FOLLOWING MORNING, Dakota drove the hour to Middletown, Maryland. The quaint town was home to ALPHA headquarters, and a quick thirty-minute jaunt to Camp David. Decades earlier, leadership responsible for creating the organization had wanted to build something far away from the nation's capital, but close to the President's secure vacation location.

The nondescript, warehouse-looking structure blended in to the area. The windows, located along the front of the building were covered with reflective glass. The only identifier was the company sign over the door. Dakota depressed the doorbell, the buzzer sounded, and he entered. After greeting the receptionist, he strode down the hallway to Luther's office.

The door was open, so he entered. Skipping the small talk, Dakota set the envelope on Luther's desk, eased into a guest chair, and waited.

Luther slipped on gloves before studying the photo of the four men in tactical gear. "I can't confirm that's you, but I can't rule it out." Then, he read the blackmail letter. "You're not going to pay this, are you?"

"Hell, no. I did that once to disastrous results."

"That was different. Your wife went missing. I would have reacted the same way."

Dakota shook his head. Conversation over. "I've got extra protection on Sammy," he said, changing the subject.

"Good." Luther slid the letter and photos back into the envelope "Wearing your vest?"

"Yeah."

"Bring me up to speed on the Hastings case."

Dakota detailed everything from the firing of Matt to the all-nighter with Providence and the police visit.

"Do you think the blackmail and the murder are connected?" Luther asked.

"No idea." Feeling like a caged animal, Dakota pushed out of the chair. "Someone knows what I've been doing and wants money to keep my secret. And that person, or a different one, wants to frame me for a murder I didn't commit. If word of ALPHA gets out, it won't matter how many alibis I have for Matt."

"If the public finds out about ALPHA, no one at the Pentagon, the FBI, or the White House will acknowledge this agency exists."

Dakota bit out a grunt. "Understood."

"Run the blackmail demand by Stryker. See if he can help you out. And keep a low profile. The less the public sees of you, the better."

Dakota strode out of the building feeling more frustrated than when he'd walked in. As he drove out, he glanced around. Anyone could be watching him from a parked car, from an office window. Someone could be flying a damn drone over his head and tracking his every fucking move.

He called Stryker. "Where are you?"

"Office, but I haven't had any coffee and my morning is booked solid."

"I'm being blackmailed for fifteen mil and the blackmailer included a photo of us on a mission."

"Fuck. *Fuck*," Stryker rasped. "I'll clear my schedule."

An hour later, Dakota strode into the Dulles building located in an area called "technology corridor", and jumped inside the waiting elevator before the doors closed.

A woman glanced over, then did a double take. "Are you the married one or the single one?"

He pushed the top-floor button. "Excuse me?"

"I know everyone who's anyone, but I don't know you. You're Dakota Luck or Sinclair Develin. One of you is married and one isn't. Which one are you?"

His thoughts jumped to Providence. He almost blurted, "I'm not available." Instead, he said, "Dakota Luck."

"Then, it's my *lucky* day." She pulled out a business card and thrust it at him. "I could be in the market for a condo. I might be available for a drink after. Possibly dinner." Her pale cheeks flushed with color.

You wouldn't last one day with me. I'm dangerous, I'm wanted, and I'm an assassin. He smiled. "I'm flattered, but I have to pass."

Her mouth dropped open. "Pass on me? I'm Stacy Blunk, B-L-U-N-K. Pronounced blanc, like the wine." Again, she jabbed her card at him. "I'm an influencer. An *influencer!*" The doors slid open.

Dakota didn't take the card. On a huff, she exited the cab and spun toward him. "You're a first-class jerk. And here I was willing to risk my life. For all I know, you killed that guy and dumped him in the—"

The elevator doors closed. *I've gotta listen to Luther and keep a low profile until this mess blows over.*

The upscale offices of Truman Cybersecurity were bustling with activity. Stryker's company was the premiere cybersecurity company in the region. Their goal? Stop hackers from infiltrating computer systems and holding companies' data hostage. Stryker knew everything about hacking because he'd once been a helluva hacker himself.

"Stryker is expecting you," said the receptionist.

Dakota strode past the cubicles that filled the expansive office space, then the executive team's private offices. Stryker's door was closed, so he knocked.

"Go away."

Dakota opened the door.

"That never works," Stryker said.

His desk was covered with a large computer display and four laptops.

"You've got a hoarding problem," Dakota said as he eased into a chair at Stryker's conference table.

Stryker flipped him off. "Coffee?"

"No." Dakota pulled the envelope from his computer bag.

After slipping on disposable gloves, Stryker examined the blackmail envelope and its contents. "This sucks."

"I've got a giant target on my back. For all we know, he'll be coming after you next."

"Have you told the guys?"

"No."

Stryker dragged a laptop off his desk and started typing. "Offshore accounts are hard as hell to hack into. That's why they're so popular." He looked at Dakota. "This might take days and I might not be able to hack in."

"You're good. You'll get it done."

"Thanks, bro. What's your strategy when the ransom isn't paid?"

"Make sure my daughter and her nanny are safe."

"What about you?"

"As soon as I figure out who he is, I'm gonna rip his fucking heart out."

Despite not hearing from Patricia Stearns, Providence had shown up for work at The Dungeon on Tuesday and Wednesday. Stryker didn't know her job was a cover and she wasn't going to bail on her cousin. But she was treading water, at best.

The knot in the pit of her stomach hadn't gone away. Her decision to sleep with her target could result in a misconduct violation. She'd be removed from the case and placed at that desk job Patricia had warned her about. Being Dakota's sole alibi didn't help her situation, especially if he was the vigilante the FBI believed him to be.

Dakota hadn't shown up at the club, nor had he reached out to her. She kept telling herself it was for the better. But she didn't feel that way.

On Thursday, she got a text from her dad. "Mom is worse, but won't go to doc. Call me when you can."

She phoned him right back. "What's going on, Dad?"

"Hey, honey. I'm hoping you can talk some sense into your mom. The nausea has gotten so bad, she's had to cancel a bunch of appointments with her patients, and she never does that."

"I'm sorry to hear that."

"She doesn't want me to know, but I heard her throwing up. And the dizziness is getting worse."

"Where is she?"

"Camped out in the family room. She insists she's just overexcited because Randy is back, but I don't think that would make her sick."

"I'll swing by on my way to work."

"That would be great. I made her an appointment for next week, just in case we could get her to change her mind. Please don't make a big deal about it, okay?"

"I'll be chill," Providence said and hung up.

Later that afternoon, when she arrived at her parents' house, Randy was sweeping out the empty garage. He extended both arms, gesturing at the empty space. "What do you think? Am I pretty damn amazing, or what?"

Providence laughed. "I'm impressed. You guys work fast."

"What guys?" He chuckled. "I did this. Pocketed a wad of cash, too."

"Where's Lizzie?"

"At work. She teaches preschoolers, remember? We already told you that."

She couldn't miss his annoyed tone. Providence had forgotten about her brother's short fuse. Rather than respond, she stayed silent.

He swept dirt into a dustpan. "What brings you by?"

"Checking in on the folks."

"Just in time for happy hour." Randy set the broom aside and they walked inside together.

As clean as the garage was, the kitchen was a mess. The counters were cluttered with unopened mail, cans of beans and boxes of pasta. *What's going on here?* As she walked past the table, she spied her mom's will. *Hmm, I haven't seen that in years.*

Providence found her mom lying on the sofa. Her face was ashen white and her hair was oily and untidy. Normally, her mom did circles around everyone else. Not today.

"Hi, honey," her mom said, while forcing herself up. "Looks like Dad called in the big guns."

It was impossible to get one over on her mom.

"Why would he do that?" Randy asked.

Ignoring her brother, Providence sat beside her mom. "What's going on?"

"Just relaxing."

"I'm going to make myself a well-deserved drink," Randy said. "Can I get anyone anything?"

"No, thanks," Providence replied.

"Mom," Randy said. "How about a wine spritzer?"

"Nothing for me," she replied, but Randy had already left the room.

"Where's Dad?" Providence asked.

"He was hovering, but since he brought you in as back up, he decided to take a break."

Her mom didn't look good, at all. She felt her mom's forehead, but no fever. "What's going on?" She'd lowered her voice and glanced over her shoulder. "We're alone. Talk to me."

"I think having Randy home has been more stressful than I realized. I'm just tired and a little dizzy, that's all."

"Dad is very concerned about you," she whispered. "Normally, it's the other way around. You're always on him to take his blood pressure meds. Why don't you go to the doctor so he'll stop worrying?"

"I'm good, really."

"Mom, c'mon." Providence raised her eyebrows and waited.

Several seconds passed before her mom spoke. "Fine. I'll go."

She kissed her mom's forehead. "Thank you. He set up something for next week. I can meet you guys there."

Randy walked into the room holding a glass of beer and a wine spritzer, though Providence got the feeling he had been listening. He shot them a smile. "Beer is for me because I definitely earned it today." He offered his mom the wine glass and she took it.

"You probably shouldn't have any alcohol," Providence said, taking the glass and setting it on the table.

"Don't be a killjoy." Randy shot her a glare. "The garage is cleaned out and I'm going to move your cars back in tonight. Mission accomplished." Randy drained half the beer from the bottle.

"Thank you, Randy." But their mom looked too miserable to care about the spotless garage.

Her dad walked into the room and gave Providence a hug. "What brings you by, honey?"

Providence's mom laughed. "Oh, Gordon, you and Providence are so easy to read. She convinced me to go to the doctor. Are you happy now?"

He leaned down and kissed her. "Very."

"The doctor?" Randy asked. "What for? Don't you feel well, Mom?"

"She's been lying on the sofa day in and day out," Gordon snapped. "What do you think?"

"Whoa, dude," Randy replied. "No need to bite my head off."

"I'm just worried, that's all."

Randy nodded. "Mom probably has low blood pressure. She gets wonky when she stands up too fast." Turning toward Providence, he said, "Did you hear about the realtor who turned up dead in the Potomac?"

Providence's guts churned. "Yeah, it's all over the news."

"The primary suspect—his name is Luck—offered me a job. I'm an excellent judge of character and he seemed like a total tool. I was right. Good thing I turned him down. That could have been *me* in the river."

Providence didn't want to discuss Dakota, so she congratulated Randy on cleaning out the garage and kissed her mom goodbye. "Feel better."

Her mom smiled, though the sparkle in her eyes was gone.

"I'll walk you out," her dad said.

Once outside, he said, "Thanks for convincing Mom to go to the doctor."

"You're right. She's not okay."

"I think Randy might be stressing her out. He's here all the time."

"Why don't you suggest he find an affordable apartment to rent?"

Her dad stopped at her car. "They don't have any money."

"Can you loan him some?"

"Years ago, we loaned him thousands and never saw one penny repaid. Mom and I don't want to go that route, yet."

"I understand."

"So, how's the job at Stryker's club?"

Again, Dakota popped into her head. She wished she had someone she could confide in about the mess her life had become.

"It's fine." She opened her car door. "I saw Mom's will on the table. What's that all about?"

"She wants to amend it to include Randy." Her dad shrugged. "I don't have an issue with that, but I think she should focus on her health before she makes any legal changes."

So did Providence, but she kept silent on that. "How are you holding up?"

"My golf league is starting but my heart isn't in it. I want Mom to feel better."

"You know, Mom saw right through us."

That made her dad smile. "She always does."

"Text me the appointment info and I'll meet you. Hang in there." Providence patted her dad's shoulder before slipping into her car and driving away.

She hated that her mom wasn't well and that her dad was so stressed over it. Though she doubted her parents would kick Randy and Lizzie out, she wondered if that would be the best thing for everyone. Randy had leeched off them before. Sounded like he was doing that all over again.

Providence arrived at the club to find the staff busy getting ready to open for the evening. She checked in with her line managers before heading upstairs to her office. When she walked in, her heart skipped a beat. Sitting in the middle of her desk was a giant bouquet of brightly colored flowers. In the center was a single, long-stemmed red rose. She read the card. It was from Dakota. "I haven't stopped thinking about you."

I haven't, either.

His thoughtfulness bolstered her spirits. As she logged in to her computer, one of the staff tapped on her open door.

"C'mon in, Kirsten."

"Hey," Kirsten said. "Just an FYI. We're almost out of rope."

"I checked inventory when I started working here," Providence said. "There were plenty of bondage bundles. Does the club usually go through that much rope so fast?"

Kirsten gave a little shrug. "I dunno."

"I'll order some. Anything else?"

"Are the security cams on?"

Providence studied her. "Why do you ask?"

"Mavis never turned them on."

She didn't answer my question. "They're on. Why are you asking?"

"No reason," Kirsten said before scooting out.

Hmm, what was that all about?

Providence jumped online to order more rope. Though there were a variety of colors and textures, Stryker only used black hemp in fifteen and thirty-foot bundles. As she placed the order, she remembered what the police had said. *He was bound with rope and tied to a mooring in Georgetown.*

Warren had told them Matt had been bound with black rope. A chill slithered down her back. *If I were investigating this, Dakota would look guilty as hell.*

At three in the morning, Providence left the club with the flowers. When she got home, she set the vase on her kitchen table. The pop of vibrant colors brightened her gray and white kitchen.

As she stared at the bouquet, she realized she hadn't thanked Dakota. "The flowers are gorgeous," she texted. "Thank you."

To her surprise, dots appeared. "They pale in comparison to you."

She laughed and texted back, "You're laying it on a little thick, aren't you?"

"Have dinner with me."

She stared at his text. She hadn't been on a date in years. Dating meant talking. What would she talk about? Not her job. Not her past. And talking about her unwell mom wouldn't cut it. Better to keep him at arm's length.

"I'll think about it," she texted back. She couldn't bring herself to tell him no. In her heart of hearts, she wanted to spend time with him.

"I look forward to seeing you," he texted back.

So cocky.

How could someone this attentive and this romantic be an assassin?

I'm leading a double life and my closest friends and family don't have a clue. He could be, too.

12

PROVIDENCE'S NEW PARTNER

At six twenty on Friday morning, Providence's phone buzzed with an incoming text from Patricia. "Please come into the office at nine fifteen. My conference room."

Execution day.

At nine, she passed through security and rode the packed elevator. She didn't bother stopping at her desk and she didn't grab a coffee. *No point in delaying the inevitable.*

Patricia was already seated at the head of the table and Providence's direct supervisor, Lou, was there, along with a man she didn't recognize. They rose. After handshakes and an introduction to the human resources manager, everyone sat.

Providence's heart stayed steady, but her palms were clammy. Like a Band-Aid getting ripped off, she just wanted to hear her fate.

"Providence," Patricia began. "Your career with the FBI has been exemplary. You give one hundred percent to every case."

Her guts churned.

"And you always have," added Lou.

She offered a tight smile.

"Choosing to become intimate with Mr. Luck might have been

a well-thought-out tactic," Patricia continued, "but it wasn't one we support."

"That, however, isn't the problem," said the HR manager. "You're being removed from the case because Mr. Luck is the primary suspect in a murder case and you are his only alibi. It's a conflict of interest for you to continue working it."

"I understand." She wanted to ask if she was going to be working at all. She wanted to find out if they were transferring her to another division or if she was being assigned a desk job while the police gathered evidence. But she stayed quiet.

"What HR questions do you have of me?"

"None at this time."

Both Lou and the HR employee wished her well and left, shutting the conference room door behind them.

Her attention shifted to Patricia. "How are you holding up?" Patricia asked.

"Hanging in there."

"I wanted to circle back with you on Mr. Luck's case. I've been informed that it's been closed due to lack of evidence."

That makes no sense. "But I'd only been working it for a couple of weeks."

Patricia shrugged. "I don't make the rules. I just play by them."

"What happens next?" Providence held her breath.

"It would appear you have a fairy godmother. You aren't being sidelined and you aren't being transferred to a desk job."

Providence's stomach fluttered. Patricia opened her notebook, pulled off a sticky note, and pressed it to the conference table in front of Providence.

1535 McCullah Road, Middletown, MD

"What's this?" Providence asked, picking up the paper.

"You've been reassigned. Please go straight there after you leave here."

Providence fidgeted in her seat. "I don't understand."

"The Director sent me an email stating that the Luck case had been closed. You are to turn in your badge and your weapon, then report directly to this location."

After staring at her for several seconds, Providence said, "For what?"

"I don't know."

Providence wanted to laugh. This had to be some kind of joke. But Patricia was not smiling. "You can't provide me with any specifics and you're sending me there unarmed?"

"This is coming from the Director, himself. I hardly believe he'd send you somewhere that would put you in danger." Patricia rose and extended her hand. "Thank you for your service and good luck."

What the hell? After shaking her hand, Providence placed her weapon and her badge on the table, slung her handbag over her shoulder, and walked out of the building.

Just like that, her career with the FBI was over.

She wanted to scream. She wanted to cry. Instead, she stopped on a nearby bench and dug out her nicotine gum. After popping three squares into her mouth, she chewed hard, hoping to flush out the anger. As she chomped down, the fury morphed into sadness. *Just like that, I'm dismissed and sent on my way.*

While she sat there mashing the hell out of the gum, she imagined going back into Justice, up to the executive level, and demanding to know what the hell was going on. But she would never do that.

She typed the address into the map app on her phone and enlarged the location. *This looks like a warehouse.* Now, she was full on perspiring. She was going in blind without her Glock.

Pushing off the bench, she walked up Pennsylvania Avenue and around the corner to her favorite coffee shop. Her next destination could wait a few more minutes while she bought herself what might be her last cup of coffee.

While waiting for her order, she scanned the eatery. *Oh, no.* Their eyes locked, but she didn't smile. She would be polite, but that was it. *Please don't come over.*

Jim Reynolds, known as Jimbo, pushed out of his chair and hurried over. "Hey." He started to hug her, but she stepped away.

"It's been a while," she said. *Three years to be exact.*

"What brings you in here?"

What a stupid question. "Guess."

He barked out a laugh. She always hated his laugh. Forced and shrill. "How've you been?"

"Good. Fine." That was the extent of her politeness. She had zero interest in making chit chat with her ex-husband.

"This semester has been a real bitch." Jimbo was a history professor at George Washington University. "How's your business doing?"

"No complaints." While married, she had always wished she could tell him the truth about her career. But as she stared into his dull eyes, she was relieved he knew so little about her.

"I've had you on my mind," he said as he shoved his hand into his jeans pocket.

"Well, it is that time of year."

He stared at her for a few seconds, then awareness flashed across his face. "Right. I try not to think about that."

"That? She wasn't a 'that'. She was our daughter." Glancing back, she hoped the barista would call out her name.

"I've been trying to get up the nerve to call you. I'm in a twelve-step program and wanted to apologize to you."

"Okay."

"But not here. Maybe you'd have lunch or dinner with me sometime."

"I don't need an apology. I was sorry enough for both of us."

He nodded. "I understand and I don't blame you. I'll give you a call. Same number?"

"Really, you don't have to."

"I get it. I was—"

"Providence," called the barista.

"Gotta go."

"Good to see you," Jimbo said. "You look great, by the way."

Providence collected her cup and left. On the way to her car, she unbuttoned her jacket so the April breeze could wick away the heat. Her marriage had ended terribly and she had walked away with a broken heart and a shattered life. She had zero interest in having any conversation with her ex.

As she slipped into her vehicle, she paused to sip the drink before starting the engine. "Thank God I'm not married to him anymore."

Providence didn't want to get caught up in the past, so she pushed him from her thoughts as she pulled into traffic, heading toward the unknown.

But seeing her ex had been difficult. Not because she missed him, or their marriage, but because there wasn't a day that passed that she didn't think of her sweet baby girl.

Her heart ached with a pain that never left her. But now wasn't the time to let the sorrow take hold. That would happen, like it always did, late at night, when sleep didn't come. She shoved down the myriad of emotions and forced herself to focus on the problem at hand.

Where was she going and who would be waiting for her when she got there?

An hour later, she swung into the parking lot. Her jaw dropped open as she stared at the sign over the front door.

ALPHA MEAT PACKING COMPANY

What the hell? What is this place?

Fewer than twenty cars filled the lot. The front-facing windows were covered with reflective glass, and the front door was locked, so she pressed the doorbell. *I miss my weapon.*

"Good morning," answered a woman. "Your name?"

"Providence Reynolds."

A buzzer sounded and the door clicked. She pulled it open and crossed the threshold. The woman behind the reception counter stood. "Welcome to Alpha Meat Packing. Can I see your ID, please?"

There was nothing in reception that provided a clue as to where she was. No brochures, no business cards on the counter, no nothing.

"Not until I get some information," Providence replied.

A man walked around the corner. Average height, ebony skin, clean shaven. An expensive-looking suit hung perfectly on his fit physique. "Good morning, Ms. Reynolds. I'm Luther Warschak."

As he extended his hand, he offered a relaxed smile.

She shook his hand. "Mr. Warschak, call me Providence."

"And I prefer Luther." Addressing the receptionist, he said, "We'll be in my office. I'm expecting another visitor. Tell Felipe to bring Providence's laptop to the conference room. And to wait for us."

"Yes, sir," she replied.

He gestured for Providence to walk with him.

"I'm not budging until I know what I'm walking into."

"An opportunity." Again, he motioned with his hand. "One I think you'll be interested in hearing about."

She didn't move.

"Your target, Dakota Luck, has become a primary suspect in a murder he didn't commit, and you're his alibi. We are short on time and we have a lot of ground to cover. How 'bout a coffee? Or would you rather grab the one you bought this morning at the coffee shop?"

"You had eyes on me?"

"Ever since you've been tracking my number one."

"What does that mean?"

"You're about to find out."

Providence had a choice. She joined him, or she walked. Her career at the FBI had been replaced with this one, of which she knew nothing.

Time for answers, so she took that first step.

"Thank you for making the right decision," he said. As Luther led her down a short hallway, he stopped in front of the break room. "The coffee is decent. Care for a cup?"

Her stomach was churning. No need to add more acid. "I'm good, thanks."

He poured himself one before they continued on. She entered a windowless office that could have been any CEO's office in Anytown, USA, save for the non-existent view. A large desk with an executive chair stood in front of built-in bookshelves. Two guest chairs faced his desk. A small round conference table with four chairs filled the corner of the room. On the wall across from his desk, six monitors hung on the wall—all of them dark.

No surprise there.

There was nothing in Luther's office that would identify him as the occupant of the upscale space. No photos, no awards. The desk was devoid of any paperwork or even a computer.

"Please, have a seat."

She eased into one of the guest chairs as he got comfortable in his. He grew silent for a few beats. Was this some kind of tactic to get her to start babbling? He'd summoned her, so she would stay silent.

He opened a desk drawer and extracted a laptop. After typing in a few keystrokes, he turned the device around so she could see the screen. He'd pulled up her internal FBI file, which included her entire case history for the past decade, along with her personal profile. She'd never seen it before and skimmed the information.

Her ex-husband was listed, along with their daughter. Her eyes caught the words Divorced and Deceased before Luther repositioned the computer so he, too, could see it.

Then, he toggled down to Current Position and replaced FBI Undercover Agent with ALPHA and everything in her profile was replaced with the word REDACTED.

Gone was her work history. Her personal data was no longer visible. All that remained beside her name was the word ALPHA.

That one word had changed everything.

"Congratulations, Providence. You're now an ALPHA operative. Going forward, no one searching for you in our database, or any other government database, will be able to review your case history or learn anything about you."

What the hell is going on?

"I had no idea a meat packaging company wielded that much power."

He chuckled, his eyes crinkling at the corners. "ALPHA controls everything, yet it remains the most secretive organization in the federal space. Decades ago, we were conceived by Justice, yet we stay completely buried beneath layers of bureaucracy, so we don't appear on any org chart. We don't exist, except to a handful of need-to-know individuals."

"What is ALPHA?" she asked.

"We are an elite group of operatives who hunt down and capture our country's most violent criminals."

"How is that different from any other law enforcement agency, including the FBI?"

"We target men and woman who have been arrested, tried, and convicted for the most heinous crimes. Child molesters, rapists, serial killers. DNA evidence links the criminals to their victims, but they've gotten off on a technicality or they've escaped from prison. As soon as they get out, they start killing again. What differentiates us from other law enforcement agencies is our motto, 'Dead or alive'."

Providence stared at him for a beat. "All right. I'm curious. What will I be working on?"

"One of my operatives—make that *former* operative—needs an

assist and you're the perfect person to partner with him. You're tough, you take zero shit from anyone, and you get the job done."

"So, I'm plucked from my career and now I work for you? I don't have a say in this? Maybe I liked my career and I'm not interested in teaming with one of your ALPHAs."

"Oh, I think you'll enjoy working with this one very much. If, after this assignment ends, you want to return to undercover work with the FBI, I'll make that happen."

"Just like that?"

He nodded. "Just like that." Luther pushed out of his chair. "Our IT Director has your laptop. Swing by and see me before you head out this afternoon. I'll have your weapons and other items."

As he escorted her down the hall, she glanced in the offices and saw people working. Some on their phones, others on their laptops.

"Why aren't you introducing me?" Providence asked. "Isn't that first-day protocol?"

"I'll leave that to your new partner."

"The suspense is killing me." Her sarcasm was not lost on Luther, who offered another easy-going chuckle.

They entered the conference room and he introduced her to Felipe, ALPHA's IT Director. "I'll be back." Luther left, closing the door behind him.

After welcoming Providence to ALPHA, Felipe began setting up her laptop. "If, for some reason, you misplace this, call me immediately." He gave Providence his phone number.

"I hope to hell I don't lose my phone."

"In the decade you've worked for the FBI, you've never once lost it."

Whoa. "Is there anything you don't know about me?"

Felipe shot her a sly grin, then went back to work.

"Eyes watching the eyes watching everyone else. My head is spinning right now."

"You should feel proud for what you've achieved," Felipe said. "It's an honor to work for ALPHA. Luther only hires the best of the best. And the man you're going to work with is one of a kind. More legend than man. He and Luther go way back."

Rather than ask more questions, she decided to wait until she met the legend himself.

Dakota entered Luther's office, dropped his computer bag on the guest chair, and sank into the other. "I got here as soon as I could. What's going on?"

"Can Stryker help you with the blackmail note?"

"He's gonna try." Raising his brows, Dakota threw his hands out, palms up. "Why am I here, Luther?"

"I brought someone in to work with you."

"On what?"

"Finding the person who killed Hastings. The police are going to arrest you. Won't be today or tomorrow, but I can't stall them indefinitely."

"I don't need a damn partner."

"The FBI suspects you're the vigilante who's been exterminating serial killers."

Dakota's stomach dropped. "Come again?"

"They've been tracking you for months, but I just found out. If you and your assassin team are arrested, I can't help you. I won't expose my organization."

"My assassin team *is* part of your organization."

"Not on paper, you're not. Three years ago, you went off the rails. You turned into a killing machine and I was protecting you from yourself."

"Don't throw that shit in my face now, Luther."

"Fortunately, neither of the undercover agents targeting you made any progress, so the Director closed your case for lack of evidence."

Leaning forward, Dakota asked, "Two agents?"

"The first one is a licensed realtor who worked at Goode-Luck. Like you, that's her cover. Fortunately, she found nothing and left."

"Who was it?"

"Annie Baker."

"I remember her. She worked for me for me most of last year." He crossed his legs. "And the other?"

"An agent from the Violent Crimes Division. She's been with Justice for about a decade. Stellar reputation. Hard worker, strong willed. She'll be your new partner."

"You expect me to partner with the person who's been tracking me?" Dakota chuckled. "You're joking, right?"

"No, I'm not. She's our best shot at finding the person who killed Hastings. Show her the blackmail letter and the photos."

"You've got to be fucking kidding me. I was her *target*." His chest heated. "I can't trust her. She's the damn enemy." He bit out a growl.

"Rein in your anger, Dakota."

"Like hell I will."

"You two will have a hurdle or two to get over. Once you do, you'll work well together. If you want to stay out of prison, you need to trust her completely." As Luther stood, he said, "Don't let the past dictate your future."

What the hell does that mean?

The two men walked down the hall as Felipe exited the conference room. "She's all set up."

Dakota walked in and his brain stuttered to a screeching halt.

Holy fuck. Fuuuck. Fuck me.

His personal life slammed head-on into his professional one. When he and Providence locked eyes, she could not hide the surprise. Neither of them spoke. Neither looked away. Combative energy filled the room.

She was an undercover FBI agent and she'd played him for a damn fool. She'd used him and he'd fallen for it. Now, he was supposed to work with her. Which meant he had to trust her. Fury scrambled his thoughts. He wanted to charge out the door and never come back.

Fuck her. Fuck Luther. Fuck ALPHA. Fuck it all. I don't need any of them.

At the moment that thought ended, clarity forged a crack in his anger.

Sammy. *I need to protect my daughter.* Dakota would force himself to work with her for the sake of his child.

"No introductions are needed," Luther said, breaking the silence. "Providence, you have your new laptop. Stop by my office on your way out. Your job is to find Hastings's killer. And protect Dakota."

She shoved out of the chair. "Whoa. I'm not a babysitter or a damn bodyguard."

"I don't need protection," Dakota bit out. "And I sure as hell don't want it from her."

"You both need to take this down several notches. If you don't want to get arrested for Hastings's death, you've got to work together."

"I'm not under investigation," Providence said.

"Not yet," Luther replied. "Let me put this in perspective for you two. You were at the club, alone, for hours. You're linked sexually. You both have access to rope, specifically black hemp rope. There's no surveillance camera on the back door. Your alibi is flimsy."

"I had no motive," Providence said.

"Providence, you sat with Matt at the realtor banquet. If the police find out you were there, you go down in a blaze of ego, right along with Dakota."

"What?" Dakota flipped his gaze to her. Silence reigned while he ran through the people he met that evening. "Ah, hell. You were Elaine Jones from Boston. I knew you looked familiar." He rubbed the back of his neck, but the tension wouldn't release.

This was a damn cluster fuck.

"Watch your backs...and each other's," Luther said. "I'll leave you to sort things out. Do it fast. The clock's ticking." He left, shutting the door behind him.

Time for Dakota to face the enemy.

13

OIL AND WATER

Gritting his teeth, Dakota glared at her. She'd been lying to him from the beginning. *Marketing consultant, my ass.*

While he could have been impressed that she'd been so believable, he hated that he'd been duped. He had trusted her and she had deceived him. She was the damn enemy sent to gather evidence, build a case, then arrest him.

His blood ran ice cold. He was furious with himself for letting his guard down.

Fuck me a thousand fucking times.

For the next few hours, Dakota had to man up and manage through this. He couldn't let his anger at her, and himself, get in the way of protecting his daughter, clearing his name, and figuring out who was blackmailing him. "Looks like someone's got some explaining to do."

"It would appear *you* do," Providence replied, crossing her arms.

Providence crossing her arms wasn't helping. But he did not glance at her breasts.

"I'm getting coffee." He opened the conference room door. "You want a cup?"

"Whatever." They walked down the hall in a frigid silence. He couldn't deny that being around her was intense and exciting, yet infuriating as hell.

He filled two mugs while she went hunting for what he assumed was milk.

"In here." He opened the refrigerator door and pulled out a carton of creamer.

"Uh-huh," she grumbled.

They returned to the conference room. Dakota shut the door, sat at the head of the table. They sipped their hot drinks and glowered at each other. The standoff continued while they drained their mugs.

"Do you always sleep with your targets?" he bit out.

"We didn't sleep. There was zero snoozing." She flipped open her laptop. "I don't much like this, either. I get plucked from my job and forced into an organization I didn't know existed two hours ago. Now, I'm tasked with protecting you. Oh, yeah, and if you get arrested, I probably will, too. No fuck is worth that."

With his thoughts pinging from problem to problem, he unearthed his laptop. "The quicker we can move forward, the faster we can end this partnership. I don't trust you, but I'm out of options."

She shook her head, blew out an exasperated breath. "At least you're not pretending you like this, and you're certainly not kissing my ass."

"No, I already did that." He stared at her, wishing she wasn't so beautiful, especially when she was madder than hell.

"My job," she began, with a cutting edge to her tone, "is to find the person or persons trying to frame you for murder. Since I know next to nothing about you, I'm going to have to start at the beginning. The more information you provide me, the more we have to work with. There are clues everywhere, so we can't overlook anything. Nothing is insignificant. Nothing can be assumed."

Dakota might be pissed as fuck, but she was right. They needed to stay ahead of the police so they didn't get arrested.

"I sat next to Hastings at the banquet," she continued. "He admitted to me that he'd taken kickbacks before he got completely trashed and told the entire crowd. Is that why you fired him?"

He appreciated that she was jumping right in. There was no long, drawn out conversation, no getting into the weeds about who did what to whom. No flinging words about who screwed who over. The fury that had overtaken his thoughts stood down and he took a calming breath.

"My business partner, Juanita Goode, found out he was taking kickbacks from a mortgage banker, so we fired him for cause the day of the banquet. I could have pressed charges or reported him to the national realtor association, but I didn't."

"Why not?"

"Everyone deserves a second chance. He could have made a good living without the kickbacks, but he got greedy."

"Do you think the hit was real estate related? Had Matt pissed off a client? Maybe the president of the mortgage company wanted him dead so he wouldn't talk."

"Possible, but doubtful. Once that video went viral, an opportunist wanted Matt dead. There's been too much happening to me to make me believe it's a coincidence."

"What else is going on?"

He dropped the envelope on the table. "Blackmail letter."

She glanced around the conference room. "I need gloves."

"In the lab." He rose. "Have you seen the facility?"

She shook her head.

"I'll show you around."

Though neither uttered a word, he couldn't ignore the constant tug. Rather than keep their distance, they walked side by side and in step. On their way to the lab, he introduced her to the

ALPHA operatives who weren't on the phone or in a closed-door meeting.

After Providence met the check-in tech in the lab, Dakota grabbed two pairs of disposable gloves. Several employees sat hunched over microscopes, while others worked at their stations. The space was clean, the conversation kept to a minimum.

They returned to the conference room where she slipped into the gloves and extracted the envelope's contents.

NOW THAT I HAVE YOUR ATTENTION

If you want your ALPHA secret to stay that way, wire transfer $15 million to offshore account 1-87623-487721 Bank of the Princes. Deadline is midnight Thursday.

"You are getting slammed," she said. "Was yesterday the deadline?"

"Yes."

"Did you do it?"

"No."

"Have you heard from them today?"

"No."

After re-reading the letter, she asked, "Does Stryker know about this?" He nodded as recognition flashed in her eyes. "Oh, no. Is Stryker part of your vigilante team?"

Dakota remained stone faced.

"That's what I figured. So, you dragged him into your insanity."

"No dragging required."

"Can he hack into this account?"

"Said it's doubtful, but he's trying."

She pulled her laptop close and began typing. "I'm creating a file so we can keep the clues and evidence organized. Is there a way I can share this with you and give you edit rights?"

Rolling his chair closer, he showed her how. He wanted to touch her, stroke her skin or stare into her eyes. He wanted to brush her hair off her forehead, pull her close, and kiss her tempting lips. He wanted his Providence of twenty-four hours ago. But this Providence was not to be trusted, and certainly not to be kissed. He gritted his teeth, his jaw muscles flexing again and again.

As she read through her notes, she ran her tongue over her lower lip. Once, twice. On the third stroke, he realized working with her might be more of a challenge than he'd anticipated. His raging libido was interfering with his ability to think. He had to shut this shit down. But dammit, he couldn't stop staring at her.

She added more information, then turned to him. Her eyes raked over his face, the intensity of her gaze tugging him toward her. She cleared her throat, but she didn't look away. The longer they stared, the more he wanted to kiss her. How the hell was he going to keep his hands off her when all he wanted to do was strip her bare and drive himself inside her?

Her breath came out in a heated whoosh. *She's feeling it, too.*

She broke eye contact and snatched the photo of his spray-painted vehicle off the table. "Yours?"

"Yeah. That happened during the banquet, *Elaine*."

She hitched a brow. "Where were you parked?"

"The convention center garage. I didn't see anyone, but they could have been hiding anywhere."

"Whoever did this thinks you're with ALPHA." She'd been taking notes, but stopped typing and regarded him. "Are you an operative?"

"No."

"Were you at one time?"

"Yes."

Rather than jot more notes, she studied him, almost as if seeing him for the first time. The air became turbulent with an attraction that could not be ignored. He shouldn't like looking into her eyes so damn much, but he did. He shouldn't be glancing at her sexy mouth, either.

I need to kiss her.

As if sensing his intention, she severed their steamy connection and tapped the second photo with her gloved finger. "Tell me about this one."

"I don't know where or when that picture was taken. As an operative, I went on jobs with as few as three, while others had up to six."

"Everyone's wearing night goggles. I can't even see their faces." She studied the grainy photo. "Does that look like the corner of a street sign to you?"

They leaned toward the photo and their shoulders touched. Rather than move away, they each stayed anchored to the other. His body thrummed from her close proximity. For fuck's sake, this shouldn't be happening. He couldn't think clearly. Her slow, rhythmic breathing, the intoxicating smell of her hair, and her smooth melodic voice had ensnared him in a trap he doubted she'd even set for him.

"What do you think?" She angled her face toward him, giving him a front-row seat to the beautiful dark striations of gray in her eyes. Refusing to stop himself, he kissed her. Just once. But that simple peck sent blood pumping through him.

"Oh, God, Dakota," she whispered.

The achingly sexy way she'd whispered his name tugged on his heart. Years ago, he'd locked up his heart and thrown away the key. Since then, women hadn't fazed him, but this one sure as hell did.

"What do you think?" she repeated the question.

"I'm pissed. You deceived me."

"I was doing my damn job," she murmured, before pushing out of the chair. "Let's drop this picture at the lab."

"Dusting them for prints is useless. Mine are all over them."

"I want it enlarged and enhanced."

Using their phones, they each snapped a picture of it before returning to the lab. Providence set the picture on the counter. "Can you enlarge and improve the quality of this photo? I'm looking for something that might tell us where it was taken or who these men are."

"We'll do our best," said the tech. "Turn-around time is a week to ten days. And don't ask for sooner because that *is* sooner."

Walking down the hall, Dakota blew out an exasperated breath. "Do you think I'm unable to ID myself on a mission?"

They entered the conference room. "All I saw in that photo were four people in tactical gear. That picture could be of *any* SWAT team." She opened a new browser window and typed in 'SWAT team at night' and 'Night photo SWAT team'. Dozens of photos popped up. "I'm working this case like I would any other. It's not personal."

"Point well taken."

Her lips lifted at the corners. "I'll take that as a win."

Providence was on fire. That simple kiss had set her insides ablaze. She was unsure how to manage through all the feels with her new partner. At best, he was difficult. A stubborn man who was used to running the show *his* way.

But, she had been trained to be methodical in her approach. To use evidence and clues as building blocks. One step led to another, or sometimes to a dead end. But she would walk the walk and do her damn job, despite the pig-headed partner she'd been assigned to work with.

Nevertheless, being around him had a dizzying effect. Complicated, unfiltered signals flowed between them and she had to fight hard not to reach out and touch him. She was desperate to feel his whisker-covered chin or run her fingers down his sinewy arms.

If eyes were the mirror of the soul, his was a smoldering, quaking volcano, just before a torrent of lava exploded skyward, scorching everyone and everything in its destructive path.

"We need to discuss your missions with ALPHA," she said.

He glanced at his watch. "I've gotta head out. Can you work this weekend?"

"Yeah, but I'm still working at the club."

He raised his eyebrows. "Well, you don't need *that* job anymore."

She slapped her laptop closed. "I won't bail on my cousin, plus he doesn't know *that* job was a cover. I'm headed there now. I'll talk to him about my hours."

"We need a secure place to work, but this is too far to drive every day. Where do you live?"

"Arlington." She knew where he lived, so she stayed silent.

"I'll take it you know where I live...or you don't care."

"Don't care."

His lips twitched at the corners. "How'd you find me? My home address isn't listed in The Dungeon's database."

"I followed you home one night after you left your office."

He paused for an extra beat. "I've got a black site we can use that's closer to DC."

Hmm, a black site?

"Let's meet at my Tysons office around noon and we'll drive there together."

They each shouldered their computer bag and headed down the hallway. She'd been flying solo for so long, it felt freeing to work alongside someone who knew about her secret life. She didn't have to pretend with Dakota. Didn't have to change the subject the second someone asked how things were going at work. Despite their rocky start, Providence liked partnering with him, a lot.

She slowed in front of Luther's office. "I've got to pick up my service weapon."

He regarded her for a few seconds, as if trying to decide what to say to close out their day. "Drive safely." He strode toward reception, taking his fiery energy with him.

Resisting the urge to roll her eyes, she tapped on Luther's door.

"Come in."

Like earlier, a warm smile graced his face. "How was day one with ALPHA?"

"It went well, in spite of my stubborn partner."

A deep chuckle rolled out of him. "Sounds like Dakota. Have a seat."

As Providence eased into the chair, Luther set a small leather duffle on the edge of his desk. "Handling Dakota is going to be the most challenging part of your job."

"I don't doubt it." She eyed the bag.

"That's yours," Luther said. "Open it."

Providence unzipped it and peered inside. "What the—" She pulled out four different badges. FBI, DEA, ATF, and DHS. All had the name Elaine Jones with her photo. Providence smiled. "A perk of ALPHA?"

"The IDs allow you to interface with law enforcement and the public. I recommend to my new operatives that you use *one* per case, so Elaine Jones with four different agencies doesn't start popping up everywhere." He chuckled. "Years ago, I hired a seasoned DHS agent. He used a different badge every time he talked to someone for the same damn case."

Providence smiled. "Thanks for the heads up."

"I know you might want to return to the FBI after this case, but it's the ALPHA starter-pack, and I treat all my new hires the same. Everyone gets one, and that includes you."

"Thank you, Luther."

Then, he handed her two Glocks. "Strap the smaller one to your ankle."

"Understood."

"Two more housekeeping items before you head out. First, I sent you a text. Add me into your phone book as Luther. No last name."

She pulled out her phone and completed that task. "And the second?"

"If you want to learn about current or former ALPHA operatives, you can access their files through ALPHA.net."

He wants me to read up on Dakota. She collected her items. "I take my job very seriously."

"That's why I hired you."

"I'm not sure how to protect Dakota twenty-four seven if he's going to resist me."

"He's like a turtle. You just have to get past that hard-shelled exterior." Luther grabbed a large duffle bag and walked her to the lobby. "I'm sure you'll figure something out." He handed her the bag.

"What's this?"

"Your Kevlar vest. It does you no good in this bag. Wear it."

As she drove east toward the city, she had no idea how she would protect her stunningly handsome partner who was also a royal pain in the ass.

14

THINGS ARE GETTING PERSONAL

At twelve thirty, Providence rode the elevator to the top floor of the high-rise building that bore the name LUCK. Normally in control of her emotions, butterflies fluttered in her stomach. On the one hand, she couldn't wait to see Dakota. On the other, yesterday had *not* gone well...at all. The only way this situation would work is if they put aside their anger and worked together.

I can do this.

The elevator doors slid open. She threw her shoulders back and stepped into the upscale offices of Goode-Luck Real Estate.

"Good morning," said the smartly dressed woman at reception. "Nope, let's try that again. Good *afternoon*. Welcome to Goode-Luck. How can I help you?"

"I'm here to see Dakota."

"Are you Ms. Reynolds?"

"I am."

"He's in a meeting. Can I get you a beverage?"

"I'm fine, thanks."

The woman walked around the reception counter. "Please," she said, gesturing to the nearby waiting area. "If you change your mind, the kitchen is right around the corner."

"Thanks."

"Are you shopping for a new home?"

"No."

"Are you listing yours?"

Providence shook her head.

The woman stalled for a second, appearing confused. Then, smiling, she said, "Dakota will be out shortly."

Too keyed up to sit, Providence walked to the window and admired the skyline. The day was clear, the sky a vibrant blue, and the spectacular view went on for miles and miles.

She felt him standing behind her and a burst of energy skirted through her. The air crackled and her body tingled in anticipation.

"Hello, Providence." His voice was low, yesterday's anger replaced with his signature rumble that made her pulse soar.

She turned and her heart fluttered. Dakota Luck on his home turf was breathtaking. His confident smile sent endorphins flying through her. Then, she realized his achingly beautiful expression was all part of his act. And her silly, stupid little heart stopped beating so hard in her chest.

This was his billion-dollar company, and he carried himself like the CEO that he was. He didn't want his employees to detect anything was out of the ordinary. Already a primary suspect in a murder investigation, he didn't need to call attention to the fact that the woman standing inches away from him was someone he detested—and someone he was now forced to work with.

She cleared her throat. "Dakota."

He stared into her eyes another second before he said, "I'm running behind. Come on back."

Glass partitions separated workstations, giving the office an open, airy feel. He spoke with everyone he passed, asking a question about a listing or how their closing had gone.

He oozed power and charisma, yet he kept his massive ego in check. Even so, there was no question who was in charge. This was Dakota Luck's massive empire.

Could this successful businessman be hunting down and eliminating the worst of the worst? For now, she was no longer tasked with answering that question. She was there as his ally, not his enemy.

He stopped outside his office. "After you."

While she could have admired the massive L-shaped ebony desk and conference table, the stark white sofa with matching conference room chairs, or the stunning vista through his wall of windows, she did not. The man standing beside her captivated her full attention.

His striking face and killer body, paired with all that raw, animal magnetism, were a heady combination. It took all her willpower *not* to jump into his arms.

Though his threads were nothing extraordinary—a white dress shirt paired with black pants—the clothing hugged his broad-shouldered physique. Which is exactly what she wanted to do to him.

When he closed the door, the large space turned into an intimate one. "We need to reconcile our situation."

Spoken like a true businessman. That's what she was to him—a situation. Folding her arms, she hitched a brow, and she waited. *Here comes a ration of shit.*

"Going forward, no more secrets. No more lies. Can you agree to that?"

That's it? Relieved he hadn't lectured her, she offered a brief smile. "I can, if you can."

Like the professional he was, he extended his hand. She slid hers into his, but that instant connection sent sparks shooting through her. The electricity humming through her, paired with the intensity in his eyes, made for a dangerous combination. She glanced at his mouth before breaking away. Those were the most kissable lips she had ever seen and she pursed hers to quell the desire.

"I was hoping to be done working by now, but I've got a couple of calls—"

"No worries. I'll go grab a coffee." His desk phone rang. "You want one?"

He nodded as he answered. "Hold on a minute…Providence."

She turned back.

"You look gorgeous."

Her smile stayed with her all the way to the kitchen. Rather than wear jeans, she'd dressed in a form-fitting shirt, a black pencil skirt, and heels. Though she would never admit it, she had dressed for him.

As Providence poured two cups, his business partner walked into the break room. "Hello, I'm Juanita Goode."

"Providence Reynolds." They shook hands.

Juanita was friendly and personable, and the two chatted about the beautiful spring weather. "I've been looking forward to meeting you," Juanita said.

Providence wasn't sure where to go with that comment. "You have?"

"It's nice to see Dakota is doing something besides working. What do you two have planned this afternoon?"

Not wanting to stumble all over herself, Providence paused while trying to come up with something plausible. He'd created a cover but forgotten to tell her. "We thought we'd play it by ear."

"Beautiful," Juanita replied with a smile. "Enjoy."

With a nod, Providence collected the hot drinks and returned to Dakota's office.

He raked his gaze over her, then stared into her eyes while he spoke. "We can purchase the land, work with a few high-end builders, and build about thirty luxury homes."

Dakota was video chatting with a group of men. His second monitor displayed a spreadsheet filled with numbers he'd been highlighting.

As she set his coffee on the desk, one of the guys said, "Dakota, introduce us to your lady friend." She moved out of the picture.

Dakota laughed. "My *lady friend*? Who the hell talks like that?" The guys cracked up.

"Maverick, that's who," one of the other men said.

"Come back, darlin'," the first guy boomed. "Say hello to us."

Dakota's light-hearted laugh touched the deepest part of her. Whoever these men were, he was comfortable enough to be his true self.

"Providence, come meet my idiot friends."

She pulled up a chair alongside him. One by one, he introduced her. "Colton Mitus, Crockett Wilde, Jagger Loving, Maverick Hott, and that handsome devil is my brother, Sinclair Develin. This is my *lady friend*, Providence Reynolds."

She loved meeting his friends, loved hearing their good-natured ribbing as they expressed their condolences that she was spending the day with him.

"Dakota, bring her to Jagger's wedding," Maverick said.

Colton laughed. "Can someone mute him?"

Again, the guys cracked up.

"Seriously, if you can put up with that crazy one—because that's what he is—you're welcome to come," Jagger said.

"Thanks," Providence replied. "Good meeting you guys." She stepped away from the screen and stood by the window, appreciating the breathtaking landscape.

"Okay, so did everyone have their fun?" Dakota asked. Providence could hear the smile in his voice and she peered over at him. She loved seeing that happy expression on his handsome face. "Can we get back to work so I can get the hell out of here?"

"Who's the developer?" Sin asked.

"Zander King," Dakota replied.

"Maverick and I are checking out the location in a couple of weeks," Crockett said. "We're bringing Alexandra and Carly."

"I reserved rooms for all of us," Maverick said. "Let me know if you guys can make it."

"I'll check with Brigit," Colton said.

"I'll run it by Evangeline, but we'll probably go," Sin added. "Jagger, I'll video chat with you when I'm there so you can see the land."

"Thanks, bro," Jagger said.

"Dakota, can you make it?" Colton asked.

"I've got too much going on right now," Dakota said. "I'm dropping off. I've gotta touch base with Zander."

He ended the call. Seconds later, he stood beside her as she stared out the window. To her surprise, he stroked her back, then he left his hand on the small of her back.

Her skin tingled, everywhere. The need to kiss him so powerful, her body went from warm to scalding. She ached to run her fingers through his hair or jump into his arms. She became aware of his breathing, and then, her own. It was as if they were both trying to keep things under control, but the tea kettle was screaming for someone to snatch it off the hot stove.

She wanted him so badly, it hurt. This partnership was never going to work if she couldn't reel in her need.

"Thanks for putting up with my friends," he said, breaking the silence.

"You guys seem close."

"We are," he said as he wrapped his long fingers around the back of her neck, inside her collar, and gently massaged.

His rhythmic caress had her closing her eyes and relaxing into his touch.

Knock-knock-knock.

Her eyes flew open as the employee from reception walked in.

Though Dakota acknowledged her, he didn't stop rubbing Providence's neck.

"Excuse me, Dakota. Your mail, along with a client gift." She set the items on his desk and left, shutting the door behind her.

Dakota broke away to make a call, and Providence sat across his desk to finish her coffee. As he spoke with the land developer, his gaze never left hers. The more she stared at him, the more she liked what she saw. The electricity that passed between them was palpable, undeniable, and so damn magnetic.

The gift basket perched on his desk had been wrapped in clear cellophane and Providence pulled it onto her lap. Someone had sent him a collection of brightly colored tiny plastic bears. *What is this?*

At first glance, she thought someone had sent him candy, but the plastic bears were vials of liquid nicotine. There were two dozen tiny bears in a variety of different flavors, a vaping kit, and three vials of clear liquid.

What a strange gift to send your broker.

When Dakota ended the call, he pushed out of his seat and sat beside her. "What's that?"

"Someone sent you a vaping kit." She pointed to the gummy bears. "Those are liquid nicotine."

He grimaced. "That's a gift I'll never use. You want it?"

"God, no. I quit smoking. This is the last thing I need."

"Who's it from?"

She handed him the basket. "I don't see a card."

After removing the cellophane and finding nothing, he read one of the labels on a bear. "It's marked very strong." He tapped a button on his phone console.

"Yes, sir."

"Who dropped off the gift basket?"

"A courier. I didn't even have to sign for it."

"Which company?"

"Sorry, I was on the phone. I didn't see and he didn't leave a receipt."

Dakota hung up and checked the surveillance system. "He's got on a baseball cap and he kept his head down."

Providence acknowledged the footage with a nod.

Dakota checked the basket again. "I've never gotten a client gift without a card. A vaping kit with liquid nicotine makes no sense."

"No, it doesn't. Check your mail for another blackmail letter."

He thumbed through the pile. "There's nothing. I can't believe they'd give up this easily."

She shook her head. "I wouldn't let my guard down."

"Hell, no." He stood and held out his hand. "Thanks for your patience. Let's get outa here." She placed her hand in his and he pulled her out of the chair and into his arms.

But he did not kiss her.

And she did not kiss him.

She should have put on the brakes on the physical contact. She could have pushed him away. She could have told him to stop. Now, would have been the perfect opportunity to set hard limits.

But she didn't do any of those. She just let the desire build to a dizzying crescendo as they stared into each other's eyes. A low growl rumbled in his throat and she sucked down a harsh breath. The attraction pinging between them sent her rocketing to the moon. *So. Damn. Sexy.*

"You ready to grab a sandwich?" he murmured. But it was the upturn of his sexy mouth and the playfulness in his eyes that made her smile.

"Tease." She pushed out of his arms and headed for the door. Before she got there, he pulled her close and kissed her. One panty-searing kiss.

Ohmygod. Her blood whooshed through her.

"Not teasing."

The constant hum of desire burst into a vibrant inferno.

Dakota loved being around Providence, and his attraction to her was off the fucking charts. But they had a damn job to do, so he'd find a way to stay focused.

After eating a sandwich next door, they headed into the parking lot. He'd gotten his truck back, a fresh coat of black paint concealing the truth. At his truck, he lifted her computer bag off her shoulder and set it on the back seat.

"Thank you."

Those luscious lips of hers were too damn tempting and he fought against the urge to kiss her again. *Get it together.*

His black site, nestled in a woodsy area of Great Falls, was only fifteen minutes away, but a challenge to find without explicit instructions.

"I've never brought anyone from ALPHA here," he said as he turned down a dirt road.

She laid a soft hand on his arm and his gaze fell on hers. "Thanks for trusting me."

"It's part of our new business arrangement," he said with a wink.

He loved making her smile.

The unmarked building looked more like an abandoned warehouse than a first-class, black site with everything from a small surgery center, to enough bedrooms to sleep ten. What was lacking, at the moment, was grub.

He drove around back, tapped the built-in remote on his visor, and one of the oversized garage doors opened. Once inside, the door closed behind them. The cavernous room housed four identical black SUVs.

"What kind of operation are you running?" she asked.

"A top-secret one," he said, and opened the truck door.

He stilled at the door while the visual recognition screen captured his retina. When the light turned green, he pushed it open and waited for her to walk through.

When she passed by, her beautiful scent wafted in his direction. It would be so easy to pull her into his arms and kiss the hell out of her. But he did not.

No time for a tour, so he led her to the conference room. They sat side-by-side and logged in to their laptops. Having her next to him made things better...and worse.

She was damn hard to resist.

"We left off with ALPHA," she said. "When were you an operative, and for how long?"

"Seven years ago, I worked for ALPHA for five years and used my real estate business as a cover."

"Not an overachiever or anything, are you?"

He loved her sass. "I scaled back on the real estate and never had a full caseload as an operative."

"How many assignments did you work?"

"Dozens," he said, pulling up the cases.

"I'm looking for enemies. Someone who's seeking revenge. Did you testify against the people you caught?"

"Yes, but my testimony was recorded so I didn't have to appear in person and my voice was altered."

"Well, someone knew, and that someone wants fifteen mil to stay quiet."

His cell phone rang. "It's my bank." He tapped the speaker. "Dakota Luck."

"Mr. Luck, it's Darla at Sterling United Bank."

Darla was his local branch manager. "Hi, Darla. What's going on?"

"We received a wire transfer request from an offshore account. It's for fifteen million."

Providence gasped. He slid his gaze to her while anger pulsed in his temples.

"Since you've never done wire transfers," Darla continued, "I thought it would be smart to confirm with you. In fact, if you did authorize this, I'll need you to come in and sign a few docs."

"I *didn't* authorize that."

"I suspected as much. I have to report this to the FBI."

Dakota pulled up the picture of the blackmail letter. "Can I get that offshore account number?"

She rattled it off. It matched the one in the letter. The son of a bitch was not giving up. "Darla, thanks for calling me to confirm."

"Absolutely."

He ended the call. Frustration plagued him on a daily basis, but this—*this*—was insane. Someone was dead set on stealing his money.

"This person is fearless and aggressive," Providence said, breaking the silence. "We have to work harder and smarter."

Dakota called Stryker to see if he'd made any progress on the offshore account number.

"No," Stryker replied. "I couldn't hack in, so I tried calling the bank and impersonating the account owner, but there are too many layers of protection built in. I didn't make it past the first security question. I'm sorry, my man."

"Thanks for trying." He hung up. "Let's keep working. If I don't find this motherfucker, I'm going to punch a hole in a wall."

They spent the afternoon discussing mission after mission.

"How many have we covered?" he asked.

"Nine."

"With no progress."

"Let's switch tracks and—"

His phone buzzed and he glanced at the screen, then blurted, "Fuck me." He showed the text to Providence.

"You should have authorized that wire transfer. It's going to be bad for business."

Frustration shadowed her eyes. "They've upped the stakes with that threat and they want to hear from you."

"We should craft a response."

She placed her hand on his, shooting a bolt of lightning through him. "No, we shouldn't."

When his gaze met hers, the energy they exchanged grew intense. He loved how she'd taken charge of the case. How she'd remained steady and in counterbalance to his mounting fury.

She was his lighthouse in the middle of a raging sea. She was his refuge and he wanted to get lost in her for days.

After patting his hand, she offered a reassuring smile. "You're pissed over this. So are they. They want the money, like, yesterday. You didn't give in to their demand. Keep in mind, they didn't follow through on their threat to expose you as an operative."

"True." She had a valid point.

"And they didn't go public with that photo of you on a mission."

Another valid point.

"Then, they tried to take the money, and they failed there, as well." Pushing out of the chair, she paused to stretch.

Jesus, she's killing me. He had to admire the view. So, he checked out her breasts...and her ass...and every other body part available for his viewing pleasure. When she finished, she leaned her backside against the conference table, gripped the edge, and peered down at him.

"Hey," she said.

Dammit, I need to kiss her. Leaning back, he stared into her eyes. He was trying to be a damn professional and a gentleman. And he hated himself for it. Because he wanted to strip her bare and take her on his conference table.

He didn't screw his business partners. Never had. Wasn't starting now.

"Ignoring them sends a stronger message," she continued.

"Right," he bit out.

"You want to call it?"

"What I want is *you*, in my bed."

Fuck me. His mouth had taken off, unfiltered by his brain.

Her pupils blackened, her lips parted. But she did not break. "Well, you can't have me." Her eyebrow hitched and she gripped her hip. "I get that things are getting worse, not better, but screwing isn't going to fix anything."

"Like hell it won't. Fucking fixes *everything*."

Her laugh was deep and sexy, but the expression on her face reminded him why he found her so damn breathtaking. The flash of lust in her eyes told him how she really felt. She *wanted* to be in his bed.

"Promise me, no matter how many more texts you receive, you won't respond."

His phone rang. *Dammit, why all the interruptions?* It was Mrs. Morris. He answered. "Everything okay?"

"Sammy is starving, but she won't let me put the pizzas in the oven until she knows you're on your way home. What's your ETA?"

Dakota flicked his gaze to Providence. "Twenty."

"Great." Mrs. Morris hung up and Dakota pushed out of the chair.

Now, they stood inches apart, Providence's beautiful scent filling his lungs. Desire kicked up another notch until the passion whirled around them.

"I won't respond to this text or any other, under one condition," Dakota said.

Up went her eyebrows. "I don't think you're in a position to negotiate with me, but go ahead, make your case."

In the past three and a half years, he'd never brought a woman home. Not once. He'd never introduced Sammy to anyone, but Providence was different from anyone he'd ever met. His gut told him to take that leap and invite her home with him.

"Have pizza with me tonight."

"Pizza? You sure do know how to entice a girl." She studied him for a few seconds. "Fine, whatever."

Dakota waited until the warehouse garage door closed behind them before taking off. "I need you to use these." He handed her a pair of binos from under his seat. "Make sure we aren't being followed."

15

THE SURPRISE

Providence kept her eyes trained on the road. Back and forth over every car that drove into her field of vision. "Which pizza joint are we going to?" she asked as Dakota headed back toward his office.

"A local one." Though she wanted to look at him, she kept her eyes on the cars. "We've had a woman directly behind us or two cars back ever since we jumped on Route 7." She recited the license plate number into her Notes app on her phone. "Never mind. She turned into the mall."

As Dakota drove past his office, she said, "I need my car."

"We can pick it up later."

After driving into his neighborhood, he pulled over. "Thanks for being my eyes."

"Wait, we're going to your house?" She set down the binos.

"Yes."

"I'm gonna be straight-up honest. When I'm Venus at the club—"

He placed his large hand on her thigh and heat radiated up her leg. "I didn't bring you home to have sex with you. I brought you home for pizza night."

"Pizza night?" What man brought a woman home for pizza? Dakota Luck did, and she was curious enough to take the bait.

When he pulled away from the curb, she watched for cars, but the upscale neighborhood was quiet. He drove to the end of a court and into the driveway of a beautiful home with a cozy wraparound front porch. Seemed kinda domestic for a man like Dakota.

The garage door opened, he pulled in and cut the engine. "Bring your laptop into the house."

"Of course," she replied.

His kitchen was bright white and muted grays, and top-brand stainless-steel appliances. The delicious aroma of pizza made her stomach growl. They were alone, so who made the pizza?

As he set his computer bag on the floor, a small child flew around the corner. "Daddy!"

Oh, my God, he has a daughter.

He scooped her up and hugged her. "How's my angel?"

She hugged him hard. "I am soooo hungry and my growly stomach has been waiting and waiting—" The child looked at Providence and grew silent.

"Hi," Providence said, and the child gave a shy wave.

Dakota's daughter had long, dark hair and bright blue eyes. She looked so much like Dakota, it was like staring at his mini-me. Providence guessed she was five, maybe six. Hard to tell because she could have been tall for her age.

Repositioning her in his arms, Dakota turned to Providence. "Sammy, this is my work friend, Miss Reynolds. Providence, this is my daughter, Samantha Luck."

She nestled into Dakota.

Providence smiled at the tyke. "Hi."

"Let's drop our laptops in my office," Dakota said as he shouldered his bag, his daughter still in his arms.

She followed him out of his kitchen. A middle-aged woman sat on the floor surrounded by a racetrack and toddler-sized cars.

The woman stood. She was petite with a pleasant face and a friendly smile. After Dakota introduced his daughter's nanny, he said, "Pizza smells great."

"Mrs. Morris and I baked a cake, too," Sammy said. "I wanna get down."

Dakota set her on the floor and she walked over to Providence. "Do you like pizza?"

"I love pizza."

"We made two." She stared at Providence for a few beats as if sizing her up. "What kind do you eat?"

Providence started listing toppings, trying to process the situation while maintaining a chill vibe.

"Do you like black awawas?" Sammy asked.

"Black olives," Dakota explained.

"They're delicious."

The child beamed. "I love them. They are soooo yummy. My real name is Samantha and my short name is Sammy."

"What should I call you?" Providence asked.

"Sammy."

"You can call me Providence."

Sammy looked at Dakota. "Provi…"

"Pro-vi-dence," Dakota said.

"Do you have a short name?" Sammy asked her.

Providence smiled. "You can call me Provi, if that's easier."

"Sammy, let's put Providence's work bag in my office, then we can show her where the guest bathroom is so she can—"

"Do you have to wash your hands right away when you come home?" Sammy asked her.

"I have that rule at my house." Providence couldn't help but smile again. Samantha Luck was absolutely adorable.

As Providence followed Dakota down a hallway, Sammy slipped her small hand into hers. And Providence's heart squeezed so hard, she rubbed her chest to soothe the ache.

Once in his spacious office, Dakota set his bag on his desk

chair and she placed hers on the leather chair in the corner. His office was stately, yet cozy, with dark wood walls, a tray ceiling with dark wooden beams, and recessed lights that bathed the room in soothing light. As she expected, his desk was free of any papers, only a single framed photo faced inward.

The built-ins behind his desk captured her attention. The shelves were filled with books, framed artwork by his daughter, and several photos. Pictures of Sammy, Sammy with Dakota, and of Dakota with the men she'd met on the video chat earlier in the day.

Mrs. Morris popped in. "Pizza's ready."

"Yay." Sammy bolted, leaving Providence and Dakota alone in his office.

She slid her gaze to his. He was waiting. For the first time since she'd laid eyes on him, she was seeing him for his true self. The wealthy real estate mogul and businessman—and possible vigilante—was a father. And because she hadn't accessed his file like Luther had suggested, she'd been blindsided by the news.

He stepped close. "I assumed you knew, but you didn't, did you?"

"No, I haven't read your file. Total rookie mistake."

He stroked her cheek. "I wasn't ready to say goodbye to you. There's nothing like pizza night with a four-year-old that screams romance." He pointed to an open door. "You can use the bathroom off my office." And then, he dipped down, but instead of kissing her, he whispered, "Thank you for coming home with me."

He flashed that killer smile and was gone.

Providence didn't need a man to complete her. But this man was slaying her with his words.

She walked into the bathroom on rubber legs and shut the door. *He has a four-year-old.* Annabel's face crashed into her thoughts. *She would've been four, too.* Her heart felt heavy, but she washed quickly, not wanting to keep them waiting.

They were seated, but they hadn't started. "Please eat," she said. "Sammy is starving."

Without delay, Sammy picked up her slice and bit into it. Her eyes lit up as she chewed. Forcing down any lingering emotion, Providence asked, "Sammy, which pizza should I try first?"

"This one."

Providence picked up a slice covered in black olive pieces and took a bite. "Mmm, you and Mrs. Morris make the best pizza."

The child beamed at her.

Dakota asked Sammy about her afternoon and she chatted away between bites. When they'd devoured the slices, Mrs. Morris retrieved a covered cake tray and set it in the center of the table.

"Daddy, close your eyes." Dakota shut them while Mrs. Morris removed the cover. "Okay, you can open them."

The chocolate cake had a border of delicate pink flowers with green stems. Providence's heart stuttered as she read the words in red icing.

BEST DADDY EVER!

"We spelled the words and Mrs. Morris, she did the flowers!"

"Wow, Sammy, that's beautiful. What a great surprise. But it's not my birthday and it's not Father's Day."

Sammy placed her small hands on his cheeks. "You are the best daddy ever!"

Providence's heart swelled. This was one special little girl.

After Dakota hugged her, he snapped a picture of the cake and one of Sammy with the cake. Then, he showed her both photos. "Thank you, honey, I love it." Dakota cut four slices and passed them out. "Who wants coffee?"

"If you're making it, I'll have a cup," Providence replied.

Miranda shook her head. "None for me."

"Are we having movie night?" Sammy asked.

"I have to work tonight with Providence," he replied.

Sammy's expression plummeted and Providence's heart broke. Not wanting to interfere, she stayed quiet.

"We can watch the movie together, Sammy," Miranda said.

Tears filled her eyes. "I want Daddy to watch *Lady and the Tramp* with me."

"That's one of my favorite movies." Providence knew she shouldn't have said a word, but work could wait ninety minutes.

Sammy gasped. "It is?"

"Oh, yeah."

"Oh, boy, I'm outnumbered," Dakota said while making coffee.

"Will you and Provi watch with us?" Sammy asked.

"Yes, we will, but after, you are going right to bed. Do you understand?"

"Hurray. Movie night!"

Once the coffee had brewed, Dakota filled two mugs and returned to the table. After trying the cake, he said, "Wow, this is fantastic."

After dessert, Dakota cleaned up while Miranda helped Sammy change into her jammies.

Providence cleared the table, refilled her mug, and sat at the kitchen island sipping her drink. With the dishwasher loaded, Dakota sat beside her. "I'm not sure now is the best time for a movie, but I appreciate your flexibility."

"You're a lucky man to have such a wonderful child. Enjoy every moment with her."

He laughed. "You haven't seen the *other* Samantha Luck. The one who hurls her LEGO across the floor or flat-out refuses to take a bath."

Sammy appeared, dragging a worn blanket. "I'm ready."

Providence made a beeline for the recliner in the family room. As soon as Dakota sunk down in the center of the sofa, he got busy pulling up the movie while Sammy climbed up beside him, her blanket in tow.

Miranda walked into the room. "My sister wants to FaceTime

with me. Sammy, would you mind having movie night with Daddy and Providence so I can talk to my sister now?"

"That's okay," said Sammy.

"Dakota," Miranda said, "I'm out early tomorrow, so you and Sammy have a fun Sunday together."

Dakota nodded. "Thanks for a great dinner, Miranda."

"It was good to meet you, Providence," Miranda said.

"You, too," Providence replied. "Thank you for dinner."

With a smile, Miranda vanished around the corner.

"Does she live here?" Providence asked.

"She has a private suite in the basement with her own entrance," Dakota replied. "Sammy, Providence is all alone on the other side of the room. Should we invite her to sit with us on the sofa?"

Sammy crawled over Dakota and patted the empty cushion. "There's room for you, Provi," she said before scrambling back over onto her spot.

Moving beside Dakota would be a mistake. "I'm comfortable here."

But when Dakota patted the sofa cushion and said, "Please join us," she couldn't resist. The second she sat next to him, she became hyper aware of his close proximity. *Oh, God.*

With a tap of the remote, the lights dimmed, and the movie started playing.

Though she snuggled against the end of the sofa, his large frame and muscular legs were inches away. And so damn tempting. The electricity running between them sent tingles racing through her.

Sammy crawled onto Dakota's lap and snuggled close, her thumb in her mouth, the blanket draped over her small legs. A rush of emotion tightened Providence's chest and her eyes misted. She couldn't change the past, couldn't bring back her child. As she watched the kid-friendly movie, she struggled to keep it together.

If she excused herself to the bathroom, she'd ruin Sammy's evening. So, she bit back the sorrow, and forced herself to focus.

As if he could sense she was struggling, Dakota clasped her hand. Being here, with this family, was wrong. This was a job, an assignment, not an opportunity to bond. It was bad enough that she was starting to develop feelings for this man, but he had a child.

When this case ended, she'd be on to the next. And she'd say goodbye to Dakota. Emptiness filled her soul.

Maybe pizza night wasn't such a smart idea. Yet, her broken heart yearned for a deep, meaningful connection and a family of her own.

The movie ended and a sleepy Sammy said goodnight to Providence. Dakota carried her upstairs while Providence waited on the sofa. She needed to leave, but not before she set some serious ground rules.

16

THE INCRIMINATING PHOTOS

After helping Sammy brush her teeth, Dakota tucked her into bed.

"Can Provi come back for movie night?" she asked.

As he sat on the edge of her small bed, he smiled. "I can ask her, how's that?"

"Okay." In went her thumb, she rolled over, and her eyes fluttered closed.

He kissed her forehead and returned to find the family room empty. Thinking Providence had started working in his office, he went in search of her, but she wasn't there.

"Hey." She stood in the doorway and her beauty halted his breath. He wanted to carry her upstairs, too, deposit her into *his* bed, and love her all night long. "I was in the bathroom."

The fire in her eyes burned brightly, but something was wrong. Something was definitely off.

She shouldered her computer. "I'm gonna take off."

"I'm sorry about the movie," he said. "It set us back—"

"It's not the movie. Mixing business with personal is a bad idea. This is a challenging case and we've got a lot of work ahead of us. I don't want things to be strained. I called my sister for a ride since I've got my work laptop."

"Don't go."

"It's too late to work and I'm not here for a booty call." She crossed her arms.

She sure as hell was fired up about something.

Her phone binged. "My sister's here. Thanks for inviting me for pizza night. See you Monday." And just like that, she was gone.

He fought the urge to go after her. Maybe introducing her to Sammy had been a mistake. In truth, he wouldn't have been able to concentrate on work anyway. Providence had done what no other woman had been able to do. She'd gotten to him. And from her abrupt departure, she was struggling, too.

All evening, he'd wanted to touch her. Not kissing her was an exercise in frustration. If she had stayed…*It's better that she left.*

No, that's a damn lie. I wanted her to stay.

He locked up, set the house alarm, and retreated into his office. *Time to learn about my new partner.*

He accessed ALPHA's database and found her file. Her career as a special agent with the FBI's Violent Crimes Division spanned a little over a decade. About four years ago, she transferred to undercover work. Most of those assignments had taken her out of town. She'd received numerous accolades within the organization. Without question, she was well qualified to work as an ALPHA operative. Her career was stellar, save for one disciplinary action for misconduct.

Him.

But it was the personal information about Providence that caught his eye.

Spouse: *Jim "Jimbo" Reynolds. Divorced.*
Children: *Annabel Sylvia Reynolds. Deceased. SIDS.*

"Oh, God." His heart broke for her. She had suffered an

unimaginable loss. Based on the dates provided, her daughter had died four years ago. And her marriage had ended not long after that.

This explains a lot.

"Thanks for the ride," Providence said to her sister, Megan. "My car is at Goode-Luck Real Estate in Tysons."

At the red light, Megan glanced over. "What's wrong?"

Providence had been staring out the window, trying not to think about her evening, but that's all she could think about. "I've got this client and…" She paused. "It's nothing."

"Why is it that I tell you all my secrets and you never reciprocate?"

"I don't have any."

"Everyone has something. C'mon. I'm a good listener and I might even be able to help." Her sister's cajoling smile was the tipping point.

"I've got a client, and it would appear we're…well, we're attracted to each other."

"Nice." The light turned green and Megan rolled forward. "What's the problem?"

"I don't mix work with pleasure."

"All you do is work, so when would you ever meet anyone, if it wasn't through work? You don't date and you haven't put yourself out there since your divorce. Maybe this guy is good to…you know…practice. You get your dating mojo back and then, BAM! You're out there."

Providence chuckled. "He's got this adorable daughter. She's four, the same age—"

"As Annabel would have been."

"You remembered."

Megan pulled into the real estate parking lot. "Of course, I do.

She will never be forgotten. Not by any of us." She paused for a beat. "Do you like this man?"

Providence grew silent while she thought about the question.

"I'm not asking if he's the one," Megan continued. "I'm simply asking if you like spending time with him? Does he push a button or two?"

That made Providence smile. *He pushes a lot of buttons.* "I guess," she replied, wanting to keep things on the down-low. "I struggle with letting myself be happy."

"Have you talked to Mom about this?"

"Years ago, but not lately."

"For what it's worth, you deserve happiness. Annabel's passing was the worst thing, but it wasn't your fault." She put her hand on Providence's shoulder. "Bad things happen that have the power to ruin us if we let them. Annabel wouldn't want that for you. She would want her mommy to thrive, if for no other reason than to honor her memory. Be the best you can be *for* your child."

Fighting back the tears, Providence nodded. After a few seconds, she got control of her emotions. "Thanks for being such an awesome sis. Please don't say anything to Mom or Dad."

Megan crossed her heart. "Not a word. Oh, I sent you a text earlier, but never heard back. Leigh and I made brunch for tomorrow. We've been concerned and want to check on Mom and Dad. Can you swing by?"

"Sure. What time?"

"Around eleven."

"What can I bring?"

"Just your beautiful self." Megan leaned over and hugged her. "I hope I helped. You helped me find my happy when I was struggling with coming out. I want you to find yours."

"I love you, Meg." Providence grabbed her computer bag and made her way to her car.

The two women drove out of the parking lot toward their respective homes.

When Providence got into bed, she checked her phone. She found herself smiling as she read the text from Dakota. "Sammy asked if we could invite you over for another movie night. Having you here meant a lot to me, too. What should I tell her?"

She could shut him down and keep things professional. But this was her opportunity to take a chance, like Megan had suggested. Was she willing to put herself out there and let herself feel again? *I might not find joy. This could turn into heartache and loss all over again.*

Even though she didn't believe she deserved a second chance at happiness, she couldn't disappoint the child. "Tell her I'd love to," she replied.

"I'm not sure who's happier. Sammy or me," he texted. "Sleep well, Miss Rhode Island."

He was doing everything possible to break down her walls. If they came tumbling down, would she?

AT ELEVEN TWENTY, Providence entered her mom and dad's house. Megan and Leigh were busy in the kitchen. Their puppy was crashed out in the family room. Through the window, she spotted Randy mowing the backyard. But her mom and dad were noticeably absent.

"Hey." Her sister-in-law, Leigh, broke from setting the table to hug her.

After a moment of small talk, Providence asked where everyone was.

"Randy is mowing," Leigh said. "Lizzie ran to the liquor store."

"Mom's not doing well," Megan said. "She's upstairs and Dad is with her."

Providence found her dad sitting on the edge of the bed, staring at the floor. Her stomach dropped. He didn't look so good, either. "Hey, Dad."

It took a few seconds, but her dad shifted his attention to her.

"Hi, dear."

She sat beside him and that's when she heard her mom retching in the bathroom. "What's going on?"

"Mom is getting worse."

"I'll meet you guys at the doctor tomorrow."

"Thank you."

The bathroom door opened and Providence stifled a gasp. Her mom looked pale, gaunt, and sickly. Heather Sharpe ambled toward them. She and her dad moved out of the way and her mom got into bed.

"I'm not feeling so good," her mom said.

Her dad held her mom's hand.

"Maybe you should go to the hospital." Providence felt her mom's forehead. No fever. Then, she placed her finger over her mom's wrist and timed her pulse. "Hmm, well, your heart rate is slower than I would have expected."

"Probably because she's so weak," said her dad.

Megan appeared with a glass of water and set it on the night table. "Brunch is ready."

"Thank you, honey," said their mom. "Take Dad and enjoy. I'm going to rest."

Providence glanced at her sister. "Can we bring you something? How about a piece of toast with jelly and tea?"

"I'm not sure I'll be able to keep it down, but sure, that would be nice."

"I'll be back with it." As Providence kissed her mom's forehead, she struggled with just how ill her mom was.

"Dad, do you want me to bring you a plate so you can stay with Mom?" Megan asked.

He nodded.

The sisters left, closing the bedroom door behind them. As they headed down, Providence voiced her concern and her sister echoed her sentiments. They entered the kitchen to find a sweaty Randy guzzling a glass of orange juice. Leigh was seated at the table, surrounded by covered dishes, while Lizzie poured champagne in a flute, then added orange juice.

"Hey, guys!" Randy raised his glass. "The lawn is mowed. I'm taking a quick break for grub, then heading back out to weed the gardens."

"Who wants a mimosa?" Lizzie asked.

Those two sure are happy. "No, thanks." Providence placed a piece of bread into the toaster and pulled a mug from the cupboard.

"No one is having a cocktail?" Randy asked.

"No," Megan replied, sitting next to Leigh. "I can't drink. I'm too worried about Mom."

"Poor thing," Lizzie said. "I was hoping she'd be feeling better by now, but she's getting worse."

Randy walked past Providence and she grimaced from his body odor. He sat and started serving himself. "Am I the only one who's eating?"

Leigh dished out a plate for herself, then passed a serving bowl to Megan while Providence waited by the microwave for the tea to heat.

"What's your story?" Randy asked Megan and Leigh. "Are you two roommates?"

"We're married," Megan replied.

Silence.

"That's wonderful," Lizzie said. "Isn't that great, honey?" she asked Randy.

On a nod, Randy shoveled food into his mouth. "When did the whole lesbian thing happen?"

Another chilly silence filled the air.

Beep-beep-beep. Providence's skin was crawling as she opened the microwave and pulled out the hot mug.

"I mean, when did you decide to become a lesbian?" Randy was digging himself deeper into a hole.

"Randy," Lizzie said, her tone abrupt. "Let's not go down that path."

"What?" Randy asked. "I thought she liked men. I was just wondering about it, that's all."

"I was a kid when you left," Megan said. "You've been gone for years and have no business questioning me about my sexual orientation."

Leigh placed a hand on Megan's arm. "We fell in love, just like you and Lizzie did. No different."

Bing! Providence pulled out the toast and rolled a light layer of jelly on it, wondering how much longer she could stay silent.

"Not *just* like us," Randy protested. "I mean, you're *both* women."

Slowly, Providence pivoted. "Randy, you have a right to your opinion, but keep your mouth shut if you can't be accepting of *everyone* in this house."

Scowling at Providence, Randy pushed out of his seat. "I can say what I want, whenever I want. I live here. You don't."

"*Sit. Down.*" The harshness in Lizzie's voice caught everyone's ear. "I'm sorry," Lizzie said to Megan and Leigh. Then, she frowned at her husband. "Be quiet."

Providence set the mug and toast on a tray, then plated food for her dad. "I'm taking these to Mom and Dad."

Lizzie jumped up. "I'll do it."

Too angry to respond, Providence left the room.

Her brother had soured her stomach and killed her appetite. She'd forgotten how closed-minded he was and how his negative rants had always been a conversation killer.

When she walked into the bedroom, her mom was resting and her dad was pacing. She set down the tray. "What time is Mom's appointment tomorrow?" she whispered.

"Eight fifteen."

"Text me the address."

Her mom pushed up and leaned against the propped pillows. "That tea smells good."

Providence handed her the mug and her mom sipped the drink. Then, she sat on the bed beside her. "I think you guys should ask Randy and Lizzie to move out."

"Where would they go?" her mom asked.

"They're adults. They'll figure it out. You two need a breather."

Her mom and dad exchanged glances, but remained silent on the subject. Providence didn't want to push. They were both stressed enough.

On the way back downstairs, she promised herself she would stay calm, no matter what crap came flying out of her brother's mouth. Providence walked into a silent kitchen. Lizzie complimented the meal, but Randy ate in a brooding silence. Between he and Lizzie, they downed that bottle of champagne in no time. Providence poured herself an orange juice and sat at the table.

And then, Providence did what she always did. She walked *toward* the fire, not away from it. *Time for some answers.* "Randy, how's the real estate business treating you these days?"

"Never better."

"He's a natural salesman," Lizzie added. "His new clients love him."

"Most realtors hold open houses on Sundays. Do you have any today?"

"I do, but I got a couple of the other agents to sit them for me."

That made no sense. "As a rookie agent, why aren't you holding your own open houses? Isn't that how you find new clients?"

"Randy is managing the agents who are doing the open houses for him," Lizzie said.

Whatever the hell that means...and why can't he answer his own damn questions? "Who do you work for again?"

"Larke Realty," he replied.

"Which office?"

"Damn, girl, you ask a lot of questions." He shoved out of the chair and left the room.

Providence helped clean up, then took off. She wanted to spend the rest of the afternoon familiarizing herself with ALPHA's extensive databases.

That evening, she texted Dakota. "Meeting my folks at the doc 8AM. Mom not well. What's the plan for tomorrow?"

"I'll call you in ten," he texted. "Putting Sammy to bed."

Not long after, her phone rang. *This is work.* But she couldn't stop the excitement that lit a fire in her belly when his name popped up on her phone. "Hey," she answered.

"Hey, yourself. What's going on with your mom?"

"Not sure, but she's definitely not okay."

"I'm sorry to hear that."

She wanted to ask him about his day. What did he and Sammy do? Had he thought about her at all? In spite of the stress with her mom and her brother's unacceptable comments, she'd thought about him and Sammy. But that wasn't what this call was about.

It's business. That's it.

"We've got to find a different place to work," he said. "It's too risky to use my black site every day."

As his deep voice rumbled through her, she locked onto his cadence, the way he kept his voice low, like he was telling her a fantastic secret, just for her to hear.

"Agreed."

"ALPHA HQ is too far."

She knew exactly where this conversation was headed. Her body warmed, but she needed to pull her thoughts from the gutter. "And we can't work at your real estate office. Hmm, maybe we should each work from home and sync up daily?" She bit back the smile.

Silence.

And then, she laughed. "Not the answer you want to hear?"

"Hell, no."

"So, what are you proposing, Dakota?"

"We work at my house."

"What about Sammy?" *And your bedroom? And your bed? And your hard, sexy body? And the fact that we're having a hard time keeping our hands off each other. What about all that?*

"She's at daycare twice a week and Miranda has her the other three. I've worked at home plenty since she was born and she knows I can't play during the workday."

"I was just giving you a hard time. We can give it a try. It'll work or it won't. If it doesn't, we'll figure something else out."

"Thanks for being flexible. Good luck with your mom."

She hung up and tossed her phone on the sofa. "This new work arrangement is never going to fly."

Dakota woke at five in the morning in order to work out before the day got away from him. After lifting and running on the treadmill in his home gym, he checked his phone on the way upstairs to shower. *What the hell?*

He had several missed calls and texts. And it was only six thirty.

His phone rang with a call from Crockett Wilde's wife, news anchor Alexandra Wilde. "Hey, Alexandra. What's going on?"

"We received an anonymous letter about you, along with two photos. I snapped pictures of everything and texted them to you about twenty minutes ago. My producer wants to run with the story. Can you comment on it?"

His stomach dropped. "I haven't seen it. Hold on."

The letter was pieced together from magazine clippings.

Dakota Luck is doing a helluva lot more than running a real estate company. It's time the public knew his real story.

The photos were the same ones the blackmailer had sent to

him. *Jesus. This is crazy.*

To cover his concern, he chuckled. "You know, I thought the graffiti on my truck was from a disgruntled woman." He kept his voice steady, but he was so fucking angry.

"Dakota," Alexandra said. "It's me you're talking to. I haven't interviewed you about Matt Hastings's death but I think you need to tell your side of the story. How about an exclusive?"

The fury he kept in check broke free, sending adrenaline pounding through him. Talking about this would send the media into a feeding frenzy. He'd be hounded day and night.

He needed to deflate the problem before it blew up in his face. "I'll call you back in five."

He hung up and called his brother. If anyone knew how to handle the press, it was him. Sin answered, "Turn on the TV."

He did. A different news station was airing the story, along with the photos.

"I'm so fucked," Dakota bit out.

"The son of a bitch sent the letter to all the local stations," Sin said. "Did Alexandra get a hold of you?"

"Yeah. I'll give her an exclusive."

"Schedule it at my office and we'll strategize first," Sin said. "Come by as soon as you can."

"Do me a favor," Dakota said. "Call your dad and let him know I'm giving Alexandra this interview."

"Got it," Sin said and hung up.

Dakota called Luther to keep him in the loop.

"I'm confident you and Sin will handle this," Luther said. "Just find this person before they ruin your life altogether."

Dakota called Alexandra back and scheduled the interview for later that morning. After he showered and dressed, he found Sammy at the kitchen table drawing a picture while Miranda organized flash cards.

"I'm making this for Provi."

Despite the fact that his world was imploding, he would do

everything in his power to shield his child. Dakota sat beside her. "That's beautiful."

Sammy had drawn the three of them watching a movie on the sofa. He glanced at Miranda.

"When Provi comes back for movie night, I'll give this to her."

"Samantha."

"Uh-huh." She continued coloring.

"Honey, stop for a minute."

She did.

"You know when Daddy works from home, you don't come into my office because I'm busy."

"But sometimes I come in and you stop for a little while." Her smile melted him.

"For the next few days, Providence and I are going to be working here in my office."

Her eyes lit up. "I can give my artwork to her, today!"

"We have a big project and I'm going to need you to wait for us to finish working."

"Sammy and I can spend some time in my apartment," Miranda said. "She loves playing downstairs with me, right, Sammy?"

"Okay."

Despite not getting a break, Dakota wasn't going to lay down the hammer with Sammy. He would wait to see how the afternoon played out, first. "Who wants scrambled eggs?"

"Me!" She finished her juice.

Dakota made enough eggs for all of them, ate breakfast at the table like it was a normal Monday, kissed his daughter goodbye, and left.

But there was nothing normal about this Monday, at all.

Slogging his way through rush-hour traffic toward DC, he called Providence.

"I saw the news," she said. "I hate that we're playing defense."

He loved that she said 'we'. After he brought her up to speed, he told her about Sammy. "I adore my child, but I'm concerned that she'll want to spend time—"

"Don't sweat it. One day at a time."

"I am not getting a damn break," he growled.

"You haven't been arrested. The police haven't returned to question us. That's a good sign. Maybe the evidence is taking them in a different direction. If your sweet daughter wants a few minutes of my attention, I'll give it to her. If we have to work after she goes to sleep, we'll do that."

"You're rock steady."

"That's me."

"And drop-dead gorgeous."

"Okay, cowboy, enough of the sweet talk. I've gotta go."

"Meet me at Sin's office in Georgetown."

"Will do. Good luck."

"You, too."

After parking in Sin's private lot, he went upstairs to Develin & Associates. Sin was on the phone, and waved him in. Dakota shut the door behind him and sat on the arm of the sofa.

"If you'd contacted him directly, he would have given the exclusive to you," Sin said. "You aired the story and ran the photos." As he listened, he slid his gaze to Dakota and a devilish grin filled his face. "When you find yourself in a position where you need me to fix some scandal for you, don't call me." He grew silent, then added, "Get yourself out of your own fucking mess. You have a good day now." Sin hung up. "What a douche bag."

"I'll assume that was the news director who chose to run the story about me."

"Sure was, and he's going to regret it."

"Where's Evangeline?"

"In her office. She's working on questions for Alexandra. We'll strategize the best way to answer them."

In general, Dakota despised the press and kept them at arm's distance. "Is that how it's done?"

"That's how I do it," Sin said. "I trust Alexandra will stick to the plan."

"When I talked to her this morning, I admitted to the graffiti," Dakota said. "I told her I assumed it was from a disgruntled woman."

"Smart move," Sin said.

Knock-knock.

Evangeline poked her head into the room. "Safe to enter?"

The men smiled. "The only one I'm going to kill is the person responsible for this," Dakota said.

"I'll pretend I didn't hear that." Evangeline sat at the conference table and both men joined her.

She ran through the list of questions and they strategized Dakota's answers. Then, Sin got his dad on the phone and they ran through the list of questions, along with Dakota's prepared answers.

"Great job, guys," Warren said. "I'm not thrilled you're discussing Mr. Hastings, but the answers are sound. Keep in mind, the detective in charge of the case will be watching."

"Thanks for the feedback," Dakota said.

"Talk later, Dad," Sin said and hung up.

As soon as Alexandra and her cameraman arrived, the receptionist set her up in the conference room.

"Let's give the public a story they'll find entertaining and forgettable," Sin said. "You ready to play nice?"

Dakota narrowed his eyes at his twin. "Fuck, no."

"Dakota," Sin warned.

"I'm gonna do it, but you know I'm furious."

"Smile through that anger, brother. And remember, the person who sent the letter will be watching, so you've gotta play this one real laid back."

Dakota, Sin, and Evangeline entered the conference room. After hellos and small talk, Alexandra ran through the approved list of questions. "Any wiggle room to add additional questions?"

"None," Dakota replied.

"I didn't think so."

The cameraman started recording.

"I'm here with Dakota Luck, CEO of Goode-Luck Real Estate," Alexandra began. "Dakota, let's jump in with the question on everyone's mind. Did you murder Matt Hastings?"

"No, I didn't. Matt brought a lot of energy and professionalism to his job. He was a strong realtor and we loved having him as part of the Goode-Luck family. Unfortunately, my partner and I had to let him go for cause. Because the murder investigation of Mr. Hastings is ongoing, I'm not at liberty to discuss the details. He took a swing at me at the awards banquet because he was angry. Hell, I get that. He was pissed he got fired, but the situation would have all blown over by morning if someone hadn't killed him."

Alexandra asked a few more Matt-related questions, and Dakota answered them as he'd been coached. He defended his innocence without bringing Providence's name into the interview.

Then, Alexandra moved on to ask him about the letter and photos.

"What's ALPHA?"

That's when Dakota chuffed out a laugh. "While I don't kiss and tell, I might have pissed someone off, and she opted to tell me what she *really* thought of me. I'm an Alpha male. But I've gotta say...I'm surprised she didn't paint the word 'jerk' or 'a-hole' on my truck." Leaning back and crossing his ankle over his thigh, he offered another relaxed smile. "Alpha is kinda flattering, don't you think?"

Alexandra pressed on. "The letter our news station received said—and I quote—'Dakota Luck is doing a helluva lot more than running a real estate company. It's time the public knew the real story'. What is that story?"

"I'm the CEO and broker of a well-known real estate company

with offices in Northern Virginia, suburban Maryland, and DC. That's not newsworthy. What the public doesn't know is that I'm also involved with Maverick and Carly Hott's foundation. Helping Others To Thrive. The organization helps veterans get back on their feet, and Goode-Luck Real Estate has purchased and donated several homes for area veterans. I'm just a regular guy trying to make a positive difference." He paused to smile. Out of the corner of his eye, his brother nodded in approval. "I appreciate the free publicity the letter and photos have afforded me, but I'm not sure what all the fuss is about."

She held up the picture of the four men in tactical gear. "When was this taken and who are you with?"

Dakota shrugged a shoulder. "No idea who's in that photo, but it ain't me. That looks like stock photography. There are hundreds online just like it."

Alexandra asked a few more open-ended questions and Dakota answered them as planned.

"I'll give you the last word," she said.

"I'm confident the person or persons responsible for Matt Hastings's death will be found."

Alexandra closed out the interview and turned to her cameraman, who gave her the thumbs-up.

"So, Dakota, off the record, what's really going on?" Alexandra asked.

He looked her in the eyes and said, "Damned if I know."

After Evangeline walked Alexandra and her cameraman out, Dakota dragged his hands through his hair. "What a fucking shit storm."

"You were relaxed and believable," Sin said.

"If the guy blackmailing me shows his face, I'll rip his heart out."

"I pity him. He has no idea what you're capable of."

"No," Dakota replied. "He sure as hell doesn't."

17

THE PARTNERSHIP

As they headed toward reception, Sin asked Dakota, "How are things with Providence?"

"I keep telling myself to slow down, but I can't. That this is just work, but I can't stop myself from wanting her. And it's not just about the sex. She met Sammy."

Sin glanced over. "That's big. How'd it go?"

"Well," Dakota replied.

They entered reception and heat infused his chest. Providence stood there talking to Evangeline, looking ultra-hot in a form-fitting jacket and skin-tight jeans.

She slid her gaze to his and a sly smile curved the corners of her mouth. His body hummed with energy, the desire to kiss her took hold. They were locked in a smoldering gaze neither could break.

Dakota stopped inches away. "Miss Rhode Island."

Sin and Evangeline laughed.

That elicited a bigger smile from Providence. "Dakota."

"Good to meet you in person," Sin said to Providence.

"Same," Providence replied.

"I see you've met my better half," Sin said.

"Sure have." Providence turned to Evangeline. "Our conversation was very...um...enlightening." The two women exchanged smiles.

"We should have lunch," Evangeline said to Providence. "Give me your number and we'll figure something out."

After Providence rattled it off, Dakota said, "The press will hound you."

"Good point," Evangeline said. "We'll have you guys over for dinner."

Providence flicked her gaze to Dakota. The energy that passed between them was charged with passion and he ran his hand down her back. He didn't want to touch her, he *needed* to. And the spike of electricity that passed between them ignited his pent-up passion.

"We should get to work," Providence said. "Good meeting you both."

Dakota thanked his brother and sister-in-law before he and Providence entered the waiting elevator. The instant the doors closed, he snaked his arm around her waist, pulled her close, and kissed her. No permission asked. None granted. He couldn't hold back and he sure as hell wasn't going to behave. Not when she was standing inches away and looking so damn hot.

He didn't deepen the kiss, just let his lips linger longer than they should have.

"Dakota," she murmured as the doors slid open at the lobby.

Rather than exit, he tapped the button to Sin's floor. The doors slid closed, and he pulled her flush against him and kissed the hell out of her. Her throaty groans turned him hard. They were full-on making out like two libido-fueled teenagers when the doors split apart.

Providence nudged him away.

"You didn't get very far," Sin said with an amused grin.

When the doors closed again, Providence said, "We have *got* to stop."

"I'm done fighting this."

"It's unprofessional."

"Fuck that. I think about you all the damn time. I want to kiss you and bury myself inside you. I want to touch you, to learn everything there is to know about you. It's consuming the hell out of me."

The doors opened but he didn't move. She stepped off, turned toward him. "We can't have this conversation now."

He didn't like that she was pushing him away. "I'm putting myself out there, Providence."

Several people were trying to step into the elevator, but they couldn't get around Dakota, so she took him by the arm and led him out of the building. "Let's talk at your house."

Thirty minutes later, he pulled into his garage while Providence parked on the street out front. The house was quiet.

"When is Sammy at daycare?" she asked as they made their way into his office.

"Mondays and Thursdays." He pushed the button on the bookcase and the wall slid open, revealing his safe. After punching in the code, he placed his weapons inside.

"That's a great hiding place." She pulled the Glock from the back of her waistband and stored it in there.

"Where's your second piece?"

"At home. The ankle strap broke and I need to get another one." Then, she surveyed his office. "Someone made some changes."

He'd added a second desk and set it up so they were facing each other. "I had Sammy hauling furniture in between tea parties and LEGO."

She laughed as she set down her computer bag. "You did not."

"I want you to feel at home."

She appreciated how he'd gone out of his way for her. "Thanks for doing this."

He held her gaze, sending electricity racing through her.

"Coffee?" he asked.

"Sure."

Once in the kitchen, she sat on a barstool while he poured their drinks. "I got you almond milk." He set their mugs on the island, then pulled the carton from the fridge.

Her expression softened. "Thank you." He sat beside her.

"Evangeline said the interview went well," she said. "I'm sorry I missed it."

"I denied everything. Not sure how long this will hold the son of a bitch off. He's determined to take me down." He placed his hand on her shoulder because he had to touch her, and damn, if she didn't feel fantastic. "What's going on with your mom?"

"A few weeks ago, she started feeling dizzy and nauseous. It's so bad now, she can't work and just lays on the couch. Yesterday, she was vomiting."

"What did the doc say?"

"Her blood pressure is low, her heart rate is down, too. He's not sure what's wrong, so he drew blood and is running a bunch of tests."

"Has she had this problem before?"

She shook her head. "She's super active and healthy. She works full-time and power walks with my dad. They play tennis and ride bikes. The only thing that's changed is my brother and his wife moved back into the area. They're strapped for cash and moved in. At first, I thought it was the stress of long-term guests, but I don't know." Providence paused. "I wish I could help her."

He held her hand, stroked her skin. His tender touch was slaying her. She could stare into his bedroom eyes all day long. How in the hell were they going to get any work done?

"I'm sorry to hear that," he said. "If you want a second opinion, I've got a great doctor."

"Thanks for the offer. Let's see what the test results show." Though she didn't want to sever their connection, she tugged her hand away and pushed off the stool. "We should get to work. There are a lot of moving parts to this case."

"Not until we talk about us."

"There is no 'us', Dakota."

"Like hell there isn't. I'm being honest with myself, Providence. It's time you were, too."

Providence bit down on her lower lip. She did *not* want to have this conversation. Despite the fact that she knew how she felt, she didn't want to share it with Dakota. Feelings got in the way of her doing her job and, considering the lack of progress they were making, she didn't feel especially confident in her abilities there, either.

"I spent time yesterday getting more comfortable using ALPHA's systems," she said. "I reviewed our notes and added next steps."

He lifted her hand, kissed her finger. "Stop. Avoiding. This."

She stilled. The longer she stared into his eyes, the more alive she felt. Yet, she was terrified to discuss her feelings. "I like working with you. You're okay to hang with. The sex works, too. There, are we good now?"

He dropped a soft peck on her lips and she fought the desire to throw her arms around him and kiss him for hours. "I see how you look at me. How you love kissing me. If I were to carry you to my bed and love you, you wouldn't say no."

"You're wrong. I would say no." She walked around the granite island, the distance helping her focus. "I'm afraid of putting myself out there and getting hurt. I worry because you have a child and I don't want this to end badly. She's an innocent bystander in all of this."

"Do you trust me?"

She stared at him for a long moment. "I trust what I know, but I know so little."

"Fair enough. Trust that I will answer any question honestly, despite the fact that I was *your* target and you were hunting me down."

"Are you a vigilante?"

The warmth in his eyes drained, and he said nothing. She let the silence linger, but he stayed quiet. Though she now knew the truth, she pushed on.

"You want me to explore a relationship with you," she said. "If that's the case, I want to know everything about you. What side of the bed do you sleep on? What's your favorite meal? Why did you become a realtor? What happened to your first wife? I've got a million questions that will be answered in time. What I do know is that you love Sammy unconditionally. You're protective and loving and patient with her." She walked over to him and stood close. "But I don't know what you're capable of. Are you the man who's been tracking down these violent criminals and killing them? Are you a vigilante?"

This time, she waited out his silence.

"I am," he replied.

His answer didn't scare her. Now, she knew who she was dealing with. "How many?"

"Seven."

"Do you work alone?"

"No."

"How do you find them?"

"Someone at ALPHA feeds me the info."

Whoa. I wasn't expecting that.

"The difference between an ALPHA operative and my team is that we don't bring them in alive. When they meet me, they're out of options."

"Do you like killing?"

"No. But I like stopping them from preying on the innocent. I like taking out the guy who's spent decades stalking women, torturing and raping them before he kills them. When I found the man who'd been slaughtering homosexuals, I liked ending his killing spree."

She didn't condone what he was doing, but she admired him that much more because of his conviction. "You're not afraid of getting caught?"

His confident smile sent heat blasting through her. "No."

"Thank you for answering my questions."

"Have your feelings changed now that you know the truth?"

She slipped her hand in his and started walking toward his office. "I'm not sure there's anything you could tell me that would change the way I feel about you. And that terrifies me most of all."

He pulled her close and held her in his arms like he owned her… body, mind, and soul. Because he did. His kiss was filled with tenderness. "I'm crazy about you, Providence Reynolds."

Her heart fluttered wildly. "I like you, so damn much," she murmured, hardly believing she'd been bold enough to utter those words. "All right, cowboy, time to work."

After entering his office, she pulled her laptop from her bag, sat at her desk and ran through her checklist, while Dakota pulled out his laptop from the safe. "Let's start with the convention center's surveillance cameras the night Matt was killed." And then, she sighed. "I have a confession."

"Are you wearing a wire?"

"God, no." Then, she offered him a playful smile. "Wanna frisk me?"

"Hell, yeah." He started to get up.

"Sit. We have to work. Do you want my confession or not?"

"Go ahead."

"As a special agent, I had worked with Warren Hott when he was DC's chief prosecutor. I asked him not to mention that the night he came to the club."

Dakota paused. "No more secrets."

"Thank you for being succinct, and I agree. No more secrets." She logged in to ALPHAnet. "I reviewed some more of your cases while you were an operative. You had to have pissed someone off while you were there."

"I pissed everyone off."

She rolled her chair beside his. "Someone's angry enough to extort you and we're going to find him."

The hours flew by while they discussed case after case. She loved working with him. Dakota was brilliant and hardworking, but with each case they reviewed, he grew more and more frustrated.

Tap-Tap-Tap.

Providence wasn't sure what she'd heard, the sound was so quiet.

"Come in," he barked.

The door opened and Sammy peeked inside. When she locked eyes with Providence, hers lit up. "Daddy, Mrs. Morris wanted me to tell you she's starting dinner." She grinned at Providence. "And she said that there's plenty to share for Provi."

Providence returned the child's smile. She was being so respectful and she was so happy to see her daddy.

Dakota's expression softened. The knot between his brows vanished and his smile was filled with love. "Hi, sweetheart." He pushed out of the chair, walked around the desk, and lifted her into his arms.

"Daddy, can Provi stay?"

"Why don't you ask her?"

"Provi, can you have chicken with us?"

Providence didn't want to impose, yet, as she stared from the child to her dad, she didn't want to leave. Going home to an empty condo would only magnify her deep-seated loneliness. She rose. "I would love to. I'll wash up and see if I can help Mrs. Morris." She turned to Dakota. "Thanks for your efforts today."

"We made zero progress." She couldn't miss the annoyance in his voice.

"Not true. Narrowing the scope of possibilities is progress."

"Daddy, put me down."

Dakota set her on the ground and she scampered over to Providence. "I made you a picture."

"You did? I would love to see it."

Together, they headed into the kitchen, leaving Dakota in his office. Sammy pulled the artwork off the island and handed it to her. "It's from our movie night! That's me and you and Daddy."

Providence admired the picture. "It's so beautiful. You are very good at coloring. Thank you so much, Sammy. Can I hug you?"

"Uh-huh."

Providence knelt down and gathered her in. When Sammy wrapped her delicate arms around her, her heart squeezed. When the hug ended, she asked Miranda if she could help with dinner.

"I'm all set," Miranda replied. "I've got my system."

"Are you sure?"

"Positive."

Providence turned to Sammy. "I hear you have some very special dolls."

She beamed. "Uh-huh."

"I would love to meet them."

The child gasped. "Really?"

Sammy led the way into the family room and plunked down beside her toy box. Providence joined her. One by one, the child introduced her to her dolls. The joy on Sammy's face, and the tender way she cared for each of them, touched Providence.

Sammy scooted a little closer and held out a doll. "This is Miss Lady. She's my favorite."

After taking her, Providence admired her. "She's beautiful. I love her outfit."

As Sammy prattled on, Providence reminded herself that she and Dakota weren't a couple. They'd been thrust together in a time-sensitive work situation and had hooked up a few times. Still, she couldn't stop herself from getting drawn in. Samantha Luck was capturing her heart...same as her dad was doing.

Her phone buzzed with a text. "Sammy, I have to check my phone."

"Okay." Sammy got busy playing tea party.

The text was from her brother. "It's Randy. Gordon gave me your number. Lizzie and I are eating out. Wanted to talk to you about mom. Can you join us?"

"Can't tonight. How's she doing?"

"Same," he replied. "Can we swing by on the way to the restaurant?"

"I'm not home," she texted.

"What's your ETA?"

"Couple of hours."

"We'll talk another time," he replied.

Providence returned to playing with Sammy. At some point, she glanced up. Dakota was watching. How could she not feel something for this man and his child? Were they the missing pieces that could fill her life with joy?

"Hey, you two," Dakota said.

"Daddy, can you play with us?"

"It's time for dinner."

"But...but Provi said she'd have a tea party with Miss Lady."

"Samantha—"

Sammy popped up and stomped her foot. "I want to keep playing."

Dakota shifted his attention to Providence and arched an eyebrow. "Well, Providence told me she was starving. What should we do about that?"

Sammy spun toward Providence. "You can wait to eat, right?"

"Well, Sammy, what about all the wonderful food Mrs. Morris has made? Wouldn't it be better to have dinner now, then have a dessert party after?"

"What's that?"

Providence rose. "They're just like tea parties only we pretend to eat all our favorite desserts."

"Okay." And just like that, Sammy took Providence's hand and they headed toward the kitchen.

As she passed Dakota, he ran his hand over her backside, then fell in line beside her. She glanced over and scowled at him, then shook her finger at him. "You, behave."

"Never."

Providence had no idea what she was getting into with these two, but she was following her sister's advice and taking a chance.

After dinner, she and Sammy had a dessert party with Miss Lady. It took a little convincing, but Sammy put the cartons of cookies away so they could *pretend* to eat all kinds of delicious treats. Providence hadn't used her imagination in a long time, and she found herself laughing along with the child.

"Let's mix the cookies into the ice cream," Providence said and Sammy giggled.

She took joy in the simple game they were playing together. Once they'd eaten all the imaginary sugar they could consume, Providence told the child she had to go home.

"Can you come back and play with me tomorrow?"

"Maybe. Your daddy and I haven't looked at our work schedules yet."

They found Dakota in his office on his computer, his brows knitted together as he peered at the screen. "Maybe your dad will have a dessert party with us next time."

"Daddy, will you?"

He blinked, then refocused on them. "You two sounded like you were having a good time."

"Uh-huh," Sammy said. "Provi is soooo much fun."

"All right, I've got to get going," Providence said. "What's the plan tomorrow?"

"We'll work here. Come over as early as seven." He pushed out of his chair. "Sammy, let's walk Providence out."

Dakota's jaw muscles were flexing so hard, Providence asked him if he was okay.

"I just spent the last hour reviewing more of my cases. Most I'd forgotten about, but not a single one stands out. We've hit another dead end."

She laid a calming hand on his shoulder. "We have plenty of other clues to chase down. I'm leaving my laptop, and I'll be back in the morning."

Providence slung her handbag over her shoulder and collected her very special artwork. "This goes on my refrigerator."

Dakota lifted Sammy into his arms and they walked her to her car. "Text me when you get home."

She drove off, feeling like she was leaving her heart behind.

Back at her condo, she flipped on lights as she made her way to her bedroom. Light spilled from the door crack of her walk-in closet. *I never leave that light on.* Her heart rate shot into the triple digits. She went to grab her Glock, but she'd left it in Dakota's safe. *Dammit.*

She bolted to her night table drawer, where she had stored her second weapon. It was gone.

Oh, God, no.

Shoving down her fear, she grabbed a kitchen knife and rushed back to her bedroom where she flung open the closet door. She was alone.

With adrenaline surging through her, she checked under her bed, in her shower, the guest room, the coat closet, and the pantry. After clearing her home, she stopped to catch her breath. Then, she checked her front door, but couldn't tell if the lock had been tampered with.

Her television hadn't been moved, her personal laptop lay untouched on the kitchen counter. Starting there, she checked every cupboard to see if the intruder had taken anything.

Nothing. He'd taken nothing. Even her spare house key was still in the kitchen junk drawer.

When she returned to her bedroom, the center drawer to her desk was ajar. Inside, her checkbook had been placed on the other side of the drawer. But no checks had been taken.

There's no way I can stay here tonight. Randy and Lizzie were in the guest room of her parents' house, and Megan and Leigh were tight on space. Crashing on their sofas wouldn't work. She fished out her phone and called Dakota.

"Make it home okay?"

"Someone broke into my place."

"I'll be there as soon as I can. What's your address?"

She gave it to him and hung up. She didn't even need to ask him for help. Relief washed over her. She pulled out an overnight bag and threw in some clothing.

Her doorbell chimed and she froze. "Hey, Providence, you there?"

It was her ex. She confirmed through the peephole before opening the front door. "What are you doing here?"

"I'd mentioned wanting to talk to you. Is now a good time?"

"No, it's not. Why didn't you text me first?"

"I was driving by. It's almost ten, and I figured you'd be here. I won't stay long."

She wanted to close this chapter of her life, for good.

"Five minutes." She stepped aside and he entered. He was wearing a white button-down shirt, loosened tie, and navy pants. Looked like he'd come from work.

"Can we sit?"

"No. Just say what you have to."

He shoved his hand in his pocket and shuffled. A few more seconds passed. "I'm sorry. I ruined our marriage with my drinking and cheating. I regret that I wasn't there for you, for us. I'm sorry I turned to someone else when the only person I've ever wanted has been you."

She'd give him props for an actual apology. "Thanks. I appreciate your saying that. It was a terrible time, for both of us."

He studied her. "Are you okay?"

No, I'm not. "Yeah, sure, why?"

"You look pale and totally stressed." He headed toward the kitchen. What had once been *their* kitchen. She followed. He poured her a glass of water and she drank it down.

"Are you over-worked?"

"Thanks for the apology. Now, you can cross me off your list and move on."

"Providence, I don't appreciate that."

Ah, crap, here comes the lecture. If there was anything Jimbo Reynolds loved, it was the sound of his own voice. She pitied his students. All she picked up from his nonstop babble was, "Let's try again."

"Whoa, what did you say?"

"Let's try again," he repeated.

"Try what again?"

"Us. A family. I can move back in—"

"Jimbo, I'm not a do-over. Our marriage ended a long time ago. You moved on, then I moved on. It's over. Look, I accepted your apology—" She returned to her small foyer, but when she glanced back, he hadn't followed her. "You need to leave."

He meandered toward her. "C'mon, let's have a conversation, a real conversation. That's all I'm asking."

The hair on the back of her neck prickled. "Did you come by earlier tonight?"

"What? No."

"You sure about that?"

"Yeah, I was teaching a night class."

Knock-knock. "Providence, it's me."

She flung open the door and the tension running down her back fell away the second Dakota pulled her into his arms. "You okay?"

"Yeah."

"Who the hell is this?" Jimbo asked.

Providence broke away. "Jim Reynolds, Dakota Luck."

Dakota's eyes narrowed and his jaw muscles started ticking in his cheeks. The two men nodded to each other. Neither man smiled.

"How do I know that name?" Jimbo asked.

Ignoring him, Dakota stepped into her home, his gaze cemented on Providence. "Tell me what happened."

"What do you mean, what happened?" Jimbo asked.

"It doesn't concern you," Dakota replied.

Jimbo's eyes grew large. "I know who you are. You're that guy suspected of killing his employee." He regarded Providence. "You can't be hanging out with a murderer."

"Goodbye, Jimbo," Providence said. "You said what you needed to say."

"But...but, we had a marriage. I think we should at least—"

"I accepted your apology," she said. "Please leave, and don't come back."

On a huff, Jimbo pushed past Dakota, shoving him in the shoulder.

Providence shut and locked the door. And then, she threw her arms around Dakota. "Thank you for getting here so fast. Does Miranda have Sammy?"

He kissed her forehead. "Yes, she does." He clasped her by the hand and brought her into the living room. "Tell me what happened."

All Dakota cared about was Providence's safety. When she finished explaining, Dakota asked her to walk him through her place.

"And you're sure you put your spare Glock in here?" He peered inside her night table drawer.

"Of course." Her shoulders drooped. "I'm sick to my stomach over this. You've got so much going on right now, you don't need this hassle."

He placed his hands on her shoulders. "I'm glad you called me. Did you and your ex live here?"

"Yes. How did you know he was my ex?"

"I read your profile."

"So, you know…everything."

"I do, and I'm sorry." He held her in his arms and caressed her back. Her heart was pounding so hard, he could feel it beating against his chest.

Her sad smile tore at him. "Thank you."

"You want to talk about your daughter?"

"Maybe another time. Right now, I want to get the hell out of here."

"Let's circle back to Jim. When did he get here?"

"Right after I'd cleared the condo."

"Did you know he was stopping by?"

"No. I ran into him last week. He's going through a twelve-step program and wanted to make amends."

"I didn't see cameras in the hallway." He glanced around. "Do you have surveillance?"

"No."

"I'm gonna check your lock. Can I borrow your key?" He returned to her front door and slid the key into the lock. "It's been picked." Dakota glanced up and down her quiet hallway. "Do you know your neighbors?"

"A few of them, why?"

He pointed diagonally across her hall. "There's a doorbell cam. It's late, but maybe your neighbor will show us the video."

Providence knocked on the door. "Hello, Providence," said the white-haired man. "Everything okay?"

"Someone stopped by tonight and slid a card under my door, but it wasn't signed."

Her neighbor chuckled. "I didn't think young people did those types of things nowadays."

"Is your doorbell camera on?" she asked.

"Sure is." Her neighbor fetched his phone and checked, then showed Providence and Dakota.

Someone cloaked in a dark hoodie walked past. Fifteen minutes later, the same person walked by, heading toward the elevator.

"Can you forward those to me?" she asked.

He did, then said, "I hope you find your mystery admirer."

She and Dakota returned to her condo.

"Let's get you out of here," Dakota said.

"I'll stay in a hotel until I can figure out—"

Stepping close, he stroked her shoulders. She was okay and that's all that mattered. Still, he wanted to rip the perp's face off. "I have a guest room, not that I want you in there. I want you in my bed. But, I have a child and we need to be smart about this."

"I panicked and called you, but I don't want you to feel obligated—"

This time, he stopped her with a kiss. And she moaned into him, wrapping her arms around him and holding him so hard, he smiled. Her lips curved as she ended the kiss.

"I will tell you this as many times as you need to hear it. I want you to come home with me. I want you safe. I want you in my bed, but we have to take this slowly. Not for me. Maybe for you. Definitely for Sammy."

"Okay. Thank you."

He returned with her to her bedroom while she finished packing. "Bring your laptop and your checkbook. And your passport, if you have one." He spied a picture on her night table. It was of Providence and her adorable baby. In the picture,

Providence wasn't just smiling, she was radiant. Like before, his heart ached for her loss.

"This must be Annabel. She's beautiful."

A rueful smile touched her eyes. "Thank you." Without another word, she finished packing. He wanted to go to her, comfort her, but something kept his feet cemented in place. His gut told him that she needed space when it came to her daughter, and he wanted to respect that.

As soon as she finished packing, they left. Providence followed him back to his place and parked on the street in front of his house.

After pulling into his garage, he walked out to her. "You can park in the driveway in front of the other garage door."

"Doesn't Miranda park in the garage?"

He pointed to the car parked along the curb. "That's her car. I keep my sports car in the garage."

"That sounds fun."

"When I turned thirty-five, I bought myself a Porsche Spyder, but I rarely use it."

Once in his office, he opened his safe and handed her a house key. "This is for the front door and the door from the garage, but we only lock that door at night."

"Got it."

He led her upstairs. "Sammy's bedroom," he said as he passed an open door. "Mine's at the end of the hallway."

He entered the guest room, flicked on the light, and set her bags on the bed. "You've got your own bathroom. It's fully stocked with towels and soap." He didn't want to linger, didn't want her to feel uncomfortable that he was standing in her bedroom. But damn, he could not leave.

"Thanks, this is great." She sidled close. "Between the break-in and Jimbo's pop-in, I'm not sure I'll be able to fall asleep right away."

He knew exactly how to help, but rather than go there, he said, "How 'bout a nightcap?"

"Will I be drinking alone?"

"Never." Clasping her hand confirmed she was safe, but touching her turned the heat way, way up. "Let's sit outside."

They took their cognacs onto his screened porch. She got comfortable on the sofa. After easing down beside her, he tapped the remote. The gas fireplace roared to life. They sat in silence, admiring the flickering flames in the hearth, while sipping the liquor.

"What should we tell Sammy?" she asked. "The truth will scare her, so we'll have to make up something."

"She'll be so happy you're here, she won't ask why. If she does, we can tell her you're getting new wood floors and there's a lot of dust."

Being around Providence wasn't just easy. It was necessary. He laid his hand on her thigh. To his surprise, she threaded her fingers over his.

He shifted his gaze from the roaring fire to her. He could stare at her for hours. Not just because she was beautiful, but because this...whatever the hell this was...felt real...and natural...and so damn right.

"I don't know what to make of the break-in," she said, her gaze still cemented on the fire. "He leaves my electronics and takes my Glock. You'd think he'd already have a gun."

"The whole thing concerns me. The guy on the video could've been anyone."

"I'm not gonna lie. I was scared pretty good. I thought he was in my closet."

"I take it you checked."

"Damn straight."

"You should have gotten the hell out of there, but badasses don't run. You, Providence Reynolds, are a badass."

Her lips curved as he kissed her. He had to feel her soft lips on his. Had to taste her, so he pressed onward and she welcomed him. Their kisses were soft, yet the energy she brought was powerful. She broke away, took his drink, and set both glasses on the table.

Then, she straddled him and kissed the hell out of him. And he couldn't hold her tighter or kiss her long enough. One kiss rolled into so many they found themselves grinding on each other.

And then, she laughed. "This is insane," she said as she sucked down a breath.

"No, this is two people who are highly charged around each other."

"Like a battery?"

"Like I need you in my bed or I'd be happy to do a sleepover in yours. Lady's choice. Or you can say no. You can always say no."

"I have no willpower around you. I almost didn't call you for this exact reason." She moved off him and sat beside him again.

"Don't ever hesitate to call me when you're in trouble. Ever."

"Thank you." She handed him his drink and sipped hers. "Tell me something to help me understand you better."

After several seconds, he broke the silence. "My wife was taken when Sammy was six months old."

"Oh, my God." She stared into his eyes. "I'm so sorry."

"I was a primary suspect back then, too. Until I received a blackmail letter. Then, the focus of the investigation shifted."

She furrowed her brow.

"They wanted half a mil. I wired two hundred thousand in a show of good faith."

"And?"

After tossing back the alcohol, he pushed off the sofa and leaned against the porch railing. He hated talking about how he'd failed his wife. How the guilt of her abduction haunted him. "The kidnapper sent me a GPS location. It led us to her car, abandoned in a remote area of Virginia. Her blood was found in the interior. I never saw her again."

"I'm so sorry."

She set the glass on the table and rubbed her neck. "Who told you to give them that amount?"

"I did it on my own. The detective, along with Luther, advised me *not* to give in to their demand until we knew who we were dealing with."

"What does Sammy know?"

"Since Beth's body was never found, she was presumed dead. When Sammy started asking about her mom, I told her that she had died."

Providence pushed off the sofa. "Do you have the blackmail letter?"

"The detective took it as evidence, but I have a photo." He scrolled through his phone until he found it. He hadn't seen the handwritten letter in years.

IF YOU WANT TO SEE YOUR WIFE AGAIN, DEPOSIT $500,000 TO BANK TAHITI, ACCOUNT 84739083. NO MONEY, NO WIFE. YOU HAVE ONE WEEK.

"I know this must be difficult for you," she said, stroking his back. "Thanks for showing me that."

It pained him to discuss this. He couldn't bring Beth back and, as he stared into Providence's eyes, guilt grew in his heart. For the past three and a half years, he'd kept women at a comfortable distance. The longer he knew Providence, the closer he wanted her to be. And he wasn't sure how to reconcile his newfound feelings.

For now, all of that could wait. Over the next few hours, he had something in mind that didn't require any reconciling at all.

18

THE AWAKENING

Providence was grateful Dakota had offered her refuge, but her thank you extended beyond what was deemed appropriate guest behavior. She wanted to screw his brains out, for starters.

"I should go to sleep," she murmured, fighting against the mounting need thrumming through her.

He cupped her chin, dipped down, and kissed her. "Your bed or mine?"

"Someone has to do the right thing."

"We will, and we'll do it together."

"That's not why I'm here."

"But you are here and we can't control how we feel."

"*We?*"

"We're crazy attracted to each other. We have commitment phobia. We haven't loved in a long time. And we're the kind of people who take one day at a time." He dropped one more soft kiss on her lips before murmuring, "I'm leading with my heart on this one."

She glanced at his crotch. "I think you're leading with your teeny tiny man balls."

He laughed. "My compass is pointing due north toward Miss Rhode Island."

That made her laugh, then the smile fell away. "I don't want Sammy finding out."

"We'll make sure you're in the guest room before she wakes up."

"You want me to *sleep* in your bed?"

"I'm not having sex with you, then tossing you out. I want to hold you and keep you safe all night long."

She melted from how much he wanted to protect her. His sensual kiss was a tease for all the other ones she would receive as soon as she crawled into his bed.

He locked up and activated the house alarm. As they climbed the stairs, he took her hand. At the top, he kissed it. "I'm glad you're here."

"So am I. I'll be in shortly." She brushed her teeth, dressed in a tank top and panties, then threw a sweatshirt over them.

The hallway was dark, save for a night light. *My vigilante boyfriend uses night lights.*

No, he's not my boyfriend.

When she entered his bedroom, he was propped up in bed waiting for her. And her heart took off in her chest. He was shirtless. And his chest—his rock-hard chest with those amazing broad shoulders and sinewy arms—stole her attention. But the heated look in his eyes lured her in.

"Hello, beautiful." His sexy voice thundered through her.

She closed and locked his bedroom door, then removed the sweatshirt. His gaze strayed from hers as he checked her out, the intensity in those piercing blue eyes stripping her bare.

"Are we making a mistake?" she whispered as she slipped in beside him.

Wrapping himself around her like an oversized blanket, he kissed her. "Does this feel like a mistake?" He kissed her again.

"No," she whispered. "This feels right."

"Then embrace it."

She ran her fingers through his soft hair while he caressed her back. He slid his hand inside her tank and teased her nipple with his thumb. Soft, gentle strokes that had her undulating against him. Her eyes fluttered closed as the pleasure pounded a direct line to the small, heated space between her legs.

And then, he removed her tank and slid off her panties. Naked, they pressed closer. Skin against skin, her nerve endings were on fire. Every muscle she stroked felt like steel beneath her fingers. The harder she clung to him, the more she desperately wanted him inside her.

When his mouth found her nipple, she shuddered in a breath. He licked and teased, nibbled and tugged. She loved everything he gave her and she begged him for more.

Their whispers floated through the silence and their quiet moans riled her. She nudged him away and began stroking his shaft. His wetness trickled onto her fingers and she couldn't wait to taste his sweet, sweet juices. Kissing her way down his body, she took his long, hardened shaft into her mouth. Wetness flooded her core and she sucked down a harsh breath.

"Jesus, Providence, you feel so fucking good."

His voice was raspy, his cock hard like steel. She rolled her tongue over the smooth head before taking him into her mouth again. She was on fire, her desire to pleasure him had her writhing in place. She needed him inside her, so she slowed her sucking and licking, then pulled off.

After dropping a trail of kisses up his torso, she found his mouth once again. And she kissed him hard and fast.

Their collective groans pierced the silent night.

"I love how good you suck me." His hooded eyes were sky blue, his cheeks pink.

"I'm dying for you," she said. "Where's the condom?"

"I want to make you come with my mouth first."

"Not tonight."

"This relationship is too one-sided for me."

"It's okay, really. Now, where's that condom?"

He pulled it from under his pillow, covered himself, and pulled her onto him. "How do you want me to love you?"

She froze.

He slayed her with a playful smile. "Too much?"

"You're an idiot."

"I'm confident you won't feel like that in about fifteen minutes."

She pressed her index finger to his lips. "You need to stop talking."

"Then, shut me up."

Their mouths met in a scorching kiss, tongues clashing, bodies writhing in an intoxicating rhythm. Gasping for air, Providence sunk down on his massive cock. His low, guttural groan ripped through her while he dragged his hands down her bare back.

"Fuck, you feel so good," he murmured. "I can never get enough of you."

Scratching and clawing his biceps, she repositioned so he could fill her completely. And she started moving. Then, she sat up and glided on his shaft. Though she made no sound, their heavy breathing reverberated through the quiet of the night.

"You are too beautiful. And so fucking sexy." He caressed her breasts and slid a hand under her ass. "If I don't slow us down, it's going to be over before I've had my fill of you."

In one fluid move, he pinned her beneath him and stilled. "My God, what am I going to do with you?"

"I can think of several naughty things."

His kiss was passionate and powerful, his embrace strong, yet loving. He moved over her slowly, as if they had nothing but time. Gentle touches and soft caresses morphed into a frenzy of energy that had them gasping for air and grinding hard against the other.

Instead of climaxing, Dakota slowed down until he stopped moving altogether. "This isn't about me fucking you," he murmured. "This is about *both* of us finding pleasure in each other. We're not playing at The Dungeon. You're in my home, my bed. You're in my arms. And I need to understand how I can be the kind of lover who brings you sexual fulfillment."

She stared into his eyes, questioning whether she should tell him what she'd never told anyone. "If you'll let me bring you to orgasm, I'll tell you why I don't."

He dropped a kiss on her lips. "I don't need to come. I need to understand you. That would bring me pleasure."

She bucked her hips and he smiled. "Let's finish what we started, then we'll talk," she whispered.

The build was hypnotic, the feeling of him inside her, filling her to her limit, sent her higher and higher. Every touch, each caress had her body bowing to his.

Wrecked from the onslaught of his powerful thrusts, she felt the orgasm building inside her. The ecstasy taking her higher and higher.

"Relax and let it happen," he murmured. As he released inside her, he murmured her name like she was his entire world.

Even with his encouraging words, the mounting orgasm retreated, until it was gone.

Still rooted inside her, they snuggled close, neither wanting their intimacy to end. He kissed her again and again before he retreated into the bathroom, returning a moment later.

"I could get damn used to having you in my bed."

Snuggling close, she ran her fingertips down his chest and around his nipple. "This is temporary. It's a work thing."

"Hey. Hey. Look at me." She lifted off him. "Don't push me away." He leaned against his elbow, stroked her shoulder, let his fingers graze her nipple. "We have an agreement. Help me understand how I can be a better lover."

"It's not you, it's me."

"Do you like your clit stimulated?"

"I love that, but I still won't come."

"Have you ever climaxed?"

"Yes, but I stopped after Annabel died."

He grew silent for a beat. "I'm a good listener."

She sat up and pulled on her tank top. "When I got pregnant, Jimbo lost interest in me, sexually. After Annabel was born, we resumed sex. He seemed distant and I was having trouble climaxing. When I told him, he brushed it off as being a new mom. I was able to achieve orgasms on my own, so I knew it had to do with him, or his lack of interest."

He nodded.

She never spoke of Annabel's passing. It was too painful. But the compassion in his eyes spurred her onward.

"When Annabel died, I kind of did, too," she said. "Instead of turning toward each other, we grew apart. That's when I switched to undercover work. I loved becoming someone else because I didn't have to think about my own life. I can't totally blame Jimbo, because I was out of town for weeks at a time. Four months after she passed, Jimbo told me he'd moved on to someone else."

"I see."

"Even though the doctors told me Annabel's death wasn't my fault—that there was nothing I could have done to prevent what happened—I blamed myself. I stopped touching myself because I didn't think I deserved that much pleasure."

"Did you talk to anyone about this?"

"My mom is a psychologist. Her specialty is helping couples overcome sexual issues, so I spoke with her."

"That was smart."

"We concluded that my issue was on the subconscious level. I was punishing myself for Annabel's death and my failed marriage."

He traced her heart tattoo with his finger. "Is this for Annabel?"

"Yeah."

"Thank you for telling me." He ran gentle fingers through her hair, tucking some behind her ear. "I think we should stop focusing on your orgasm and start focusing on what makes you feel good. What makes you happy. I think if we did that, you might start to feel like you deserve a fulfilling life."

Tears filled her eyes. Surprised by the onslaught of emotion, she dropped her head so he couldn't see.

He lifted her face to his. "You deserve to be happy, Providence. I want to help you find that."

"I would have expected that from my husband, but you don't have to extend yourself. I appreciate that you're an attentive lover, but—"

"If you won't say yes, we can go back to being work partners." He kissed her. "But that would suck, for both of us. Because we like each other too damn much."

He was right. So right. "Can I sleep on it?"

He patted his chest. "Come on in."

She kissed him. "Thank you for being an amazing man. I've never met anyone like you. It's hard for me to wrap my brain around your *other* job. You are so caring and such an attentive dad, then you turn into a—" She stopped, searching for the right words.

"A cold-blooded killer?"

"Luther is right. You're a complicated man."

The alarm clock woke Dakota from a deep sleep. He and Providence were still wrapped around each other. Five thirty had come way too fast.

She slid out of bed and pulled on her clothes before he could kiss her good morning. "I'll see you for breakfast," she whispered.

Dakota sat on the edge of his bed, his boner pointing to the ceiling. "I hate to waste a perfectly good erection."

With a sleepy smile, she said, "I'm confident that won't be your last."

He wanted to pull her on top of him and love the hell out of her. She was just as beautiful in the morning as she was in the evening. Her hair was tussled, her voice deeper. It was as if he saw her for the first time without the protective armor she wore as a shield.

"I'll get downstairs around seven," he said. "We can all have breakfast together. Sammy will love that."

"Thank you for…for everything." She kissed him, then closed the door behind her.

Dakota wasn't ready to get up, so he reset his alarm and rolled over. As he drifted to sleep, he thought about what Providence had told him about herself. Though she had been through a lot, he felt confident she could find happiness. And he had the perfect little accomplice to help him achieve his goal.

At six forty, he got ready, then went downstairs. As expected, Sammy was eating breakfast with Miranda.

"Good morning." He kissed the top of Sammy's head. "Sleep okay?"

"Uh-huh." She ate a piece of French toast.

"We have a house guest," Dakota said after pouring himself coffee.

"What's that?" Sammy asked.

"A visitor who stays for sleepovers."

"Who?"

"Providence is staying with us for a little while."

Sammy gasped and her eyes grew large. She set down her fork and started to climb out of her booster seat.

"Whoa, there, Missy, where do you think you're going?" Dakota asked.

"To see her."

"Samantha, she's getting ready and we have to give her privacy."

"Good morning," Providence said as she entered the kitchen.

"Provi!" Sammy smiled at her.

"Wow, what a great greeting," Providence said. "Hi, Sammy. Morning, Miranda."

"Can I make you something?" Miranda asked.

"Oh, I'm fine."

Miranda smiled. "I'm making French toast. One slice or two?"

"Two would be great, thanks." After pouring herself coffee, she sat at the table.

Sammy climbed back into her booster seat and resumed eating her breakfast.

After Sammy talked about what she and Miranda were doing that morning, Dakota said, "Samantha, Providence and I will be working here today."

"I won't int-rupt you," Sammy said.

"Thank you, honey."

When Sammy finished, she played in the family room. With just the adults in the room, Dakota said, "Miranda, with everything going on, we need to be extra vigilant with Sammy's safety."

"I don't take tai chi for the hell of it, Dakota."

Providence laughed. "Girl power is strong in this house."

"I am so outnumbered," he replied.

After breakfast, Dakota and Providence retreated into his office and shut the door.

"I need to let Luther know someone broke into my place and stole my backup weapon." Providence dialed, put the call on speaker.

"Good morning, Providence," Luther said. "How are things going?"

"You're on speaker and Dakota is with me. Things are progressing slower than we'd like. Someone broke into my home last night and stole my secondary weapon."

"Are you okay?"

"Yes, I wasn't home."

"Did they take anything else?"

"Not that I could tell."

"Did you contact the police?"

"No."

"You're not safe at home. Where will you be staying?"

"At Dakota's."

"Good. If you two don't stay ahead of the police, Dakota will end up in jail. Maybe both of you."

"We're doing our best," Dakota replied. "It's hard to find someone who's doing one helluva job staying hidden."

"Dakota, I have something to discuss," Luther said. "Call me back." The line went dead and Providence headed for the door.

"Where are you going?"

"To make my bed so you can have your top-secret call." Her phone rang. "It's Stryker." She tapped the speaker button. "Hey," she answered. "Dakota's with me."

"A Detective Beeker stopped by the club last night with a warrant for rope," Stryker said.

"Dammit," Dakota bit out.

"I had to give him a bundle of black hemp," Stryker said. "Sorry, guys."

"Not your fault," Providence replied.

"Making any headway?" Stryker asked.

"No," Providence replied. "You?"

"Not yet," Stryker said. "I'll keep you posted." He hung up.

"I'm failing you," Providence said.

"Hey, don't go there. We're doing our best."

She painted on a smile. "Let me know when it's safe to come back in." She shut the door behind her.

Dakota called Luther.

"We've located the Midnight Raper," Luther said. "Local law enforcement has spoken to him, which means he's getting ready to run again. As much as I want you and your team to carry out this assignment, you need to stay focused on your own case."

"I can do it. Isn't he the one who's been arrested twice?"

"Three times," Luther replied.

"Refresh me."

"The assaults started over twenty years ago when he was a college student in Florida. He started helping coeds with their computer problems. He got to know them, then he targeted them, and assaulted them. Over the past two decades, he's lived in more than thirty college towns. We estimate he's assaulted over two hundred women. He rents a home and sets up his home-based computer repair business. It's legit and he makes a good profit. But the business is a front so he can meet college girls. He gets their home address and phone number. His M.O. is always the same. He strikes right around midnight. After the authorities question him, he takes off, only to reemerge in a different college town under a new alias. He's been arrested three times. Twice, he was released on bond and vanished. The third time, bond wasn't set, but he managed to escape. His DNA is linked to over seventy-five women. Law enforcement is close to making another arrest."

"I need to stop him before he vanishes."

"You sure you want to do this?"

"Positive."

"He's in Portland, near the University of Southern Maine. He's renting a house close to campus. He works alone, so you can bring a small crew for this job."

"Send me his file. We'll take care of it."

Dakota hung up, then went in search of his new partner. All he had to do was follow Sammy's giggles. He found her and Providence in the family room. Providence was showing Sammy a yoga pose. Sammy was mimicking her, but couldn't stop laughing.

He loved watching them interact and his hardened heart softened, just a little more.

"This is called the Yogi squat or Garland pose," Providence explained. "You're doing a great job, Sammy."

"It's the pooping pose," Sammy said. *Pfffft.* "'Cuse me. I tooted."

Providence laughed. "You're excused."

Dakota caught Providence's eye. "You two look like you're having fun."

"Daddy, Provi is teaching me yoga."

"I can see that." Dakota pulled out his phone and snapped a picture of them both. "Have you shown Providence your karate stances?"

Providence ended the pose and sat cross-legged on the floor. "You study karate?"

Sammy grinned. "Uh-huh. With Uncle Crockett. He's the best sensei!" She went into a basic defense stance.

"That's fantastic." Providence slid her gaze to Dakota. "You have a wonderful daddy to put you in karate class." She stood. "If you want, we can do more yoga and karate tonight."

"Okay." Sammy went back to playing with her dolls.

As he and Providence returned to his office, he said, "Thanks for going out of your way to spend time with her."

"It's my pleasure. She's a sweetheart."

They entered his office and he shut the door. "I'm going out of town tomorrow, returning on Thursday afternoon."

"You're taking a huge risk, Dakota. If you're caught, you're going to prison for a long, long time."

"My target is the Midnight Raper. Familiar with him?"

"No."

Dakota told her what he'd learned from Luther. "I'll know more once I read his profile, but I wouldn't be doing this if his DNA hadn't been found on dozens of victims. He's a vicious predator who's got to be stopped."

"Do you want me to leave while you're gone?"

"What? Hell, no. You better not leave. When I'm on a job, I go dark."

She opened her laptop. "Where are you headed?"

"Portland, Maine. I've got to line up a crew."

"Before you do that, did you pinpoint any enemies while in ALPHA?"

"No, but that doesn't mean I don't have any."

"Then, I'll move on. Let's circle back to the night of your banquet. Show me how to access the surveillance system at the convention center."

Sitting side-by-side, he hacked into the database. She plugged in the date and they located the files from the cameras in the ballroom and the atrium. They fast forwarded to the event and watched as attendees filtered in and out of the ballroom.

"It's going to be impossible to ID anyone," Dakota bit out. "Everyone is wearing a fucking mask."

Providence placed a calming hand on his. "I've got this. You want me to work in my bedroom so you can put together your team?"

"Stay. I trust you."

That elicited a smile.

She's so damn pretty.

He spent the next hour calling his guys. On such short notice, only Stryker was available. Since Quincy was tentative, Dakota called his brother.

"Hey," Sin answered.

"I've got a job in Maine tomorrow."

"Need my plane?"

"Yeah, and I'm one short. Can you do it?"

"I need specs."

After Dakota told him about the Midnight Raper, Sin said he'd call him back.

Dakota chuckled. "Checking with the boss?"

"Yeah, and the Mrs. just walked into my office. Give me five." Sin hung up.

Dakota eased down beside Providence. "Find anything?"

"There's a couple who stuck pretty close to Matt once he landed at the bar. The guy is wearing a three-quarter mask and the woman's been keeping her head down. It's like they know where the cameras are because I can't get a clear picture of them. The guy left, but the woman stayed with him."

Providence fast-forwarded the video. "About ten minutes later, the woman and Matt exited through the main entrance of the convention center. The man might be waiting in a car at the curb, but the cameras don't cover the street."

"Rewind," he said. "I recognize that other couple nearby."

An unmasked man and woman were leaving the building at the same time. "That's Kelly and Kevin Borenstein. They're a husband-and-wife real estate team with Larke."

Providence made a note. "Luther gave me a slew of federal agency IDs. Alias Elaine Jones. Looks like Elaine is going to pay the Borensteins a visit. Maybe they saw something that can help us find this masked couple."

Dakota growled. "That video is a major fucking problem."

"Problem? This is the first real clue we've gotten."

"That masked man and woman with Matt could have been us."

"*Us?*" As she played back the video, the color faded from her cheeks. It would be hard to prove it wasn't them. Two people concealing their faces, plying Matt with liquor, then ushering him into a waiting vehicle.

"Since the police are looking at me…and possibly you…that could be very damaging."

"Show me how I can access the streetlight cams."

It took some doing, but he was able to access one down the street from the convention center.

"There's a four-door sedan." She froze the frame and enlarged the picture. "That's our masked driver." She zoomed in, then jotted down a note. "It's a Maryland license plate." She jumped to a different website, logged in, and punched in the plate number.

"Tell me you've found the killers."

She shook her head. "The license plate was reported stolen. One step forward, a bunch back."

"We're not dealing with amateurs," he bit out.

"No, we're not," she replied. "I'm going to try to follow this car."

They worked nonstop until dinner.

While eating, Sammy chatted about the farmers market and the petting farm. Though Dakota stayed present for his daughter, he wondered how much circumstantial evidence the detective was finding to build a case against him. He hated that the masked couple cozying up to Matt could easily have been him and Providence. Their disguises made it impossible to ID them.

After dinner, Providence spent time with Sammy before Dakota took her upstairs to read her a story and tuck her in. When he emerged, he found Providence in his office, working.

"I'm meeting with Kelly and Kevin Borenstein in the morning," she said.

"Good." He sat on the sofa.

"And I'm meeting with the manager of Sequoia tomorrow," she added. "It's the Georgetown restaurant where Matt's body was found."

"Thanks for your efforts." He patted the cushion next to him. "Come sit with me."

She did.

"Miranda knows to contact Sin or Maverick Hott if I don't come home. If Sin doesn't make it, Maverick and his wife, Carly, will take Sammy."

"Does Sammy have grandparents?"

"No, they're deceased."

"I'm sorry."

"Thanks." He held her hand, stroked her skin. "You can continue to live here."

"Dakota, please."

Then, he shot her a cocky smile. "But, we're going to get this son of a bitch and fly home on Thursday."

She nodded in approval. "That sounds more like you."

"I have an idea I want to run by you."

She'd been watching the tender way he caressed her fingers. When she lifted her face to his, he said, "I'm going to help you with your grief and survivor guilt."

"*What?* No. Absolutely not."

"I am, and we're starting tonight."

19

PROVIDENCE GOES BROKE

Providence slipped into bed beside Dakota. She expected he would want to bring her to orgasm manually, but he didn't remove her tank top and panties. Instead, he rolled toward her and kissed her forehead.

"This isn't about sex or orgasms. Mine or yours."

Boy, did I call this one wrong. "Then, what?" she asked.

"I want you to feel safe. Having you in my bed isn't just about sex. It's about you living with the loss, but letting the blame go. It's about keeping Annabel in your heart, but making room for others so that you can have the most fulfilling life for yourself...and for her."

He had this amazing way of making her feel special and grounded, and loved. He was doing everything possible to tear down her walls and protect her heart. How could she not fall in love with this man?

"Thank you. I would love that." His kiss elicited her smile. "But what if I want to have sex and I want *you* to come?"

"Keep in mind, the only time I don't want to have sex with you is right after we have sex."

She smiled. "How do you know how to help me?"

"I had to go through this myself."

"So, you blamed yourself for Beth's death?"

"I blamed myself for not protecting her, for not keeping my wife safe. But, this isn't about me, it's about you. What do you like to do when you're not working?"

She didn't want to keep him up into the wee hours, so she kept her comments brief. "I love to cook, especially on the weekends. But I don't cook big meals for myself. I love taking yoga classes, but I haven't done that in a while. And...I've wanted to take racing lessons at Summit Point, but I would need a sports car to do that."

"Those are great. Tell me about your sexual preferences."

"Vanilla sex is always fun, but I like role playing on occasion and my club profile was accurate. I like sensory play and deprivation. How 'bout you? What do you like?"

"You. So damn much." His kiss was heartfelt, and the passion kept them anchored to each other. Desire spread like wildfire, devouring the landscape with its scorching heat.

As the kissing continued, sex would have been a natural, next step. Instead, he slowed the embrace down until it ended.

They gazed into each other's eyes. This man was the epitome of strength and danger. He was fearless and ruthless, and yet, she was drawn to him in such a powerful way.

"I can't wait to do all those sexy things to you." He pulled her onto him and held her close. "While I'm gone, consider doing something that would make you happy. Something just for you. Like taking a yoga class or cooking a big meal."

"I will." She snuggled close. "Thank you for caring."

PROVIDENCE WOKE BEFORE DAWN. "Be safe," she murmured before kissing Dakota goodbye, and heading down the hall to her bedroom.

Her chest tightened when she heard him leave. She didn't

agree with his methods, but she would wait until the right time to voice her opinion. All that mattered was his safe return home.

After breakfast, she read Sammy a story, grabbed the FBI badge, and headed out to speak with the husband and wife team at Larke Realty.

"Elaine Jones for Kelly and Kevin," she said to the receptionist.

A short time after being led into a small conference room, the Borensteins entered. Kevin set his laptop on the table. After introductions, Providence showed them the surveillance video where she'd spotted them outside the convention center at the same time Matt was leaving.

"Yes, that's us," Kelly confirmed. "Poor Matt."

"Did you see Matt at any point throughout the evening?"

"I didn't," Kevin said.

"After the banquet, I'd gone to the bar in the atrium to get us drinks and I heard him ranting about Dakota," Kelly said.

"We've known Dakota for years," Kevin said. "He's a well-respected broker and a total pro to work with. I don't believe for a minute he killed Matt Hastings."

"Can you tell me anything about this woman?" Providence pointed to the masked woman with Matt.

"I saw her—and the man she was with—at the bar. He was the only person with a mask that covered most of his face. Kevin and I have been realtors for years, so we knew most everyone at the banquet, but we didn't know them."

"Kelly, did you see Matt leave?"

"No, but I spotted him outside on our way out."

"Was he with the same woman from the bar?"

Kelly paused. "I think so, but I was paying more attention to Matt than to her."

Providence made a note. "Why?"

"He seemed super drunk, like she had to help him walk. I was thinking of hurrying over to ask if he was okay, but they got in the car and took off."

"Do you remember anything about the car? Two doors or four? A dent or anything else that caught your eye?"

"I don't remember the car," Kelly said. "But I remember the guy behind the wheel. I thought it was strange that he hadn't taken his mask off."

"Did you tell the police about this, especially since you can vouch for Dakota's reputation?"

They both shook their heads.

"But you're here now, taking our statement, so we're good, right?" Kevin asked.

Not exactly.

"If you think of anything else, call me." Providence jotted her cell phone number on the pad of paper on the conference table.

"No FBI business card?" Kevin asked.

"Unfortunately, I ran out and keep forgetting to order more."

"So, is your job as exciting as the TV shows portray?" Kevin asked.

"Definitely," Providence replied with a sarcastic edge. "It's non-stop action from morning to night."

They laughed, but she wondered if they actually believed her. "My brother just got his real estate license, and he's with Larke," Providence added.

"Awesome," Kevin said. "Does he have a mentor?"

Providence stood. "No idea."

"We've mentored a lot of rookie agents," Kelly said. "Does he work out of this office?"

"He didn't say," Providence replied.

Kevin opened his laptop. "I'll look him up in our directory. What's his name?"

"Randy Maddox."

He plugged in the name. "He's not coming up."

Providence peered over Kevin's shoulder. "Are you sure?"

"Let me ask the manager if the new agents have been added to the roster." Kelly popped out of the conference room and returned a moment later. "The website's current."

"Thanks for meeting with me." Providence saw herself out. *If Randy doesn't work for Larke, where does he work?*

Before heading to the Sequoia restaurant in Georgetown, she pulled up Goode-Luck Realty on her phone and checked the list of realtors. Randy wasn't listed there. She sent her sister a text. "Which real estate company does Randy work for?"

"Larke," Megan replied.

Rather than ignore what might be a blatant lie, Providence sent her brother a text. "Hey, Randy, it's Providence. I have friends who are realtor shopping. They want to work with a realtor from Larke or Goode-Luck. Which one are you with?"

As she started her vehicle, he replied. "Larke."

"Can I pass along your number to them?"

"I'm swamped right now and can't give them the attention they need," Randy texted back. "Tell them to call the office. They'll assign someone."

That makes no sense. A realtor who turns down referrals? What the hell is going on with him? Baffled, she headed toward Georgetown.

The upscale eatery didn't open until noon, so she texted the manager when she got there.

A woman opened the front door. "Can I see your identification?" Providence displayed her badge. "Thanks, Elaine. Come on in. We spoke on the phone. I'm Marcy."

After they sat by a window, a waiter delivered two sparkling waters.

"I'm investigating Matt Hastings's homicide," Providence began. "And I'm hoping the security cams on your patio picked up something."

"A detective stopped by yesterday about that. Why don't you guys work together and save a little time?"

Crap, he's one step ahead of me. "We each have our own investigation to run."

"All right, well, I'm guessing you want to see the video, too."

"Sure do."

"The detective had a warrant. Do you have one?"

"I can get one and come back later, but you'd have to take time during the dinner rush to help me out. It'll be easier if we do it now." *C'mon, don't make this so damn difficult.*

"You've got a point." She brought Providence into her office, pulled up the video, and found the night in question.

At ten past four in the morning, one of the cameras picked up a sailboat motoring over to the pier. It stayed for a few minutes before powering away.

Providence peered at the screen. Though the pier was lit, the captain's identity was concealed by a hoodie, cloaking his face in shadow. He moved to the rear of the boat, which was beyond the range of the camera. A few moments later, the boat pulled away and powered slowly up the river.

"Damn, the registration number is missing," Providence said.

"Are you done?" Marcy asked.

Providence was about to tell her to stop the video when the boat cruised by in the opposite direction. This time, she spotted the shadowy registration number on the port side. "Pause it."

"You can't see anyone onboard," Marcy quipped.

"That boat looks like it's—what—thirty, thirty-five feet long?"

"No idea."

"Rewind," Providence said. "I'm looking for the registration number on the port side."

After Marcy rewound the video, both women peered at the screen.

"Those first two letters look like VA to me," Providence said.

"Yeah, I think you're right. Nice find. The detective had me stop the video and he missed that."

Providence might have edged out the detective with the registration number, but she was still trailing him by at least a day.

"Does that third digit look like a three or could it be an eight?" Providence asked.

"It's too dark for me to make out any of the numbers," Marcy replied. "Sorry."

Providence wrote down what she thought was the registration number, along with every possible alternative. The last two digits were letters, but she couldn't tell if the first one was a C or an O. And was that last one a T or an F?

"Are there any other surveillance cams that could have picked up that boat?" Providence asked.

"No. Of the three we've got, one is broken. The second is pointed at the tables, and you saw the third one."

"Can you forward that to me?"

She chuckled. "That's the same thing the detective asked. Sorry, no can do."

Providence thanked her and left. *If I find this boat, I find Matt's killers.*

Feeling grateful she'd caught a break, she returned to Dakota's and found Sammy and Miranda sculpting Play-Doh at the kitchen island. "That looks fun."

"Can you play with us?" Sammy asked.

Sammy's adorable smile made it impossible for Providence to say no. "Sure, for a little while."

Sammy was creating a green cow and Miranda was making a pink pig. "What should I make?" Providence asked.

"Anything you want," Sammy explained. "You don't even have to make an animal."

As Providence rolled the soft clay in her hands, she asked about their morning. "We had reading time," Sammy replied.

"What did Mrs. Morris read to you?"

"I read to her."

"You can read?"

"Mrs. Morris is teaching me."

"Wow, that's pretty awesome."

Sammy's smile was filled with pride.

Miranda explained that Sammy was starting primer books, but with the one-on-one attention she received, she was ahead of her peers.

"If you keep this up, you'll be in college at fifteen," Providence said.

Miranda laughed, and Sammy asked, "What's that?"

"When you're older, you get to live at school with all your friends."

Tears welled in Sammy's eyes. "I don't want to leave my daddy."

Providence's stomach dropped. "Or, you can live here with your daddy *and* go to college at the same time."

"I'm staying with my daddy forever." Sammy set her cow down. "I'm going to make a cat." And just like that, Sammy moved on, her momentary fear abandoned for a purple cat.

After Providence finished creating an orange elephant with a corkscrew trunk, she told them she had to work. "I can make dinner for you guys tonight, if that's okay with you, Miranda."

"Absolutely. I defrosted ground turkey for meatballs."

"It's pasta night," Sammy explained. "I love 'scetti."

"I can do that." Then, Providence asked Miranda where she slept when Dakota was out of town.

"Upstairs in the guest room, but I can sleep on the sofa."

"Do you think Dakota would mind if I sleep in his bed for one night?" Providence asked. "That way, you can have the guest room."

Miranda bit back a smile. "I'm absolutely certain he'd love that plan."

She knows. "Thanks for the Play-Doh break. I'll be back to make dinner."

She retreated into Dakota's office. *Time to find that sailboat.*

Providence jumped on a website where two hundred and fifty thousand Virginia boater registration numbers were stored. After paying the fee, she did a wildcard search, plugging in suspected letters and numbers she'd written down. The system found thousands of possible matches. By filtering out motorboats, boats no longer in service, boats registered in southern Virginia, and sailboats over thirty-five feet, she was able to narrow down the number of possibilities to three hundred and thirty-seven.

I can work with that.

Her phone pinged with a text from her bank.

"Withdrawal for your mortgage payment failed due to insufficient funds. Please contact your local branch for details."

Thinking it must be a mistake, she hopped online and logged in to her account. But she was denied access. She retyped her login and password. Again, she was told one or both were incorrect. *What's going on with this?*

After resetting her password, she was able to access her bank account and clicked over to her account balance. "Oh, my God, no. No way."

Her account balance was $0.

Dread sent her pulse soaring. *That can't be right.* She had over fifteen thousand dollars in that account.

Tap-tap-tap. "Provi, can we come in?" Sammy asked through the closed door.

"Sure, come on in," she said, forcing down her growing concern.

Sammy walked in, Miranda close on her heels with a tray of food. "We made you a love lunch," said the child.

How thoughtful. The tightness in her guts released a little. "Thank you both so much."

"Do you want us to stay with you, so you don't have to eat by yourself?" Sammy asked.

A tear slipped down her cheek. "I would love the company."

"Why are you sad?"

I just lost my entire savings. "These are happy tears because you're so nice." Though her guts were in knots, she ate the chicken sandwich and a few slices of apple. Sammy chatted away and Providence did her best to pay attention. When she'd eaten as much as she could stomach, she thanked them again. "I have to run out, but I'll be back in time to make dinner."

By the time Providence pulled into the parking lot of her local bank, her nerves were so shot, she wanted to throw up.

The bank manager welcomed her into her office. "What can I help you with today?"

"I got an email that there were insufficient funds in my account to auto pay my mortgage. I was locked out of the account, so I changed the password and got back in. The balance says zero, but that's not right."

"Let's take a look." The manager logged in. "Unfortunately, that's correct. You have a zero balance."

"But I've got over fifteen thousand in that account. Where's my money?"

The manager turned back to the screen and began clicking away. Providence sat there, her foot bouncing up and down, while her head pounded and her stomach ached.

"It was withdrawn a couple of days ago and wire transferred to a different account."

It felt like someone punched Providence in the diaphragm. "Someone hacked into my account and wiped me out?"

"I'm so sorry."

Sorry? I want my money back! "Can you give me the account number where the money went?"

The manager did, then told Providence she needed to file a bank claim and a police report.

"How long will it take to resolve this?" Providence held her breath.

"The shortest I've seen is three months." The manager pursed her lips.

"And the longest?"

"Sometimes clients never get their money back."

"What?" *Oh, my God. This cannot be happening.* After the bank manager helped her fill out the online claim form, Providence closed the hacked account and opened a new one. An hour and a half later, she left the bank.

Alone in her car, she wanted to give in to the myriad of emotions rattling around in her head. But crying wouldn't change a thing. After taking a moment to breathe, she checked her wallet. Twenty-seven bucks. The asshole who'd broken into her condo popped into her thoughts. *He was looking for my checkbook so he could steal my money. That motherfucker.*

Being an action-oriented person, she drove to her parents' house where she found her dad on his laptop in the screened-in porch.

"Hey, Dad." Providence sat beside him at the table. "Where is everyone?"

"Your mom is in bed. Lizzie's at work. Randy was in the family room."

"I didn't see him."

"So, dear, what brings you by in the middle of the work day?"

"My bank account was hacked and I'm wiped out."

His eyebrows jutted into his forehead. "I'm sorry to hear that. How did that happen?"

She didn't want to tell him her condo had been broken into. He would worry about her safety and she definitely wasn't telling him she'd moved into Dakota's home. "Just one of those unlucky things."

The porch door opened and Randy strolled in. "What unlucky thing?"

"It's nothing," she replied. "How's the exciting world of real estate?"

Randy grinned. "I'm working it like a pro. How's by you?"

"Providence's bank account was hacked into," her dad blurted. She wished he hadn't said that.

"That sucks," Randy said. "Can you get your money back?"

"Doubtful." She addressed her dad. "I hate to ask...can you loan me some money so I can pay my mortgage?"

"I'll help you out," Randy said.

"That's okay," Providence protested.

"Mom and Gordon have been so generous to Lizzie and me. I've got a little money squirreled away. Let me get my checkbook." He walked into the house.

Providence slid her gaze to her dad. "I'd feel more comfortable borrowing the money from you."

"How much do you need?"

"A couple thousand," she replied.

He patted her back. "I'll help you, honey."

She sighed. "Thank you. I'll pay you back over the next—"

"It's fine. I'll write you a check." Her dad ambled inside. He looked so tired. The stress of her mom's illness was taking its toll on him, too. In the kitchen, he pulled his checkbook out of the drawer.

Randy offered her a check. "I don't have much, but please, take it."

It was for two hundred and fifty dollars.

"You should keep it, especially if you're looking to move out."

Randy snort laughed. "I'd need a helluva lot more than two hundred and fifty bucks if I want to live in *this* area." He waved the check at her. "Take it."

She collected the checks and slid them into her bag. "Thank you. I'll pay you both back. I'm going to check on Mom."

"You shouldn't," Randy objected. "She's resting."

Ignoring her brother, she went upstairs and peeked in the bedroom. Her mom was out cold. Fear sent a shiver skirting through her. Her skin was so pale that Providence watched her, just to make sure she was breathing. When her mom didn't wake, Providence found her dad back on the porch.

"Did Mom's blood tests come back?"

"Not yet. The doctor thinks she might be anemic, so he's starting her on a low dose of iron."

Providence borrowed her dad's laptop and Googled anemia symptoms. "I guess she could be anemic. What do you think?"

"I don't know what to think anymore."

She glanced around. "Where's Randy?" she whispered.

He shrugged. "He's here all the time," her dad whispered. "He's not hustling, that's for sure. I have no idea how he's going to sell a home if he has no clients. I've been thinking it might be time to ask them to move out."

No clients? He told me he had too many.

"Good idea. If you want Megan and me—and Stryker, too—to be here for support, just say the word."

"Thanks, dear. Mom has been fighting me on this because they have no money and won't have anywhere to live."

"They've been living *somewhere* all these years."

"But, we're getting a little break. Randy and Lizzie are taking off for a few days after she gets home from work today."

"Where are they going?"

"To spend a long weekend on the water."

"Good. You two need a break." She rose. "Thank you for the loan."

Once back at Dakota's, she didn't see Sammy or Miranda as she made her way upstairs. She mobile deposited her dad's check into her new account, but she didn't deposit Randy's. The guy sounded as hard up for cash as she was. Needing a moment to unwind before she made dinner, she went into her bedroom, shed her clothes, and jumped in the shower.

As the hot, streaming water pounded her back, her thoughts drifted to Dakota. What would it feel like to completely surrender to him? *Could I give myself permission to feel that good, without the guilt or sorrow?*

As she rinsed the suds from her hair, she imagined his hands on her. Those large, strong, sexy hands sliding over every inch of her. Claiming her and loving her.

And then, the image of Annabel popped into her mind. The one that sent her spiraling into the depths of sadness. She had thought her daughter was sleeping, but on closer examination, she hadn't been. Her small body had lain still. Even now, pain slashed through her heart. She adored her baby and she loved being a mom. She'd loved the middle-of-the-night feedings where she could stare into her baby girl's eyes and sing her a lullaby. She loved making her smile and watching her sleep. Except for that one time...

Providence turned off the water, dried off, and dressed in yoga pants and an oversized shirt. Then, she padded downstairs to make dinner. As the water heated for pasta, she made seasoned meatballs and slid them into the oven. Once the water boiled, she added the box of pasta Miranda had left on the counter.

As she emerged from the pantry with a jar of sauce, the front door opened.

"Mmm, something smells good," Miranda said as she and Sammy entered the kitchen.

"Are you cooking 'scetti?" Sammy asked.

Providence held up the empty box of pasta. "All the 'scettis are cooking."

"Mrs. Morris said it would be fun to have a girl party, so we made brownies in the before."

"Before we went to the playground," Miranda translated.

Providence's spirits were bolstered when she saw the smiles on their faces. Losing her life savings had gutted her, but she wouldn't let that ruin *their* evening.

"Sammy, if you want to play for a little while, I can help Providence," Miranda said.

Sammy scampered into the family room. Miranda kept her in her sights while she set the table.

"Are you okay?" Miranda asked.

That caught her off guard. "Of course. Why wouldn't I be?"

"You seemed off earlier. I thought maybe it was because Dakota was out of town."

While she had thought about him, she had every confidence he would be okay. She poured the sauce into a pan. "Thanks. I'm good, really. I appreciate your concern."

During dinner, Providence watched how loving Miranda was with Sammy. And so patient. Sammy loved to talk and talk, and Miranda was an active listener. After dinner, they each had a brownie.

Afterwards, Sammy suggested a game. Which she did not win. The smile Sammy wore so well was replaced by an angry child who stomped her foot. Samantha Luck was not a good loser, but then again, she was four years old.

"I want to play again and I want to win!"

"Sammy, it's time for your bath," Miranda said. "You have school tomorrow."

"I don't want to go to school."

"You know the best part about losing," Providence said.

"Nothing," Sammy said with a glare that reminded her of Dakota.

"It's an opportunity to congratulate someone else on their win," Providence pushed on. "It's a chance to have a good attitude even when we think we deserved to win and the other players didn't."

"I don't want to say 'good job' to Mrs. Morris."

"Congratulations, Mrs. Morris," Providence said. "You did a great job and I had the best time playing with you. Maybe we can play again sometime."

"That's stupid talk," Sammy said.

"I've never won that game, Sammy," Miranda said. "Not even once. You always win whenever we play."

Silence.

"Never?" Sammy asked.

Miranda shook her head. "You're such a great player and I can never beat you."

Sammy looked at Providence. Then, at Miranda. "I wanted to win, but you did a good job."

"Thank you," Miranda replied with a smile.

"Can Provi give me my bath tonight?" Sammy asked.

"Sure," Miranda replied. "Do you think you should ask Providence if she wants to?"

"Provi, can you give me a bath tonight, please?"

"I'd love to."

"I'll leave the monitor on," Miranda said. "I'll be down here cleaning up if you need anything."

"Thank you for a fun party," Providence said to Miranda.

Miranda offered a warm smile

"I like bath time." Sammy marched upstairs, the loss of the board game long forgotten.

Providence helped Sammy take off her clothing. While Providence ran the bath water, Sammy went to the bathroom.

Once the tub had been filled, Providence tested it, then added a little more cold water. Then, she pulled Sammy's hair into a ponytail before she stepped in and sat down. Providence sudsed the washcloth and began to clean her small body.

"AAHHHHHH!" Sammy's scream reverberated off the marble walls.

Providence startled. "What's wrong?"

Sammy pointed. "Spider."

A small spider had crawled into the corner of the ceiling. "Oh, my goodness, you scared me."

"Can you kill it?"

"Kill it? Spiders are good."

Sammy shrieked again and started to get up.

"Whoa, where are you going?"

"I'm afraid."

"Sammy." Sammy's attention was glued to the spider.

"Samantha, look at me, please." Sammy did. "I promise you I will not let that spider hurt you. I will put it outside as soon as we're done."

"No, you do it now and I'll wait here."

"I'm not leaving you alone. Show me with your finger how big that spider is."

Sammy showed her.

"Good job. And how big are you?"

She widened her arms as far as they could reach.

"I'm guessing that spider is way more afraid of you than you are of her."

"That's a girl spider?"

"Oh, sure, it's girls-only night. That's gotta be a girl spider." While talking, Providence kept washing her.

The spider started crawling across the ceiling and Sammy clutched Providence's arm. "Guess what?" Providence asked. "You did an awesome job. We are all done, young lady."

She helped Sammy stand, wrapped her in a towel, and lifted her out of the tub. She loved giving her a bath, loved spending time with her despite the attack of the arachnid.

They went into Sammy's bedroom and Providence helped her into her jammies. After Providence lovingly brushed her long hair, she kissed the top of her head. "You are clean, but more importantly, you are very, very brave. I'm sure your daddy and Mrs. Morris will be so proud of you."

"How will you get the spider?"

They went into the kitchen and Providence collected a glass and a small piece of cardboard from the back of a pad of paper. She left Sammy with Miranda and returned to the bathroom, captured the little guy in the glass and returned to show it to them both.

"Where do you put her?" Sammy asked.

"I'm setting her free in a bush, outside."

As Providence relocated the spider, she spotted a black sedan parked out front. After closing and locking the front door, she made a mental note to ask Miranda about the vehicle once Sammy was in bed.

"I heard screaming during bath time," Miranda said. "What happened, Sammy?"

Sammy explained the entire story of the spider, then at the end added, "Spiders are good, did you know that?" Then, she scrunched up her nose and turned to Providence. "Why are they good?"

"They eat bugs that bother us, like fleas and flies and mosquitoes," Providence said, tickling her.

She giggled and giggled and her joy filled a little of the emptiness in Providence's heart.

"Time for bed," Miranda said.

"Bye, Provi."

Miranda returned after reading her a bedtime story and made herself a cup of tea.

"Who's in the car out front?" Providence asked.

"Dakota's bodyguard, Marcus Freethy."

"Does he stay out there all night long?"

"Only when Dakota goes out of town. He shares the shift with another man."

"Got it. Thanks for making tonight so much fun. Not just for Sammy, but for me, too."

"You're very special to Dakota. He's never brought anyone home to meet Sammy. He's been closed off for as long as I've known him. I'm glad he's opening up his heart to you."

Providence smiled. "So am I."

Though she'd been wiped out financially, she'd gained more than she could have ever imagined for herself. She'd found the right people to help her heal. All the money in the world couldn't help her with that.

20

THE HIT

Under cover of darkness, Dakota, Sin, and Stryker entered the Airbnb on Bradley Street in Portland—their safe house while they completed the mission.

The quaint home was furnished, the curtains drawn. A single low-wattage lamp glowed from a table in the living room. The men dropped their duffle bags. Wearing their night vision goggles and with their weapons drawn, they did a sweep of the home.

They were alone.

They scattered into separate rooms to change. As Dakota pulled on his tactical gear, his mind wandered to Providence. Now, he had two reasons to return home safely. His daughter and his woman.

Earlier in the day, when The Dungeon was closed, the men had met in the Travesty room. Plans had been made, strategies discussed. Although the Midnight Raper had over thirty aliases, their target was a forty-eight-year-old white male named Jay Hill.

Luther had gotten Dakota a blueprint of the house where Hill lived. After he, Sin and Stryker had studied the map and discussed possible scenarios, they collected their gear and headed out.

Though they flew on Sin's private jet, the hit was not discussed en route.

Once dressed, and with his ski mask in hand, Dakota returned to the living room. Sin handed each of them a comm device, which they slipped into their ears. They checked their weapons, added the silencers, pulled on their night vision goggles, and pulled on leather gloves.

"No names," Sin reminded them. "We check for cameras before we go in."

Stryker pulled a tiny can of spray paint from his front pocket. "For the cams."

"Let's go surprise that mother fucker and shut him down, for good," Dakota said.

They pulled on their ski masks and left in silence. It was after midnight.

The risk of getting caught or something going wrong was greater when doing a hit in a residential area. Security cams were plentiful, and dogs heard every damn sound. Barking triggered an array of responses, none of them good.

Walking single-file, Dakota led them through the quiet neighborhood, cutting through the backyard that butted up to Wayne Street. Once there, they hoofed it up the steep hill putting them at the rear of Hill's property.

Standing shoulder to shoulder, they took in their surroundings. The house and the unattached single-car garage, situated behind the home, were both dark. Dakota's trigger finger itched to take Hill out. He'd been terrorizing and assaulting women for decades.

Ever since the police had stopped by to question him a week ago, he'd been laying low. They fully expected him to be there. This job would take no more than five minutes, tops.

They walked around the property in search of security cameras and found five. Stryker sprayed every lens with black paint. If the cameras had triggered some kind of internal alarm, it wasn't enough to bring Hill outside.

"He's not home," Dakota murmured, "or he's one sound sleeper."

As they stalked the property, they noted the walk-out basement door in the back, a side door that led to a mudroom, and the front door.

Per their plan, they would split up. Stryker was up first. He tried the door to the garage. It was locked. Within seconds, Sin picked it, and Stryker vanished inside.

Dakota and Sin took off toward the darkened house.

The storm door on the east side of the home was unlocked, so they stepped into the small mudroom. As Dakota suspected, the door leading into the house was locked. Again, Sin picked that lock.

They were in.

He scanned the kitchen, hallway leading to the bedrooms, and the living room. The curtains were drawn, the house was filled with an eerie silence. No sign of Hill.

The kitchen was tidy, but the stench of rotting food made his stomach roil. Both men walked into the main area, which served as a dining room and living room.

Per their plan, Sin strode down the hall, opened the door to the basement, and vanished down the stairs. That left Dakota to clear the first floor, or find the motherfucker asleep in his bed. Dakota looked forward to waking him.

He took off down the hallway and peered into the open doorway on the left. Dozens of laptops lined the tables and computers cluttered the floor. Hill's home office. He checked the walk-in closet. All clear.

Next, he cleared the bathroom, before making his way to the first bedroom. The linens on the empty bed were a rumpled mess, but Hill wasn't there. Again, he checked the walk-in closet. No Hill.

The bedroom door at the end of the hallway was closed, but a faint light slithered into the hall. After opening the door, he heard faint whimpering coming from the closet. With his weapon at the ready, he opened the door. *Jesus, no.*

The rage that he kept bottled up on these missions exploded in a sea of red. A young woman lay naked on the floor, her wrists and ankles bound, her mouth covered in tape. Absolute terror stared up at him.

"I'm going to get you help," he whispered. "Nod if you understand me."

She nodded.

"Have you been stabbed or shot?"

She shook her head.

"I need you to stay here for a little while longer. Then, we'll get you to the hospital."

She whimpered.

While he wanted to remove the tape and untie her, then call for an ambulance, he would not deviate from their plan. As far as anyone knew, the Midnight Raper had never imprisoned victims in his home.

"Can you stay quiet?"

Again, she nodded, but this time, she raised her arms, silently pleading for him to untie her.

"I can't," he murmured. "You're safer here." Dakota hated leaving her in the closet. He covered her with a blanket, closed the closet door, and exited the room.

He found Stryker and Sin talking quietly in the living room.

"He's not here," Dakota murmured. "What did you find in the basement?"

"Three bodies in various degrees of decomposition," Sin said. "It looks like a medieval torture chamber down there."

Dakota's blood ran cold.

"What about the garage?" Dakota asked Stryker.

"No vehicle. I checked behind the garage. I think there are bodies buried out back."

This was worse than he'd anticipated.

"There's a woman bound and gagged in the back-bedroom closet," Dakota said.

"Oh, Christ," Sin murmured. "Where the hell is Hill?"

They didn't know.

While waiting, they checked the home for surveillance. If there were any cameras, they were well concealed.

Over thirty minutes later, a car pulled into the driveway and stopped in front of the side door by the mudroom. The lights went out, the engine went quiet. A car door opened.

"Here we go," Dakota said.

"I can't fucking wait," Stryker added.

Then, a second car door opened.

"He's not alone," Sin said.

"Move into position," Dakota said.

Sin stepped into the corner of the room. Stryker moved into the kitchen. Dakota stood steadfast in the center of the room, his Glock by his side.

The storm door opened. Footsteps into the mudroom. Dakota's heart didn't beat faster, his blood pressure didn't change. He remained still, filled with the kind of hatred reserved for true evil. The door to the house opened.

"Get the hell inside," said a man's voice.

That was Hill.

A woman sobbed softly.

Oh, fuck, he's brought another victim home.

She entered. She was trembling so hard, Dakota couldn't control his rage. Stryker moved in fast, took the girl, and ushered her down the hallway toward the back bedroom.

"What the fuck?" Hill croaked out. "Who the hell are—"

Through the comm, Dakota heard Stryker whisper to the girl. "I've got you. You're safe."

Dakota stormed Hill, grabbed him by the throat, and shoved him against the wall. "You're done, Hill. So fucking done."

Hill raised his arm and Dakota spotted the tip of a shiny blade. He kneed Hill and, as he doubled over, grabbed the weapon and flung it on the carpet. Then, he lifted Hill into the air by his neck, strode into the living room, and threw him on the sofa.

Sin appeared, then Stryker returned from the back bedroom. All three men towered over him.

"How many?" Dakota bit out. "How many women did you hurt?"

A low rumbling laugh rolled out of Hill. "Not enough."

"I don't want to kill you, I want to torture you to death," Stryker growled.

"Why?" Sin asked. "Why do you prey on the innocent?"

"The only time I feel alive is when I'm sucking the life out of them. I feed off their fear, and their pain, and their energy." Hill rose. "I'm not afraid of you."

"You should be," Dakota rasped.

"You're about to spend eternity with the devil himself," Sin said.

"You get the last word, Hill," Stryker said.

"I loved every minute of it."

Uncontrollable rage billowed from Dakota. He popped him between the eyes. Hill dropped to the floor with a thud. Stryker shot him in the heart, twice.

"Confirm the son of a bitch isn't breathing," Dakota murmured before taking off down the hallway.

He opened the bedroom door. Both women were huddled together in the closet. Dakota knelt. "He's dead."

The one who'd been held prisoner started sobbing. "Oh, dear Lord. Thank you. Thank you."

"How long have you been held here?"

"Months. He kidnapped me in New Hampshire. He called me his good luck charm. I hope he rots in hell."

"Are there cameras in the house?"

"I don't know," she replied. "He might have some on the outside. He was paranoid the police were coming back."

"I'm calling them now, then we're out. They'll want information on us. Tell them nothing."

"Okay," said the second woman.

"What's important is that you're both survivors," Dakota said. "Make it a good life."

"Thank you," said the second woman.

Dakota strode down the hallway. Stryker and Sin waited in the mudroom.

"Dead?" Dakota murmured.

"Confirmed," Sin replied.

"Let's get the hell out of here." Once outside, Dakota called the police.

"What's your emergency?" asked the operator.

"Jay Hill, known as the Midnight Raper, is dead." Dakota gave her the address on Wayne Street. "There are two women being held captive in the back bedroom. There are multiple corpses in the basement, might be more buried behind the garage."

"Sir, we'll send someone right out there. What is your name?"

Dakota hung up, then called the FBI hotline and told them the same thing.

As they made their way back to the safe house, Dakota snapped the burner in two. Despite the risk of getting caught, he did not regret what he had done.

He had stopped a monster.

Sirens pierced the quiet night as they entered the house on Bradley Street. Over the next few hours, they took turns dozing, but Dakota couldn't sleep. They left before dawn, riding in a taxi to the airport.

"You guys listen to the news this morning?" asked the driver.

"No," Dakota replied.

"Well, the Midnight Raper was killed. About time someone

offed that SOB. Gals around here have been scared to death for months. Turns out, he had two stashed in his house." The guy shuddered. "I've got two daughters myself. Boy, am I glad he's gone."

"Did the FBI get him?" Sin asked.

"News report didn't say, but the house, which is right around here, was swarming with so many cop cars and media, we couldn't get down the street if we tried."

The driver dropped them at the airport. As they made their way toward private aviation, Dakota slipped into a bathroom, pulled on his leather glove and tossed half the broken burner in the trash receptacle. Before exiting, he shoved the glove into his bag.

Law enforcement officers were patrolling the terminal and one of them sauntered over.

"Here we go," Dakota murmured.

"Hey, fellas, where you headed?" asked the officer.

"Back to DC," Dakota replied.

"What brings you to Portland?"

"I'm a realtor and a land developer," Dakota said. "We flew up yesterday to scout some land near Bar Harbor."

"That's a nice area. Can I see your IDs?"

The men fished out their wallets and handed him their driver's licenses. If the cop asked to see inside their duffels, it was all over. No developer scouts land in tactical gear. And all three men were armed.

Dakota and Sin exchanged glances.

The officer handed them back their cards. "My cousins are twins," he said. "You two must've had some fun messing with people when you were kids."

"We were adopted and didn't meet until college," Sin said.

"That explains your different last names," said the officer.

"Why are you guys stopping people?" Stryker asked.

"The Midnight Raper was killed, execution style." The cop

leaned close. "If you ask me, we're all relieved. But we've gotta do our job and find the guy."

"Good luck," Dakota said.

"You fellas have a safe flight."

They didn't speak until they were jetting above the clouds. "I need a drink," Stryker said.

Sin retreated to the back and returned with three glasses of bourbon. An hour and forty-five minutes later, they touched down in DC. They deplaned, said their goodbyes, and went their separate ways.

They would never talk about what had transpired. To anyone or to each other.

On the way home, Dakota ditched the second half of the broken burner before checking in with Luther.

"It's done," Dakota said.

"In light of everything, you'll have to lay low for a while."

"Understood." He had no interest in completing another assignment anytime soon.

Eager to see Providence, he drove straight home. Sammy was at daycare, Miranda's car wasn't out front, but Providence's was. As he walked through the front door, he couldn't wait to pull her into his arms. He had missed her...a lot.

He found her staring intently at her laptop.

"Hey," he said.

No response.

"Miss Rhode Island."

She glanced up, but it was an extra beat before she actually saw him. After hurrying over, she threw her arms around him, and held him close. This was where he needed to be. Here, with this woman.

His woman.

"I missed you," he murmured, letting the last remaining anxiety float away.

Something was wrong. The spark in her eyes had been replaced with concern.

"I missed you, too. I'm relieved you're home." She hesitated for a split second. "I've got a few things to update you on. Have you eaten? Are you hungry? Do you want—"

"Whoa, slow down." He brushed her bangs off her face, dipped down, and kissed her. Her kiss was tight and over too soon.

Something was definitely wrong.

Her phone rang. She broke away. "It's Luther. I've gotta take this." She answered. "Luther, thank you for calling me back. I have an HR issue, but the only number I have is yours...well, I don't want to bother—" She paused. "I have a new bank account number for direct deposit and a starter pack of checks. Will that work?" She fished the checks from her handbag. "Thanks again," she said and hung up.

He studied her while she snapped a picture of the check. Her brow was furrowed, the worry in her eyes hard to miss. "What's going on?"

"One sec while I text this to Luther." When finished, she painted on a tight smile. "How 'bout something to eat?"

He wrapped his arm around her and guided her to the sofa. As he sat, he pulled her onto his lap. "I missed the hell out of you. You're a million miles away. We're home *alone*. All I want to do is carry you upstairs and deposit you on my bed where I can help you relax away all that tension."

"I'm fine." She pursed her lips.

"This," he pointed from her to him, "is a relationship. We're partners. Talk to me."

She stared into his eyes. "I jumped online this morning and saw that the Portland press is all over Hill's death." She stroked his shoulder, sending energy streaming through him. "I read that there were two women being held captive and the person responsible for killing him kept the women safe. You're being hailed a hero."

"I'm no hero. I'm one of the bad guys."

She hugged him. "I'm sorry. I'm here now. We can go upstairs if you want."

"Of course, I want to love my woman."

Her eyes widened. "Your woman?"

"Hell, yeah." He kissed her, letting his tongue swirl with hers. She was holding back, and she wasn't okay, so he didn't budge off the sofa. "But first, you're going to tell me what's going on."

"The guy who broke into my condo stole my bank info. He hacked into my account, did an electronic transfer, and wiped me out."

Anger coursed through him. "No fucking way."

"I filed a claim with my bank, but they might not be able to get my money back. I had to ask my dad for a loan so I could pay my mortgage this month. I'm furious, and there's not a damn thing I can do about it." She broke eye contact and let out a frustrated breath. Then, her gaze reconnected with his. He hated seeing the disappointment in her eyes, the worry lines etched between her brows.

With one phone call, he could deposit enough money to pay off her entire mortgage. But she didn't ask him for help, so, he kept quiet.

"I'd made some progress on our case, then I got slammed with this, but that's nothing when compared to what you've been through," she said. "I'm sorry. I'm being selfish. How are *you* doing?"

"I'm fine, but you aren't. Let me help you."

"No, I've got this. My brother felt so badly for me, even he gave me a few bucks."

"Did you get the account number where the money was transferred?"

She pushed off his lap and fished the piece of paper out of her handbag.

"Stryker might be able to find your money." He called Stryker.

"Busy," Stryker answered. "Stop bothering me."

Dakota chuckled. "I've got Providence on speaker."

"Hey, cuz, what's the word?"

"My bank account got hacked and my money was stolen."

"That sucks. Need some dinero?"

"I'm good, thanks."

"You got the account number?"

Providence read it to him.

"Just because it's you two, I'm dropping everything. I'll see what I can find." Stryker hung up.

Dakota shoved his phone back into his pocket. "What about this? We rent out your condo. That would give you another income stream, your place would get used, and Sammy and I could see you every day."

Her mouth dropped open, but no words came out.

"Too much?"

"I'm not sure how to process that. Is that a business proposition or..." She trailed off.

"It's the other."

"Okay, well, *wow*." More silence. "I'll give it some thought. Thank you for the offer." She opened her laptop "Let's get to work."

Undeterred by her reaction, he went to her, and drew her into his arms. "Work can wait an hour. I don't hear the pitter-patter of little feet or soft tapping on my office door. I want to show you how much I missed you."

"Dakota..." A few seconds passed. Her gaze softened. She leaned up and kissed him. "I missed you, too. So much."

Providence locked Dakota's bedroom door, pulled off her shirt, then shimmied out of her tight pants, leaving her in her bra and panties. Dakota was by her side, drawing her into his arms, and pressing his lips to hers. She inhaled his baseline scent and exhaled a sigh. She had missed him.

She worked quickly to strip off his clothing. He pulled back the linens before they tumbled onto his bed. "Condom?" she asked.

"Are you more comfortable naked or in your bra and panties?"

"It's going to be hard to have sex if I'm dressed, though you could move them out of the way."

"Let's focus on you."

"Dakota, please."

"Work with me on this. This is important to me."

"You are so good to me." She relaxed onto the mattress and stroked his bearded cheeks.

"Time to let go of the tension." He inhaled a slow, deep breath, then slowly released it. He did it again before she realized he wanted her to follow his lead.

She did, and when she released a few soul-calming breaths, the stress started melting away. Staring at him made her happy. Running her hands over his muscular shoulders and down his triceps worked, too. Using his fingers, he combed through her hair, then kissed her shoulder. He stroked her chest, but not her breasts, caressed her torso and legs, but stayed clear of doing anything sexual. His touch was tender, his words were encouraging.

"You look relaxed and happy."

She swooned.

"I could stare at you for hours."

She was his, totally and completely.

"I love touching you," he murmured, while caressing the inside of her thigh. "Does that feel good?"

"Very," she whispered, and reached down to stroke his shaft.

"Providence, not yet," he warned.

She stopped.

He pulled her panties off and cupped her sex. His gaze never left hers, his focus so intense, she wanted to lose herself in him and never find her way back to reality. When he slid his fingers between her folds, she murmured her approval and spread her legs.

He kissed her chest, this time including the swell of her breasts, while he caressed her swollen clit. Soft strokes that were light and tender. Back and forth and around and around. When he fingered her, she groaned. "I love how you touch me."

"You deserve to be happy, Providence," he whispered, then kissed her again. She stiffened. "I'm right here and I've got you."

He slid his arm under her and held her close while he continued to pleasure her. The euphoria continued to build, the intensity in his eyes never leaving hers. "Relax," he murmured.

She did.

As the pleasure continued building and she began to writhe against his touch, the guilt started to creep in. She tensed. He slowed down, dropped more worshipful kisses on her cheek, her forehead, even the edge of her mouth.

"Close your eyes."

She let them flutter closed.

"I've taken you away for the weekend," he began. "Just the two of us. We're on a private beach and I have you all to myself. You remove your bikini top."

She smiled, but she kept her eyes closed.

"I find you completely irresistible, so I tug off your bottoms and pull off my bathing suit. We start with kissing, but we're so hot for each other, that you pull me on top of you. I slide inside you and start moving. Then, I lean down and take your firm nipple into my mouth and tug."

"Show me," she whispered.

Moving with care, he stopped playing with her clit and pulled her bra down, exposing her breasts. "Ah, so perfect. You are so damn irresistible."

He took her nib into his mouth and sucked, then slid his

fingers back inside her. Her nipple plumped in his mouth and he sucked harder. The exhilaration took her higher and higher, the arousal had her throbbing with desire.

She opened her eyes to appreciate the sexy way he teased her nipple, and another jolt of adrenaline charged through her. Watching him love her was the sexiest thing she'd ever seen. He was the only man who put her first. Even while a crazed lunatic was hunting him down, he was completely committed to her. To her happiness.

He's the one.

Exhilaration, paired with that freeing realization, sent her flying high.

She started writhing on the bed, forcing his fingers in farther. "God, you feel so good. I want this so badly."

"Easy, honey," he said. "We've got this."

"I'm not sure I can come."

"Providence, it's not about that. It's about you and me and how much we care about each other."

Those words seeped into her heart and her soul. In that moment, a sliver of the guilt was carved away. And she offered a little smile. "Never before today did I think I could get there, but you give me hope. You are the most amazing man I have ever known. I'm good for today." She kissed him. "I want you inside me."

"This is for you," he protested.

"No, this is for *us*." She nudged him off her so she could pull a condom from his drawer.

As she took him inside her, she kissed him with reckless abandon and their connection was complete in all the ways that mattered.

Without question, this man was her person. Simply because he put her first.

21

THE INTERROGATION

Dakota was falling in love with Providence. He knew, because her happiness trumped his, which is why he was committed to helping her work through her issues regarding her daughter.

On the way to his office, they stopped in the kitchen for lunch, and found Miranda putting away groceries.

"Welcome back, Dakota. How was your trip?"

"Good," he said. "How'd things go?"

"We had a girls-only party and Sammy asked Providence to give her a bath."

"Where I learned about her fear of spiders," Providence said, while making sandwiches.

Dakota nodded. "Did she freak out?"

"Oh, yeah."

"Did you kill it?"

"I'm into the catch and release program."

"Everything else go okay?"

"We had a great time together," Miranda replied.

"Miranda, I'm picking Sammy up early from daycare this afternoon," Dakota said.

With plates in hand, he and Providence entered his office where a text from Stryker awaited them. "No luck hacking the bank account. Still working it."

"If anyone can find your money, it's Stryker," Dakota said.

Providence brought him up to speed on what Kelly and Kevin had seen at the banquet, and told him about the sailboat sighting at the Georgetown restaurant.

"We've got to find that masked couple." Dakota called the lab at ALPHA. "I need the status on a picture Providence Reynolds and I dropped off…how much longer will it take?" He listened then hung up.

"Well?" she asked.

"Next week." He raked his hand through his hair.

Providence showed him how she'd been hunting for the sailboat based on the various registration numbers, then suggested he search the street cams the night of the banquet for the couple Matt left with.

Three hours later, a frustrated Dakota pushed out of his chair. "These two are pros at staying hidden." Despite his efforts, he couldn't find the car with the masked couple. "I'm going to pick Sammy up. Come with me."

"I'm gonna keep working."

On the way, Dakota checked in with Juanita.

"I'm concerned," she told Dakota. "Business is down thirty percent because of Matt's death. And four more agents left to work for other companies."

"I'm not resigning. That would send a message that I'm running scared because I'm guilty."

"You are a lot of things, Dakota, but scared isn't one of them. Think about putting out a press release that you're taking a temporary hiatus until the police clear your name."

"I'll consider it. Are you doing okay?"

"I'm never okay without my business partner."

"I'll stop by soon. Hang in there." He ended the call as he pulled into the preschool parking lot.

After checking in at the front desk, he watched Sammy through the window of the four-year-olds' classroom. She was playing with two other children. He couldn't help but smile. She was having so much fun. He wished her life would always be that carefree and easy.

When he opened the classroom door, a petite blonde whizzed by him, head down. "Excuse me," she mumbled.

Dakota glanced over his shoulder, but she hurried around the corner so fast, he missed her. *Must be Sammy's new teacher.*

The teacher's assistant said hello while she attended to another child. "Hey, Leticia," Dakota said.

"Daddy!" Sammy ran over and he scooped her into his arms. She was his entire world and the best part of his life.

"How's my punkin?"

She placed her little hands on his cheeks. "Do you want to meet my new teacher?"

"Sure."

He set her down and she beelined for the assistant. "Miss El, where's Miss Liz?"

"She ran to the front office, real quick," Leticia replied.

"I want her to meet my daddy."

Beep. Beep. "Hello, Miss Leticia," said a voice over the classroom intercom.

"I'm here."

"Miss Liz stepped out for a minute. Can you manage alone for a few?"

"No problem," Leticia replied.

"I'm sorry, honey," Dakota said. "I'll have to meet your teacher another day." He fully expected her to have a meltdown.

"Is Provi home?" Sammy asked.

"She sure is."

Sammy pulled her lunchbox from her cubby, along with her

spring jacket, and a piece of construction paper. Then, she said goodbye to Leticia and hurried back to Dakota. "I'm ready."

He helped her into her coat, collected her things, and stopped at the front to check out. Crossing the parking lot, he asked about her day.

"Miss Liz said she could bring me home, but I told her only Daddy and Mrs. Morris. Can Provi drive me home?"

Dakota stopped. "Miss Liz said she could drive you home?"

"Uh-huh."

Dakota headed back inside. "Daddy, where are we going?" Sammy whined. "I want to go home."

"One minute, sweetheart." He returned to check-in. "Is the director here?"

"She's in a meeting."

"Tell her I need to speak with her, now."

The young woman stared at him. "Well, I can't...can she call—"

"*Now.*"

Her upper lip curled as she pushed out of the chair and meandered to a closed door. She knocked, then entered. A moment later, the director walked over to him. "Hello, Mr. Luck. How can I help?"

"Sammy told me her teacher said she could drive her home. What's that all about?"

The director paused, then flashed a canned smile. "She was probably just being friendly. Our staff knows they can't take students off the premises."

"I'd like to meet her," Dakota said.

"Wasn't she in the classroom?" the director asked.

"No."

"I'll go look for her." The director left the front office and headed down the hallway. While they waited, Sammy said, "Daddy, I want to go home and play."

"We will, Samantha, just as soon as I meet your new teacher."

The director returned a few moments later. "I'm sorry for the wait. Liz wasn't feeling well and left. I'll speak with her about this first thing Monday."

"Why not tomorrow?"

"She's taking Friday off."

Dakota glared at her. "This is the second incident with this new teacher."

"I'm sure it's just a misunderstanding. We'll get it cleared up soon. Have a good evening." The director returned to her meeting, leaving Dakota exasperated as hell.

As he buckled Sammy in, he told her how proud he was that she knew never to leave with anyone besides him or Mrs. Morris.

"Can Provi pick me up?"

"No." Dakota started the engine. "She's not on the list. Only Mrs. Morris and Daddy can pick you up. Do you understand?"

"Uh-huh," Sammy said, as Dakota pulled onto the street. "We had a girl party sleepover. It was so fun! There was a spider and Provi didn't kill it. She set it free. She told me the spider is sooo tiny and I'm so big. Provi helped me be brave."

He glanced at her in the rearview mirror. "I'm proud of you, Samantha."

"Is she your girlfriend?"

"How do you know about girlfriends?"

"Because Noah asked me. I said no."

"How come?"

"He spits. I don't like that."

"I agree. You can do better than a spitter." He paused. "What do *you* think of Providence?"

"She's nice. She plays with me. She showed me the poop pose."

Dakota laughed. "She *is* nice. I'm glad you like her. I like her, too."

He pulled up her favorite sing-a-long tune. He liked Providence so much so that he'd invited her to move in before he'd thought how that would affect his daughter. *I need to slow things down. Way the hell down.*

But he wasn't going to. Providence was his second chance at love. A real love that had the potential to last a lifetime.

After parking in the garage, he and Sammy went inside and washed their hands in the bathroom. "Mrs. Morris has trained us well, hasn't she?" Dakota asked.

"She says 'cooties can't hurt us if we wash them down the drain.'" Sammy dried her hands and scurried out.

As he was drying his hands, his phone rang. "Dakota Luck."

"Mr. Luck, this is Detective Beeker. I'm handling the Hastings case. Would you be able to drop by the station this afternoon?"

Dammit.

"And if I can't?" Dakota asked.

"I can pay you a visit."

"Let me touch base with my attorney. Is this your cell number?"

"Sure is."

"I'll text you back." Dakota hung up and called Warren, who said he would meet him there.

His chest tightened. *I'm going to get arrested for a crime I didn't commit. The damn irony of life.*

He found Providence in the office, and paused to appreciate her. She was so focused on whatever she was working on, she didn't see him.

"Hey."

She looked up and smiled. Even in the midst of this shit storm, his aggravation dissipated, simply because she had smiled at him. "I didn't hear you come home."

Sammy flew in, gripping the construction paper from preschool.

Providence smiled at the tyke. "Hi, Sammy. How was school today?"

"Sooo fun! My teacher said we can get our way if we do nice things for others."

Providence's eyebrows jutted up as the two adults exchanged glances.

"Samantha, you do something nice for someone because you like that person or because you want to make them happy," Dakota explained.

"Okay, Daddy."

"I'm liking this new instructor less and less," he grumbled.

"Sammy, did you tell your daddy about the spider during bath time, and how brave you were?" Providence asked.

"Uh-huh. I made you a present." She set the piece of paper on the desk. "That's us."

Providence admired the picture. "It's beautiful."

"This is me and that's Daddy. He's the biggest."

Providence chuckled. "Drawn to scale."

Dakota appreciated that, despite everything going on, Providence spent time with his child.

"That's Mrs. Morris and that's you. You can be a part of our family, too."

"This is *the* best present. I love it. I can look at this every single day and be reminded of how lucky I am to know you. Thank you."

Sammy threw her arms around Providence. As Providence hugged her, Dakota swallowed against the unexpected lump in his throat. He wasn't the only one falling for this amazing woman.

"I'm going to have a snack." Sammy skipped out of the room.

"Wow, you have one special child." As Providence stood, she swiped a tear.

Dakota pulled her in for a hug. "You are so good to her."

Providence cleared her throat. "She's easy to adore."

"Detective Beeker called me in for questioning," Dakota said. "Warren's meeting me there." Dakota texted the detective to let him know he could expect him and his attorney.

"I'm one step ahead of you," Providence said. "I heard from Beeker while you were gone and Warren is meeting me at the station, as well."

"They're going to pit us against each other."

"Their strategy will fail. I'm going to change into a suit." Providence left his office.

Dakota found Miranda and Sammy in the kitchen. "Providence and I have to go out for a few hours." He slid his gaze to Miranda. "Can I have a word?"

Miranda followed him into the foyer.

"We're headed to the police station for questioning."

"I'm sorry they're putting you both through this, Dakota."

"If they arrest me and you don't want to take care of Sammy—"

Miranda held up her hand. "Don't even go there. I've got this. And you are *not* going to jail." With that, she offered a sweet smile as Sammy skipped into the room.

Dakota picked her up and kissed her cheek. If he got arrested for the murder of Matt and was convicted, karma would be showing him who's really boss. The thought of losing his daughter made his head hurt.

Providence caught his eye as she walked toward them. She'd put on a little makeup and changed into a black pants suit and crisp white shirt. Besides looking hot as hell, she looked more prosecutor than suspect.

"You look pretty," Sammy exclaimed.

Her smile made Dakota's pulse pick up speed.

Providence stroked the child's hair. "Thank you, Sammy."

He kissed his daughter and set her down. As she walked away, his guts roiled. Losing her would kill him.

Thirty minutes later, Dakota and Providence were waiting at the police station when Warren arrived.

"How are you guys holding up?" Warren asked.

"Never better," Dakota replied, his tone filled with sarcasm.

Detective Beeker appeared. "Mr. Luck, Ms. Reynolds. I'm Aaron Beeker."

Dakota introduced their attorney.

"Mr. Luck, why don't you and I chat first," Beeker said. "Come on back."

Dakota held eye contact with Providence before he and Warren followed the detective into an interrogation room.

A female officer walked in, introduced herself, and eased down beside Beeker.

"Mr. Luck, you're a well-respected businessman in the community and have been for fifteen years," Beeker began.

That wasn't a question, so Dakota offered nothing. Not even a fucking nod.

"We're gonna get right to the point. The rope used to bind Mr. Hastings came from The Dungeon. You're one of the owners, correct?"

Leaning back in the hard chair, Dakota glanced at Warren.

"Mr. Luck provided fifty percent of the funding to open the business," Warren replied. "But he's not an owner and not involved in the day-to-day or long-term operation of the business."

"Do you have access to rope at the club?"

"If I were to use one of the private suites that supplied rope, yes, but I don't."

"Do you own a sailboat?"

"No."

"Do you ever go sailing?"

"No."

The officer opened her laptop and showed them the video of Matt after the banquet. They watched the masked couple approach the bar and talk with him. "Is this you and Ms. Reynolds?"

"No."

"This was your awards event," said Beeker. "Who are these people?"

"I don't know. I can't see their faces."

"So, it's possible it's you."

"Why would my client pretend to be someone else?" Warren asked. "That makes no sense."

"The two men had just gotten into a public altercation. Mr. Luck was humiliated in front of his professional community. Clearly, he has a short fuse because he put Mr. Hastings in a choke hold, then body slammed him."

"Mr. Hastings assaulted my client," Warren said. "Mr. Luck was defending himself."

The officer fast-forwarded to Matt exiting the hotel with the masked woman. "This woman was the last person to see Mr. Hastings alive. You and Ms. Reynolds claim to have been at The Dungeon all night long." Beeker snickered. "Come on, Mr. Luck, that's the weakest alibi I've ever heard. The surveillance system is turned off in the club, and there's a back door that conveniently doesn't have a security camera. Why don't you make this easy on yourself and confess?"

"My client is innocent," Warren said. "What *actual* evidence do you have that makes him your primary suspect?"

Beeker ignored the question and continued staring at Dakota. The evidence wasn't enough to charge him with murder. But his nightmare was far from over.

While she waited, Providence's dad texted her. "Mom's blood work results came back normal. Doc putting her on meds for Lyme and anemia."

"Glad to hear blood work is normal. I'll stop by over the weekend."

Providence was convinced her mom did not have Lyme disease. She wanted to help her parents, but she had no idea how. Stress had her massaging her aching shoulders.

Dakota and Warren came walking down the hallway. Though Dakota carried himself with an over-abundance of confidence, and looked like he didn't have a care in the world, agitation shadowed his eyes.

She was frustrated as hell over the slow progress she was making on their case. If she could ID the boat owners or find the couple Matt had left the banquet with, the police would be questioning them.

"How'd it go?" she asked.

"They're going to show you the same videos you showed me," he murmured.

She slid her gaze to Warren. "I'm glad you're here."

Despite his warm smile, her stomach was a bundle of nerves.

"Come on back, Ms. Reynolds," Detective Beeker said.

They entered the interrogation room. After introducing the female officer, he gestured for her to sit.

"I want to make this easy on you, Ms. Reynolds. I believe you're an innocent pawn in Mr. Luck's scheme."

She pursed her lips. Never before had she been on the receiving end of an interrogation. It sucked.

"Landing a wealthy, successful man like Dakota Luck is probably not a bad thing," Beeker continued.

Are you kidding me? Providence wanted to roll her eyes, then walk.

"I know that going against his alibi won't buy you any points with him. Look, while we'd be impressed if you two pulled an all-nighter at the club, we're not buying it. No one is that virile."

No one you know, maybe. She continued staring at him.

"Did you supply Mr. Luck with the rope used to bind Mr. Hastings?"

"No."

"But you had access to the rope."

She didn't respond. It wasn't a question.

"Do you have access to hemp rope at The Dungeon?"

"Yes."

"Are you familiar with bondage?"

"No."

"But you work in a kink club."

She refused to respond.

"Did you attend the real estate awards banquet?"

"No." *But Elaine Jones did.*

The officer played the video of the masked couple with Matt at the convention center bar.

"Isn't that you with Mr. Luck?" Beeker asked.

"No, it's not."

"Do you go sailing?"

"No."

The officer pulled up the video of the sailboat in front of the Sequoia restaurant the night of Matt Hastings's death.

"But your dad owns a sailboat, doesn't he?" Beeker asked.

Oh, crap. "He does."

"And you've sailed with your family, haven't you?"

"On occasion."

"Can you sail, Ms. Reynolds?"

"Please be more specific." She refused to regurgitate information freely.

"Can you operate a sailboat? Can you tie a boat to a pier?"

Adrenaline spiked through her. "Yes."

"Mr. Hastings's wrists and ankles were tied using bowline knots—a sailing knot." His insincere smile sent a shiver through her. "You work in a kink club, but you aren't familiar with bondage knots. First, you tell us you don't sail. Then, you admit you can operate a sailboat and tie a basic boating knot." He paused. "It can't be both, so which one is it, Ms. Reynolds?"

A trickle of sweat rolled down her back. He had done his homework. She knew exactly where he was headed with this line of questioning, and she swallowed down the bitter bile. "So, what? Lots of people can tie a bowline."

"Have you ever taken your dad's boat out without him?"

"No."

"But you have access to it, don't you?"

"I know where it's docked, but I don't have the keys."

"Again, I'm guessing you have access to the keys."

His comment was met with chilly silence.

"Ms. Reynolds, if you admit that Mr. Luck offered you money or bribed you with a relationship in exchange for assisting him in the murder of Mr. Hastings, you'll be doing the right thing."

Narrowing her gaze, she glared at him.

"My client did not have anything to do with the disappearance or the murder of Mr. Hastings," Warren said.

"We are trying to *help* you," Beeker said. "Mr. Luck will throw you under the bus if given the opportunity."

Wrong again.

"If you have no further questions for my client, we're done." Warren snapped his tablet shut.

She was innocent, but Detective Beeker had done a damn good job painting a very different picture.

Providence, Dakota, and Warren said nothing as they left the station.

In the parking lot, Warren said, "You did well in there. They're looking pretty hard at both of you, but they don't have enough evidence to make an arrest."

"When my late wife was abducted, the police grilled the hell out of me." Dakota slipped on his sunglasses. "I wasn't worried then, and I'm not now."

"I'm glad to hear you're keeping it together," Warren said. "I got word the M.E.'s findings will be out in the next few days. We'll talk once we see Mr. Hastings's tox report. Try to relax. I'll be in touch."

"Thanks for being here," Providence said.

After shaking their hands, Warren headed toward his car. On the ride home, Providence didn't say anything for most of the way.

"You're quiet," Dakota said as he turned into his neighborhood.

"My dad owns a sailboat."

"So?"

"Beeker asked me if I could sail. The knots used on Matt were bowline knots, not BDSM knots."

He clasped her hand. "We're innocent."

"They don't think so."

When he pulled into his garage, she told him she was heading straight to the club. "I've gotta work tonight."

"No worries. We've got this."

She appreciated his nerves of steel and his unwavering confidence. She felt like the walls were closing in, and it was just a matter of time before he—or *they*—got arrested.

22

ONE PERFECT DAY

Saturday morning, Dakota woke determined to have a normal day with his family. Not a family in the conventional sense. Hell, he hadn't even told Providence he loved her.

But all that was about to change.

Two dozen long-stemmed red roses waited in a crystal vase in the center of the kitchen table, breakfast was cooking, and he'd stashed the gift in a drawer. All he needed were his two girls so they could start their day.

Sammy plodded in first. He'd asked for her help putting together his surprise for Providence. Typically, his young daughter was the recipient of gifts, and he looked forward to seeing how she'd fair as the giver.

It took his little chatterbox some time before her energy kicked in, so he appreciated the silence as she climbed into her booster seat.

Dakota sat beside her and tucked her mussed hair behind her ear. "Sleep okay?"

"Uh-huh." She rubbed her sleepy eyes. "Are we giving Provi her present today?"

Dakota smiled. *That's a good sign.* "I think we should," he whispered. "What do you think?"

"Yes, right away."

He filled her sippy cup with juice, then added water to cut the sugar. As she sipped away, he dropped blueberries into the oatmeal.

A few moments later, Providence walked into the kitchen looking just as sleepy. When she'd gotten home from the club, she'd gone straight to her bedroom. He assumed it was because she didn't want to slink out a few hours later, but he missed having her by his side.

"Good morning," he said.

"Good morning, you two," Providence replied.

Sammy giggled when Providence beelined to the coffee pot without noticing the flowers.

As she poured herself a cup, Dakota put his arm around her and kissed the top of her head. "How was work?"

"Fine," she replied, then sipped the drink. "I met Mavis. She's a hoot. I think she's got more energy than Sammy."

"Provi, come sit with me."

"Be right there, cutie pie."

Before walking over, Providence said, "Stryker only needs me at the club once a week for another week or two."

"That's good," Dakota replied.

As she sat next to Sammy, she smiled at the child. "Hello, adorable one. What's going on with you?"

"We got you a present!" Sammy pointed to the flowers. "Look!"

"Oh, my! Those are beautiful," Providence said. "Those are for me?"

"Daddy wrote you a card. Open it."

Providence plucked out the small envelope and slid out the card.

Love eternal, Dakota

"Wow." Providence's smile told him everything he needed to know. She pushed out of the chair and dropped a light kiss on his lips. "Thank you. They're gorgeous."

"Like the note?" he asked.

"I love the note. *Love* it."

"What does it say?" Sammy asked. "Can I read it?"

Providence sat beside Sammy and showed her the card. "Love et...etra...etnal." Sammy furrowed her brow. "I can't know this word."

Dakota took his seat at the head of the table. "Eternal."

"What's that?"

"It means forever."

Dakota clasped Providence's hand and gave it a little squeeze. "Can we give Provi her present now?"

Providence's eyes grew wide. "There's more?"

Dakota retrieved the small box from the kitchen drawer and set it in front of Providence.

"For me?" Providence glanced from Dakota to Sammy. "Why am I getting a present?"

Sammy shrugged. "We like you!"

Providence smiled at Sammy. "I like you guys, too." She shifted her gaze to Dakota. "So much."

"Open it," Dakota said.

Providence put her arm around Sammy and gave her a little squeeze before she opened the box.

"It's *beautiful*." Two intertwined diamond hearts dangled from a white gold necklace. "Thank you, both. This is a very special gift."

"Daddy and I went to a store and I picked it out. Daddy told the lady that he wanted a very special necklace for a very special person."

Providence's gaze locked with Dakota's. "This was so thoughtful of you." She clasped the jewelry around her neck. "It's stunning."

After Providence hugged Sammy, she said, "You can hug Daddy, too."

"That's a good idea." Providence rose. "I think I will."

"Thank you so much," she murmured, wrapping her arms around him. Dakota dropped a soft kiss on her lips and Sammy giggled.

"Ew, kissing. That's yucky."

Laughing, Providence broke away. "Who wants eggs to go with that oatmeal I see cooking on the stove?"

"I don't like oatmeal," Sammy said. "I want my cereal."

"Samantha, oatmeal is good for you," Dakota said, using his serious tone.

As Providence got out the eggs, she asked Sammy what she wanted to do for a job when she was older.

"I want to be a race car driver."

"Whoa, that's so cool," Providence said. "You know, you have to be in great shape to do that. Oatmeal is a very healthy food."

It took a little convincing, but Providence got Sammy to eat her oatmeal.

"I should get dressed, then I've got to work on our case," Providence said after breakfast.

"Not today," Dakota replied. "Today, we're spending the entire day playing, right, Sammy?"

"Yay!"

"Dakota, I feel like I'm one step behind Detective Beeker. I need to—"

"You need to spend the day with us."

Sammy hurried out of the room.

"Where are you going?" Dakota asked.

"To get dressed for our day."

"Your day starts with karate."

Spinning around, she scowled at him. "I don't want—"

"Karate?" Providence asked. "I would *love* to watch you in class. Can I come with you?"

Still scowling, Sammy stared at her.

"I'm so impressed that you study martial arts," Providence said. "That's the coolest thing ever."

The frustration in Sammy's eyes faded and she bolted from the room.

"Headed upstairs to put your gi on?" Dakota called.

"Yes," Sammy replied as she raced up the stairs.

Dakota drew Providence into his arms and kissed her. Holding her close, he peered into her eyes. She was his missing piece, the woman who would complete his family. "I've been drowning for so long, I'd forgotten what it feels like to breathe."

"I feel like I'm failing you, but you went out of your way to buy me flowers and a beautiful necklace." She caressed his cheeks. "I don't deserve this."

"That's where you're wrong. You do. You definitely do. We both adore you, Providence."

Her joyous expression touched his soul.

"I love you," she said, with conviction. "I love you both."

"I love *you*...so damn much." Dakota kissed her and she clutched him so hard, he felt like she would never, ever let him go. Hope took root. Could this amazing woman be his forever?

"I explained to Sammy that you mean a lot to me," Dakota said. "I'm not sure how much of this she's grasping, but I trust you. I trust you completely."

Providence's eyes misted. "That means more to me than any present you could ever buy me." Then, she shot him a little smile. "But that doesn't mean I'm giving you back the necklace."

After karate class, Providence took Sammy into a changing room and helped her out of her gi and into her pants and shirt. In the car, Dakota said, "I've got a surprise for you two."

"What is it?" Sammy asked.

"Samantha, you want to be a race car driver, and Providence, you said you would love to take lessons at Summit Point, so we're going to Summit Point Motorsports Park in West Virginia to watch a few races today."

Sammy clapped her hands. "Does Provi get to race?"

Providence laughed. "Not today. I need to learn how, first. And the best way to start is by watching someone else. This sounds fun, doesn't it?"

"Super fun!"

During the hour-long trip to Summit Point, Sammy conked out. Providence started talking shop, but Dakota wrapped his hand around her thigh and gave her a little squeeze. "We get one day off. Just one. Talk to me about your childhood or about some of the cases you worked. Tell me about you, baby."

She leaned over, kissed his whiskered cheek. "I love that you care about me." She told him a funny story from childhood that involved Stryker, and the police coming to their house. Dakota laughed at the mayhem Stryker caused. Then, she confided about the last case she worked with the Bureau, finishing with, "I love that I can share my career with you."

"I love sharing mine with you, too," he replied.

When they arrived, Dakota pulled ear protection from the back seat. Before entering the park, he covered Sammy's ears. From the stands, they watched a few races, grabbed lunch, and inquired about driving lessons.

As far as Dakota was concerned, their day had been a rousing success. What he hadn't told Providence was that Marcus had been trailing them the entire afternoon. Dakota might be taking a break from reality, but he wasn't living in a fantasy land.

That evening, after dinner, Sammy asked if they could watch a movie together.

"Great idea," Dakota said. "Providence, movie night?"

Providence retrieved a gift bag from the front closet, and sat on the family room sofa beside Dakota. "I think Sammy might want to see what I bought her *before* we pick a movie."

Sammy had been busy lining up her race cars. When she

spotted the brightly colored bag, her eyes lit up. "You bought me a present?"

"Crazy, huh, because you guys bought me a present," Providence replied.

Sammy climbed onto the sofa and Providence set the bag between them.

With a smile, Sammy lifted out the tissue paper and pulled out a movie. "I know this movie! It's *Finding Nemo!*" Then, she pulled out another movie. "*Toy Story!* Hurray!"

Next came *Ratatouille* and Sammy stared at the cover. "What's this word?"

Providence held her finger over the title and sounded it out for her, then read her the back jacket.

Sammy giggled. "This one's funny."

Dakota watched the two of them interact. Providence was so attentive toward his daughter and Sammy hung on her every word. He would never have been able to get Sammy to eat her oatmeal. And this morning, the transition to karate class was seamless because of Providence.

Would Providence make a good mother for his daughter? Would she be a strong female role model, helping to teach his child about life? And was she the right life partner for him? His gut said yes.

Sammy extracted *Moana*. "I don't know this movie. Can you read it to me?"

First, she helped Sammy read it. Then, she read it to her. And finally, Sammy pulled out *Mulan*.

"I love all these movies!" Sammy exclaimed. "What can we watch tonight?"

"What do you say to Providence, Samantha?" Dakota asked.

Sammy hugged her. "Thank you for my presents." After much deliberation, Sammy selected Providence's favorite. *Mulan*.

Then, Sammy's expression fell. "Daddy didn't get a present."

Dakota pulled her onto his lap and tickled her. "My present was spending the day with you two. That makes me very happy."

That evening, they sat on the sofa, Sammy between them. And when *Mulan* ended, a very tired Sammy asked Providence if she would come upstairs with Dakota and tuck her into bed.

Somehow, Dakota had managed to eke out one perfect day. But he knew the universe had a way of balancing things out, and he expected a full-blown shit storm was headed his way.

After tucking Sammy into bed, Dakota asked, "How 'bout a nightcap?"

They entered the kitchen and Providence slid onto a barstool at the island. "What's the bartender serving, tonight?"

His devilish smile was filled with promise. "Me."

"I'm definitely interested in a nip of that."

Dakota looked super-hot in worn jeans and a Harvard T-shirt, his bare feet a reminder that he was chilling at home. *So damn sexy.*

He was the epitome of sex appeal, of power, of everything Providence craved in a man. A heady combination of brains and brawn. A vigilante who adored his child. A respected businessman who led a violent double life. This was the kind of man she hunted. Yet, as she stared into his piercing eyes, her heart confirmed his place in her life.

This was her person. And this was her forever family. Of that she was certain.

The physical pull to go to him was like a drug she had to have. She was vulnerable to falling into an abyss that was everything Dakota. A black hole that could swallow her. Was this what she wanted?

It was.

Despite everything they faced, today had been a new

beginning. Both freeing and exhilarating. But Providence wasn't lulled into a false sense of security.

He extracted a few bottles from the top cupboard and set them on the island. "For the lovely lady, I've got brandy—always a favorite—and amaretto. Then, there's the licorice-flavored Sambuca. Or I can make you a Kahlua on the rocks. Name your poison, my love."

She loved this playful, light-hearted Dakota. A rare glimpse of him relaxing. She could get pretty damn used to him like this.

"Hmm, so many good options." Pausing, she surveyed the bottles before shifting her attention back to him. "I choose...you."

"I love the sound of that."

As he shelved the bottles, she said, "You're not having a drink?"

"I don't need a drink." He rounded the island and laid his arms over her shoulders. "I need you, babe. Just you." His kiss sent sparks of energy streaming through her.

"I saw Marcus at the sports park this afternoon," she said. "Thank you for having our backs."

"I want my girls safe." His intoxicating kiss had her pushing to her feet. "Time for bed."

The grittiness of his voice would be her undoing. He threaded his fingers between hers. In silence, they walked up the stairs and down the hall to his bedroom. Once behind the locked door, she cupped his face in her hands. The intensity in his eyes set her heart on fire. As if everything were right in their world, he married his lips to hers and kissed her. Soft and gentle, yet filled with a passion that brought emotion welling to the surface.

"Thank you for a perfect day," she murmured. "Thank you for my gifts...for introducing your wonderful daughter to me. Thank you for insisting I live with you." She shot him a playful smile. "I'm like that stray cat you feed. I'm never going to leave."

His expression changed. It was subtle, but she caught the quick flash of pain in his eyes. "I wouldn't want you to," he whispered.

When his mouth found hers, the ferocity in his embrace made

her whimper. It built and built until she was panting and clutching him, kneading his glorious back with her fingers. Desperate to touch him, she slid her hands under his shirt and stroked his heated skin.

Breaking free, she started removing her jacket, but he stopped her. "That's my job."

He took his time peeling her out of her clothing. Off came her jacket, then her shirt, and finally, her jeans. Jolts of pleasure radiated through her every time he pressed his lips to her bare skin. Shaking in anticipation, she waited for him in her black push-up bra and matching thong, ravenous to take him inside her. Impatient to become one with her man.

"You do it for me in *all* the ways." His undeniable look of love took her breath away.

"My turn." She removed his shirt and pants. He'd forgone underwear, his cock ready for her.

Nudging him back, she pushed him onto the edge of the bed. With her nipples hard and aching, she leaned close. No instruction needed.

He took one into his mouth and searing heat raced through her. She watched him lick and suck her sensitive flesh. His raw groans made her moan. She couldn't stop running her hands over his shoulders and through his hair. When he gazed up at her, she trembled.

"Kiss me," he commanded.

"Make me."

In seconds, she was on her back, the mattress beneath her, a devilish grin on his face as he looked down at her. "You are so damn beautiful. And you're all mine." His radiance was as blinding as the sun. "I'm not *falling* in love anymore. I'm *immersed* in it."

God, he was slaying her with his words.

She nudged him away and pulled a condom from his drawer. He rolled it on, positioned himself over her, but he didn't press inside. His kiss was a dizzying mix of lust and love. Wrapping her fingers around his shaft, she lifted her hips so that the tip slipped inside her. He thrust the rest of the way.

"Oh, God," she murmured while the unrelenting pleasure swept through her.

He tightened his grip, protecting her in his strong embrace as he began moving inside her, but his eyes never strayed from hers. Every thrust set off an explosion of pleasure taking her higher and higher.

"I love you," he murmured, "so fucking much."

"I love you, too," she replied.

"You deserve happiness, Providence. Forgive yourself."

With shaking fingers, she clung to him, tears welling in her eyes.

His kiss was greedy, his thrusting slow and powerful. "You feel so damn good, I can't hold on," he murmured.

"Let go."

She loved the sexy sounds he made as he came inside her. But most of all, she loved that his gaze never left hers. In that moment, their connection felt like it could last a lifetime.

23

MORE SECRETS, NEW TRUTHS

Monday morning, they were working in his office when Stryker called. Dakota put him on speaker. "Tell me something good."

"I was able to ID the bank of the SOB who stole Providence's money."

"You're brilliant," Providence said.

"The money was wired to an offshore bank called The Bank of the Princes, the same bank that was in Dakota's blackmail letter."

"Whoa," Providence blurted.

"Their bank's firewalls are impressive, but I've got a few more tricks I can use to find the account owner."

When the call ended, Providence pushed out of the chair and paced. "Is it possible that we're both being targeted by the same person?"

"Why would he go after you?"

"I know you, for starters."

Dakota's phone rang. It was Warren Hott. "Hey, Warren, any news?"

"I've got a copy of the medical examiner's report. Is Providence with you?"

"I'm right here," she replied.

"The rope used to bind Mr. Hastings is the same kind used at The Dungeon, but it doesn't mean they got it from there. The report confirms what Beeker told us. Bowline knots were used on Mr. Hastings."

"The evidence is building against us," Dakota said.

"Maybe the rope was stolen from the club," Providence said.

"Mr. Hastings's blood alcohol level was 0.15%, but that's not what killed him," Warren continued. "He had so much liquid nicotine in his blood, he was already dead before he hit the water."

"Liquid nicotine?" Providence Googled it. "Could he have been partying with the people he left with? He died, they freaked, and they dropped him in the river?"

"Possibly," Warren replied. "But liquid nicotine is dangerous, especially if someone doesn't know how to use it. Even so, why bind his wrists and ankles?"

"Oh, Christ," Dakota bit out.

"What's wrong?" Providence asked.

"A few weeks ago, I received a vaping kit gift basket with liquid nicotine at work."

"Do you vape?" Warren asked.

"No. And there was no card. I've gotten dozens of client gifts over the years, but there was always a card. The receptionist said it was delivered by courier. No signature required."

"Dakota, where's that kit?" Warren asked.

"In my office."

Silence.

"Should I get it out of there?" Dakota asked.

"It's incriminating, though it's arguable that the person framing you for Mr. Hastings's murder is planting evidence. Here's my concern. If you've got employees who saw the gift and it goes missing, that only makes you look guiltier."

"This isn't going well," Providence said.

"I'm sorry, guys," Warren said. "I wish I had better news."

"Thanks for the update." Dakota hung up. "The evidence is mounting against me...against us."

Ding-dong.

Dakota pulled up the surveillance cam out front and bit out a grunt. *Fuck. Fuck me.* "It's Beeker. He's got cops with him." He tapped the secret button on the bookshelf, the shelf slid back, and he opened the safe.

Providence shoved their ALPHA laptops in there, along with their cell phones, and her handbag. Dakota closed the safe and the shelf slid back into place.

"We've got this," he said.

She nodded. "Yes, we do."

He appreciated her confidence, the strength in her voice, and the determination in her actions.

Together, they answered the door. Detective Beeker stood there holding a piece of paper. "Search warrant."

They stepped out of the way. "I've got warrants for both your residences and your office, Mr. Luck." He nodded to Providence. "Ms. Reynolds, do you live here?"

"Temporarily."

"How cozy."

Neither of them responded to his snide remark, but Dakota wanted to deck him, then kick him the hell out.

Dakota and Providence waited at the kitchen island while four officers went through every room. Only their personal laptops were seized, but that didn't stop the officers from sifting through every drawer, every cabinet, and every single closet.

"I need you to unlock the door to the basement," Beeker said.

"That's Miranda Morris's private residence. She's my daughter's nanny. She has a lease, so legally, it's a private apartment and not subject to your search warrant."

Beeker huffed out a breath. "We'll need your cell phones."

"I misplaced mine," Dakota replied.

"Sorry," Providence said. "Mine went missing yesterday when we were at Summit Point."

"You two may think you're being crafty, but you're raising yet another red flag."

Three hours later, when Beeker and his team left, Providence and Dakota surveyed the mess.

"It looks like a cyclone ripped through here," she said. "Let's put everything back before Sammy gets home."

Despite the fury coursing through him, he drew her close and kissed her. "Your life has been turned upside down because of me, and the first thing you want to do is protect my daughter. You are an amazing, loving woman. Thank you for putting Sammy first."

She kissed him back, then broke away to get started. Once they put the kitchen back in order, Dakota retrieved their cell phones from the safe, and called Sin.

"The police showed up with a warrant. If I'm arrested and they don't set bond, can you take Sammy?"

"Whatever you need," Sin replied. "I hate that I can't fix this for you."

Juanita called to tell Dakota that the police had shown up with a warrant and were combing through his office. "They took some gift basket. I tried stopping them, but they said it was important to the case."

The vaping kit. Dakota wanted to punch his fist through a fucking wall.

As they were finishing up, Miranda came home.

"The place looks great," Miranda said after they explained what had happened. "I'm sorry you're both being put through this."

"If I'm arrested, you know what to do," Dakota said.

"Call Sin first, then Maverick," Miranda replied. "I can keep Sammy here, but I'll do whatever you think is best."

"I want to keep her safe and shield her from everything that's happening." He raked his fingers down his beard. "At this point, that's impossible."

Providence's phone rang. She excused herself from the room and answered. "Hi, Mom."

"Hello, dear. I know you've been worried about me. I wanted you to know I'm feeling better."

"That's great! I'm so relieved to hear that."

"Dad and I took a walk around the block. I've been so out of it, it felt wonderful to get outside. He told me your bank account was hacked. What can we do to help?"

Providence smiled. This was the mom she knew. The active, energetic spirit who was on top of things and always there for her family. She had to see her mom for herself. "I'll swing by in a bit."

"Can't wait, honey. See you soon."

Returning to the kitchen, Providence told Dakota about her mom. "I'm going over there now to spend some time with her and my dad. How 'bout I grab us something for dinner on my way home?" *Home. This feels like home.*

Dakota's smile said it all. Somehow, in the midst of everything going wrong, that one word had made things better. "Sounds great, babe."

At the front door, he draped his arms over her shoulders. "You," he kissed her, "are the bright spot in all this darkness."

She kissed him back. "It goes both ways. I'm sorry to bolt. I should be working to ensure we don't get arrested."

"I'll put the squeeze on the lab tech at ALPHA," Dakota said. "We're outa time and need to know who's in that photo."

"I'll be back soon." One more kiss and she was gone.

When she got to her parents' house, she found them sitting on the screened porch sofa, holding hands. Her mom looked better than she had in weeks, but her dad's nonstop smile reminded Providence how much he adored her mom.

Her mom rose and hugged her.

"You both look fantastic," Providence said, easing into the cushioned chair.

"How'd I get lumped into this?" her dad asked.

"You weren't looking so hot yourself." Providence flipped him a playful smile.

Her mom sat back down and patted Gordon's thigh. "As always, your dad was my rock."

"Where are Randy and Lizzie?" Providence asked, relieved they weren't underfoot.

"They extended their weekend," her dad explained. "They were having so much fun sailing, they said they'd be home later tonight."

"Are you going to ask them to move out?" Providence asked.

"I'd like to," her dad replied.

"I think it's time," her mom agreed. "Dad and I are bringing up the subject tonight. We're giving them a couple of weeks to find something."

"He claims he's a realtor, so that should be easy," Providence said.

"We aren't sure he's actually working," her dad said. "The realtors we know put in long hours."

"And they're always on the phone or email with clients," her mom added. "Plus, they drive them around and show them homes. Randy is here a lot."

Providence tucked her hair behind her ear. "I don't think he's a realtor, either." She hoped they'd go through with their decision to kick him and Lizzie out. Both her folks seemed more relaxed with them gone.

"What's the deal with your will, Mom?" Providence asked. "I saw it on the kitchen table a while ago."

"Randy asked to see it."

"And?"

"I explained to him that I've left everything to Dad. If he passes first, you three each get one third of the estate. And that I made you the executrix."

"What did he think of that?"

"He told me he should be the executor, since he's the oldest."

A chill slithered down her spine. *He wants control of Mom's estate.*

"But I'm not dying, so enough of that," her mom said. "How are you doing, dear?"

I've fallen in love with an assassin who has a child Annabel's age... and I'm being investigated for murder.

"Before I answer that, I'm going to grab an iced tea. Any takers?"

Her parents declined.

As Providence headed into the kitchen, she spied a pile of magazines and a pair of scissors in the corner.

She opened a bottle of iced tea, poured herself a glass, and returned to the porch. "I thought the old magazines went to the dump weeks ago."

"Lizzie is working on a preschool project," her dad explained. "So, she kept some."

"Providence, what's been going on with you?" her mom asked.

While she wanted to tell her folks about Dakota and Sammy, she decided to wait. Her mom was improved, but not recovered. "I've got a new marketing client that's been keeping me busy, and I stepped in to help Stryker at his club, but that gig is winding down."

"You work so much, honey. What happened to getting out and socializing?"

"Thank you, Dr. Sharpe."

Her mom's lyrical laughter made her smile. Redirecting the conversation back to her mom's health, they chatted for a few more minutes.

"I love you both." Providence hugged her dad, then her mom. "Stay healthy."

On her way out, Providence pulled a magazine from the pile and flipped through it. All the pictures were intact, but some of the words had been snipped out. The blackmail letter and the letter sent to the news stations popped into her head. The hairs on the back of her neck prickled. *Could Lizzie have sent those letters? That's ridiculous. There's no way.*

She checked a second magazine and found the same thing. Words were missing, but the pictures remained intact. That made no sense. If she were working with preschoolers, she would cut out the pictures, not the words.

After taking one of the magazines, she left, stopping on the way home for carry-out. When she returned home with dinner, Sammy ran to the door to greet her.

"There she is!" Providence exclaimed. This tiny tot had stolen her heart, along with the man close on her heels. She had fallen hard for them both.

Later that evening, after Dakota had tucked Sammy into bed, he joined Providence in his office. She'd been combing through the database for the owner of the sailboat.

"Hey." He rubbed her shoulders. "For a woman who looks completely chill, you're pretty tight."

"Mmm, that feels incredible." After a moment, he kissed the top of her head, then pulled his chair around to sit beside her. "Make any headway?"

"I've narrowed it down to seventy-one sailboats."

"That's progress."

She tossed the magazine on her desk and flipped it open. "I found a pile of these at my parents'. According to my dad, my sister-in-law is doing some project for work." Providence continued turning pages.

"So?"

"She hasn't cut out any of the pictures. She's only cutting out words."

Dakota cocked an eyebrow. "And?"

"She's an early childhood educator and little kids can't read."

"Maybe she's teaching them."

After a beat, her shoulders slumped. "I'm losing it. I'm looking for clues where there aren't any."

"Why do you think your sister-in-law would target me? I haven't even met her."

She sighed. "I have no idea."

"I give you props for staying vigilant." He dragged his laptop over and logged in. "I called the lab at ALPHA and waited on the phone until they sent me the enlarged photo of the men in tactical gear."

"Please have good news."

"You were right. I'm not in the picture."

They stared at the enlarged photo. "Can you ID any of these men?"

He pointed to one of the men in the front. "This might be Luther. I forwarded it to him and texted him to call me ASAP."

It was after eleven when Luther video chatted them.

"This photo was taken before you became an operative, Dakota," Luther began. "I'm in the front row on the right." He hesitated for a beat. "Your dad is next to me."

What the fuck?

Dakota stared at the photo. "What are you talking about? My dad was a civil engineer."

The silence was deafening.

"I'll give you two a minute," Providence murmured.

"Stay," Dakota bit out.

Luther's heavy sigh set the tone. "That was his cover, Dakota.

Your dad and I went through Quantico together. Then, we were undercover with the FBI. Years later, we both worked as ALPHA operatives. Your dad ran the group for over five years."

What the hell? Muscles running the length of his shoulders turned to lead. "Why is this the first time I'm hearing about this?"

"Your dad couldn't tell you. As close as he and your mom were, she never knew the truth. After he was killed on a mission, I replaced him as head of the organization."

"I thought he died in a car accident."

"That was the story I was forced to tell you."

Another fucking lie. "Tell me the damn truth, Luther."

"We were on a mission and it went bad. Your dad was killed and another operative was critically wounded."

Dakota needed the pounding in his head to stop. He was struggling to wrap his brain around the words he was hearing. His dad, an ALPHA operative?

"Who are these other two men in the photo?" Providence asked.

"The one behind your dad is Brady Kilpatrick. The three of us worked well and went on a number of missions together."

"Where is he?" Providence asked.

"He retired in California near the grandkids."

"And the fourth man?" she asked.

"He's looking down and I can't tell who it is," Luther replied. "I've asked around."

Providence continued probing. "Who took the photo?"

"I'm guessing this was a training class and the instructor took it."

"Can you find out who that fourth person is?" Providence asked.

"I will," Luther said. "Dakota, I know this is a shock. Once we get past this—and I know we will—I can tell you more about what a brave man your dad was." Luther wished them a good night and hung up.

Struggling to process the truth, Dakota rasped out, "One more fucking lie to add to all the others."

"I'm sorry," she whispered. "He couldn't tell you, just like you can't tell Sammy. It's the life we've chosen. We keep the secret to protect the ones we love."

Too angry to respond, he said nothing.

"If you get arrested, you'll lie to your daughter, because you need to protect her. Our truth is complicated. You know that. So, we create lies and we live with them."

He dragged his fingers through his hair. "My parents kept my adoption from me. My birth mother was a lunatic who separated Sin and me because she could make more money by splitting us up. I thought my dad was a civil engineer. Nope, wrong again." He glared at her. "You lied to me. Are you still lying to me? Is this relationship a lie? Is your love a damn lie, too?"

"Dakota, I—No. My love is real. My love for your daughter is real, too."

He needed to burn off this hostility. "I feel like a caged animal. I can't leave my house without Marcus or someone from his team detailing me all over the damn place. Most of the time, I'm holed up here chasing an invisible fucking killer." He huffed. "I'm going to run on the treadmill."

"Don't shut me out. Let me help you through this." She grasped his hand and led him upstairs and into his bedroom.

An instant after closing his bedroom door, he hauled her against him. Their lips met in a fiery kiss and she ground against him.

Clothing, gone in seconds. He wanted to fuck her hard and fast. He wanted to forget reality and get lost in her beautiful essence, in all things Providence.

But this latest lie had nothing to do with her. She was his protector, his partner. He believed her when she told him she loved him. He could see it in her eyes, feel it in her touch. Even now, she was willing to take his anger from him.

But she was not the problem. She was the solution. Her relentless pursuit of the truth had forced Luther's hand.

"I fucking adore you so much," he rasped out. "I should be worshipping you instead of taking my anger out on you. It's because of you that I learned my dad was an operative."

"Even so, I think a good, strong fuck would do you good."

That made him smile.

"Get on the bed, Dakota. I'm going to screw your brains out."

Together, they tumbled into bed, their raw, gritty passion taking them higher and higher. When he reached for the drawer, she stopped him.

"No condom," she whispered.

"That's a big step."

"I'm on the pill, and I'm healthy."

"I always wore condoms and I'm clean, too." He kissed her shoulder, her chest, her mouth. "I love you and I want you to know that in your heart."

She stroked her necklace. "I do know that."

Moving slowly, he slid inside her. She couldn't tear her gaze from his. But not because he was a beautiful man. Because he was loving her with his entire soul.

As she loved him back, the happiness she had denied herself blossomed from the deepest part of her, the part she'd walled off from everyone.

They began moving faster, the euphoria spiraling through her. She accepted that there would always be a hole in her heart that she could never fill. A loss that would never leave her. A child that she loved, and lost, but would never, ever stop loving. No matter how many children she might be lucky enough to have, her Annabel would always be her first.

And there was nothing she could have done to save her.

As she went over the edge, tears streamed down her temples. He was there for her, comforting her and holding her while waves of pure, sweet ecstasy washed over her, shattering her into a thousand pieces.

"I love you, Providence," he murmured. "With everything I am."

Sobbing quietly, she floated back to earth, fortified by his strength and set free by his love.

24

THE POISON

Late afternoon, and club employees were filtering in to begin their shift. Providence had insisted Dakota join her, but she wouldn't tell him why. As he stared at the bundles of bondage rope in the supply closet, he flicked his gaze to her.

"What?" he asked.

"Look at all that rope," she said.

"Yup," he replied.

Her eyes shone brightly as she clasped his hand and took off toward her office. As he slid into the guest chair, she logged in to the computer. While waiting, he glanced around. A clean ashtray sat on the desk and a small stack of newspapers had accumulated in the corner. Mavis had definitely returned.

After several minutes of scrolling, she said, "I found it."

"What are you talking about?"

"Right after I started working here, one of the employees told me we were low on rope, so I ordered more. I didn't think anything of it, until this morning."

Providence spun the monitor so he could see the screen, tapped the keyboard, and the video surveillance started playing. Kirsten stopped in front of the retina scanner outside the supply closet on L1. The light turned green and she entered. Seconds later, she exited, carrying several bundles of rope. Providence worked the surveillance system so she could follow Kirsten. Instead of taking them to private suites on L3, Kirsten walked out the front door and offloaded the bundles to a man in a black hoodie and a three-quarters mask. In exchange, he handed her cash. Providence zoomed in. "He's paying her for that rope."

"No fucking way," Dakota blurted. "That's the guy from the banquet."

"It sure as hell is." She smiled at him. "That's our killer."

"I'm impressed."

"I should have figured this out weeks ago."

Knock-knock. Stryker stood in the doorway. "Hey, cuz, I got your text. What's going on?"

"Come check this out," Dakota said.

As Stryker reviewed the video, he said, "I need her to get her ass in here so I can fire her."

"Tread easy," Providence said. "We need her to tell us everything she knows about the guy she sold the rope to."

Stryker blasted off a text to his employee. "I told her to get her ass in in here the second she gets to work."

Providence's phone rang. "Hey, Dad."

"Mom is in the ER."

"*What?*"

"She had a seizure and collapsed."

Oh, God, no. "Which hospital?"

"Reston."

"I'm on my way."

"Providence, wait," her dad blurted. "I forgot my reading glasses when I rode with Mom in the ambulance. They need me to sign a bunch of forms."

"I'll grab them on the way. Did you tell Megan?"

"No, can you call her...and Randy, too?"

"Isn't he at home?"

"No, he left right before she had the seizure."

Providence got off the phone. Both men were staring at her. "What happened?" Stryker asked.

"My mom's in the ER. She had a seizure."

"Oh, hell, no," Stryker said. "You want me to come with you?"

"No, stay here and get answers from Kirsten."

"I'll drive you to the hospital," Dakota said.

As he started to get up, she said, "I'll grab an Uber to my parents' so I can pick up my dad's car for him."

"Keep me posted," Stryker said.

As the driver headed to her parents' house, Providence called her sister, but the call rolled to voicemail, so she sent a text. "Mom had seizure. In Reston hospital. Call me ASAP."

She jumped out of the car, ran up the driveway, plugged in the garage door code, and hurried inside. The house was quiet. Her dad's glasses weren't on the kitchen table or in the family room. As she bolted upstairs toward the master bedroom, she heard an alarm clock beeping. *Who sets an alarm for five in the afternoon?*

The annoying sound was coming from the guest room, where Randy and Lizzie slept. Providence knocked, then stuck her head inside. "Hello, anyone here?"

Neither Randy nor Lizzie were there, so she turned off the alarm. The night table drawer was open and several small, brightly colored, bear-shaped containers caught her eye.

Curious, she pulled one out. It was a gummy bear vial of liquid nicotine marked "extra strong". *What the hell?* She thought back to the family brunch when Lizzie had said vaping made Randy sick to his stomach. And the gift basket delivered to Dakota's office.

Her heart picked up speed. She snapped a pic of the inside of the drawer, then dropped the vial into her handbag. As she turned to leave, she glanced inside their walk-in closet. A bath towel hung on the open door and a mask dangled from the inside doorknob.

It looked like the one the man had worn at the realtor event, the same one she'd just seen in the video with Kirsten. *It can't be.*

But in her gut, she knew.

Fear hammered through her. Her mom and dad were living with cold-blooded killers.

She didn't have to look far to find the second mask. It was on the closet shelf. After snapping more pictures, she strode into her dad's home office. His reading glasses weren't there, but she rummaged through his desk drawer for his boating paperwork. When she found the sailboat registration number, she groaned. Though she didn't have confirmation, she felt confident she'd found the boat used to transport Matt's body.

Hurrying into her parents' bedroom, she found her dad's glasses on the floor. Adrenaline pumped through her on her way downstairs. Just as she grabbed his car keys, the door from the garage flew open.

Randy startled when he saw her. Then, a twisted smile filled his face. "Hey, sis! I just had a fantastic showing. The house practically—"

"Mom was rushed to the ER." She pushed past him and ran to her dad's car. On the way to the hospital, she made a call.

"Detective Beeker, it's Providence Reynolds. We need to talk."

Leaning back in the executive chair in his office, Stryker chuffed out a laugh. "For a man who's got some serious shit goin' down, you seem—I dunno—*happy*."

Dakota shifted on the sofa. "Happy? Hell, no, but I am crazy in love with your cousin."

"I can't believe it. She's been in my life forever. This love affair could have started years ago, man."

"It's happening now and I'm good with that."
Knock-knock.
"Yup," Stryker said.

Kirsten opened the door and glanced from one man to the other. Though her smile faltered and her spine stiffened, she stepped in. When she started to close the door, Stryker said, "Leave it open."

She sat in the guest chair.

"Tell me about the man you sold the hemp rope to," Stryker said.

Kirsten swallowed. "I...um...I don't know what you're talking about. What rope?"

Stryker spun the computer screen around. "That's you. That's my rope. That's some guy buying my rope, but he's giving you the money. Your turn."

Her cheeks flushed with color and she squirmed. "He flagged me down in the parking lot one afternoon. He told me the place he buys rope was out of stock and offered me a hundred bucks for some bundles."

"What was his name?" Dakota asked.

"He never told me."

"Describe him to me," Dakota said.

"White guy, about five ten. Short, dark hair." She shrugged. "He told me he'd be back at the end of my shift to pick it up."

"How old do you think he was?" Stryker asked.

"Maybe fifty. No, wait. Forty-five."

"What kind of car did he drive?" Dakota asked.

"I didn't see his car."

Dakota shook his head. "Did he have a scar, a tat? Anything that stood out?"

"He looked like he was in the military, because of the short hair. Later, when he picked up the rope, he wore a mask. I wasn't even sure it was the same guy."

"You do that again, you're fired," Stryker said. "You clear on that?"

"Yes. I'm sorry. Thanks for the second chance." Kirsten left, closing the door behind her.

"One step closer," Stryker said.

"Feels more like one step backward," Dakota bit out. "A white guy in his forties with short brown hair. There's probably a hundred guys that fit that description who walk through these doors every night."

"Well, lucky for you, you only need to find one of them."

Providence found her parents in a triage room, and her heart stuttered to a stop. Her mom was lying in the bed, her skin sallow, her breathing shallow. Her dad was holding her hand. He looked like he was about to lose the best part of his life.

He rose and hugged her. Then, tears filled his eyes. "I don't think she's going to make it."

Fear streaked through her. "Don't say that." Providence handed him his reading glasses and his car keys. "I need to speak with the doc."

She left the room and flagged down a nurse. A few moments later, the attending physician walked over. "I'm Dr. Modling. How can I help?"

After introducing herself, Providence said, "I think my mom was poisoned with liquid nicotine."

His eyebrows jutted up. "That's deadly. What makes you think that?"

Her symptoms fit. "She's been nauseous and dizzy. She's been vomiting, too. Her blood pressure is down and so is her heart rate. Plus, she had a seizure and collapsed, which is why she's here." Providence pulled out her ALPHA-assigned FBI badge. "I've been working an undercover case and have reason to believe my brother is behind this. Please keep that between us."

"Of course," he said. "Her blood was drawn. I'll add that to the order."

Providence waited while he called the lab. When finished, he said, "They're working on her blood panel now."

"My mom isn't safe here," she continued. "I need her moved where my brother can't get to her."

"Let me see what I can do," Dr. Modling tapped his tablet. "I need to wait until her blood work comes back before I give her activated charcoal as an antidote."

"What does that do?"

"It counters the poison by stopping the absorption of nicotine into her blood."

Providence gave the physician her cell phone number. "Please call me as soon as you get her results."

"Shouldn't be too long. Can you stick around?"

"I'm meeting with the detective now," she replied.

"I'll call with the results."

Providence returned to the triage room and her heart broke. Her mom lay still, and her dad's eyes were red from crying. Before confiding her suspicions to him, she needed to talk to Beeker. After telling her dad she'd be back in ten, she hurried out. Beeker was waiting out front in his car.

She slid in beside him. "Thanks for meeting me."

"You ready to talk?"

"I sure am," she replied.

When Providence showed him her Elaine Jones FBI badge, he couldn't hide his surprise. "What the hell is going on and why am I just now learning about this?"

"You'd zeroed in on us, but we didn't do it. Until today, I had no suspects." She gave him a rundown of everything from the blackmail letter, to her hacked bank account, to the suspected nicotine poisoning of her mom. Then, she showed him the vial from Randy's bedroom, along with the photos.

"If you hadn't shown me that badge, I would have accused you of planting evidence," he said.

"Why would I kill my own mother?"

"Why would he?"

"Money. My parents are very comfortable. Their house is paid for. My brother and his wife just moved back to the area. He has no job and they've been mooching off them, plus, he has a history of borrowing money and never paying them back."

Her phone rang. "It's the hospital." She answered. "Hello?"

"It's Dr. Modling. Your mom has elevated levels of liquid nicotine in her blood. I'm moving forward with the charcoal."

"Will she be okay?" Providence held her breath.

"I feel confident we caught it in time."

Providence sighed out her relief. "That's great."

"We're moving her to a private room."

"I'll let Detective Beeker know," Providence said and hung up.

"Well?" Beeker asked.

"She tested positive for nicotine poisoning." Overcome with emotion, tears clouded her vision. "Sorry, I need a minute."

"Take your time," Beeker said. "This is a lot to take in."

After a brief respite, she composed herself. "I've got a plan I want to run by you."

"All right, Providence. What did you have in mind?"

25

THE TRUTH

Luther set the empty brandy snifter on the end table in Dakota's home office, then relaxed against the sofa cushion. Here, the two men could speak freely. Sammy was sleeping downstairs at Miranda's, and Providence was still at the hospital.

"I'm here to tell you the truth," Luther said. "I'm here to fill in the missing pieces to a story that began decades ago."

"About damn time." Dakota picked up the photo Luther had brought with him. It was a close-up of the four men in tactical gear.

"The fourth person in that photo is Randy Maddox," Luther said.

Dakota drew a blank. "Who is he?"

"Maddox had been a Marine for a decade and was ready for a change. He came highly recommended, so your dad brought him in as an operative. After Maddox completed his training, your dad and I took him with us on several missions. He progressed well, so he began leading his own. Fast-forward two years. Your dad confided he thought Randy had turned."

"Against ALPHA?"

Luther nodded. "As you know, a lot of prep work goes into an assignment. We had several jobs where the target never showed. That happened, but it was rare. I tailed Randy to find out what was going on. Turns out, he was alerting the wealthy criminals of their pending arrest in exchange for a payoff."

"Jesus."

"Back then, protocol required your dad to discuss his concerns with the operative, so he talked to Randy, who denied everything. On your dad's next mission, he was killed. I was certain Randy had murdered him, but the evidence was circumstantial. Randy was cunning. Very cunning."

Anger slithered into his marrow, and he pushed out of the chair. He wanted to hunt Randy down and kill him. Take his life in exchange for killing his beloved dad. But he needed information, so he shoved down the hatred. "I don't remember the name Maddox."

"He used his ALPHA alias, Scott Sanders."

"Didn't he go to prison?"

Luther nodded. "For extortion. But he got out early on good behavior and was released three months ago."

"And he's back for revenge."

"Exactly." Luther rose. "You caught him once. You've got to do it again."

"I want to kill the SOB."

"I sent you his profile. When you strategize, include Providence. She's very smart and needs to be kept in the loop on this. She'll be instrumental in catching him." He eyed Dakota with a hard stare. "Keep your anger in check."

"I'll do my best." Dakota walked Luther to his car.

"Watch your back and do *not* kill him. He's cunning and manipulative."

"He won't win," Dakota said. "I can promise you that." Dakota went inside and spent the next thirty minutes beating the hell out of the punching bag in his home gym.

Covered in perspiration, he returned to his office and read

Randy's profile. He'd met the guy briefly years ago and hadn't thought of him since. When he got to the bottom of the page, every muscle in his body stiffened.

Spouse: Lizbeth Maddox
Parents: Father, Keith Maddox, deceased. Mother, Heather Sharpe
Siblings: Providence Sharpe Reynolds, Megan Sharpe

Dakota stared at Providence's name. *What the fuck. They're siblings?* This had to be a mistake. Was she in on this? Had she been playing him from the beginning? Dakota checked his phone. Providence had texted him while he'd been working out.

"Lots to tell you. On my way."

Dakota had moved past her deception because she'd been doing her job as an FBI agent. But this...this was unforgivable. He'd invited her into his home. He'd introduced her to his child. He'd brought her into his bed and he'd fallen in love with her.

Who the fuck is she...really?

He showered and dressed, then paced in the family room. The relief he'd gotten from boxing the punching bag had been short lived. Had he made the biggest mistake of his life?

The front door chimed. "Dakota," Providence called out.

He stopped pacing. "Family room."

Looking relieved, she rushed into his arms and hugged him. He couldn't touch her. Backing away, she stared into his eyes. "What's wrong?"

"What did you want to tell me?" Dakota asked.

"This is going to sound *insane*, but my brother is behind it all. He's been poisoning my mom with liquid nicotine...and almost succeeded in killing her. If that's not bad enough, I'm confident he killed Matt Hastings and is trying to frame you for his death."

Silence.

More silence. He stared into her eyes, unsure if he could trust her.

"Dakota, say something. Aren't you relieved to hear this? This is *huge*."

"Randy Maddox is your brother, Providence. Your *brother*."

"Right." Then, she furrowed her brows. "How did you know his name? I never told you his name."

"Have you been scheming with him this entire time? You deceived me once. Are you *still* deceiving me?"

The light in her eyes flatlined. She crossed her arms, pursed her lips. "For weeks, he's been slowly killing my mom with liquid nicotine. According to Beeker, you were days away from getting arrested for a crime you didn't commit. I've fallen in love with an assassin, for fuck's sake, and I'm a damn FBI agent. What the hell is wrong with you?"

She turned on her heels and marched out. He blew out a heated breath and went after her. She took the stairs two at a time, strode into the guest room, and shut the door.

Knock-knock.

She opened the door. "I'll be outa here in ten."

"I'm sorry. I overreacted."

"My life has been turned upside down and you think I'm in cahoots with him? He's a psychopath."

"I don't want Sammy to wake up. Please, I'm sorry. We need to talk. If, after we've discussed everything, you don't want anything to do with me, I'll let you go."

Silence.

"No, that's a fucking lie," he continued. "I will fight for you for as long as it takes to win you back."

She barreled into him, her kiss ferocious and brutal. He welcomed her intensity, and the ruthless way she raked her fingernails down his back. Her passion riled him. She broke away. Panting, she closed and locked the door. Then, she came at him again.

She was on fire, the fury in her embrace detonating his own desire. They stripped each other naked, and she jumped into his arms. When she rose up and sunk down on him, they masked their groans with another explosive kiss. Tongues crashed against each other, she ground against him, gliding fast on his shaft.

"I love you so fucking much," he ground out.

"Shut up, Dakota. I am so, so pissed at you. So damn pissed."

She was taking him for her own pleasure. The euphoria pounding through him had nothing to do with him and everything to do with her. All he cared about was her. Her beauty, her strength, her anger, but most of all, her happiness.

As she rode him, her heavily lidded eyes darkened, her soft moans morphed into low, guttural utterances. Her orgasm wracked her body and she convulsed hard against him as she groaned through the release. When she finished, she slowed the kiss, then ended it.

This woman was his partner, his soul mate, his forever.

"I fucking adore you," he said.

"You didn't come," she whispered.

"You did, and that's all I care about."

"I might be furious with you, but I think we can do better."

Five short minutes later, they were *both* sated. And each had been forgiven.

After showering and changing, she told him how she found the liquid nicotine and masks in Randy's bedroom, how she'd brought the ER doc into her confidence, and about her conversation with Beeker.

"Do your mom and dad know?" Dakota asked.

"No. I've got to get back to the hospital and check on my mom. Plus, I need to tell my dad what's going on."

"I'll drive you," Dakota said.

"I don't think now's the best time to meet my folks."

That made him smile. "I'll wait outside." He kissed her. "I'm sorry I accused you of working with your brother."

"I get that you have trust issues, but I'm *not* the bad guy. If you can't trust me—really trust me—this isn't going to work."

"I will *never* make that mistake again."

"You'd better not." She paused. "My God, though, the sex. The sex." Her joyful expression fell away. "Tell me how you know my brother."

On the way to the hospital, Dakota filled her in on his run-in with Randy. "My dad brought Randy in as an ALPHA operative, then mentored his career." Dakota explained how Randy had turned and Luther had suspected him of murdering Dakota's dad.

"I'm sorry," she interjected. "My brother is evil."

"After my dad passed, Luther took over. It was at that point he solicited my help in capturing Randy."

"But he never told you about your dad?"

"No. He knew me well enough to know I would have killed Randy. My dad and I were very close. I loved my parents a lot." He stopped at a red light. "Luther was concerned there were other operatives who might have been on the take, but he trusted me."

"So, you weren't in ALPHA?"

"No, I was with Goode-Luck. Once I completed that assignment, I told Luther I wanted in."

"How'd you get in without law enforcement or military experience?"

"I didn't take no for an answer. When Luther gave in, I cut back on work, trained hard for months, then he mentored my career."

"How did you capture Randy?"

"I posed as a criminal who used his real estate business as a cover. When Randy found out I had money, he told me he could ensure I didn't get arrested if I paid him. I wore a wire during the payoff, he got arrested and ended up in prison."

Her eyes grew wide. "*Prison?* He told us he retired from the Marines after serving twenty years."

"That's a lie. He got recruited into ALPHA after ten."

"When did he get out of prison?"

"A few months ago. He's back to blackmail me and set me up for murder. In the meantime, your folks were bankrolling him."

Awareness flashed in her eyes. "He's the one who broke into my condo, stole my Glock, and wiped out my account." A low, rumbling growl shot out of her. "What a pig."

Dakota pulled into the hospital parking lot. "Where is he now?"

"Where he always is…at my parents' house. After I left the hospital, I stopped by to update him. He tried to hide his disappointment that my mom wasn't dead, but I saw right through him. I lied and told him she's in ICU, to ensure he won't visit her."

He pulled up at the hospital. "You've got a plan, don't you?"

"I sure as hell do," she replied.

Three days later, Providence entered her mom's hospital room and found her sitting up in bed, her dad in the chair nearby. Though relieved, Providence knew the nightmare wasn't over… yet. "You two look much better today."

"You just missed the doctor," her mom said. "He said I've turned a corner."

"It's the best news," her dad added.

Two days earlier, Providence had confided in her dad that Randy had poisoned her mom, but the doctor expected her to make a full recovery. She'd never seen her dad so angry. But that information helped him stay vigilant against his stepson.

Then, last night, Providence had stopped by the house to pick up her dad's laptop, but she'd really gone there to check on Randy. He and Lizzie were enjoying a filet mignon dinner, compliments of the money he'd stolen from her.

Per her plan, she told Randy their mom was dying. The flash of glee in his eyes had sickened her to her soul.

Providence sat on the bed, beside her mom. She'd been lying to her parents for years, but that was all about to change. "I need to talk to you guys about my work."

"Now?" Her dad glanced at her mom.

"I'm not really a marketing consultant. I've been working as an undercover agent in the FBI's Violent Crimes Division." While she wasn't coming clean about being an ALPHA operative, she was telling them more than she'd ever planned to say.

Her parents stared at her for several beats.

"Wow," said her mom. "That's a lot more suited to your personality, and it explains the vague answers I've been getting all these years."

"I'm so proud of you, Providence," said her dad. "That's prestigious, but it's so dangerous."

Providence smiled. Their reactions didn't surprise her. "I love my job. I've been working on a case that led me to believe you were poisoned with liquid nicotine."

Her mother gasped. "What? Who would poison me?"

"Randy."

"No, dear, that can't be right," her mom protested.

"Heather," her father began. "I know this sounds far-fetched, but you were healthy until Randy came back. I think we should listen to what Providence has to say." Her dad clasped her mom's hand as tears rolled down her cheeks.

"During the four days when Randy and Lizzie went sailing, you started feeling better because he wasn't around to poison you. As soon as he returned, he upped the dosage. You had a seizure and almost died. Your blood test showed a life-threatening level of nicotine."

Providence explained that Randy had been in prison for seven years, without disclosing his career as an ALPHA operative.

"Why did he go to prison?" her mom asked.

"Extortion and bribery. He went to prison because he's a criminal. He tried to kill you because he's a psychopath."

"I can't wrap my brain around this," her mom said.

"I know it's shocking," Providence said. "Our hunch about him was right. He's not a licensed realtor."

"We'd figured that out weeks ago," her dad grumbled.

"I think Dad was his next target."

"Oh, God," her mom blurted.

Providence confided how he'd hacked into her bank account and stolen her money. "I need your help if we're going to arrest him."

"My heart is broken," her mom said, "but you have it."

"Whatever it takes," her dad agreed.

Dakota pulled around to the rear of the hospital and parked outside an unmarked exit. Providence's parents were being escorted out through the morgue in the middle of the night in order to ensure their safety. As he got out, a doctor wheeled her mom over to his truck, and Providence's dad helped her mom out of the chair.

"Good luck," the doctor said.

"Thank you for everything," she replied.

"You wouldn't be here if it weren't for your daughter." The doctor offered a warm smile. "She's excellent at her job."

After the doctor left, Providence introduced her folks to Dakota.

He shook their hands. "Let's get you somewhere safe."

Once everyone was in the vehicle, Dakota pulled away. Using the binos, Providence kept a watchful eye. Even though Beeker had someone trailing Randy—and had confirmed that Randy and Lizzie were home sleeping—Providence was leaving nothing to chance.

They said very little en route to his black site. Once inside, Dakota led them through the building and into one of the larger bedrooms with a private bathroom.

Providence sat on the bed beside her mom and her dad relaxed in a chair. Dakota retrieved a chair from the room next door. "Can I get you guys something to drink?"

"A water, if it's not too much trouble," Heather said.

After retrieving bottled waters from his kitchen, he asked, "How are you both?"

"Under the circumstances, we're doing well," Gordon said. "Providence told us we can't ask any questions, so forgive us if we seem rude."

Everyone laughed. The ice had been broken and Dakota relaxed. "This is my black site, which also functions as a safe house. You're both welcome to stay as long as you need to. I'll be working with Providence and law enforcement to ensure things go smoothly and no one gets hurt."

In truth, he wanted to hurt Randy. He wanted to punish him for everything he'd done, but he couldn't do that, not this time.

"Thank you for letting us stay here," Gordon said.

Heather offered a warm smile. "I'm a psychologist, so I'm trained to ask questions. Perhaps I could ask just one."

Providence laughed. "Couldn't resist, could you, Mom?"

Dakota smiled. "You're welcome to ask me whatever you'd like."

"Are you FBI, too?"

"Mom."

"I'm the CEO of Goode-Luck Real Estate."

"That's why you look so familiar," Heather said. "I remember your commercials."

"I'm also the person the police thought had killed Matt Hastings," he added. "You might have seen that on the news."

"I did," Gordon said. "I'm sorry my stepson was framing you for a murder you didn't commit."

Dakota slid his gaze to Providence. "Like the doctor said, you have a very smart daughter who figured it out *before* I got arrested."

He and Providence held their gazes for an extra beat. He adored this woman and would do whatever it took to keep her by his side, always.

"Dakota, what do you do besides work?" Heather asked.

"I'm a widower and I have a four-year-old daughter who keeps me pretty busy. We live in McLean. When Providence's condo was broken into—"

"What?" her mom exclaimed.

Providence arched an eyebrow at Dakota. "I wasn't home."

"The reason I mention that," Dakota continued, "is because I insisted Providence move in with us. We've all fallen in love with her. Me, most of all."

Tears filled her mom's eyes, and her dad got up from the bed and shook Dakota's hand. "That's wonderful."

"Hey, maybe I haven't reciprocated those feelings," Providence replied.

Her mom laughed. "I knew something was different about you. You don't have to say a word, Providence. I can see how you feel. Well, that's the best news. Thank you, Dakota, for sharing that with Gordon and me. We could use something uplifting. What is your daughter's name?"

"Samantha, but she goes by Sammy."

"We can't wait to meet her."

Dakota's phone rang. "Excuse me. The nurse is here." He walked down the hallway, opened the garage door, and waited while Baker Dean drove inside.

As Dakota escorted him down the hall, he brought him up to speed. Dakota introduced Nurse Baker, who set Heather up on an IV.

"We need to make sure you stay hydrated," Baker said.

"I've scheduled a cook to swing by in the morning," Dakota explained. "Which is just a few hours away."

"Thank you so much," Gordon said. "This is more than we would have ever expected. I'm happy to cook meals for us."

"You've both been through a lot." He slid his gaze to Providence. "Your daughter put me in the doghouse last week, so I'm doing my best to get in your good graces, if it'll help my cause."

That elicited another round of laughter from his grateful guests.

"We've got to go," Dakota said. "There's a rec room where you can watch movies. The kitchen is stocked if you don't want to wait for the cook. My office is the only door that's locked, but you're welcome to wander around. Just don't leave the facility. I'll check in with Baker later this morning."

"We're not going anywhere," Gordon promised.

Providence hugged her mom and dad. "You'll be safe here. If I don't come by for a day or two, no worries, okay?"

"No worries," her mom said. "Thank you both for taking such great care of us."

When Dakota and Providence entered the spacious garage filled with his fleet of SUVs, she pulled him close and kissed him. "Thank you."

"Did I score some points?"

She kissed him again. "Enough to bump you into next year."

One more kiss before they jumped in the truck. "You ready to catch a criminal?" he asked.

"So damn ready," she replied.

26

EXECUTING THE EMERGENCY PLAN

Once back at home, Dakota locked up and set the house alarm. It was after three in the morning, but despite the lack of sleep, he was on edge and full of energy. Randy was unpredictable, at best.

Before heading upstairs, Dakota sifted through the mail Miranda had left on the counter.

"Fuck, no," he said. His chest tightened as he lifted the envelope from the stack.

Providence hurried over.

"He's getting bold," Dakota said as he opened the letter.

A photo dropped out, this one of Sammy and Miranda at the neighborhood playground.

Providence stared at the picture. "God, no."

Like the others, the handmade note had been pieced together from magazine clippings and glued to white construction paper.

**Last chance to buy your way out.
Wire transfer $25M or you lose it all.**

A growl shot out from the back of his throat. "One shot," he bit out. "All I need is one shot to take him out."

"You can't kill him."

"Why the fuck not? He can't hurt us if he's dead." He shoved the letter and photo back into the envelope.

"We have to stick with our plan." She caressed his shoulder. "Let's take Sammy and Miranda to your black site."

"She won't feel comfortable staying there without me, especially since she doesn't know your mom and dad."

"Miranda will be there. Could Sin and Evangeline spend a day or two with her?"

"We'll do it your way, but I still say, I can end this tonight."

Together, they hurried up the stairs. Providence tapped on the partially open guest room door. "Miranda, it's Providence."

Dakota strode into Sammy's room. His angel slept peacefully, unaware of the danger that lurked beyond these walls. For her sake, he would play this Providence's way. He packed her clothes, then hurried into the family room and packed two large bags with toys.

Providence and Miranda hurried into the kitchen. "I'll load the truck, but I won't open the garage door," Providence said.

"I'm sorry, Miranda," Dakota said.

"No apology necessary," she replied.

Taking the stairs two at a time, Dakota hoofed it into Sammy's room and sat by her bed. "Hey, punkin." He didn't want to scare her, so he gave her a second. Her eyes fluttered open and she gave him the most adorable sleepy smile. "Is it time for school?"

"I have a special surprise for you. We're going somewhere fun for a couple of days."

She bolted upright. "Okay."

"I packed some of your dolls, including Miss Lady. You don't need to get dressed. Providence and I are driving you and Mrs. Morris there now."

He lifted her out of bed, this time remembering her security blanket. Once he buckled her into her car seat, he set the house alarm and drove out of the garage. Within minutes, Sammy had fallen back to sleep.

They drove in silence while Providence kept a watchful eye out the back. Once there, Dakota carried Sammy inside and Miranda followed, while Providence went to alert her sleeping parents.

Dakota brought them into a bedroom with two double beds. Never did he think he'd be bringing his daughter to this location. Yet, there he was, holding his precious child in his arms.

He would do whatever it took to keep her safe.

As he tucked Sammy into the bed, she woke. "Are we here?"

He smiled. "We sure are."

"Yay." Sammy slid her thumb into her mouth and closed her eyes.

The bass drum pounding in his head subsided. She was well protected and unaware of the imminent danger. That was all that mattered. In that moment, he understood why his dad had kept his secret from him, and why Luther had, too. They were trying to protect him, like he was now, for his own child.

"Are you staying tonight?" Miranda asked him.

"Yeah. I'm going to ask Sin or Maverick Hott to come out here for additional protection."

Providence tapped on the doorframe. "We're staying tonight, right?"

He loved how in sync they were. How he didn't need to explain. She just knew. "Yeah, we're staying."

"That's perfect," Providence replied. "I told my mom and dad they've got company." Her sweet smile assuaged some of his fury. "Sammy's gonna love this little getaway, especially when we tell her it's a family retreat."

His love for Providence grew tenfold. She, too, was putting put Sammy first. *How could I live without her? I can't.*

"Try to get some sleep," he told Miranda before he and

Providence left the room, closing the door behind them.

Dakota texted Sin and Maverick. "I need your help." When no dots appeared, he checked the time. It was after four in the damn morning.

His phone rang. It was Maverick. Dakota answered. "Hey, sorry for the—"

"What's going on?" Maverick asked.

Dakota wasn't surprised that Maverick jumped in without hesitation. That was the kind of friend he was.

When Dakota gave him the short version, Maverick said, "We'll be out the door in fifteen."

"Watch your six."

"Always do, brother. I've got the dog."

"Even better. Isn't he trained to protect?"

"That, plus a bunch of other things. He'll keep Sammy entertained for hours. I'll text you when we get there. Gotta fly."

Dakota found Providence pacing in the hallway outside Sammy's room. He pulled her into his arms. "I thought you'd be catching some z's."

"I can't sleep. I can't believe my brother is this evil."

"He's about to be stopped." He dropped a kiss on her forehead. "Maverick and his wife, Carly, are coming out here. Maverick runs ThunderStrike. It's a private, para-military security firm based out of DC and Carly is a private investigator. They'll keep everyone safe."

An hour later, Maverick, Carly, and their German shepherd, Whiskey, arrived.

"Whiskey, heel," Maverick said, and the unleashed dog stood by his side.

Once in the kitchen, Maverick got the dog a bowl of water, then had him lie down. Providence made a pot of coffee and the four sat around the kitchen table.

After Dakota brought them both up to speed, Maverick said, "We've got this, bro. No worries. Do what you've gotta do. Sammy will think this is the best vacation of her life. Your mom and dad will get plenty of rest."

"And Miranda will get some quiet time of her own," Carly added.

"I haven't heard back from Sin, yet," Dakota said. "You want me to tell him not to come out?"

"Hell, no," Maverick said. "I'm always up for seeing one of my boys, and Carly loves Evangeline."

"Show us where we're sleeping," Carly said.

Dakota started to get up, but Providence said, "I've got this."

After the two women had left the kitchen, Maverick stepped closer. "You two look pretty damn tight. Providence seems perfect for you. Someone sane to balance out your insanity."

Dakota chuffed out a laugh. "She's awesome."

"My license as an ordained minister is still valid. In addition to marrying Jagger and Taylor next month, I can marry you two."

"I gotta pop the question first."

"What does the little boss think of her?"

"Sammy adores her and vice versa."

"I'm happy for you, Dakota. Sounds like you've found your missing piece."

The short time Dakota spent with Maverick lightened his spirit, but the fury that fueled him wouldn't be quieted until Maddox was arrested…or dead.

The first light of day came fast. Dakota and Providence were crashed on the sofa in the rec room when Sammy came running in. "Daddy! Provi!" She climbed on the sofa. "Mrs. Morris said this is a stay-tion."

"A stay-ca-tion, Sammy," Miranda corrected, still in her robe.

Dakota and Providence laughed.

"My mom and dad are here," Providence said.

Sammy scrunched up her face. "Your mommy and daddy are here?"

"They're sleeping now, but they'll be up soon."

"Sammy, two of your favorite people are here, but they're still sleeping, too," Dakota said.

"Who?" Sammy asked.

"Uncle Maverick and Aunt Carly," Dakota replied. "And they brought Whiskey."

Sammy started jumping up and down while clapping her hands. "I love Whiskey! He's the best dog ever."

Dakota's phone buzzed and he read the text. "Sin and Evangeline just got here."

"Hurray," Sammy said. "This is so much fun. Where are we going?"

"Going?" Providence asked. "Nowhere. The party is here. It's a family reunion!"

A moment later, Sin and Evangeline walked into the room. Sammy ran over and Sin lifted her up. "Looks like someone is having a great time."

"This is soooo fun." Sammy's smile was exactly what Dakota needed to see—the green light for him to proceed with business.

The business of arresting Randy Maddox.

As planned, that evening, Providence entered her parents' home. The kitchen and family room looked like a dump. Unwashed dishes filled the sink and empty beer bottles were strewn about.

"Hey, guys," Providence said. Though she forced a smile, her blood ran cold.

Randy was eating a giant piece of chocolate cake and watching a video on his phone. Lizzie was too busy cutting out those damn words from a magazine to even notice her. But the disposable gloves she was wearing were a dead giveaway. Providence wanted to rip those scissors out of her hand and—

"Hey, sis!" Randy said. "What brings you by?"

"I have the best news," Providence said. "It's an absolute

miracle."

Randy's expression fell. "What?"

"Mom has been moved out of ICU and into a private room."

He and Lizzie exchanged glances.

"Great!" Lizzie exclaimed, joining them in the kitchen. "When can we visit?"

"Good idea," Randy echoed. "How 'bout tonight?"

Providence couldn't believe how easily they were falling into her plan. "Yes and no."

"I don't think it's fair—" Randy protested.

Providence held up her hand. "Hold on. She's turned a corner, but she's very weak. Visitors are restricted to family, and one at a time."

"How 'bout tonight?" Lizzie asked.

"Randy can, and if she continues to improve, you can go next."

This time, when they exchanged glances, Lizzie nodded. "That'll work," Randy replied.

"Megan is there now," Providence said.

"And the gay wife?" Randy asked.

Providence pursed her lips. She wanted to slap him, hard. "Leigh said that Lizzie can visit Mom tomorrow. She'll wait to see her."

"That's nice," Lizzie remarked.

"I'll take Dad to the cafeteria before you get there, so you can have some alone time with Mom," Providence said.

"Good, because I don't want to have to deal with him," Randy replied.

What an ass wipe.

"Come by at nine." Providence jotted down the room number and left, mumbling a string of obscenities under her breath as she drove away.

At eight thirty, the stage was set. Once an adversary, Detective Beeker was now their biggest ally. Staff and patients on the floor had been temporarily relocated for their safety. The hospital room light had been turned off, but the light in the corridor was sufficient for the security cams to work.

Providence, posing as her dying mother, lay in the hospital bed, her Kevlar vest and street clothes concealed by a hospital gown. The IV bag was bedside. The drainage line had been taped to her arm, lying beneath the blanket, the needle removed. Dakota waited in the dark bathroom, behind the partially opened door, and Detective Beeker stood at the foot of the bed, acting as Heather Sharpe's doctor. Four plain-clothes police officers, posing as patients, were in the hallway or milling around the nurses' station.

Providence had pulled the sheet up so that it covered most of her face, and she'd worn a salt and pepper wig. She didn't care that she was overheating from the Kevlar vest. All that mattered was catching her brother attempting to murder their mom.

And she believed, if given the chance, he'd do it.

Everyone was in position. All they needed was their star villain.

At nine fifteen, Randy sauntered into the room.

"Mrs. Sharpe," Beeker began, "you need to take it easy or I won't permit any more visitors." Beeker turned to Randy. "Hello, are you family?"

"I'm her son."

"Your mom is very weak," said Beeker.

"I won't stay long."

"Please limit your visit to ten minutes."

"Sure thing, doc," Randy said as the detective left the room.

It was up to Providence. She'd worked dozens of assignments over the years, but none more important than this one. Failure was not an option.

"Hi, Mom." Randy pulled a chair over. "Sounds like you're doing better."

Providence offered a soft moan.

"We're taking good care of the house. Lizzie and I moved into the master bedroom. But just as soon as you guys come home, we're back in the guest room."

Providence let out a garbled sound.

"I'm doing great," Randy continued. "Been busy with my clients. Sold a house already. I'm on my way to becoming a superstar realtor."

Damn liar. Providence's blood boiled, but she remained still.

Then, he grew silent for several long seconds and Providence peeked to see what he was doing.

He leaned close and his stale breath warmed her cheek. "I like living in your house. I like spending Providence's money, and I'm about to become a millionaire. A goddamn millionaire. Can you fucking believe that? I'm going to kill you, then I'm going to kill my stepdaddy. Gordon Fucking Sharpe. Brainless nitwit that he is."

She forced herself to take a slow, calming breath, but she wanted to take the son of a bitch down.

"I'm going to finish you off." When he removed the cap from the secondary IV line and attached the syringe, she flinched.

"Easy does it, Mom. I'm injecting nicotine directly into your vein. This isn't sweet like the others. This is tasteless, odorless, and colorless. It's the perfect poison. Poor Mommy, the past few months have been hell for you. Except when Lizzie and I went sailing. Imagine how pissed I was to find you feeling better when we got back."

Providence wanted to unleash her hatred on him for everything he'd done to her family, to Dakota's family, to Matt Hastings, and to the countless others he'd hurt. But she remained motionless, playing the part of her dying mother.

He stood and peered down at her. "Goodbye, Mother."

And with that, he headed toward the door. Providence pushed out of bed and ripped off the drainage line. Beeker blocked his exit, his weapon pointed at Randy. Dakota stepped out of the bathroom shadows.

"You're under arrest," Beeker said.

Rather than stopping, Randy charged Beeker. The two struggled in the corridor as he went for Beeker's weapon. Dakota strode forward, grabbed Randy, and yanked him away.

Randy pointed Beeker's gun at Dakota's head.

With lightning speed, Dakota grabbed the Glock, spun Randy around, and put him in a choke hold while he pressed the barrel of the gun to Randy's temple. Dakota was breathing hard and his eyes were wild. "I could end this in two fucking seconds," he growled. "And there's nothing I'd like more."

Beeker grabbed the gun from Dakota, while the other officers stood there, their weapons aimed at Randy.

"Randy Maddox, you're under arrest for the murder of Matthew Hastings," Beeker said. "And for the attempted murder of Heather Sharpe."

Dakota shoved him away. Gasping for breath, Randy clutched his throat. One of Beeker's guys pulled Randy's hands behind his back and cuffed him.

"I loved killing your dad," Randy bit out.

Hatred filled Dakota's eyes and his jaw muscles ticked again and again.

"I went to prison because of you." Randy sneered at him. "This isn't over, Dakota. You better keep a close eye on that sweet little girl of yours."

Dakota's rocking right cross to the jaw sent Randy to the floor.

"Whoa," Beeker said, moving Dakota away.

"I'm gonna press charges," Randy said. "You assaulted me and I've got witnesses."

"Fuck you," Dakota bit out.

"Sis, you disappoint me," Randy said. "You've aligned with the enemy. And now, I've got you in my crosshairs. Bang, bang, you're dead, too." An eerie grin spread over his face. He threw his head back and laughed, his shrill cackle heard down the corridor as the officers led him away.

"Go pick up his wife," Beeker said to the two officers who stayed behind. "Try the house."

When they left, Beeker glanced from Dakota to Providence. "Anyone hurt?"

"Motherfucker," Dakota growled, flexing his hand. "I'm fine."

Providence studied him. Rage shone in his eyes, his nostrils were flared, and his stance screamed aggressor. He was not fine.

Providence stroked Dakota's back. "I'm good."

"Nice work," Beeker said. "Especially, you, Providence. Cool under fire."

She tossed him a nod.

"I'll be in touch." Beeker left them standing alone in the hallway.

Dakota pulled her close. She wrapped her arms around him, never wanting to let him go.

"You did a great job." He kissed her. "Beeker and I agree on one thing. You are damn cool under fire." His smile was fraught with tension. She leaned up, kissed his cheek.

"I want this nightmare to be over," she whispered.

"As soon as they pick up his wife, it will be. Let's get out of here."

They left the hospital and headed for his black site. Using night goggles, Providence watched out the back window.

When they turned onto the quiet, residential side road, Dakota pulled over. A car stopped a hundred feet back. "Check this out." She handed him the goggles.

"They're turning around," Dakota said.

"Follow them."

"Probably took a wrong turn."

He handed her the goggles and waited another few minutes before he drove forward. It had been a stressful day, so she let it go. But as Dakota turned down the deserted road that dead-ended at his black site, she couldn't shake the feeling that someone was still on their tail.

27

LIZZIE GOES MISSING

Providence's phone rang as the garage to Dakota's black site opened. "It's Beeker." She tapped the speaker button. "Hi, Aaron."

"Lizzie Maddox isn't at your parents'."

Providence shifted her gaze to Dakota. "Are you sure? Maybe she's not answering the door."

"I've got a warrant. I don't want to break down the door. Any chance you can swing by and let us in?"

"Absolutely," she replied. "I'll be there—"

"*We'll* be there in thirty," Dakota said, then waited for the garage door to close.

"Thanks," Beeker said. "See you soon."

Providence hung up. "Dakota, you need to check on Sammy."

"She's asleep and well cared for. You and I—we're partners. I'm not letting you walk into that house without me."

"Randy's in jail."

"But his wife isn't."

She clasped his hand. "Thank you." Using the night goggles, she kept watch as they made their way back to her parents' house.

When they arrived, the house was dark. With their weapons by their sides, the officers entered the home. Providence flicked on the kitchen lights. Nothing had changed. The place was still a mess.

"I'll show you where I found the evidence."

Dakota pulled out his cell phone. "I'm calling a locksmith."

"You'll never get anyone at this late hour," Beeker said.

"Watch me," Dakota replied.

Three hours later, every room in the home had been searched. The police took laptops, the vials of liquid nicotine, and the masks. But Providence's stolen Glock had not been found.

Providence and Dakota stepped outside with Beeker.

"Thanks for everything," Beeker said to Providence. "Let me know if you hear from your sister-in-law." He shifted his attention to Dakota. "Mr. Luck, you are no longer a person of interest in the Matt Hastings homicide case."

Dakota had a few choice words for Beeker, but opted for, "Good to know."

A van rolled down the street and parked in front of the house, a locksmith decal displayed across the side of the vehicle. A guy got out and walked up the driveway. "You Mr. Luck?"

"You got him."

"Looks like you got yourself a locksmith after all," Beeker said.

Dakota wanted to tell Beeker that, once again, he was right, and Beeker was wrong, but he kept his mouth shut and showed the guy into the house. An hour later, the locks had been changed and Dakota handed the guy his credit card.

"You aren't paying for this," Providence said.

"You can pay me back," he said with a wink.

When the locksmith left, they made sure all the windows were locked, changed the code on the garage door, and headed out. It was three in the damn morning. Dakota was running on adrenaline. When they got to the black site, they crashed in an empty bedroom.

Late morning, they woke. Once dressed, they headed down the

hall toward the sound of Maverick's booming voice and hearty laugh. Dakota smiled. Then, he heard Sammy giggling and his fury fell away. She was his cure-all.

They entered the rec room and stopped short. It did look like the best staycation he'd never planned on having. Sammy was holding Maverick's hand while Whiskey appeared to be getting obedience training from a four-year-old.

"Good boy, Whiskey." Sammy grinned up at Maverick.

"You got this," Maverick said. "Tell him to stay and we'll walk away from him."

As they did this, Dakota shifted his attention to the other end of the spacious room. Sin was talking with Heather and Gordon Sharpe. Evangeline and Carly were at the table, working on a laptop together. Miranda was chatting with Nurse Baker.

"Daddy!" Sammy ran over to him. As he lifted her into his arms, the tension in his back loosened. His daughter wasn't just safe, she was loved by a family he'd made from the lifelong bonds of friendship.

"Hi, Sammy," Providence said. "Are you having the best time or what?"

She held her arms out to Providence, and Providence took her. When Sammy hugged her, Providence's eyes misted and Dakota fought against the emotion. This was a special moment.

"I'm having so much fun!" Sammy said. "Uncle Lalla said this is a—."

"A staycation?" Dakota asked.

"No, he said it's a vacation on the inside!" She giggled. "I want a dog, Daddy."

Oh, boy, here we go.

"Do you like dogs, Provi?"

"I love them."

Maverick joined them, Whiskey heeling by his side. "What did Uncle Lalla and I tell you about a dog, Sammy?"

Sammy shook her head vehemently. "I don't want to do that."

Maverick pulled Dakota in for a hug. "Hey, bro."

"Samantha, what did Uncle Lalla and Uncle Maverick tell you about a dog?" Dakota asked.

"To wait until I'm ten." Sammy scowled. "I don't want to do that."

"I tried," Maverick said. "She's strong willed. I wonder where she gets that from."

"Sammy, did you meet my mom and dad?" Providence pointed to her folks.

"Uh-huh. They're nice. Please put me down."

Providence set her down and she patted Whiskey.

"I'm going over to talk to them," Providence said. "Why don't you come with me?"

"Okay."

Providence extended her hand, and Sammy clasped it. With a heartwarming smile, Providence said, "See ya, boys."

As Dakota watched them walk across the room, he knew. Without question, those two were meant to be together.

"How's everything going here?" Dakota asked.

"We're having a blast," Maverick replied. "Sammy hasn't even asked to go outside. As far as she's concerned, inside vacations are the way to go."

"Thank you for this."

"You got it, brother."

Sin joined them and Dakota pulled him in for a hug. "Everything go okay?" Sin asked.

"Maddox's wife went missing," Dakota replied. "Police took evidence from Gordon and Heather's house and I had their locks changed so the lunatic can't get back in and ambush them."

"I heard Maddox was arrested," Sin said. "How'd that go?"

"I about killed him."

"I'm not surprised," Sin replied. "Smart *not* to do that in front of the police."

All three men laughed.

Dakota's phone rang. "It's Stryker." He answered. "Tell me something good."

"I'm so good at my job, I amaze myself," Stryker said. "The offshore account is owned by a Lizbeth Maddox."

"That's Randy's wife."

"Where is she?" Stryker asked.

"Vanished."

"She's probably hauling ass outa town."

"Or she's right around the corner," Dakota replied.

Over the next twenty-four hours, Dakota tried to relax, but he was on edge. Where the hell was Maddox's wife? Was she a threat to his family or an innocent spouse? Was she Maddox's accomplice or the one in charge?

TWO DAYS LATER, Providence's mom was well enough to return home. While everyone was hanging out in the safe house's rec room, Heather Sharpe pulled Dakota aside.

"I'm very grateful for what you've done for Gordon and me," she began. "I've got to tell you that Sammy was instrumental in my speedy recovery. She's precious and so smart."

"Thank you," he replied. "But I think Nurse Baker had *something* to do with your recovery."

Heather laughed. "It's been a godsend to see Providence happy. You and Sammy are helping her heal."

He nodded. "She told me about Annabel, and I'm sorry for your loss."

"Thank you. I only tell you this because she's found love again and a real chance for happiness."

"I've fallen in love with her. Sammy has, too. Your daughter is an amazing woman."

"You're a good man, Dakota Luck," Heather said.

Dakota's friends were heading out. They had lives to lead and businesses of their own to run. After Dakota discussed the situation with Providence, they decided they should head back home, too. While leaving the black site was risky, he couldn't stay there indefinitely.

As soon as night had fallen, everyone began filing out.

Once at home, Dakota and Providence cleared the house while Miranda waited in the truck with a sleeping Sammy. Dakota tucked his exhausted daughter into bed, then called Marcus. "I'm gonna need eyes on the house at night."

"You didn't get my voicemail," Marcus said.

Dakota glanced at his phone. "I missed it. What's up?"

"It's not my year for holding on to employees. Craig is moving out of town and I had to let Hillendale go. For now, it's just me and I've got to split my time between work and hiring more people."

"I understand."

"I'll work out a schedule and send it over." Marcus ended the call.

Providence walked into Dakota's office. "What's wrong?"

"Nothing."

"Nope, that doesn't work with me. Spill it." She crossed her arms.

God, he loved when she did that, and he glanced at her chest. "You're so damn sexy, even when you're not trying."

Her smile was good for his soul. "Marcus lost his security crew, so he's dropping to part-time until he can beef up his staff."

"No worries, Dakota. We've got this."

In the morning, Dakota didn't wake Sammy for school. During breakfast with Providence and Miranda, he told them he was keeping Sammy home until Lizzie had been arrested.

"Smart move," Providence said. "I'm happy to spend time with her so Miranda can have a break."

"Thank you, Providence," Miranda said. "I'll take you up on that when I grocery shop."

"Between the three of us, she'll be well protected." Dakota had no appetite and he'd barely slept, having spent most of the night running through strategies to find Lizzie Maddox. But he'd come up empty. For all he knew, she could be hiding in plain sight.

"If Sammy asks about school, what should we say?" Miranda asked.

"Tell her we want to spend extra time with her." He topped off their coffees. "If I knew where Lizzie Maddox had gone, I'd hunt her down myself."

Miranda cleared her plate. "I'm going to put together some extra lesson plans. Gotta grab my laptop."

"I'm calling the daycare center," Dakota said. "My phone's in my office."

"I'll come with you," Providence said. "I'm going to start digging into Lizzie's past. Everyone has one, right?"

As Providence jumped on her computer, Dakota made the call and tapped the speaker button. When a staffer answered, he told them that Sammy wasn't going to be there this Monday and Thursday.

"Thanks for letting us know," said the employee. "I'll let Miss Leticia know."

"What happened to Miss Liz?"

"Liz?" Providence blurted and Dakota glanced over at her.

"She resigned," said the staffer.

Dread filled his chest. "What's Liz's last name?"

"Give me one second." The staffer put him on hold.

Providence was staring at him. "No, please, no," she whispered.

"Sorry about that," said the employee. "I couldn't remember and had to ask. It's Maddox. Liz Maddox."

Dakota felt like the air had gotten sucked from his lungs.

"Oh, my God," Providence said. "Oh, my God."

"Did Liz say where she was going?" Dakota asked.

"Not that I know of. Let me ask the director. She's right here." Dakota wanted to put his fist through a fucking wall. "No, Liz didn't say. She called in last week and quit. No notice or anything. We're gonna miss her. She was great with the kids. We used to joke that she could get them to follow her anywhere."

Hell, no. Don't say that.

Dakota thanked her and hung up, his mind racing, yet none of his thoughts were coherent.

He stared at Providence for several seconds, unable to speak. Lizzie had wormed her way into Sammy's life in order to gain her trust. This woman was *not* an innocent spouse. Liz Maddox was every bit as guilty as Randy...and every bit as dangerous.

A shadow darkened Providence's eyes. "She worked there to target Sammy."

"Sammy told me disturbing things Lizzie had said to her. At the time, they made no sense, but they do now."

"She was the one crafting those blackmail letters," Providence said. "We need to warn Miranda."

"I've got to tell Sammy. If she saw Liz, she'd run over to her."

They found Miranda working at the dining room table. "You two don't look so good."

There was no way to soften the news. "Sammy's daycare teacher, Miss Liz, was Randy's wife, Lizzie Maddox."

Miranda's eyes widened. "Well, that's terrifying. Sammy was quite fond of her. Are you telling her?"

"We've got to," Dakota replied. "I can't risk her getting anywhere near Sammy and—" A sharp pain lanced his heart. He refused to finish that sentence.

Sammy plodded into the room dragging Blankie. The feeling of dread returned, but he forced a smile. "Hey, punkin. Sleep okay?"

"Uh-huh."

After a quiet breakfast, father and daughter went upstairs. As he helped her into her clothes, he was relieved she didn't ask about going to school. "Samantha, I need to talk to you, honey."

He sat in the chair, the one that was too small for his large frame. "Your teacher, Miss Liz, left your school."

Sammy's expression fell. "I'm sad."

"Honey, she's not a good person and she can't be around children."

"Nuh-uh, Daddy. She's nice," Sammy protested.

"She's just pretending to be nice, Samantha. I found out she's done some very bad things. If you see her, you have to tell me or Providence or Mrs. Morris right away, okay?"

Sammy was staring at him, hard. This was more of a challenge than he thought it would be.

"You cannot—absolutely *cannot*—go to her. Do you understand?"

He waited, watching her struggle with this. Finally, she muttered, "Okay."

He kissed her forehead. "Good girl."

Hand in hand, they went downstairs and found Miranda. "Are you ready for an exciting day?"

"My teacher is bad," Sammy blurted.

Miranda glanced at Dakota. "Yes, that's right. It's good we found out the truth." Then she showed Sammy the computer screen. "I found a fun game that's going to teach us about numbers."

Dakota left his daughter in the competent hands of her nanny and found Providence working in the office. "I'm not finding any social media accounts for Randy or Lizzie."

"No surprise there," he said.

Providence pulled her phone off her desk. "I'm letting Beeker know."

"What does Liz look like?"

"Blonde, usually wears her hair in a ponytail. Slim figure. Not much makeup. Maybe five-five. Nothing stands out, like a tat or an accent."

Providence put the call on speaker.

"Detective Beeker," he answered.

"Hey, Aaron, it's Providence Reynolds. Lizzie Maddox was Samantha Luck's preschool teacher. We're concerned she'll make a play for her."

"Thanks for the update. I've got a BOLO out on her and will let you know if we get a hit."

Providence thanked him and hung up.

"They'd better be on the lookout for her," Dakota grumbled. "If she comes near my child, I'm gonna kill her. You know that, right?"

"Not unless I kill her first," Providence replied.

That evening, Dakota made sure Sammy's bedroom window was locked. After he and Providence kissed her goodnight, they sat at the top of the stairs—two sentries guarding the innocent.

THREE DAYS LATER, no one had left the house, except when he and Providence had taken Sammy to the playground, or when Miranda had gone to the grocery store, escorted by Marcus.

Dakota had reached out to Luther, but ALPHA couldn't take on the case since Lizzie wasn't a convicted criminal. His own extensive search had turned up nothing. It was like she'd never even existed.

At night, he snoozed on the sofa, waking at the slightest sound, and checking surveillance for anyone skulking around the house. Providence caught a few hours of sleep in the hallway outside Sammy's bedroom, or on the floor by her bed. Twice, Sammy woke, excited to see Providence was having a sleepover in her bedroom.

Dakota had reached his breaking point.

After tucking Sammy into bed, they were sitting at the top of the stairs when Detective Beeker called Providence.

"Hey, Aaron, tell us some good news."

"Lizzie Maddox's car was found at a shopping center in Berkeley, West Virginia. It's about an hour and a half northwest."

"Was her decomposed body in it?" Dakota asked wryly.

"No," Beeker replied. "We're working with the Berkeley P.D. and hope to pick her up in the next few days."

Dakota would stay vigilant until she was behind bars or dead. At the moment, she was neither.

The call ended and Providence turned to Dakota. "We can't stay locked in the house forever."

"I know, babe."

"My mom and dad are having a small dinner party tomorrow to celebrate her recovery. They'd love for us to come. Miranda is invited, too. My sister and Leigh will be there. I think we should consider going. My sister is socializing a puppy they hope will become a guide dog for a visually impaired person. Sammy would have a blast with Beacon." Providence's sweet smile was like water on a raging inferno. It tamped down on his burning frustration, but didn't extinguish it.

"I'll give it some thought."

"Getting out for a few hours would do us good. I can't imagine Lizzie making a move with so many people around."

That night, as Dakota kept watch over his loved ones, he acknowledged that he had to do something to get his life back on track. *Maybe Providence is right. We've got to get out of here.*

He climbed the stairs, checked on Sammy, and walked down the hallway to his bedroom. After stripping off his clothes, he got into bed. Providence rolled toward him and lay her head on his chest.

"You're right," he said. "Tell your folks we'll see them tomorrow."

"Sammy will be so excited."

"I'll see if Marcus can cover us."

She kissed him. "I'll bring my Glock with me." Then, she lay back down and snuggled close.

"We'll get through this and come out stronger for it," he said as he held her close.

But, those words fell flat. Dakota was a man of action and a man who always had a plan. This time, he was neither.

28

DAKOTA'S BADASS QUEEN

The following evening, Sammy beamed as she was introduced to Beacon. Seeing her like that gave him hope that they could find their way back to normal. She patted the dog, then listened to Megan explain why Beacon lived with her and Leigh.

Her smile fell away. "You don't get to keep him?"

"Right. We help him to be the best puppy he can be, then we pass him along to someone else."

"I would be sad if I had to give my dog away."

"We like helping other people, so if Beacon gets to live with a person who has trouble seeing or can't see at all, that makes us happy," Leigh explained. "He becomes their eyes and their partner to help them for years and years."

Sammy grew silent for a few beats. "That's good."

Leigh tied the rope around the handle of the refrigerator and everyone watched as Beacon tugged open the door. After applause, Megan pulled a toy from her bag and Beacon's tail swished back and forth.

"I'm going to take her out back and play with her," Megan said. "Sammy, would you like to come with me?"

"Okay!"

"Can I come, too?" Providence asked.

Sammy slipped her hand into Providence's. "Of course, everyone is included."

Heather said, "I love that, Sammy. That was such a kind thing to say."

Dakota stayed behind with Providence's mom and dad. "How are you feeling?" he asked Heather.

"Good as new." She studied his face. "How are *you* doing?"

He hesitated, unsure how much of the truth he wanted to reveal to them. "We're holding up."

"Hmmm," Gordon replied.

"Yeah," Heather said. "I'm not buying that."

"Lizzie's car was found in West Virginia, but she's missing. Since she and Randy were blackmailing me for money, I won't let my guard down."

"We're so sorry our family has caused you this much trouble," Gordon said.

"No apology necessary," Dakota replied.

Sammy came racing into the kitchen. Providence close on her heels. "Daddy, this puppy. He's soooo smart!"

"I think Beacon is smarter than I am," Providence said.

Her dad laughed.

"Doubtful," her mom replied.

After dinner on the screened porch, Gordon brought out a few board games that were age appropriate for a four-year-old. For the first time in weeks, some of the tension gripping Dakota's back slipped away. The vibrant pink sky melted into the horizon, replaced by a star-filled night sky.

His phone rang. It was his home security system. Pushing away from the table, he answered.

"Mr. Luck, this is Bob with Secure Home Systems. We got an alert that your home security system was triggered. Did you or someone in your household set off the alarm?"

"No. I didn't get an alert that my security system detected motion. Hold on." He checked his home surveillance system, but there was nothing. "Which door?"

"The garage door into the kitchen. The police have been notified."

"Is the alarm still ringing?"

"No, sir. I turned it off."

Dakota thanked him and hung up. Providence was by his side. "What's going on?"

"The home alarm went off. The police are on their way. I'll meet them over there and walk through the house with them."

"Do you think it's Lizzie?"

"Could be."

"Do you have your weapon?"

He lifted his pants. The smaller Glock was in his ankle holster.

"I'll stay with Sammy. Call me once you've cleared the house."

One quick kiss and he bolted. From time to time, the alarm had gone off while he'd been at work. Neither he nor the police had found any sign of an intruder. Would Lizzie be so bold as to break into his home? He was about to find out.

He parked in his driveway and tapped the garage door opener as an officer walked around from the side of his house.

"Are you the homeowner?" he asked, flashlight in hand.

"I am." He extended his hand. "Dakota Luck."

"Officer Brentwood. Sorry to ask, but can I see your ID?"

Dakota showed him his driver's license.

"Thanks," Brentwood said. "I walked the perimeter of your home and didn't see a point of entry."

Dakota brought him through the garage and into the kitchen. The kitchen was how they'd left it.

"These security systems have minds of their own sometimes," Brentwood said.

The two men surveyed every room. Dakota checked windows. Still closed and locked. He checked closets and beneath beds. All clear. He led the officer through Miranda's basement apartment, but they found nothing out of place. No window had been broken, and the back door remained closed and bolted.

"I'm sorry for the inconvenience," Dakota said.

"Happens all the time. We chalk it up to ghosts." The officer showed himself out through the garage.

Standing in his kitchen, he pulled out his phone and called Providence. "Hey, babe."

"What happened?"

"False alarm. We walked through the house. No one was in here and nothing was—"

The door from the garage opened and Dakota turned. Everything went into slow motion as his brain screeched to a halt. His late wife stood there staring at him, a glazed look in her eyes.

"Hello, Dakota," Beth Luck said. "It's been a while."

His brain shorted. "No way...Beth, you're back."

"Dakota, what's going on?" Providence asked. "Dakota!"

Beth pulled her hand from her jacket, aimed her taser, and fired.

"AAAAYYYYYY!" Jolts of searing pain pummeled him and he dropped to the floor. Blinding agony had him writhing on the ground.

Beth moved into action, but he was powerless to stop her.

In less than a minute, she tied his wrists behind him and secured the rope to the kitchen table. Both his ankles and knees had been bound with black hemp rope. His legs had been tied to a kitchen chair. His cell phone lay a foot away, next to his Glock. So close, yet utterly useless.

With the effects of the taser gun gone, he acknowledged the cold, harsh truth. He was a prisoner in his own home.

Dakota barely recognized the woman glowering down at him. Her dark, brown hair hadn't been combed in days, her clothes were filthy, and he couldn't get past the deranged look in her eyes.

Instead of pointing the taser at him, she was pointing a handgun at his head.

She'd killed the first-floor lights, save for the stove light, which bathed her in shadow.

"Life is fucking irony, you know that?" Beth began. "You fucked my life up once, now you fuck it up again. What are the chances the same man—*the same freakin' asshole*—fucks it up twice?"

"I'm the one tied up, so I'd say you've got the upper hand." He was stalling, trying to figure out a way to free his hands, or to beat her at her own game.

She stopped pacing and stared at him. "Do you know who I am?"

"My wife, Beth Luck." While he should have been elated his missing wife had returned, he was not. She appeared to be a shell of her former self…and a violent one, at that.

"No, I'm *not* your wife and I never was. I'm Randy Maddox's wife, Lizbeth Maddox."

What? What the hell is she talking about? He clenched down on his jaw and remained stone-faced.

"You're going to transfer twenty-five million into my offshore account, Bank of the Princes." Beth flipped open a laptop perched on the island. "This is your computer. Password?"

"Fuck you," Dakota growled.

"I'll kill you if you don't give me what I want." She pointed her handgun at him. "All I have to do is pull this trigger. Bang, bang, you're dead, Dakota." She waved the weapon around like a lunatic. "This is Providence's gun. I'll be long gone and she'll be the one in the hot seat." Her creepy laugh pierced the otherwise silent house.

"You can't get money from a dead man."

That got her attention. For several seconds, she stared at him. "Where's the booze?"

"Over the stove."

She grabbed a bottle of vodka and guzzled it down.

"You'll get your money after you answer my questions." Behind his back, he was trying to undo the knot, but she'd secured it well.

"Fine, whatever. What do you want to know?"

"Everything."

She started pacing back and forth. "Seven years ago, Randy went to prison because of you. Me and him were on a fucking roll. We were making more money than I ever coulda working my stupid daycare job. He was with some super-secret group that gave him access to the worst criminals. He tipped them off and they paid him for their freedom. You come along and he gets caught. I did what any loyal wife would do, I avenged him."

Jesus, this can't be true.

"I glammed myself up and got a job at your real estate company. I wormed my way into your life, sucked it up, and married you, but that marriage wasn't binding because I was *already* married. I thought that would get me your millions, but it didn't. God, I was so pissed! So, I got pregnant. Even after I had that stupid baby, you still wouldn't give me access to your money. I mean, c'mon, Dakota. I was your goddamn wife. What was up with that?"

"You had the checkbook," he said.

She stopped pacing and glared down. "You had millions and you gave me access to less than a hundred grand. Big fucking deal!" She was flailing her arms and waving the gun around.

"So, you staged your abduction."

"Bingo!"

A low, deep growl shot out of him. She'd put him through living hell when she'd vanished.

"I cut myself, dripped blood in that fancy-ass car you gave me, and cut out of town. That blackmail letter worked good enough. You wired enough cash to keep me going until Randy got out." Her crazed smile made his blood run cold.

"Your husband didn't mind you whoring yourself out to me?"

"No choice. He was behind bars, and I needed money." Her

soulless eyes sickened him. "I found myself a wealthy mark and I played the part of doting wife." She shrugged. "Beats living in a shithole apartment. But I never loved you and I sure as fuck never wanted a snot-nosed kid." She glanced around. "You never changed the locks, never changed the garage door code or your checking account. Thanks for making things easy for me."

The fury he kept below the surface reared up like a tsunami. "You're insane."

Again, that chilling grin split her face. "What can I say? I love my husband, and we wanna be rich." She tapped her fingernail on the keyboard. "C'mon. Be a good boy and give me that password."

Providence slammed on the brakes and bolted from the car. She ran down the street toward home, her weapon drawn. The neighborhood was quiet, front porch lights illuminating her way.

Her pulse soared, but she remained laser focused. All that mattered was getting inside the house and finding Dakota.

She cut through the neighbor's backyard and ran over to the side of their house. Using Miranda's house key, Providence slipped in through the basement door. Once inside, she listened, and heard a muffled voice was coming from upstairs. She skulked up the carpeted steps and slowly opened the door to the first floor.

"I told you everything," said a woman. "I'm not your wife, never fucking was. If Randy gets convicted, he's *never* getting out. This time, I'm not waiting for him. I'm starting over, somewhere warm, like the Bahamas."

What the hell? It's Lizzie. Providence froze in the dark family room, unable to see them. She didn't know if Lizzie had a weapon or if Dakota had been tied up…or shot and was bleeding out. She hated flying blind.

"Password?" Lizzie demanded. Dakota told her and Lizzie

started typing. "I'm in. I've been waiting for fucking ever to clean out this account."

"It's a big day for you, Lizbeth Maddox. You've been playing me for years. You should celebrate."

"I'll celebrate when you're stone-cold dead."

Oh, God, no. Providence inched her way toward the kitchen.

"Tell me why you killed Matt Hastings." Dakota's voice was calm and slow, like he was deliberately trying to stall her.

"We went to that stupid event so I could get the skinny on you. That idiot realtor was one of the luckiest things that has ever happened to us. What a perfect set up! He punches you, you body slam him, and the video goes viral." Her haughty laughter made Providence grimace as she took another step forward.

"Why did you poison Randy's mom?"

"Money, stupid. She and Gordon were low-hanging fruit. We had already moved in. All we had to do was get them outa the way, then live off their savings until we could steal your money."

Providence's muscles tensed while her breathing roared in her ears.

"You know what we were planning next?" Lizzie asked.

"Fuck you, Beth," Dakota growled.

"Kidnapping your daughter. Sweet little Sammy adored her teacher. We figured she was worth at least twenty-five mil."

Rage exploded through Providence. She stormed into the kitchen. Lizzie—now a brunette—was glaring down at Dakota, a gun pointed at his chest. He'd been tied up and secured to the kitchen furniture. "Put the gun down. *Now!*"

Lizzie raised her gun and fired. As Providence staggered backwards, Lizzie aimed her gun at Dakota.

BAM-BAM-BAM-BAM-BAM!

Lizzie hit the floor, blood pouring from her chest.

Providence staggered over to Dakota. "Are you okay? Were you shot?"

"No. Where were you hit?"

"She got me in the chest, but I'm wearing my vest." Though wracked with pain, Providence untied him. "These are bowline knots."

Once freed, he checked her. A bullet had struck her dead center. "Jesus, she would have killed you."

"I'm fine."

"Like hell you are. Sit. Now."

Hugging herself, Providence folded into the kitchen chair.

Being as gentle as possible, Dakota removed her shirt and the vest, then checked her chest. "Nice, easy breaths, babe," he instructed. "You might have a cracked rib."

As he helped her back into her shirt, she flinched, then winced. "This could have been a lot worse."

"You, Providence Reynolds, are my badass queen."

Despite the discomfort, she smiled.

Dakota called Beeker. "Aaron, it's Dakota. Lizzie Maddox tried to kill me. She's at my house…Providence has been shot… Maddox is dead." Dakota hung up and kissed Providence's cheek. "He's on his way and he's calling for an ambulance."

She was sweating and her heart was pounding so hard, she was having trouble catching her breath. Dakota got her a glass of water. After she drank it down, he held her hand while her heart rate slowed and she breathed easier.

"She was the mastermind," he said. "She was in charge of everything."

"Not everything," Providence said, staring at Lizzie's lifeless body. "And not anymore." She peered into his eyes. "Your nightmare is over. She can't hurt you and she can't take your daughter."

A tear slid down Providence's cheek. "Sammy's the one child I *could* save."

29

R & R

Providence walked inside ALPHA HQ, her man by her side. What seemed like a lifetime ago, she had driven there with a chip on her shoulder. But now, she had a renewed sense of confidence and accomplishment. So much had changed.

Together, they entered Luther's office.

"Congratulations to you both," Luther began after they sat down. "You two make one impressive team."

"Thank you," Dakota said. "While I might have a stubborn streak in me—"

Providence and Luther laughed.

"I will admit you were right," Dakota continued. "Working with Providence was for the best."

"For us both," she agreed.

"It's also good for the agency." Luther offered a warm smile. "Providence, I gave you my word that you could return to the Bureau after this case ended. You don't need to give me an answer today, but I'd love to have you stay on as an operative."

"I would like that, but I want Dakota to return here, working cases as his schedule allows."

"You didn't mention that to me," Dakota said.

"We've had a *lot* going on," Providence replied.

"I've been doing some thinking myself," Dakota continued. "I'm done being an assassin."

She smiled. "Seriously?"

Luther leaned back in his chair. "Then, my next offer comes at an opportune time. Dakota, I'm retiring at the end of next year. I would love to groom you to be my replacement over the next eighteen months."

"Oh, wow," Providence said.

"Thanks for the vote of confidence," Dakota replied. "I'll give it some thought."

"I'm confident your dad would echo my sentiments," Luther added.

On the ride home, Providence said, "I love that you know about my career. You understand what's at stake. You get me, and I love that I don't have to live my life in isolation because of the secrets I keep."

"You will never be alone again, babe."

She leaned over and kissed his cheek as his phone rang. "It's Juanita," he said. "Do you mind?"

"Of course not."

He put the call on speaker. "What's the word?"

"First, congratulations and hallelujah!" Juanita exclaimed. "What a relief that debacle is behind you."

"I couldn't agree more."

"I sent out a company-wide email letting everyone know the charges against you have been dropped. I've heard from all the agents who bailed. They want to come back, but I'm not sure that's in our best interest."

"Why?" he asked.

"Their lack of loyalty."

"I'll back your decision."

"And that's why we make a great team. So, how did the police find the real killer?"

"I heard an undercover FBI agent was working the case," Dakota replied, glancing at his woman. "And she was a total badass."

Providence stifled a laugh.

"Ooo, that's so exciting," Juanita said.

Dakota stroked Providence's thigh. "*Very*," he replied.

"When are you coming back to work?" Juanita asked.

"I'll be in next week."

"I look forward to it," Juanita said and ended the call.

Dakota pulled into the garage. "I've got a surprise for you."

They walked into the quiet house. Sammy was at her new preschool, and Miranda had flown to Michigan for her son's wedding.

"We're home alone," Providence said. "That's surprise enough for me."

Dakota laughed.

"I was invited to Jagger and Taylor's wedding. With everything going on, I wasn't going, but we've gotta get away."

"We?"

"Hell, yeah." He kissed the tip of her nose. "Like Luther said, we make one impressive team. The assassin and his badass queen."

She smiled. "When's the wedding?"

"This weekend in Malibu."

"I'm there," she replied. "I'm so there, I'm going upstairs to pack."

"Pack, now? No way in hell. We've got something way more fun to do."

She palmed his ass. "I couldn't agree more. Lead the way."

"After you, my love. I can't pass up the view of your sexy wiggle."

PROVIDENCE COULDN'T WAIT to get away. And what better place than beautiful, sunny Malibu to cleanse her soul and clear her mind from the whirlwind of everything that had transpired over the last few months.

She, Dakota, and Sammy boarded Sin's private jet to the applause of those already seated. She laughed as Dakota took a bow and Sammy jumped up and down. On the way to her seat, she said hello to Sin and Evangeline, Maverick and Carly, and Crockett and Alexandra. Though she'd met Colton Mitus during the video chat in Dakota's office, Dakota re-introduced her to him, and she met his wife, Brigit.

"This guy," Dakota said, pointing to Colton, "is the reason I became a realtor."

"I don't remember that," Colton replied.

"You said, 'If we're gonna buy these apartment buildings and duplexes, one of you needs to get his damn real estate license.'"

Brigit laughed. "That sounds like Colton. Always bossing everyone around."

"Smartest business decision I ever made," Dakota said.

After they took their seats, Dakota buckled Sammy in, then handed her Miss Lady. Once the plane was airborne, the guys got out of their seats and started talking with each other. Sammy fell asleep and Evangeline came over and sat beside Providence.

"I was with the FBI," Evangeline whispered.

"Me, too," Providence replied.

"I know," Evangeline said.

"Should I assume Dakota and Sin have no secrets?"

Evangeline nodded. "They're very close. They missed out on the first eighteen years together, and from what Sin has told me, they're making up for it."

Dakota's friends made Providence feel welcome and her pre-flight jitters vanished before the plane touched down in Los Angeles. The groom, Jagger Loving, and his fiancée, Taylor Hathaway, had arranged for limos to pick them up at the airport and whisk them to the Loving Resort in Malibu.

Providence gasped when they entered the posh hotel. "I'm never leaving," she murmured to Dakota.

When the guys saw Jagger, the hooting and hollering made everyone in the hotel stop and stare. It was touching to see how close these six men were and how much they'd missed their friend.

The rehearsal dinner was more about the guys being together than about rehearsing. Providence loved seeing Dakota with his friends, but his easygoing smile and entertaining stories didn't fool her. He was on edge. The truth about Lizzie had been both shocking and disturbing. But Dakota was a strong man. She had complete confidence he would process what Lizzie had done to him and move on, and she would support him however he needed. Despite Lizzie's evil ways, they'd had a child together. Samantha Luck was a true blessing.

The wedding took place in the large ballroom. Since Maverick officiated, and Dakota, Sin, Colton, and Crockett were groomsmen, she and Sammy sat together. Providence loved having the little one by her side.

Taylor looked stunning in her off-the-shoulder, white silk wedding gown, and Jagger was a handsome groom in his traditional tux, but it was their words of love and adoration that touched Providence the most. Without question, these two were meant for each other.

Providence wanted that for herself. Her gaze slid to Dakota, who looked flat-out gorgeous in his jet-black suit. Their eyes locked and her heart fluttered. Was he her soul mate? In her heart of hearts, she believed he was her forever.

Following the ceremony, guests moved to a different ballroom for the reception. The wall of sliding glass doors facing the beach had been opened, and the warm sea breeze and breathtaking view of the Pacific Ocean beckoned. Excusing herself, Providence stepped outside. She slipped off her stilettos and let the sand squish between her toes.

Not long after, Dakota joined her. "Want some company?" He slid his hand through hers.

"No, I'm good." She shot him a smirk while squeezing his hand. "This is beyond beautiful. Thank you for inviting me. I didn't realize how stressed I was until I saw the ocean. It's good for the soul, you know?"

"*You're* good for the soul."

With a smile, she caressed his back. "I didn't think I would get a second chance at love, but every time I'm with you, I know it more and more."

He kissed her. "We're supposed to be together. I'm positive about that."

She loved this man with her entire being.

The sit-down dinner was first class all the way, and the reception continued late into the night. Jagger and Taylor's wedding was the highlight of her year. She couldn't remember the last time she'd had that much fun.

"How 'bout we take a morning walk on the beach?" Dakota suggested as they slid into bed that evening.

"I can't wait," she replied and snuggled close.

The following day, Providence found Dakota and Sammy in the living room of their hotel suite. "It's eight o'clock in the morning. How is it that you're both ready to go?"

Sammy giggled.

"We're on East Coast time," Dakota said. "You ready to take that walk?"

Sammy jumped off the sofa and ran to the door.

"Someone's excited," Providence said as they headed out.

Sin and Evangeline were waiting in the lobby and Sammy ran over to them.

"Are you guys coming, too?" Providence asked.

"We're taking Sammy to breakfast," Evangeline said.

"Join us when you get back, we'll be sitting outside," Sin said.

Again, Sammy giggled.

"We'll be back soon," Dakota said.

Hand in hand, they headed down to the beach, slipped off their sandals, and strolled along the water's edge. The ocean air was crisp and the newly risen sun cast their shadows over the lapping waves that kissed the shoreline again and again. Providence had her man by her side and, for the moment, life was perfect.

After watching the seabirds show off their fishing skills, he suggested they retrace their steps and head back to the hotel.

"We've been through a lot together," he said, breaking their comfortable silence. "From the moment we met, I was wowed by you."

She gave his hand a little squeeze. "Thank you. Same here."

"We make a good team."

"You think?"

His beautiful smile sent excitement careening through her. "Yeah, I do."

He stopped on the beach in front of the resort. "I love you, and Sammy loves you. We've been doing our best, but we've been missing someone strong and kind, smart and funny, patient and loving. We've been missing you." He pulled out a small box from his pocket, dropped to one knee and smiled up at her.

She gasped and her heart ka-chunked in her chest, then started beating wildly.

"Providence Sharpe Reynolds, I love you with my heart and soul. I can't imagine my life without you. Will you do me the greatest honor of marrying me and being my life partner?" He opened the ring box.

Her gaze darted to the diamond ring, sparkling brightly in the morning light. While the ring was magnificent, it was the adoration in his eyes that made her heart soar.

"I would love to be your wife, and Sammy's mommy." She placed her hands on his face, leaned down, and kissed him.

He slipped on the emerald-cut diamond surrounded in a halo of smaller diamonds and flanked with baguettes.

"That ring is…it's beyond gorgeous."

When he rose, she jumped into his arms and kissed him again and again. These kisses…these hummed in her bones and overflowed with love.

"I adore you, Miss Rhode Island."

"I adore you back," she replied with a smile.

Cheering and applause snagged her attention.

Dakota's band of brothers and their wives waited by the hotel, Sammy in Sin's arms. All of them were grinning, and everyone was wearing a T-shirt that said,

She said YES!!!

Providence gave a thumbs-up before kissing Dakota again. "So cocky. My refusing you never crossed your mind?"

"Hell, no."

Sammy ran over and Dakota lifted her into his arms.

"Are you going to marry my daddy?" Sammy asked.

"I am. What do you think of that?" Providence asked as Dakota's friends formed a circle around them.

"It's soooo good. Are you getting married today?"

"Not today," Providence replied.

"But Uncle Maverick can do it," Sammy explained. "He marries everyone!"

Laughter filled the air as Jagger's hotel staff brought out mimosas and orange juice in flutes. The group lifted their glasses in a celebratory toast.

"Congratulations," Sin said and everyone raised their glasses. "We love you guys."

"To the six," Dakota said.

"To the six," the guys repeated.

After everyone toasted, Dakota said, "To our women. The best part of us."

Providence and Dakota shared a tender kiss as everyone

pulled out the cameras and snapped pics. Jagger asked his staff to take photos, and the thirteen of them posed on the sand.

Overcome with joy, happiness filled Providence's lonely heart.

Dakota spent the first few days after Beth's death processing the harsh truth. She had never loved him, had never been his legal wife, and she had staged her own abduction. After Randy had been released from prison, the psychopathic husband and wife team had become hell-bent on taking his millions and destroying him in the process.

Had it not been for Providence, they would have succeeded.

When Providence rubbed his back, Dakota blinked away the past. Her loving touch made all the difference, and he turned toward his future.

"You okay?" she asked.

"Never better." He had found his true love. Together, they would raise Sammy...maybe even have a child or two of their own. "How 'bout you, babe?"

Her relaxed smile said it all. "I am loving this vacation."

While she sported a fading black-and-blue mark from her bruised rib, that hadn't stopped her from wearing a bikini. And damn if his woman didn't rock it out. He planted a kiss on her, eliciting another smile.

"Mmm," she murmured. "I love kissing you."

"Good thing, because there's going to be sixty years of it."

Her light-hearted laugh made him smile.

Crockett and Alexandra had taken Sammy for the day, so Dakota had his beautiful fiancée all to himself. Hand in hand, they strolled along the private Malibu beach. Nothing but miles of sand, clear blue sky, and the morning sun ahead of them. The lapping of waves helped wash away the nightmare that had almost cost them their lives.

Down the beautiful beach they walked, with no agenda and no plan. Dakota inhaled the fresh, salt air. For the first time in years, he could breathe…really breathe.

Though his world had been rocked, he was ready to move forward. His child was safe and deeply loved. His fiancée was alive and by his side. Together, they were building their new life.

While they were in California, the house was being scrubbed and the furnishings replaced with all new. He'd been living with a ghost. Time to exorcise it from his life…for good.

"I've found some homes I want us to tour next week," he said.

"What for?"

"I want us to move into something that's ours. What do you think about that?"

She pulled him to a stop, leaned up, and kissed him. "I love that idea."

"What do you want to do with your condo?"

"I used to be afraid that if I sold it, I would be leaving Annabel." She laid her hand over her heart. "She lives in here." After a pregnant pause, she nodded. "I'm ready to sell."

"Luther said he wants my answer when we get back."

They held each other's gaze.

"I'm returning to ALPHA, part-time, as long as you'll be my partner."

"Yes! That's the best news. I am so stoked about that." She paused and her winsome smile fell away. "We're making a lot of changes. Too many at once?"

"Hell, no. Based on the past few months, we can handle a lot."

"I want to run something big by you, too. I'd like to adopt Sammy. Is that something you're open to?"

This time, he kissed her with so much passion, she melted into him. "Wow. My God, you can kiss," she said. "I'll take that as a 'hell yeah.'"

"Damn straight."

"She's so young, but her thoughts and feelings are what matter most. I would never adopt her if she didn't want it."

"She adores you, Providence."

"I love her so much." She stroked his arms, sending jolts of energy powering through him.

"We can talk to her about it and see what she thinks."

"I would love that."

"You are the most amazing, loving, brilliant, gorgeous, badass woman I have *ever* met."

She laughed. "You're pretty badass yourself, you know that?"

"Yeah, I do," he replied with a playful wink.

As they resumed their stroll down the beach, Dakota dropped his arm over Providence's shoulder and kissed her temple. "I'm going to love you forever, Miss Rhode Island."

"Right back atcha, cowboy."

EPILOGUE

TWO YEARS LATER, SEPTEMBER

"This is so exciting," Providence said. "I can't wait to hear all about it."

"Thanks, Mom," Sammy said. "But it's no big deal."

Dakota chuckled. "There was a lot of bedroom discussion last night about what to wear."

A year and a half ago, the Luck family had moved to a different McLean neighborhood where they could make new memories. Sammy could walk to school, and Miranda had her own home on the Luck property. Mornings were father-daughter time and Miranda picked her up in the afternoons.

But on this day, she was accompanied by Dakota, Providence, *and* her one-year-old brother, Graham.

Ever since she'd turned six, Dakota's little girl had morphed into a little lady. Providence had curled the ends of her long hair and she was wearing a new outfit from a recent mother-daughter shopping spree.

"Give me a hug goodbye."

With a smile, she threw her arms around him. "I love you, Daddy."

"I love you, punkin. You're gonna rock first grade, Samantha Lynn."

Providence lowered Graham so Sammy could kiss his cheek. Graham just grinned at her.

"Bye, Gray-Gray," Sammy said before turning her attention back to her parents. "I found a spider in the bathroom. I captured it in a cup and put it outside."

Dakota high-fived her. "Nice job."

"I'm proud of you, honey," Providence said. "Was it big?"

"Not as big as me," Sammy replied with a smile.

Providence put her arm around her daughter and kissed the top of her head. "Have a great first day of first grade and keep my suggestion in mind."

"What suggestion?" Dakota asked.

"Sammy has a bunch of friends from kindergarten, but there's probably going to be someone new who doesn't know anyone," Providence said.

"I'll be nice to them. Do we have yoga tonight?"

"They canceled class because it's the first week of school," Providence replied.

Sammy's expression fell.

"We can still do it, just the two of us."

"Yay! I love you, Mom."

"I love you, too, honey," Providence said with a smile. "Mrs. Morris will meet you here with Graham this afternoon. Make it a great day."

Sammy gave a little wave and set off toward the front doors where the principal and staff waited to welcome the students back from summer break.

Graham started fussing. "She'll be back this afternoon, little one." Providence pulled a rattle from the stroller and handed it to him.

The baby held out his arms for Dakota. "Dadda."

Providence kissed her son before passing him over.

"There's my big guy." Dakota kissed Graham's chubby cheek again and again, and the baby started giggling.

Providence snapped a picture of them before taking one of Sammy, then she started videoing her.

As Sammy walked away, Dakota's heart clenched. She was growing up so fast. All he could do was savor all the good moments and manage through the challenges of being a parent. But he had a great life partner who cherished *all* the moments, regardless of what they encountered. Providence would say, "We've got this because we've got each other."

As Sammy vanished into the building, Providence swiped a tear.

Dakota caressed his wife's back. "You okay?"

"She looks beautiful and she's *so* confident."

"That's because she's got a great mom who's the best role model."

"Thank you, baby, but I'm only half of this dynamic duo."

Dakota chuffed out a laugh as he placed Graham in the stroller. "The crime-fighting duo of Luck and Luck, ALPHA's kick-ass operatives."

"That sounds like a T-shirt that will *never* get made." Providence smiled down at her son before they headed toward home. "I'm getting my third tattoo this week."

"Another tiny heart?"

"Yes. One for each of my babies."

"I can't wait to admire it on your perfectly beautiful chest," he replied.

"And I can't wait to show it to you," she said as she stroked his back. "I signed us up for the intermediate racing class at Summit Point. It starts in a couple of weeks."

"That'll be fun." His phone rang. "It's Maverick."

"Carly must've gone into labor," Providence said.

Dakota answered. "What's the word?"

"We just got to the hospital," Maverick said. "Sin and

Evangeline have Ian and Whiskey, but they've got an event tonight at their children's center—"

"We'll take them. How's Carly doing?"

"She's great. I'm the nervous one. Oh, before I forget, I got your text about donating two homes a month to our charity. That's crazy generous of you guys."

"We love helping veterans find their forever homes," Dakota replied.

"Righto. Gotta help bring my baby girl into the world. God, I hope I don't pass out this time."

Dakota chuckled. "You've got this."

"Thanks, bro." Maverick hung up.

"They're at the hospital," Dakota told Providence. "We're taking Ian and Whiskey tonight."

Providence's phone rang. "It's Evangeline." She put the call on speaker. "Hey."

"Did you hear? Carly went into labor."

"We can take Ian and Whiskey tonight."

"Thank you," Evangeline replied. "I got your text. This criminal is...well, he's super dangerous."

"And that's why we're chasing him," Providence replied.

"I did some digging and can fill you in later," Evangeline said before hanging up.

These days, Dakota counted his wealth differently. He considered himself a rich man because of his family. He adored his wife and his two beautiful children. He loved co-running Goode-Luck with Juanita, and ALPHA with Providence.

And he savored their close-knit relationships with his five friends from college, their wives, and their children. He was a lucky man, indeed, and he never took his good fortune for granted.

On the short walk home, he pulled his beloved wife to a stop, captured her face in his hands, and gave her a tender kiss. "Love eternal," he murmured.

"Love eternal," she replied with a smile.

Another Happily Ever After by
Stoni Alexander

**DESPERATE FOR MORE
SIN & DAKOTA?
Keep Reading!**

You'll find them both in...
DAMAGED
THE VIGILANTES, BOOK ONE

...and readers first meet and fall in love with Sin in
THE HOTT TOUCH
BOOK FOUR OF THE TOUCH SERIES

A NOTE FROM STONI

Thank you so much for reading DAKOTA LUCK, the final book in The Touch Series. **The Harvard Six** have found their true loves and are enjoying their happily-ever-afters.

These stories have taken me on an amazing journey and I'm so thankful to the many people who have helped me along the way.

As far as my next series, Stryker Truman takes the lead, picking up where DAKOTA LUCK leaves off. Where Stryker goes, trouble follows...

It's always fun to hear from readers. You can drop me a note at Contact@StoniAlexander.com.

To learn about my upcoming releases, be the first to see a cover reveal, or participate in a giveaway, sign up for my Inner Circle newsletter at StoniAlexander.com. When you do, I'll send you my steamy short story, MetroMan.

All of my books are available exclusively on Amazon and you can read them FREE with Kindle Unlimited.

Cheers to Romance!
Stoni

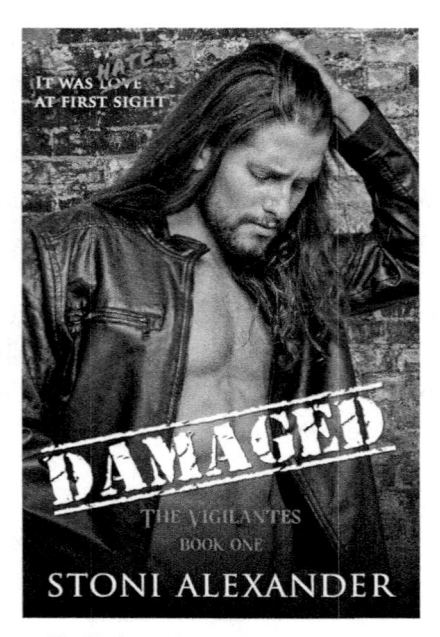

The Vigilantes Series - Romantic Suspense

I'm *not* one of the good guys...not even close. I'm a heartless savage hunting down the thug who murdered my mother. Watching her die in my arms has turned me into a killing machine. Revenge runs bone-deep for me. It's burned into my soul, baby.

When I become the one with a damn target on my back, my life turns into a raging dumpster fire. But not because my company gets breached or because some SOBs are trying to off me.

There's this woman...the *one* woman I can't freakin' stand. An impulsive cop who arrested me for a crime I didn't commit. She gets too close to me, she's gonna learn about all the ones I *did* pull off.

The problem is, I'm crazy attracted to her. Insane, over the top, can't-get-her-outta-my-head kind of attraction. She pushes all my buttons and makes me madder than hell. If anyone can bring me to my knees, it's her.

Turns out, I took a vow of celibacy. And I don't break so easily.

Except the hot cop is now a detective...and I gotta help her with a serial-killer case 'cause I got wicked-good hacking skills. But that's all I'm gonna help her with...
 Grab DAMAGED or read FREE with Kindle Unlimited!

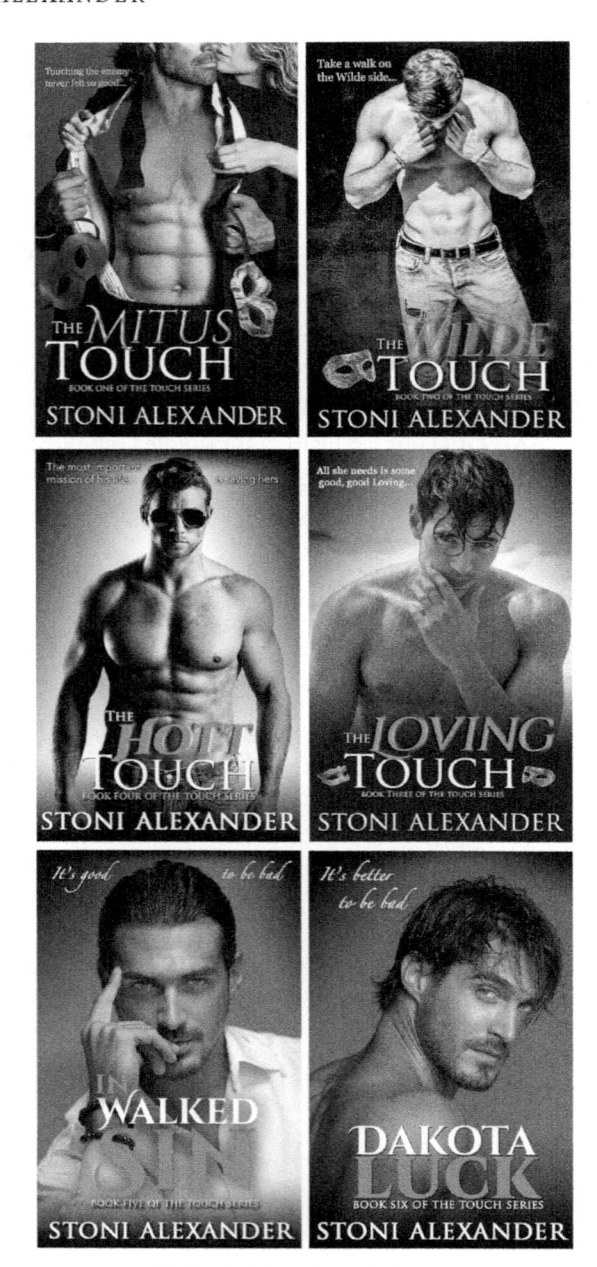

The Touch Series - Romantic Suspense

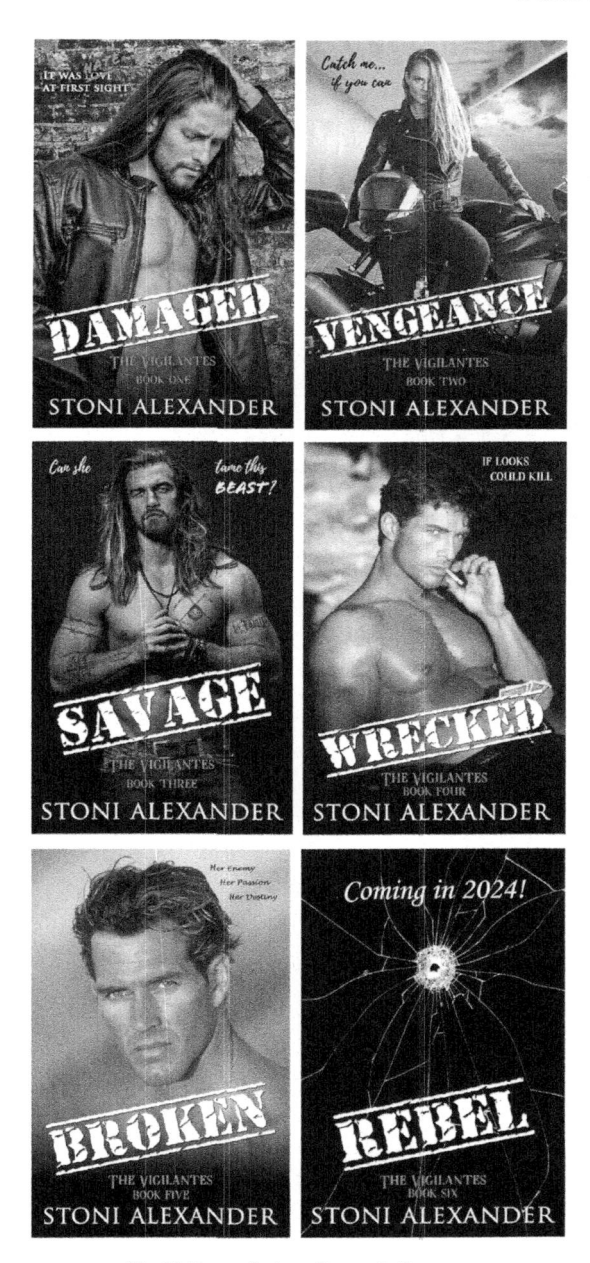

The Vigilantes Series - Romantic Suspense

Looking for a sexy standalone?

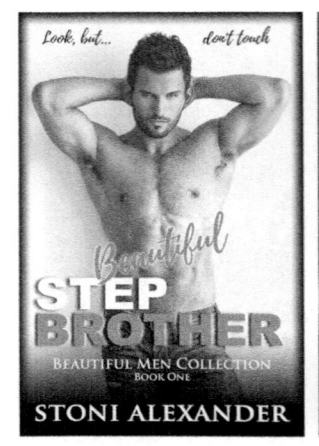

Beautiful Men Collection - Contemporary Romance

Grab them or Read FREE with Kindle Unlimited!

ACKNOWLEDGMENTS

This series was an absolute joy to write. I am forever grateful to my husband for his life-changing words that set me on a very different, and much beloved, career path. Johnny, thank you for loving me so damn much and for making our life one that is filled with such goodness. Love eternal.

Mom, I miss you every day. Your loss left a hole in my heart that can never be filled. But I have a lifetime of memories that fuel me forward and make me smile. We had a one-of-a-kind bond that I appreciate every single day. Thank you for being an *amazing* mother. I was truly blessed to be your daughter. Rest in peace and soar with the angels.

Son, we got through the challenges of 2020 as a family. Now, it's time for you to fly. Godspeed.

Bruce and Patricia, thank you for sharing your story with me. Your heartbreaking loss became the most important part of Providence's character.

Nicole, you are amazing. You work your magic every single time. I'm grateful you're my editor.

Family and friends, thank you for your unwavering love and support. And thank you for all the laughter, especially through all the craziness of 2020.

Readers, thank you for spending a little time in my imaginary world. You are deeply appreciated.

Muse, rest up. Things might get a little darker with Stryker…

ABOUT THE AUTHOR

Stoni Alexander writes sexy romantic suspense and contemporary romance about tortured alpha males and independent, strong-willed females. Her passion is creating love stories where the hero and heroine help each other through a crisis so that, in the end, they're equal partners in more ways than love alone. The heat level is high, the romance is forever, and the suspense keeps readers guessing until the very end.

Visit Stoni's website:
StoniAlexander.com

Sign up for Stoni's newsletter on her website and she'll gift you a free steamy short story, only available to her Inner Circle.

Here's where you can follow Stoni online. She looks forward to connecting with you!

amazon.com/author/stonialexander
bookbub.com/authors/stoni-alexander
facebook.com/StoniBooks
goodreads.com/stonialexander
instagram.com/stonialexander

Printed in Great Britain
by Amazon